LITERARY AGENTS BEWARE

AN INTERNATIONAL ROMANTIC THRILLER

BY
JOHNNY RAY

LITERARY AGENTS BEWARE

To someone else, the rejection letter might be perceived as a simple piece of correspondence. But when Amy, who suffers from bipolar disorder, receives a form rejection letter from Edward, an agent she had an affair with at a recent convention, she takes the rejection as both personal and professional—in short, a declaration of war.

Amy quickly embarks on a plan to get revenge by destroying Edward's literary agency. However, Amy is soon not the one to be feared the most. Her actions create a copycat who targets literary agents and viciously murders them. Living with the knowledge that she has created a monster, a serial killer, is one thing, while doing nothing to stop the madness is another. But how could she track down a killer when she has no training in such? Thinking like a mad man might be the only way—but could she go there and survive herself?

When the winds of fate rekindle the romance with Edward, thus making him the next target—she really has no choice but to help the FBI. But will she be too late?

ALL RIGHTS ARE HEREBY RESERVED
BY
JOHNNY RAY

JOHNNY RAY

Johnny Ray is an award winning novelist who won the Royal Palm literary award for best thriller and is quickly making a name for himself as the master of the romantic thriller. He loves social interaction with his readers and can be found on

Twitter **www.twitter.com/sirjohn_writer**

Facebook **www.facebook.com/authorjohnnyray**.

He can also be reached by e-mailing at **sirjohn@wwisp.com**,

Or you can just follow him on his blog at **www.sirjohn.us**

For updates and future releases.

OTHER NOVELS BY JOHNNY RAY INCLUDE

SCANDAL—THE DEATH OF A LEGACY
Published by Sir John Publishing in 2012

MODELS AND LOVERS
Published by Sir John Publishing in 2012

HER HONOR'S BODYGUARD
Published by Sir John Publishing in 2012

FOR LOVE AND VENGEANCE
Published by Sir John Publishing in 2012

THE SALSA CONNECTION
Published by Sir John Publishing in 2012

THE JOURNEY TO WHITESTONE
Published by Sir John Publishing in 2012

CHAPTER 1

He envisioned his own tombstone:

Mitchell Lloyd

Literary Agent Extraordinaire

Killed in the Line of Duty

Damn, he knew he could die any minute. A blurred object moving mere inches in front of his eyes materialized, as a flash of light reflected from the cold steel. Focusing on the razored edge of the curved knife ascending into a sharp tip designed to kill, he stopped breathing. His body stiffened, and froze solid where he sat with his back against a hard cold wall. He felt scared that any further movement on his part might agitate his attacker. The pain radiating from the back of his battered head dulled his vision and his thoughts, as a wire tying his hands together cut into his skin, increasing the unbearable terror ravaging his body.

He inhaled the smell of blood and sweat as he gazed into the darkness, hoping to gain his bearings. Again, a fist smashed into his forehead, slamming the back of his head into the wall behind him as the world faded. He fought his way back to reality, only to stare into the slicing blade carving the side of his face.

"DAMNNNNN!" His voice erupted and echoed off the nearby walls and in his head. The pain shattered the remaining will to remain still. He struck out with his head, his arms, and his legs. In return, the hand slammed his head back against the wall again.

He forced his mind to stay conscious, as the warm blood flowed from his face. "What do you want from me?"

"Satisfaction."

"Satisfaction for what?"

"Ruining my life, that's what!"

Another slice sheared off an ear.

"OHHH SHIT, stop, please stop. I'll give you anything you want—anything!"

"That's impossible."

The knife retreated as a face leaned forward, one he recognized only so slightly.

"You? Why you crazy—."

A vicious kick to his crotch blasted his tortured soul to new levels. "Oh God, why me? Stop, please stop."

"I know you think you have the balls to do what you want. Being a literary agent doesn't make you God—you stupid bastard!"

The next kick to his crotch made his stomach deliver its contents to his throat. The bitter taste forced a gagging convulsion. He knew then that he was going to die soon. "I'm sorry. I'm—"

"You should've thought about your actions earlier."

Another punch to the face bounced his head off the concrete wall. Thoughts of his life rushed forward to fill in the fading minutes. Would his life end like this? His family, his agency, his friends, his clients—what would happen to them?

His world collapsed as the remaining blood drained from his body.

CHAPTER 2

Four months earlier, Amy Jenkin's apartment in Atlanta, Georgia.

"Mom, I can't talk anymore! Please, just leave me alone," Amy's voice trailed off, trembling in one small sob after another.

"Amy, are you sure you are taking your medication right?"

"Yes . . . and I know how to regulate my damn medication!" Amy let the phone slip below her ear as she attempted to avoid her mother's persistent interrogation.

"Okay, okay, but please try to get some sleep, and I'll come by and check on you later."

"Just leave me alone. I need to do some thinking." Amy disconnected before her mother could reply. She knew her mother meant well, but it wasn't the time to tell her the news.

Amy read the rejection letter again, as though for the first time. The blood in her veins pulsated, making her face flush with heat, but still dim compared to the burning desire inside her to strike back. There must be a mistake. How could she have been deceived into thinking this agent was any different? She knew she had already lost control, and the medication she had swallowed would be too little too late. She knew the tightness in her chest and the nausea in her stomach resulted from the boiling venom in her brain, but fighting the evil was useless. The computer in front of her became her weapon of choice as she clicked on the word processor and started to type.

Hello Jerk,
I received your rejection letter today. It hurts—a lot!

When I met you at the writers' convention, I thought you were everything I could ever dream of in an agent and a friend. Now I know you are just another arrogant and conceited asshole who has used and misled me. The rejection letter from you shows just what you really are—a true jackass. I thought you would be different, not such a prick.

However, this time your egotism will not go unanswered. Do not worry about "only" watching your back—I will get even with you any way I can, and soon. You will learn just how bad you screwed up. I can promise you—I will be the worst nightmare you ever dreamed of. You Jerk!

Amy clicked on the print button and heard the printer spring into action. Without reading the letter again, she folded it, placed it in an envelope and added his address, but did not include a return one. To make sure he opened it, she wrote "expected mail" at the bottom of the envelope. She licked a stamp and placed it on the envelope as she walked out to the mailbox.

Amy's cell phone rang. She, at first, decided not to answer the call, but changed her mind when she noticed the call was coming from her best friend. "Hello, Lenny."

"Amy, how are you, girl? I've been trying to call you all day."

"I'm not doing well at all. It's been a bad day."

In his take-care mannerism that exemplified his gay lifestyle, Lenny nevertheless continued to be a trusted friend as he responded, "I'm so sorry. You know, I think I'll bring you some soup I wanted to make today. It's just delicious and you'll just have to try it."

"Lenny . . . ."

"Not a word. I'll not let you stop me. It'll be a few hours before I can make it, but I'll just not take *no* for an answer. I'll see you as soon as the soup's ready, girl." He disconnected before Amy could say another word. Lenny always amazed her with his bossy way of taking over like a mother hen. Of course, Lenny always acted more feminine in many ways than most of the girls she knew.

A feeling of relief flowed through her body as the envelope slid into the mailbox. The feeling would not last long—it never did. When it reached this state, she knew she could do very little. Perhaps she needed to give her psychologist, Dr. Lankford, a call and ask her what she would recommend. She hated feeling so helpless, but it was something she had gotten accustomed to.

She retrieved some mail in the box addressed to her, Amy Leigh Jenkins, which consisted of the normal bills and junk mail. While she always received mail from someone wanting something from her, she would have loved to receive an old-fashioned letter from a friend, but she couldn't remember the last time that had happened.

Thinking about how few friends she had sent her mood plummeting. It also didn't help to concentrate on how bad her case of bipolar disorder had become. After becoming an expert on her condition over the years, her entire medicine cabinet represented the many past attempts to regulate her moods. It contained all the remains of failed wonder drugs; including Lithium, Pramipexole, Zoloft, and Divalproex, just to name a few.

As she stood by the mailbox for a minute to think, a car eased to a stop as it passed along the street beside her. A man in a small blue sports car turned his head toward her as he lowered his window. Maybe her long blonde hair or big breasts caught his attention. Those were her two saving graces; or, at times, her greatest curses. Everything else about her looked pretty normal. Then she realized that she was still wearing her white bathrobe, and it wasn't completely wrapped around her to cover her body. Since it was the middle of the day, she guessed she did look a little ridiculous.

"Hello, how are you today?" he asked, obviously eager to make conversation.

She adjusted her robe to ensure that it covered her breasts, offered a cute little smile in his direction, and started to walk back toward her apartment. Her legs felt almost lifeless, and as if weights had been tied to her ankles. She knew he was still there, watching her, so she turned briefly toward him. "I'm not feeling well today. Have a good day."

"Okay, you have a good day yourself." He raised the window as he uttered a deep low whistle that was just loud enough for her to hear.

On any other day, she would have adequate words for this wolf on the prowl, but not today. She felt too drained. As this was so typical of the way men had constantly caused her problems it represented nothing new, yet it was a constant reminder.

The rejection letter she had received from Edward Lawson symbolized the worst thing that could have happened to her. While her mood had recently regressed, she had hoped that, just maybe, it would pass soon. And then she received the letter from the son of a bitch. It was a good thing he didn't live in the same city that she did. Because if he had, it would have been so tempting to drive to his house and claw his eyes out.

Even the plain front door to her apartment looked depressing. It made her feel like she was hiding in a small prison while she waited for her day of salvation to come. While Amy appreciated her Mom and Dad and how they still helped with the bills, all of her past screw-ups would make a good book. In spite of being great and wonderful parents, they'd finally had all they could stand and forced her out of their house a year ago.

Memories of how over the last several years she went

from one job to another and bounced from the company superstar to the company embarrassment echoed in her head. One end of the cycle led to feelings of prominence and confidence which made people love her for a while as she out-produced everyone. Then the mood shift came, causing it all to tumble down. Yes, she enjoyed some normal times. These times reflected her golden periods . . . if only those times would last. Dr. Lankford had always reminded her that she needed a stable life, but that didn't appear to be possible.

She could still hear the words of Dr. Lankford in her head. "Amy, while it's important to properly use your medication, I can't express enough how important it is for you to avoid putting yourself in stressful situations."

Amy remembered how she always responded, "Listen, I'm young and I don't want to be stuck in such a dull life with nothing to look forward to." While she wanted to have fun now, it was later in the ensuing depressed state that she hated life in general and saw no way out.

She opened the door to her apartment and stood still for several moments to allow her eyes to adjust to the darkness. With the curtains pulled and no lights turned on, the dreary apartment matched her mood. Her relentless memories surrounding the rejection letter tormented her. She knew she wasn't the first person who felt like they had been screwed and wanted to fight back, but she still felt frustrated. No, not frustrated—she felt mad as hell. After all, she had gone to bed with him.

But . . . who was she to fight a top literary agent who represented so many great authors? She wondered how he managed to acquire them. It would only be a matter of time until they learned the truth about him, and Edward would get his payback.

As she turned on the lights, she glanced at the cheap pictures decorating the walls and the bits and pieces of furniture that didn't match. With glasses and empty snack bags covering the coffee table, she would have to do something about her wreck of a place, maybe tomorrow. Today, she felt too tired.

After she slouched on the sofa, she noticed a small writing pad on the table in front of her. With nothing specific in mind, she picked the pad up and started to doodle. Then she added a small heading at the top which read, "Edward Lawson's hit list".

As her mind slowly started to focus, she had a small sense of a goal that must be accomplished. She wanted to get this guy one way or another. She didn't know how or where, but in time she would do it.

Since Edward thought she didn't have a career in writing, it would be nice to make sure he didn't have one as an agent, but what could she do? In the back of her mind, she considered making a martini to drink as she worked on the list. She forced herself to avoid the temptation and stared hard at the empty list.

She knew he liked to frequent conventions and conferences that were attended by writers. Perhaps she could follow him and harass him there. While the idea appeared tempting, it wouldn't be too effective and would probably just make her look like a psycho.

She realized her mind was starting to function. Perhaps the thoughts were evil, but for the first time in days she felt like the fog in her mind was clearing. She doodled some more on the paper as she plotted.

She needed to get the word out about the bastard so no one would dare use his services. She remembered seeing sites on the Internet listing predatory agents. That could be one place to start. If she could find a way to ensure that publishers never accepted books written by authors he represented, the authors would be forced to move on to other, more competent agents. She would love to accomplish such a feat, but learning exactly how to do it would require a lot of research.

Publishers are in business to make money, and they do so when the books they publish sell. It would be nice to watch Edward fall flat on his face by recommending bad books that lost money.

The words in his letter burned in her mind. "You might want to take some courses in writing." *Did he really think I'm some dumb high school blonde*? Then he added insult to injury when he avowed, "Sorry, this isn't the kind of book we're looking for at the present time. I wish you luck in finding someone to represent you."

At the convention, Edward told her paranormal romances were hot right now, and that was precisely what she had finished. In fact, it was one of the reasons she wanted to use him as her agent. "Oh you jerk! You told me nothing but damn lies," she yelled, but she knew others hated to be misled just like she had been deceived.

Suddenly, she wondered more about which books he preferred to promote, and which authors he represented. It would take some time, but she would find out. She walked over to the little table in the small eat-in kitchen where she ate her meals and operated her computer.

With the computer still on, she started to do some research and quickly located many sites with his name on them. She knew this would take a long time, so she adjusted her chair and started clicking on one site after another while printing the best ones. She had soon compiled a lot of information about him, and felt like she had accepted a mission with a very precise goal of totally destroying Edward Lawson as a literary agent.

When a loud knock on the door shattered her concentration, she suddenly remembered how Lenny had promised to bring her some soup in an attempt a cheer her up. "Hold on, I'm coming." She ran from the small kitchen table to let him in.

"Hello, girl." He said while holding a large pot. "This is just what the doctor ordered, and I know you'll just love it." Lenny had always looked like a model when he ventured out to take care of errands or helping out friends, and as usual his coordinated clothing looked perfect.

"Lenny, you shouldn't have!"

"Not a word. This is what friends are for." He stopped and looked at her intensely. "You do look terrible and definitely need some cheering up."

"Thanks." From anyone else she would consider the comment an insult, but she knew he spoke honestly and really cared about her.

"What's upsetting you so much today?"

"It's everything." That was a lie, but she didn't want to go in to all the details right now. Perhaps later she would tell him. It was so embarrassing to receive such a letter from someone she had held such high expectations, but instead was kicked to the curb, as if she was some kind of stray dog.

"I do hope you'll call your doctor tomorrow. It's so hard to see you in such a state of depression."

"I swallowed another pill a few minutes ago and I'll feel better soon. My mother has already made me promise to call Dr. Lankford."

Lenny walked over to the kitchen and placed the pot on the stove. "It's still warm. I can stay for a while, if you want me to."

"No. I have some things I want to do on the computer, and I need to be alone."

"Are you still working on a novel?"

Tears started falling down her face. "No, I think I might as well give up on my dream."

"That's nonsense. It's simply a matter of time until the literary world finds out about you."

Amy lowered her head again. She felt too weak to reply to his encouragement. "I think I need to rest for a while."

"I agree, and I hope you enjoy the soup." He stepped over and offered her a small hug. "Call me if I can do anything for you."

She would find a way out of this depressing mood somehow, but for now, she only had strength to hold on to the few friends she had, and she hoped that they would be patient with her. "Thank you for the soup. I'll call you soon."

Lenny walked over to the door. "Everything will be fine, you'll see." As he walked out the door, he closed it behind him.

After she poured a large bowl of the soup, Amy went right back to the computer. She tasted it a little at a time as she concentrated on her research. Four hours later, she had used all of her paper. She almost felt like she was working as a private investigator by conducting background checks on a suspect.

It amazed her how much information she had discovered on the Internet, but she knew this would only be the beginning. To accomplish what she wanted to do, she needed to know everything she could about him.

She continued to work as the time slipped away. During the day, she usually felt so tired and drained that she simply stayed in bed all day. Today, however, she continued to click and read. While she often ordered pizza, which had contributed to a large part of the problem with her weight, she was too busy today. She didn't think she looked like a washing machine or anything close, but she knew she could benefit from shedding some pounds.

After finishing the entire pot of soup, she walked over to the refrigerator and opened it, hoping to find anything that might taste good. She slightly laughed as she discovered some items placed inside by her mom. While her mom had always expressed concern about her weight, she didn't exactly nag. While she knew fat-free yogurt and raw vegetables, for some reason, wouldn't fill the void in her stomach, she picked up a container of yogurt anyway and headed back to the computer.

After Amy found many more sites with information, she finally located a site listing the authors that Edward represented. It felt like she had hit gold. Since she had no more paper, she clicked on favorites and saved the site. Next, she started searching for his authors and the books they had written. After she finished the yogurt and started feeling better, she located a review of a book that one of Edward's authors had recently released. The book reviewer praised the book and recommended it, making Amy immediately start to relapse. She felt as if this book reviewer knew nothing. As she continued to read the article, her plan came into clear view. It couldn't be too hard to write a book review.

Yes, this would turn the tables on the jerk. She wondered how he would like being criticized, and in front of the entire world. The payback would satisfy her much more than anything she could have ever dreamed for. It would take some work, but now she knew that she was creating a perfect way to make sure that Edward's career would come to a grinding halt.

CHAPTER 3

Amy rushed to the elevator and hit the up button. She hoped to arrive on time. Eager to make Dr. Lankford proud of her, she had worked hard to look presentable today. The last time they met, she'd arrived in an old sweatshirt and faded jeans. Today, she wore a bright red dress and three inch heels. For the first time in a week, she had also washed and blow-dried her hair. Her long blonde hair grew thick and required at least a half hour to dry and style. Applying makeup was another task altogether. While her eyes looked expressive, she often thought they were too large, and they required a lot of work to make them look nice. Thanks to the weight problem, she had, to some extent, fat cheeks. Luckily, with good makeup she could hide that problem. As far as her long nose was concerned, she had considered surgery, which scared her, so she had decided a long time ago to accept life as it was. Anyway, she considered her looks okay, especially with everything else going on these days.

Finally, she reached the entrance to the doctor's office. Since dear old dad was paying for these expensive sessions, she needed to arrive on time. Also, if she didn't keep her appointments, Dr. Lankford might cut off her medications. Sometimes she resented the medications complicating her life, but without them she couldn't imagine having any life line at all.

Dr. Lankford's receptionist looked up at her as she walked in. "We were hoping you would make it today. Dr. Lankford's waiting on you. Please go on in." The receptionist smiled at Amy as she glanced at her dress.

"Thank you. I'm sorry I'm running a little late."

The office looked impressive and professional, as it should be based on the massive amount of money she knew that her dad was shelling out to Dr. Lankford.

Dr. Lankford stayed at her desk as Amy entered. While busy reading a book, she stopped, looked up, and placed it to one side. "My goodness, you look nice today!"

Amy knew she must have blushed. "Thanks. It does feel good to dress up."

"I take it that you're feeling good today."

"I feel slightly better . . . but only slightly. This is more of a desperate attempt to get back on track."

"Are you taking your medication as we agreed?"

"I'm not sure, but I think so. The last few days have been very bad."

With a look of concern, the doctor pointed to the chair beside her. "Has anything happened to cause you extra stress the last few days?"

Amy allowed an expression of sorrow to flow across her face, which gave no doubt that it had been a bad week. It would be hard to get through all that happened in only one hour.

"I guess we need to get to it then. Tell me what happened to you this week."

Amy drifted over to the seat next to Dr. Lankford's chair and glanced around again at the expensive and elaborate furnishings in her office. She wondered if Dr. Lankford possessed such a gift for decorating, or if she had a designer put it all together for her. Her executive style desk set the tone for the rest of her impressive office. She did manage to give the office a female touch with the fresh flowers scattered around on several small tables. While admiring the hundreds of books she neatly displayed, Amy wondered if she really read them, or if she added them simply for decorations.

Dr. Lankford looked at her patiently, and though she didn't rush her, Amy knew she needed to concentrate, and to stop allowing her thoughts to wonder. After shrugging her

18

shoulders, Amy glanced toward the ceiling. "It's more of the same things that always happen to me." She lied, but she found it much easier than jumping into the true story of what triggered her depression last week.

"Perhaps we should review your life chart for a minute to better understand how this week fits in, and where you are with your true moods. I want to know if anything in your past resembles how you feel now."

Dr. Lankford pulled out a long chart she had made earlier for Amy. Amy had seen it many times before. It listed the major events in her life, and marked the periods when she had her highs and lows. They both knew what Dr. Lankford was doing as she tried to pinpoint what caused Amy's enormous mood shifts. While Amy's environment had a part in it, the genes causing the chemical imbalances in her brain caused most of her problems.

"I think we need to start at the beginning." Dr Lankford pointed toward the top.

"We've covered this many times before," Amy responded in a weary voice.

With the chart open in front of her, she recognized the first major turning point in her life. She had just become a teenager and it was the time when boys discover girls and girls discover boys. It was always a dramatic point for both. In her case, she had several problems. She reflected on being overweight, and how her breasts had become fully developed by the time she had reached fourteen. It had been both a blessing and a curse. Although her breasts brought her attention, she also became the center of jokes. The boys often made fun of her and gave her bad names—always related to her breasts.

Dr. Lankford nodded toward Amy. "I know how hard it is for a young girl to get a handle on her sexuality, especially with immature boys around that don't understanding their own feelings."

"These . . ." she said, as she pointed to her breasts, "have always caused me problems."

Then there was the first boy in her life. His name was Jason. He was the guy all the girls in school fell in love with. She had felt surprised when Jason sent word to her that he wanted to talk to her. After all of this time, she could still remember the ecstasy she felt when one of her friends said, "Jason told me he likes you and wants to talk to you." It was one of the greatest highs she could remember. In that mood, she could see nothing wrong and saw only what she wanted to see. She would learn later that when she felt this way, it usually resulted in her making most of her worst mistakes. Yes, she had made many stupid decisions when she drifted into this state.

She didn't know that his friends had put him up to it. He was a charmer and very good at deceiving her. It wasn't long until he asked, "Can you meet me in the woods behind our house?" Deep in the woods, they were all alone when he then told her, "If you like me, you would show me your breasts." The first time, she told him no, and she had hoped he was just teasing her and that he really liked her.

Over the next few days he acted cold to her, and she really wanted him to be her boyfriend. She remembered how her girlfriends had teased her about him and how embarrassing it would be to tell them he wasn't her boyfriend anymore. Needless to say, a week later, she told him, "Meet me in the woods in a few hours. I really want to be your girlfriend."

After he walked over to where she was waiting for him in the woods, he made his move. "I have a secret place not far from here. Let's walk over to it." When they arrived at his secret place, he reached over and kissed her. It was her first true kiss from a boy.

After he finished kissing her, he stepped back and waited for her. Since she had promised him she would let him see, she started by unbuttoning her blouse and pulling her bra to one side to expose one nipple. He soon told her, "I want you to take both your blouse and your bra off."

"No." While she didn't want to be naked and fully exposed, she gave in when he looked like he was going to simply walk away. She would never forget the next few minutes. As soon as she removed both and stood in front of him, he snatched her blouse and bra and shouted, "Come on out guys, I have her bra!" His buddies suddenly appeared from out of nowhere, as they laughed and pointed at her breasts. To them it was hilarious, but to her, she felt like dying. In fact, that is what she tried to do a week later.

Amy's voice lowered to a whisper as her thoughts turned inward. "I still have nightmares of this, or of being naked in public somewhere."

"Being naked in public is one of the most common nightmares for most people, but in your case I know it can be especially frightening. Hopefully, time will help you get over what they did to you."

Finally, a year later, her dad had decided to listen to her school psychologist and move to another city to help her obtain a fresh start. It was hard to think about how badly she had been ridiculed that year before she moved. She knew those scars would be inside her forever.

Everything eventually went well until she entered high school and she discovered alcohol, as well as the problems associated with it. For a while, she was the party girl. Everyone loved her. She thought she stood above the law and immune from all possibilities of getting hurt, as she was making great grades and looking forward to going to college.

Then, another boy came into her life. They went everywhere together, and life was wonderful, but in some ways she felt as if she was missing out on life. She eventually went out with some of the girls from her school one night to a party at a nearby college, and pretended to be college-aged girls as well. It was amazing what makeup could do for a girl.

The party, which had many kegs of beer and plenty of hard liquor available, became wilder and wilder, as the guys had a grand old time with the girls they had invited. While the music played loud, the house became crowded with drunks who lost control, which also included her.

When she saw two of the girls dancing on small tables with the boys shouting for them to show some skin and to *take it off*, she vaguely remembered some girls actually stripping slightly for the guys. After one guy next to her reached over and poured straight vodka in her glass, she drank too much too fast and soon found herself sitting on the couch to keep from falling.

This guy knew he was getting her totally drunk as he pulled her to him and kissed her. She had no strength to resist him. His slow, tender kisses became much more passionate as his hands started to explore her breasts. At first she resisted, but he kept pressing and pressing. This caught the attention of others in the house, as another boy on the other side of her leaned over and kissed the back of her neck.

It felt so good to have the attention of two boys at once, and she was the party girl—right? It was when the new boy slid his hand up her dress that she knew she was in trouble. She managed to slap his hand and make him stop the first time, but he became as persistent as the first guy. "Please don't do that," she pleaded. But his hand found its way up her dress and to her panties, where he managed to fondle her through them. It wasn't that it felt bad, and it actually felt erotic and sensual at the time, but she knew what she was doing was wrong and that she now had a boyfriend. She remembered how this escalated with them abusing and molesting her more every minute. At that moment, she didn't care. No one would ever know, she thought.

At first, she didn't notice the flash of lights as several guys started taking pictures. When she looked down, her dress was all the way up and her legs spread enough to make a centerfold layout for Playboy.

Amy quickly struggled to force her dress down. "What do you think you're doing?" She shouted as she suddenly becoming fully aware of the situation. The first guy had managed to unbutton her blouse and lowered her bra enough to kiss one nipple for the cameras. "Stop," she yelled, as she tried to clear her head from the vodka.

Somehow, she managed to regain the strength to stand. As the guys realized she was mad and now becoming cognizant of what was going on, they quickly realized it would be better to stay out of her way. She remembered locating one of her friends and a different group of guys that were using the same tactics of getting her friend drunk. Amy yelled as she shook her friend. "Wake up, they're taking photographs of you."

While her friend slowly gained consciousness as well, she appeared to be in worse shape than Amy. If Amy hadn't showed up when she did, she felt sure they would soon have started raping her.

Fortunately, another one of the girls staggered in who had been separated also, but she wasn't nearly as drunk as they were. They were all lucky when this girl called a taxi before she held up her cell phone and yelled to the group, "Who wants me to call the police?"

"Don't do that." All the guys yelled, or pleaded in some sort of fashion. They knew their fun was over and they could be in some serious trouble.

"I want all the photos erased now!" she yelled at them.

Some of them complied, but not all since Amy remembered the day her boyfriend received his copy. The fight was bitter. She had ruined something which could've been so special. They never talked again.

Depression set in as one thing after another started going bad for her. Her grades dropped and she stayed at home most of the time, just sleeping or lying around. She wasn't able to function, and the medication she received made her mood swings worse. It would be years later before they diagnosed her with bipolar disorder.

That was four years ago, and when Amy had first started working with Dr. Lankford. Amy was lucky that another psychologist had recommended that she try Dr. Lankford, who specialized in treating the kind of wild mood swings that she had. During those four years, Amy had educated herself about her condition, but knowing about it was one thing—controlling it was totally different.

Dr. Lankford appeared to be about fifty years old, and had a soft and gentle nature about her. Amy assumed her mannerisms had been perfected from long hours of listening to wretched souls like her. Her large brown eyes looked like those of an adorable puppy, begging for attention.

Amy filled her lungs with air and let it out slowly. "Several days ago, I received a rejection letter from an agent I wanted to represent me. He was the one I met a month ago at the writer's convention I told you about."

"Yes, I remember you had such high hopes, but as you know, it's hard to find a good agent to represent first-time writers."

"You know, I feel like this jerk led me on. He was like so many men in my life from the past. However, this time I'll not be walked over like I'm nothing. I thought we had made a connection at the convention." Amy briefly covered her eyes with her hands. "I think it's time for someone to stand up and get even with people like this. It's hard for me to explain just how much he hurt me and how mad I am at him right now."

"This is different from you. I know you've received

many rejection letters in the past. Why is this one rejection so earth-shattering for you?"

"Like I said—we had something special . . . humm, very special, at the convention."

Dr. Lankford shifted her weight and leaned forward. "Are you suggesting that you had an affair with him at the convention?"

"I was in one of those moods where I was above it all and doing crazy things. I don't remember all the details, but yes I did get drunk that night." She returned her hands in front of her eyes and started to cry.

Dr. Lankford handed her a tissue, as usual. "Amy, I think we need to talk more about this trip to the convention."

Amy knew she was right, but she wouldn't like what she was about to hear. Dr. Lankford remained quiet as Amy started to tell all the details of the story surrounding the convention. "I arrived at the convention like many other want-to-be authors. My mood was in a *high swing* and I knew that was dangerous. I knew I was in the kind of state where I might do many crazy things I would regret later, but those states are also the times when people love me and I'm most productive. My energy level felt extraordinary. I expected to find the perfect agent to represent my new book. For several months I had worked endless nights and days on it." Amy looked over to her for approval.

"I know you're working on a novel, and it's a good use of your creative energy, but it's this trip to the convention that I'm worried about."

Amy studied Dr. Lankford, and it felt as if she was truly interested in her story. "Perhaps I should've listened to you, since it's hard to predict what my moods will do to me. I know that I can act normal for a period of time, and also swing so much in such a short time also. What is so upsetting, however, is that it's hard for me to tell where I am in my moods."

"Precisely, and that's one of the reasons I want you to attend the group sessions I'm starting the day after tomorrow. You're still planning on coming, I hope?" She paused briefly before she continued. "I think having others around that are going through the same problems you are will help you. This has been working for a number of other psychologists across the country to identify early shifts in moods."

"I'm not so sure about this, but I might give it a try."

"I'm glad. Now tell me the full story about this convention. Something tells me there's much more you haven't told me. I promise to simply listen and not judge you."

For the remainder of the hour Amy told Dr. Lankford details of the convention she hadn't revealed earlier. She knew she could talk openly, but decided to close her eyes as she went through the details as best she could remember them. "I saw many agents and publishers at the conference. I had completed as much research as I could on them, and I had planned my three days at the convention to ensure I would make as many contacts as possible with the agents I had hoped would offer me the best shot in being accepted. It was during one of the first group meetings that I attended where I first saw Edward Lawson walking into the room. He was tall, slightly over six feet, and slim. His hair was dark and combed straight back, which revealed a receding hair line that at first made him look older than he was, but from my research, I already knew that he was thirty-two years old."

Amy breathed in deeply and continued. "As he walked toward the front of the room, many people moved toward him to shake his hand. It was obvious that he was very well known. His movements became slow and measured, and as if he wanted to make sure he was doing things properly and using correct etiquette. With a smile plastered on his face, I knew that time would tell if it was for the crowds, or if it was genuine."

Amy shifted her weight. "After his speech, I wasn't able to move close to him because of the small mob surrounding him. His talk had appealed to everyone, since he had participated in a group discussion with other agents on what was hot, what kind of manuscripts they were interested in, and what kind they didn't want to see. I remember my heart being full of excitement when I heard him talk about what he liked. He was interested in paranormal romances, and that's exactly what I had just completed. I had worked hard on it to make sure it was polished, and then polished again. It was at that moment I knew, somehow, I would find a way to talk to him."

Amy opened her eyes to study the expressions on a face calmly encouraging her to continue. "After two days of nothing but disappointments, I received the break that I had been waiting for. As I waited in line to shake his hand at the end of one session, I heard him tell someone that he planned to go to a local bar later that night for some drinks. Come hell or high water, so to speak, I knew I would visit that bar."

Amy blinked her eyes and continued. "After the person in front of me left, I came face to face with Edward for the first time. I remember the same frozen smile he had while he was speaking as he extended his hand to me and said hello. His teeth were perfect and obviously whitened by a dentist. It was, however, his eye brows that captured my attention. They were heavy and thick and seemed to give his face added expressions when he talked. Since it's not too often I'm at a loss for words, I know I went into super mode and started talking too fast. As you know, it's the one part of the bipolar condition that's so hard to control when I enter that phase. Oh god, I must've made a fool out of myself, but to my surprise, I think it impressed him—I really do."

Amy fought back a small sniffle. "He asked what I was writing and I told him a paranormal romance. He looked pleased and said to send him a query letter and the opening chapters, which he would love to look at. Wow—that felt great!"

She briefly tightened the muscles in her hands before she continued. "His eyes looked small, but penetrating. He kind of reminded me of a teacher who could look right at me and dare me to not tell him the truth. Thinking about it, he even dressed like a young professor. When he reached out to shake my hand, I still remember how soft it felt, almost feminine. It was obvious that he wasn't an outdoor type. While he was tall, he had a lean body from what I assumed was very little physical activity. Eventually, I thanked him and moved on as I knew many people wanted to talk to him."

Amy concentrated on the events before she continued. "That day I went all out getting ready for the night, and I spent a lot of time working on my hair, and my makeup. When your hair is this naturally curly, it takes a lot of time to make it look good. Then, I tried on every piece of clothing I brought with me, and nothing seemed to fit right. So I went shopping and spent more than I should, but I found the perfect little red dress that I hoped he would like. While most of the time my large breasts are a nuisance to me, but right then I was willing to use whatever I had to attract his attention. The dress was a solid red party dress that tied behind my neck and left my back exposed. It was a dramatic look that also helped to lift my breasts and highlight them. It has a single fake diamond pin that held the material together between my breasts. It was expensive, but I knew I had to have it, and I would worry about paying for it later."

Amy raised her hands to cover her face as the embarrassment flooded in. "And of course when I was in the store, I had to have a new pair of shoes to match it, as well as a cute pair of earrings, which complimented the diamond pin. I knew the seven hundred dollars I charged on my credit card would take a while to pay off, but it's not the first time I've made mistakes like this and regretted it later. Yes . . . and I know it won't be the last time. You know, I think part of my current bad mood is from the bill I received for all the money I spent. Anyway, I finally drove to the bar where he was going that night. Since I wasn't sure what time he would show up, and I definitely didn't want to miss him, I had arrived early. I had prepared to wait all night if I had to in this quaint little place where the crowd was mainly professionals stopping by on their way home for a quick cocktail."

Amy paused. "After all the time I had spent getting ready, I was really hoping for some attention when I walked in, but I was mainly ignored. Many of the women in the bar looked very beautiful, making the competition very tough that night. I remember thinking that I needed to lose some weight and that there had to be a way to do it. After I had decided to wait at the bar, a bartender soon drifted over to me and asked what I wanted to drink. Since I didn't know how long I had to wait, I decided to order a glass of white house wine, hoping that this would be easy to sip on and I could easily wait out the time."

Dr. Lankford interrupted for a second. "How many drinks did you have?"

"Too many before the night ended." Amy sniffed. "Not long after I ordered the second glass, I watched Edward and two other guys coming in. Edward was in the same bright blue shirt he had worn earlier, but he'd removed his sports coat and tie. He also no longer had the plastered-on smile and looked much more relaxed and natural. While he wasn't an extremely handsome guy, he had a few good qualities."

Amy knew this story was taking some time, and that she

had to hurry to tell it all. "The two other guys looked much like him, and I assumed that all three were single. One of the two men I vaguely recognized from the convention. After studying his face for a minute as they moved around the room, I eventually remembered who he was. He was one of the speakers in a meeting and had written several books. I could only guess that he was one of Edward's authors."

"The three finally walked to the bar where I was sitting and selected seats close to me. With only about twenty seats at the bar, and most of them taken, I felt happy the seat between us stayed empty and accepted it as a good sign. It would make a move over to them easy enough."

"Since they weren't laughing or talking much, it quickly became obvious that they didn't do the bar scene too often. I watched them constantly looking around, as if trying to evaluate the place before deciding what to do. They offered passing shots over at me while trying to hide little comments between themselves. It would've been good to know what they were saying, but as I've learned before, they were probably talking about my breasts."

"Suddenly, Edward stood and rushed for the door as he pressed his cell phone to his ear. Apparently he had received a call and wanted to take the call outside. While it wasn't extremely loud in the bar, it wasn't too easy to carry on a conversation in there either. After he left, the two guys ordered a beer and started talking as they often turned and looked around the room to check things out."

"The writer I had recognized was on the side closest to me. He was in his thirties and wore jeans and a nice pullover, which looked new. His brown hair was cut fairly short, and he was slim like Edward, but not nearly as tall. I tried to remember his name, but my mind wouldn't function as it should."

"When he turned to survey the room the next time, I decided to flash him a smile, which he returned in a somewhat friendly, but boyish manner. Since he appeared to be shy, it looked like I was going to have to make the first move.”

“A few minutes later he turned toward me again as I spoke first and asked him if he was one of the speakers at the writer’s conference. At first he acted surprised, and then he flashed a small smile and told me that his name was Michael Hadcock. I reached across the empty seat so that I could reach his hand. Of course, I had intentionally left one seat vacant for Edward when he returned.”

“After I told him my name was Amy, he then introduced me to Larry Waterman, who was next to him. Larry had slightly long blond hair, and he appeared to have a little bit of a Swedish look, including the classical deep-blue eyes. He looked to be around forty and an inside type guy as well.”

“We were busy talking about the convention when Edward walked back in to the bar. He slid into his seat and looked at his two friends who had already managed to attract a lady to talk to. I saw the look of approval on his face as he sneaked them a quick wink.”

“Michael started to introduce us when I again took the initiative and extended my hand to Edward and told him I remembered him from the convention. At first, he stared at me, and then he acted like he remembered me. I’m not sure if he did or not. I know he meets so many people at the conventions it would be difficult to remember everyone. However, I was hoping he remembered me. Suddenly, he looked up with his beady eyes beneath his heavy brow and told me that *now* he remembered how I was writing a book.”

“I told him I had finished it and it was a paranormal romance. He looked pleased. I prayed for once in my life I was on the right track, and that this was it for sure.”

“After his beer arrived, he turned and saluted his two friends. Apparently, I was still not in the thick of the group, but the night was young. My energy level was high, and I was determined to land him as my agent. I felt lucky when he turned and asked me again about my book. He acted extremely polite."

"When he talked, his words were measured and precise. I had no doubt he was extremely intelligent as well as highly educated. The questions he asked me about the book were pointed and direct. I assumed he wanted a straight answer, which I provided. He looked pleased."

"I ordered another wine, and I don't remember much of anything after that. As you know, my limit is around two glasses of wine, but I was determined to stay and talk to him as long as I could. I don't know for sure if I left him with a good or bad impression of me. In fact, I remember nothing but waking up the next morning in my room. I'm sure he learned I can't go past two glasses of wine, and I really can't remember how many glasses of wine I had before I left."

Amy stopped talking for a while, unable to focus, but then continued. "I do remember him being friendly and staring intensely at my breasts for a long time. I was in a mood to do whatever I could to get him as my agent. While it's too bad that I still don't remember exactly what happened that night, I do know we became very friendly with each other. I think we danced and I may have even kissed him several times while we danced. I must've blacked out mentally. Perhaps, I'll never know."

When Amy finished the story, Dr. Lankford twisted her lip to one side. "I see you had a very dramatic episode in your life . . . again. Some people go long periods during their cycle. You're one of those who can cycle fast or stay normal for a long time. That makes it hard to decide which medication to keep you on. It's extremely important for you to tell me things like this. I hope you understand what I'm saying."

"Yes I do, but it's so hard to understand my moods

myself."

"That's why I think it'll be good for you to attend the new group therapy session I'm starting. You really need to attend."

"I know I should, but I also know this is costing my dad a lot of money. I don't want to be any more of a burden on him than I am already."

"Since I think you'll truly benefit from this, and I also feel like you'll be a big help to me in understanding others, I'm going to make you a special offer. The first month is absolutely free. Of course, I don't want you to tell anyone else about this. Is this okay with you?"

"Yes, and if you don't mind I'd love to attend. I really do appreciate what you're doing for me. You've helped me so much and I'm not always the best patient in the world."

CHAPTER 4

While thinking about the group meeting over the last two days, Amy worried about sharing her feelings and behavior with perfect strangers. Also, she didn't know how she would react to other people who suffered with the same type condition she had. If she hadn't promised Dr. Lankford that she would come, she wouldn't even think about attending the group meeting at her office at all.

As she held her breath and opened the door to Dr. Lankford's office, the reception area looked empty, but she could hear people talking from inside of Dr. Lankford's private office. She had only taken a few steps when Dr. Lankford walked out into the reception area from her office.

"Hello, Amy. I'm glad you're here. Come on in and have a seat. We'll start in a few minutes, and everyone else is already inside."

As usual, at most events she arrived last. "Thanks. I'm still not so sure about this."

"Don't worry. You'll do fine here and hopefully you'll make some new friends." Dr. Lankford followed behind Amy to close the door, which had been left open by Amy as she stepped into her office. Dr. Lankford had rearranged her office to make room for the group session. She had pushed her desk as well as her couch to one side. In a circle of small chairs occupied by about seven or eight people, Amy watched various degrees of interest coming from the group.

As Amy walked over to one of the two empty chairs, she assumed Dr. Lankford would occupy the last one. No one said a word, but a few occasionally offered her a small curious smile. She was relieved to see Dr. Lankford walking to her seat. With her big smile which seemed to light up the room, she was the one common element bonding the group together and maintaining their trust.

Dr. Lankford began talking as she walked to her seat.

"I'm so glad to have all of you here today. This is a new group and I'm sure everyone has some mixed feelings with all the new faces, but I think every person in this room will benefit greatly from the exchange of information each of you can share."

She paused for a moment to glance around the room. "I don't have a lot of rules, but I'd like to ask for one rule to be observed, if nothing else. As you can imagine, it's important for everyone to openly share their thoughts and feelings with the group, and because of that I think we should all agree that what's said in this room stays in this group. I hope everyone will agree with this rule. If so, let me see you raise your hand in agreement."

Amy could definitely agree with this rule, as she checked around the room to see that all complied. For the first time, she carefully studied the small crowd of people, where she counted four women and three guys. The ages ranged from the early twenties to around the late fifties. She couldn't believe she had joined a group like this. This wasn't the way she thought life was supposed to be, but here she was.

"As one added layer of security, I think we need to do one more thing. When we go around introducing ourselves in a minute, it would be good to only provide your first name. Is that agreeable with everyone?"

Everyone agreed again by raising a hand into the air. Amy quickly concentrated on what she could say about herself in a few minutes.

With a big smile on her face as she looked over the group, Dr. Lankford continued. "Who wants to go first and tell us your first name and something about you?" The room remained quiet, since no one wanted to go first. Many glanced toward the floor and waited for someone else.

Finally, one guy who had good posture and one of those super large smiles raised his hand and started talking. "My name's Stephen, and I was recently diagnosed with having a bipolar condition. I'm lucky to have a great family supporting me to seek help. It's something I think I've lived with for a long time, but I had no idea what caused me to do so many crazy things in my life, things I've regretted later. Sometimes, like now, I feel like I'm on top of the world, but over time I have also realized that this is when I make my worst mistakes. I've started projects in the past that there's no way I could ever complete, and because of it I've had many financial crises in my life. It has also cost me a divorce several years ago." He looked around the room to see if anyone wanted to ask him a question. When no one offered any, he lowered his head and waited for someone else to talk.

A girl next to Amy started next. She had short black hair pulled across her forehead from a part on one side. "My name's Judith, and I always wondered why I felt depressed so often. I'm single, but have a Mom who looks after me, and has worked with my periods of depression and aggression for years. While my doctors would prescribe medication for me, it always appeared to make it worse. There are many times I felt like I can do no wrong, but it never lasted long. With the medication I'm taking now, I'm finally getting a handle on life, but it's something I have to work at all the time."

Judith also looked around for questions before lowering her head. While Amy guessed that she was around thirty-five or so, her sunken posture indicated she had suffered with depression and the lack of exercise for a long time.

As Stephen offered her a small approving nod, Dr. Lankford appeared to welcome the exchange. "Who's going to be next?"

The next woman to speak sat across from Amy and looked to be in her mid-fifties. She had the look of a grandmother, the one who acts like she cares about you, understands you, and always wants to bring you fresh baked cookies. "Hello, I guess I'll go next. My name's Nancy, and I never thought I'd be in this situation. I didn't have many problems with my moods until a few years ago when my husband became sick, and I lost my job while taking care of him until he died. He was the world to me, and it was something I couldn't cope with for a long time. When I was put on medication, I went wild and thought I should make up for a lost life. When all was said and done I'd spent a lot of our savings, which was intended to cover our retirement. It's been a battle ever since to have a normal life again. If you're like me, you've had all of your friends tell you to simply snap out of it. I wish it was so easy. It's going to be good, I think, to have friends who understand what it's like to be bipolar."

As she finished, a small man off to the other side of Amy raised his head to talk. He appeared to have been a drunk for a long time, and someone who might even be a homeless person, even with the nice clothes he wore. She assumed that his lean body came from missed meals and not a great exercise program. "I'm Wendell, and thank you for letting me join the group. I've recently stabilized somewhat because of a nice guy who has given me a chance to work for him. He understands me because his own son suffered from the same condition until he committed suicide two years ago. Since his son and I shared some common interests, he decided to help me as if I was his son as well. I don't know how long I'll stay in the normal range. He knows and I know, but it's been something I've faced all of my life."

Dr. Lankford glanced over to one guy who was in his mid-fifties, who looked back at her with ghostly eyes. They froze as they connected with each other. "Okay, my name's Ernest, and this is one of the few times I've been out of bed in months. It does feel good to venture out, but I'm tired of having to fight this day after day. I know you'd like to see me better, but there has to come a time when you have to admit you're a failure."

Dr. Lankford spoke quickly. "That's not exactly true. Many in your field consider you way ahead of your time and, in fact, brilliant. You've received many awards and honors for your work, and I think soon you'll be at the top of your game again."

Dr. Lankford next glanced at Amy, who lowered her head. She wasn't ready for this, since she felt just like the last guy who had introduced himself. *Damn! Why am I here*?

Fortunately, another girl looked as if she was suddenly given a signal to spring into action. "Okay, like my dad's making me come to these sessions. I don't think I'm sick or anything like that. I'm still young and hey . . . I love to party. Yeah, like sometimes it does get a little wild, but that's life. When things don't go my way, I get depressed, like most people. I'm not here to be anybody's friend. The courts and my dad are forcing me to take counseling, and it's the only reason I'm here. I just thought I'd say that so we can be honest with things here." Her short black hair bounced lively as she looked around the room, daring anyone to challenge her. When no one did, she became silent and slid back in her chair. "My name's Brittany." She looked back down at the floor.

Amy noticed how Brittany dressed with interest. She wore jeans cut extremely low, exposing her lean, well-toned stomach almost all the way to her crotch. Her thin pull-over t-shirt stretched tight over small breasts revealing the shape of her nipples. She looked like a girl asking for trouble.

Amy next looked across the room at the one lady who hadn't said a word. She looked like she didn't belong here in any form or fashion. She appeared to be in her late thirties, tall and beautiful. Every aspect about her shouted money and lots of it. Her long blonde hair layered flawlessly in a style which fit her to perfection. She reflected poise and elegance in every movement she made. Her face had been frozen in a fake smile ever since Amy had first noticed her. Amy suspected her teeth had been veneered because they were too perfect. She looked almost like she belonged in a beauty pageant, rather than a group therapy session with a bunch of losers like her and the other misfits.

When it became obvious the beauty queen meant to be last, Amy glanced around to gain her thoughts. Finally, she started, choosing her words with care. "My name's Amy, and I guess I've the same mood problems as everyone else. My mood swings from high to low and can take years, or it can be less than a month. That's what makes it so hard to regulate my medication and to make life normal. A month ago, I was feeling fine, and then I went into another depressed mode. Until a few days ago, I just wanted to stay in bed and sleep all the time."

Stephen raised his hand. "Did anything bad happen to you which caused this, or do you think it was a shift in a chemical imbalance?"

Amy considered his questions before she continued. "A month ago I went to a writer's convention, and I met what I hoped was a guy who would also be my agent. It was the greatest feeling in the world."

Stephen spoke again. "Then what causes your problem?"

Amy looked around the room as she remembered the letter. Since it made her angry, she didn't mind letting everyone know how she felt as she spoke loudly. "He sent me a rejection letter, which I received a few days ago. While it hurt me, it was his side comments that ripped me apart. He suggested that I go back to school to learn to write. I've studied English for a long time, including working on my Masters in English, and I know I'm good at it. After telling me he was looking for my kind of book at the convention, he reversed himself and said my novel wasn't what he was looking for. I know that to be a lie. It turns out that he's like so many jerks in the literary agency field who think they're so much better than everyone else. It's almost like they expect writers to bow and worship them. They know you have to use them to get to the major publishers."

The rich woman soon raised her head, as her eyes flashed around to catch everyone's attention before she spoke in a soft and caring voice which revealed how much Amy's story must have touched her. "I completely understand how you feel. Some people are arrogant, and it's like fighting city hall with nothing you can do about it."

Amy couldn't control her anger as she shouted back. "That may be true most of the time, but this time . . . I'll get even. It might take some time, but this agent will never forget what a bad mistake he made." She couldn't stop the tears as she lowered her head.

Dr. Lankford raised her hands. "I know we all get hurt, but making threats toward someone isn't a positive way to resolve anything. I can see that we need to work on this some more, but time will help heal the pain you feel, and I'm sure you'll find an agent soon. I've read your work, and I think you're very talented by the way."

Amy paused before sending her a small smile. "It's not a threat—it's a promise. I plan on doing to him exactly what he did to me. We'll soon find out how he likes to be criticized."

After the room settle, all eyes focused on the beauty queen and wondered what her story would be. "I guess it's my time to tell all. My name's Estella, and I do have a lot I'm thankful for. My parents have been very good to me while I was growing up, and they have provided me with everything a girl could want. My husband's a professional man that I rarely see anymore, but he spoils me in spite of my problems. So, why do I get so depressed? I think maybe because I've not been allowed to try anything on my own. I know I've humiliated my family often with my drinking, but it's my easiest way of escaping life and living it up for a while. It's my one way to establish that I'm in control. I know I'm lucky to have them cover up all the bad spells I've had."

Estella glanced at Amy. "I admire you for wanting to fight back. At least you know what you're fighting for, and you have a goal. I feel like I'm in an ivory tower sometimes with no way to escape."

After she finished, everyone returned their stares to Dr. Lankford as she stood and smiled at Estella with approval before looking directly at each person, giving them a similar smile. "You all have different problems, but over time you all go through the same problems others are having. I think by sharing with others in the group, everybody can benefit from the combined groups' knowledge. I think you should all give each other a large pat on the back for taking the first step in this group. It'll take some time, but I'm sure the trust will build in the group and all of you will be able to share more and more." After stating a few goals she had established for the group, she continued, "We'll meet every week at the same time. I want to thank all of you for coming."

As everyone slowly glanced around and stood to walk toward the door, no one offered small talk or goodbye hugs. She would have to wait and see how this group advanced.

CHAPTER 5

Amy's heavy head felt so good on her soft pillow, while her body felt warm and snuggly under the covers on her bed. She couldn't believe how she had tossed and turned all night after the group meeting the day before. Images of Edward spun in her head all night, haunting her and making sleep impossible. She knew that her hatred for this guy she barely knew was consuming her, but now she was becoming more determined than ever to ruin him.

While she felt sure he wasn't the only prick in the publishing industry, he had totally stepped over the line with her. It was time for him to pay his dues for not only ruining her dreams, but possibly the dreams of many other writers.

She felt a small wicked smile cross her lips as she remembered one famous saying, "Hell hath no fury like a woman scorned." Well, he should soon find out exactly what that means. Somehow she knew what she was doing was wrong, but at the same time she felt like her actions were justified.

After Amy managed to drag herself out of bed and walk toward the shower, she slowly dropped her night dress by the door before stepping under the flow of hot water. With the water invigorating her, she started to feel alive again as she slowly opened the bottle of body wash and started to bathe. The soft silky feeling was exactly what she needed. Not only were her breasts large, they were sensitive. As she reflected on all the past opportunities at love which never worked out, she couldn't believe she was still a virgin. The stupid hang up she had about her breasts had ruined many chances for romance. Like most girls she knew, she wanted someone to care about her and not *them*.

With her eyes closed, she slowly visualized Edward's face as his beady eyes with heavy but well groomed eyebrows stared at her. His frozen smile softened, as he focuses on her. She knew they could've been so good together. While he wasn't exactly a stud, he did have a certain charm about him. The vision of him standing so close to her felt so real in her head, and it was as if she had actually been this intimately close to him before.

She remembered the morning after meeting Edward and how she fantasized about making love to him. Visions of holding his penis in her hand and slowly massaging it, even sucking on it appeared so real. No way! Her mind shifted back to who he was—the jerk. *What am I doing*? *I must be going crazy*. One thing was for sure—she felt wide awake now.

After she stepped out of the shower, she examined her body in the mirror. Damn, it looked scary. The long wet hair exemplified the ruined mess of her wretched face and a plump white body badly in need of some sun tanning and exercising.

With no energy to work on such a large project, she decided to go over to the computer and do some more research on Edward. She needed to know everything she could about him. He had a web-site with the basic information about him. While he operated a successful agency, which is one of the reasons she wanted him, it appeared he devoted all of his life to his work.

Several hours later the phone rang—her mother. "Hello, honey. How are you?"

"I'm fine, and I'm just doing some research on the computer."

"Good for you, but I just wanted to remind you of your work today."

"I haven't forgotten. Don't worry. I'll make it on time. Thanks for checking on me."

"You're welcome. Call me back later." Her mother quickly ended the connection.

While not a big job, it was easy work inside a large

coffee shop at a bookstore. The few hours she worked there generated her a little extra spending money. While she was always amazed at what people would pay for coffee and snacks, she gladly accepted the tips for something the store paid her to do anyway.

Most of the time she worked fast and furious, but at times she could read a book or two from the store. Since she always loved to read, this provided a perfect job for her. She would have to see how this day went.

She clicked on a list of recently released books by authors that Edward represented, and wrote them down on a small piece of paper lying on the table. She needed to find a copy of some of the books, and read what kind of reviews the store had written on them.

As her plan to destroy Edward kept materializing, she became more motivated to keep digging. Amy could picture the look on his face when he read the papers and saw the reviews she planned to write about his superstars. When people stopped buying his clients books, she felt sure the publishers would quit looking at the manuscripts he recommended.

While the bad press would hurt, she knew it wouldn't complete her mission. She would love to hear that some of his authors had signed with other agents. If word circulated that he acted as a predatory agent, or was caught in a scandal where one of his books was falsified, he would be branded for life. She also had heard of an association of agents she felt sure he belonged to. She wondered what it would take to have him expelled from it.

After she selected one of the reports she had printed about him, which contained his photo on the front, she immediately drew him some pointed ears and a devil's beard. She had the most fun with his piercing eyes. When she finished, she scratched at them with her nails. Unable to concentrate on anything else, she taped the remains of the photo to the front of her computer. It looked befitting in terms of her feelings for him.

The idea of having access to information about his authors and their books made her want to hurry to work. As she slipped into the bookstore uniform they provided, she went to work on her hair and makeup. While the uniform looked plain, it at least managed to make her breasts a little less noticeable.

CHAPTER 6

The bookstore didn't look very busy as Amy walked through the large double doors, which were left wide open by the management to invite the general public in. Slightly inside the door is where the process of selling books began, with the best sellers and books of local interest strategically placed. She glanced at the books as she walked past them. Her hopes of having a book among them appeared to have disappeared now due to the asshole. After receiving various other rejection letters in addition to this one, she had lost interest in writing to some extent, but she knew that one day she would try again. It was the rejection letter from Edward, however, which finally broke the camel's back, so to speak. Still, she admired the writers who dedicated their life to writing and made the sacrifices to get published. Amy especially envied them in finding the right agent to help them. All she had found was Edward, and now she assumed her writing future was over. With an evil smile, she quickly visualized how she planned to ruin his career.

As she walked through the store, she passed rows and rows of books on her way to the back meeting room. The sheer number of books written every year impressed her. It would be fun to know more about how all of these authors lived. You know, like what made them tick. She liked working in the bookstore in many respects, since the work was easy and she had a really nice boss.

After Amy walked into the meeting room and located her time card, she stared at how little time she had worked this period, but it did provide a good part-time job. Since it had become harder and harder to find a real job, she appreciated any money she earned. Her dad paid her major bills, but she knew he couldn't do it forever. She hoped to get her life back under control at some time, at least she hoped so since she knew she had put her dad through a lot.

Amy saw her boss coming through the door as she clocked in. "Hello, Amy."

"Hello," she answered back and managed to give him a small cheerful smile.

"I think I'll let you take the front cash register right now. I don't see much going on, and I think you can handle it by yourself. I'll let you work the coffee shop when traffic picks up in a few hours."

"That works for me. I'm happy to be working today." He looked pleased as she walked toward the front of the store. While sometimes a boring place to work, it would give her access to a computer where she could do some research without anyone caring.

As Amy walked behind the small counter and had a seat, she listened to the background music before she touched the mouse and the screen came alive. After she connected to the internet, she looked for more information on Edward. After finding the authors he represented, she searched for the books the store carried that were written by them. They had many. After making a list of some of the books, she glanced around for a minute to see if she would be needed before she went to find them.

With several of the books in the romance and paranormal sections, a small smirk crossed her face as she whispered, "Imagine that. Edward wrote in his rejection letter that my book wasn't the kind of book he represented. What a bald faced liar."

Amy quickly retrieved the ones she found and headed back to the counter since she didn't need to stay away too long. She started by reading the book's jackets, where each carried the basic story line and a small blurb about the author. Only on one of the books did the author give thanks to his fantastic agent. What a real suck up this guy must be.

She reconnected to the internet, looking for any book reviews on these books. After locating several on all of them, she enjoyed reading the various opinions on the books. While the styles all looked different, she knew it couldn't be too hard to write a review.

She started to wonder how much they paid writers to write such articles. There had to be an easy way to get a list of newspapers and their e-mail addresses. She assumed all they could say was no to her articles.

Soon, she had completed a lot of research on the internet concerning how to write articles. She also found many sites giving advice, and where she would do more studying later.

When an older woman came to the check out and placed several books on the counter, Amy stopped to take care of this lady who patiently waited on her to do her job. Amy thought how she must represent most widows with nothing else to do but read. "How are you?"

"I'm fine and I'm glad to find these books. Do you know anything about them?"

Amy looked at them and noticed that they were erotic romance novels. She ventured a small smile. "I'm not sure that I do." She felt curious about why a woman of her age would read such racy romance novels, but she guessed there was no time table for someone to dream of romance and a time that might be.

"I read where this one was recommended by your store's magazine. Since you wrote rave reviews on it, I hope it lives up to the billing."

"I'm sure you'll like it. I know of nothing better than a good romance."

"I know." She tilted her head and winked. "I try to read four or five every week." This woman had to be typical of what drives the book market and makes the publishers happy. It felt so amazing how she looked to the publication for advice on which book to buy. Maybe a reviewer's point of view did make a difference after all.

As the lady left, Amy picked up the in-house publication

and read the articles the woman had been looking at. The relatively large magazine had been written by many different reviewers. All the articles had positive reviews. With the bookstore trying to sell books, she guessed she wouldn't find anything negative about a book in a bookstore publication, which only made sense.

Amy knew if she planned to write articles about the books Edward's authors wrote, she needed to write under an assumed name. The more she considered it, the more sense it made. Now, all she needed to do was to select a dynamite new name. As she selected one book again and started to read it, she decided to make this book the first one she would ever review. She felt sorry for the author who had chosen the wrong agent, just as she had.

Soon, her boss walked over. "Since the traffic will be increasing shortly, I think it will be good for you to work over in the coffee section. Your friend Lenny will clock in soon, and I hope I can trust the two of you working together."

Amy offered her boss a sideway smile, which sneaked out of the corner of her mouth. Being gay, they both knew the only problem they had with Lenny was his admiration of all the young athletic guys who ventured in. Still, she remembered the fun they had when they worked together. After all, Lenny had recommended this job for her.

They had become friends when they attended a writing class at a nearby college. Lenny knew all about her wild mood swings. She felt supportive of his decisions in life, and he tolerated her problems, making them an odd couple of sorts. One thing for sure, she didn't have to worry about him making a pass at her, or her breasts, and she loved how easy she could tell him things she couldn't discuss with other guys. "I'll be glad to, if you don't mind."

As she closed her account on the register, she watched her boss motion to another girl to work behind the counter.

The duties at the coffee shop rotated often like this to keep work from becoming too boring for anyone. She knew that for the store to keep good help at such a low rate of pay, the management had to do what they could to retain their employees.

When she found no one behind the coffee counter, she quickly surveyed the condition it was left in and studied which coffee they advertised today as the daily special. Amy loved the fantastic smell of the coffee, as she placed her books on a side counter. She knew she wouldn't finish them in the store, but would consider buying them with her employee discount to read later at home.

Lenny soon arrived, and flashed smiles as he walked into the coffee section. He looked almost like a little kid. His long lean face radiated so clean and smooth, with an almost pretty pink color to it. Amy wondered if he ever had to shave. He had pulled his long streaked blond hair into a pony tail behind his head. "Hello, girl. How are you? Since you look much better today, I think my soup must have been good for you."

She offered him a smile and shrugged her shoulders. "The same old story—how about you? Is anything new happening with you?"

"Not really. I had to spend all morning cleaning my apartment. You know how I do hate it when anything is out of order. I really do need to paint the den again."

"Again? I heard you just painted it."

"It wasn't too long ago, but I had a friend of a friend talk me into that dreaded color. It really is just not working for me, if you know what I mean."

"I hear what you're saying, but it sounds like too much work for me."

"So, have you seen any hot guys in here this morning? You know, I think that's the only reason I work in this place. The coffee here really draws in some nice ones." He tapped his fingers on his chin as he glanced around.

She rolled her eyes. "You're unbelievable. Do you ever think of anything else?"

After acting almost like she had insulted him, he straightened his posture, including a slight raise of his chin. "I've many interests—do you really think I'm that dull?"

"Hey, don't get upset. I was just messing with you, but I'll tell you what. If I see any hot guys in here today, they're all yours."

Sensing something in her voice, he raised a slightly waxed eyebrow. "What is it that has your panties all in an uproar?"

"Men in general—they're all such pricks."

Needling her a little more, he continued as he offered a small smile. "Is this really *all men,* or do you have a problem with one guy I can help you with?"

She knew she could talk to Lenny in trust from time to time, and she hoped that he wouldn't go telling this to all of his friends. "Yes, there is this one guy I know, well kind of know, who is a real prick." Lenny's ears appeared to perk up, since she knew he liked nothing better than a good juicy story about some guy. "This guy's a literary agent from New York. He handles clients all over the world, and that's why I had hoped he might be interested in me. I was wrong about him, and now I think he's just a plain old asshole. Damn, I want to kick his butt!"

"Amy, I never knew you had such passion in you like this. This guy must have really lit a fire in you."

"I don't think I'd call it . . . passion, but I know if it takes my whole life, I'll get even with this jerk. He sent me a rejection letter on the novel I had worked hard on for a long time."

"I read your novel. It was fantastic for me, but do tell me more about this intriguing guy you're so crazy about."

"I'm not crazy about him! He's an arrogant, egotistical

bastard who thinks all of us want-to-be authors should bow down and worship the ground he walks on. They know they hold the keys to us getting in with publishers. However, I think just once . . . this particular little *want-to-be author* is going to fight back."

"Oh, I do like a good fight." His eyes, highlighted by his long, almost feminine lashes, lit up.

"In fact, I'm already working on a way to handle him. I know of nothing better than beating someone at their own game."

The color of his greenish-blue eyes intensified as he appeared to understand that he was in on the planning of Amy's revenge. "May I ask how you plan on doing this?"

"I've thought about it, and I'm still working on some details, but for starters, I think he should receive a dose of his own medicine."

"What do you mean?"

"I'm going to start writing book reviews. Take a guess on whose books I'm going after . . . with a passion as you mentioned."

"I don't understand. Is he a writer also?"

"I don't think so, but I'm talking about the books of authors he represents. If I can make those books look terrible, and ruin their sales, it has to affect his ability to sell future books to the publishers."

"It'll be fascinating if you can pull that one off. There are many book reviewers, and the authors have many loyal fans. You'll also be fighting the powerful money of the publishers."

"I know what I'm up against, and that it'll require a lot of work. I also have many others ideas I'll use."

"Do say . . . what else do you have planned for our little . . . boy toy?"

"Well, for one thing, I'd love to talk to the authors he represents and see if I can talk any of them into changing agents."

"Do you really think talking to his authors will be easy to do?"

"I'm sure I can if I put the time into it. I also think I can reach them in some sort of fashion. You'll be amazed how certain rumors can spread across any profession."

"You know what you are planning can have some serious legal implications?"

"I know the law has many gray areas. I'll stay out of trouble with the law, but I'll get even with the bastard."

"Wow, I never knew you had it in you, girl!"

"I've been pushed and pushed around all of my life. This time I won't be shit on anymore. Call it what you want, but today I'll take it no longer."

A customer, who was perhaps in his late twenties, walked to the counter and ordered a latte. Lenny catered to his every desire. "I do hope you enjoy it," Lenny said, as the guy walked away not knowing exactly how to take him.

"I just love a guy with a hard body and tight ass."

Amy rolled her eyes. Lenny was hopeless, but still he was a friend in those moments when she needed someone. It was something she had learned to live with when she was around him. "I didn't notice."

"Oh really?" He smiled. "I would so hate it if we had to fight over him."

Shaking her head, Amy went back to her discussion about Edward. "I need to learn how to write reviews. It can't be that hard."

"Since it's your opinion you write in your article, I guess you can just say what you want. Finding someone to buy it, and publish it is something else."

"Listen, I know you know a lot about books. Will you help me?"

"Girl, I wouldn't miss this for the world. I just hope to meet this guy you're so hot for."

"I'm not HOT for this guy. You do love to tease me, don't you?"

"Well, yes I've been known as a tease before." He batted his long eye lashes in fun.

"By the way, I'll need a name to write under. I don't think I should let anyone know exactly who I am, as I'm likely to create some enemies."

"I agree that you need a name, someone that will puts fear into any authors heart who knows you're about to rip to shreds his or her life's work. It has to be someone who has a keen eye. Maybe you could use something like *Lady Hawk.*

"Not too bad, and I think it's close. I might use the name *The Literary Hawk.* What do you really think?"

"It works for me." He raised his hand in a high five. "I think it will then be . . . *The Literary Hawk.*"

CHAPTER 7

Amy stayed extremely busy the next few months working out of her apartment, and like today, she spent countless hours reading book after book before writing her reviews. Her mood returned to normal for a while as she felt like she was finally getting a handle on her new craft. She didn't make too many sales, but the money wasn't why she wrote, which was a good thing since the most she made for an article was only twenty-five dollars.

Her boss often congratulated her at the bookstore on how pleased he was that she had developed into a knowledgeable source of current books being released. The store's regular buyers asked for her more and more when they came into the store. A small raise also helped some.

The more she worked on writing her reviews, the more she could see Edward's destruction. His day was coming. It was simply a matter of time. Still, it was her late night dreams of him that confused her. Sometimes, she imagined him closing his shop in New York and running away with his tail between his legs. At other times, they were together acting like intimate friends and perhaps even lovers. She had discussed these crazy dreams with her psychiatrist, but somehow the explanations she received appeared far from the truth.

While in the middle of another daydream about possible ways to ruin Edward, her phone rang—Lenny. "I know this is your day off, but I just heard something I think you'll be interested in knowing."

With a teasing type tone to his voice, she knew he discovered something special. "What is it?"

"I just heard of a convention being held next month for book critics. They've sent out invitations to some of the major bookstores, including ours, so some of their employees can attend."

"That could be something I'd like to join."

"Yes, but I see some problems. If you join, then everyone will know who you are."

"I'd still like to sneak into the crowd and learn. It would be nice to meet the other critics at the conference and learn how they work." She owed Lenny for this.

"Actually, this might be your perfect opportunity, girl. You could go as a bookstore representative, and no one will ever know you're also a critic."

"Do you think the store would send me?"

"If you agree to pay your own way, I'm sure they would love for you to go. It's not too far away, and you could drive and stay somewhere cheap."

"I'll think about it. Thanks for letting me know."

"I knew you would love this information. Let me know if you can work it out. You can tell the store I'm willing to cover for you while you're gone. It's only a two day convention."

"I owe you for this."

"Hummm, I do love it when someone owes me."

"You're totally deranged, but a good friend. Thanks again."

As she ended the phone call, she looked over at the growing collage of Edward's photos. She had penciled over most of them with images of the devil or some other crazy monster. While her hatred for him never ended, the more she deliberated, the more she wanted to get even with him. It was something she had a hard time understanding since she generally wasn't like this. Some of her feelings she had explained to Dr. Lankford, and some to Lenny, but she definitely couldn't talk about it to anyone else.

After she went to the mail box and retrieved her mail, she felt astonished to see three envelopes from different newspapers. One by one she opened them and examined the signed agreements and checks. It was slow, but she was gaining a few newspapers at a time. The checks made her feel ecstatic. She had to celebrate later tonight, but for now she needed to do some more research on this convention.

She walked back into her apartment and adjusted her chair in front of the computer. While on her blog, she wanted to share the good news of her new newspapers to her loyal fans of maybe a hundred people. At this point, she kept the actual number of people coming to her site a secret. She felt it best to let everyone guess how many hits she received.

As she wrote news on the blog, her mind started to wander back to the convention where she had met Edward. She remembered the bar she had followed him to, and how she had been introduced to two of his authors. That part of the night was crystal clear. The time afterwards gave her problems. The wine did her in, and left her with only vague recollections of what happened next.

She had managed to somehow return to her room from the bar, but exactly how she ended up back in her room remained a mystery to her. She did remember waking in the bed naked the next morning and thinking of how much she planned to live a full life with her fabulous new agent. That had turned into a joke, she suddenly thought, as she laughed out loud.

She focused on a vague image of her slow dancing with Edward. While his eyes seemed beady and perhaps not too attractive to many people, she remembered how they also penetrated deeply when he focused his attention on her. Thoughts of him dropping his pants and her servicing him with oral sex still haunted her. *Did I do that? Surely not.*

Her mind wondered to the letter she had mailed to him. He must have had a good laugh about it, but perhaps he had received letters like it many times before. Still, if she had a shot at ruining him, she needed to know more about the publishing game. She was learning, but it was going to take some time.

58

Amy clapped her hands in a small celebration at the possibility of going to a convention. While she knew the people at them would be intelligent and exciting to talk to, she also considered it to be the next step in make good on her promise.

CHAPTER 8

Finally, after driving all day, Amy arrived at the hotel in Orlando, Florida where they held the convention. It looked large and almost intimidating. With the men in front of the building wearing typical hotel uniforms, and handling the arriving visitors, she studied the special lane for valet parking.

Her nerves stood on end as she studied the parking area in front of the hotel. She would soon come face to face with many new people. Sometimes she loved to meet people, and at other times she couldn't function. It was hard for her to know how she would react over the next few days. Her moods were so unpredictable, and they often hinged on random events of the day. She felt determined to do her best as she prayed for help.

Since the cost of this trip drained most of the money she had left, she knew she needed to watch every penny. There would be no expensive night outs, unless she could find someone else to pay for it. The chances of that happening were slim, and she knew it. She had packed some food in her car that she could sneak into her room later if she needed to.

Since many conventions provided free snacks and refreshments, she hoped this would be one of them. She didn't want to spend time worrying about money and needed to concentrate on how to sell her articles. She needed to learn some tricks of the trade.

Amy lifted her lone suitcase out of the back of her little Honda, and headed for the front door. The traffic came and went swiftly as several cars arrived in line to use the valet service. This hotel clearly catered to an upper class clientele.

When she arrived at the door, a doorman moved over to open it for her. The large and elaborate atrium shocked her. The marble floors brilliantly shinning and matching the various marble pieces in the center of the large entrance dominated everything else. On top of these beautiful stands, fresh flowers arranged perfectly in oversized flower pots added the perfect touch. She saw many visitors scampering around and taking care of arrangements or meeting other members of their party. Many of them had numerous suitcases being attended to by bellhops.

After finding the front desk, she strolled over to it. A man in his late fifties turned in her direction as she approached him. "Can I help you?"

"Yes, I've a reservation for the next few days." She handed him her confirmation.

He looked at it for a minute before typing on the keyboard. Satisfied, he looked back at her. "It's a good thing you booked early—the hotel is fully booked this weekend. Are you here for the convention?"

"Yes, I work for a bookstore, and they thought it would be a good idea for me to meet some of the book critics."

He handed her a key. "We hope you have a great stay, and if we can do anything for you, please let us know. By the way, I think you'll find many of the attendees at the bar on your right."

"Thanks. I appreciate that."

Being close to happy hour time, she hoped to meet some of the people attending the convention in an informal manner. She would have to check it out as soon as she placed her luggage in her room. While she had planned on eating some of the food she brought with her in her room, she hoped she could, at least, have one drink in the bar.

She walked over to the elevator and pushed the up button. The door opened and she noticed the inside of the elevator being every bit as elaborate as the rest of the building. The highly polished walls looked like solid cherry.

After she pushed the button for her floor and moved to the back of the elevator, three women entered the elevator behind her. They all looked professional, but not so over dressed like others in the lobby.

The tallest one in the center spoke first, "I can't believe I was talked into coming to this convention. I saw some critics here that it's killing me to be nice to. Damn, I'd kill if I could get away with it."

An older woman on the right added with more authority in her voice. "Remember it's more about damage control than anything." It was easy to tell she was someone accustomed to getting matters taken care of and one you didn't want to mess with. Her silver hair shined brightly and had been expertly cut and styled.

The girl on the far side looked much younger, perhaps in her late thirties. She carried several folders as she nodded. "We have everything in place as you wanted. I'm sure it will all go smoothly."

Amy felt as if this last girl was a secretary or assistant of some kind, and probably the one doing all the work, but, of course, the old blues received all the credit. She would love to know their names, since she felt sure they were connected to the convention somehow.

After realizing someone was standing behind her, the gray haired lady turned and offered Amy a sly little smile. Amy thought that this lady would at least be smart enough to not say too much in front of someone she didn't know. "Hello." She leaned closer toward Amy.

"Hello," Amy replied as the old lady still hadn't sized her up yet, but continued to play it safe. This was going to be a fun convention before it ended. The bell sounded as Amy recognized her floor. "Excuse me. I need to get off here."

The ladies parted as Amy prepared to exit the elevator. The gray haired lady quickly asked in a friendly voice. "Are you here for the convention?"

"Yes I am, and I know I'll enjoy meeting some new people here. My name's Amy. I hope to see you around."

She had almost exited the elevator when the secretary shouted after her. "We're having a small reception later in our room. If you wish to come, you're welcome. It's in room 1802."

"Thanks. What time does it start?"

"It will be after happy hour ends in the bar. I think the crowds will drift in between seven and eight."

"I think I might make it. Thanks for inviting me."

Amy chucked as she walked off the elevator, recognizing the smart thinking by the assistant. If they wanted damage control, then finding out who everyone at the meeting was becomes important, especially when that person had been listening to you throughout the elevator ride. Amy felt proud of the way she had handled the conversation. She had said just enough to make them have an interest in her. Also, she'd now have a way to get something to eat for free.

After opening the door to her room, she had to catch her breath for a minute. It looked much nicer than she could have ever imagined. While not extremely large, but well decorated, she breathed in deeply, thinking of the next few days. The polished headboard of solid oak had intricate carvings, and the matching secretarial desk off to the side had a beautiful lamp magnificently glowing above it.

She knew this trip had ruined her checking account, but she hoped it would pay off in new newspaper orders she might acquire. She had come to learn secrets in selling her articles, and she didn't need to look like an amateur. Of course, she wore two hats and she needed to remember that. Yes, she worked as a book critic, but officially she represented the bookstore.

After unpacking, she left for the bar she had noticed earlier on the far side of the atrium. Since the hotel looked massive, she decided to check out the rooms where the meeting would be held tomorrow as well.

She soon saw the large bar opening onto the atrium. As

she walked in, she watched the happy hour crowd coming alive. On the right side she studied a long bar, with bar stools occupied by patrons in front of several over-worked bartenders. With the laughter echoing around the room, she knew many had already had several drinks.

The inside lights that were softer than those outside created a more intimate setting, one that was missing from the hustle and bustle of the outside atrium. On the left side of the bar, she saw many tables petitioned off and providing some privacy, but most of those tables were full as well.

Amy walked the length of the bar, but found no where to sit. Luckily, on the way back to the front, she watched several men paying their bill and leaving. She gracefully slid into one of the available seats as a bartender walked over and collected his tip before cleaning off the top of the bar. "What can I get for you?" He asked as he offered her a large grin.

"A glass of your house red wine would be exactly what I need."

He smiled and went to the end of the bar to pour her a glass. Yes, she knew he had seen her kind before; ordering the cheapest drink possible and waiting on someone else to order the next drink. He quickly arrived with the drink. "That will be eight dollars."

She paid him and added a small tip, as she was surprised by the prices in the bar. The smoothness of the cabernet tasted exactly like what she wanted.

The bar had the feel of an expensive country club, with virtually all the patrons appearing to be in a good mood and knowing each other to some extent. While the two seats next to Amy were vacant, she knew this would change soon. On the other side of these two spots were two middle age men facing each other while engaged in a deeply heated discussion. She couldn't hear the details of what they were discussing, but she watched their intense interactions as they paid no attention to anything else around them. Two attractive women in their early thirties were having a good time on the other side of these two men. With both being blonde, slender and dressed to kill, Amy knew they came to have fun.

She felt a small bump to her left arm, as the man next to her laughed while engaging with four others in his small group. Apparently realizing he had bumped into her by accident, he turned to her. "I'm sorry. You'll have to excuse us. Sometimes we get a little out of control."

"Not a problem. It's good to watch friends having fun."

He nodded at her and extended his hand. "I'm Charles."

"Good to meet you. I'm Amy."

He quickly mentioned the names of the others next to him, but the noise in the bar overrode his voice. She couldn't hear him well, especially when he turned his head to introduce them. She waved at them as they waved back, but she assumed they didn't really hear her name either. Still, she did feel like maybe they were welcoming her into their small group.

After Charles turned back around to face her, she asked him, "Are you here for the convention?"

"Yes. We all work for a magazine that tailors to writers. What do you do?"

"I work for a bookstore." She considered saying she was a book critic, but she had already decided to keep that part a secret. Since she planned to write under an assumed name, she would have to stick with it.

"Have you been to this convention before?"

"No, this is my first time at this one. I've been to many others, but not this one."

"You'll find it about the same as most. Almost every large publishing house will have people here, especially since they have a lot of interest in making sure their books are being properly publicized."

"I can imagine they would."

"I'm glad to see that more people like you are here from the bookstores. I know you also have an interest in which books receive good reviews, since it's nice to have books in the stores that sell. Having the wrong books can cost you money."

"I'm happy to be here. This will be a learning experience for me, and I always enjoy meeting people."

He reached in his pocket and handed her a card. She felt a little embarrassed when she realized she didn't have one. "I'd love to give you my card, but I don't have one. I don't have much need for one at the store."

"No problem." He handed her another card. "Here, write your name and e-mail address on the back. I'd like to send you some information about our magazine."

"Thanks, I would really like that."

Another woman soon walked in and joined them at the bar. Since it looked like she had been crying, Charles rushed out of his seat and hugged her. She returned a small smile and slightly bit her lips, as if to maintain control. "I'll be fine."

Charles turned to Amy to introduce her. "This is Beth Sherman. She's a writer."

"Yes, I've heard of you. It's a pleasure to meet you."

"Thanks. I apologize for the way I look. It's been a bad day."

Charles looked over to Amy and whispered, "Her agent was discovered this morning. He had been brutally murdered."

Wild images flooded Amy's mind. "Who was he?"

"His name was Mitchell Lloyd. Have you heard of him?"

"Yes, I think so." Amy thought she might've sent a query letter to him, but she wasn't absolutely sure. She would check on it when she returned home.

Beth lowered her head and looked like she was going to cry again. Amy slid over one seat to give Beth room to sit. "Here, please have a seat."

"Thanks. I guess I could use a good drink right now."

Charles picked up on the request quickly and waved at the bartender. "What would you like?"

"Scotch . . . on the rocks." Beth trembled as she lowered her head again.

Looking over at Amy, Charles pointed toward her glass. "What would you like?"

Amy glanced at her glass. "I think I need to stay with my cabernet." As Charles ordered the drinks, Amy felt compelled to place a hand on Beth's shoulder.

Beth appeared to appreciate it as she spoke slowly. "I don't know if I can stay or not. I know I have to speak tomorrow, but I'll leave as soon as I'm finished. When I talked to his wife, they were still making funeral arrangements."

When the drinks appeared, Beth finished the entire drink in one long gulp. It was obvious she intended to get drunk. Charles looked over at Amy as if to say, "I think I'll need some help here."

When Beth asked for another drink, Charles reluctantly ordered it for her. That one lasted two sips, but she did seem to relax as it hit her and she closed her eyes while repeated over and over, "I will be fine, I will be fine."

Amy knew that maybe tomorrow she might be fine, but tonight she was going to be drunk. Charles leaned closer to Beth. "Perhaps I need to help you to your room, so you can get a good night sleep."

"It's too early to go to bed."

Charles pursed his lips. "With one more drink, you'll not know what time it is."

"I guess you're right. One more drink and I'll turn in." With the effect of the first two drinks in her system showing, Charles winked at Amy, as he ordered Beth one more drink. They left the bar as soon as she finished it. While Charles appeared to be a nice, reliable guy who could be trusted to take care of her, Amy wondered just how well they knew each other.

As soon as they left, the girl on the other side of Charles moved over to Amy. "I'm sorry, I couldn't hear your name a few minutes ago."

"It's Amy, and what was your name again?"

"It's Glenda. I work with Charles. It looks like he has his hands full with Beth. Charles is one of the top writers for our magazine. Anyone else would take advantage of this situation, and have a heyday with an article, but Beth knows she can trust him. I'm proud of Charles and his professionalism."

"So . . . Charles is also one of the book critics here. Will he be speaking tomorrow?"

"Yes, he'll be speaking on several of the panels tomorrow."

Curiosity quickly set in as Amy asked, "What do you do at the magazine?"

"I'm the editor," Glenda said.

"Wow, it's good to meet you." Amy smiled, knowing she had just made a great contact.

"What do you do?"

"I work at a bookstore. Since my boss insisted we should have someone represent us, here I am."

"It's good to see you made it. I think you'll learn a lot tomorrow."

"I hope to meet many of the book critics tomorrow. It appears to be a . . . remarkable occupation."

"Remarkable is an understatement, but it does have its moments. It also requires a tremendous amount of time to read book after book, and each one of them you have to read intensely in order to properly evaluate them."

"It still sounds like a *remarkable* job."

Glenda shifted closer to Amy. "There's always a need for a good critic." She reached in her purse and handed Amy her business card. "I hope to see you around the convention."

"I'm sure I'll see you later. This is, shall I say, very intriguing for me."

Glenda stood and said goodbye to her other friends as she walked out the door. It was very obvious that she had some place to go. Amy enjoyed the ease she had in making new friends. Life felt good.

After two glasses of wine, she needed to go to the restroom. When Amy looked around for it but didn't immediately find one, she remembered one in the lobby and decided to go visit it. As she made her way across the lobby, she froze and studied a man getting on the elevator. While he was too far away for her to know for sure, he looked like Edward.

He quickly disappeared before she could be sure, but the idea of Edward attending sent her mind racing and out of control. She wasn't expecting to see him at this conference. Perhaps, it was just her imagination. She would have to check the list of those attending tomorrow morning. Until then, she would have to be careful. She didn't want to confront him right now, not knowing how she would react. Her crazy mood swings were so unpredictable, especially when she faced such events in her life.

She didn't go back to the bar. Instead, she returned to her room. She needed to rest for a minute and bring herself together before she made it to the reception she had been invited to earlier.

After a short rest, she opened the door from her room and walked toward the elevator as she whispered, "Please don't let me run into him on the elevator, especially with no way of escaping." Finding an empty elevator, she breathed in deep. She pushed the button and proceeded toward the reception. All looked good.

As soon as she exited the elevator, she heard voices coming from one room. Apparently this little group had grown much larger than they had anticipated. As she entered into an impressive suite, she discovered it full of people laughing and having a good time. She slowly walked around looking for the three ladies she met on the elevator, but only saw many faces she didn't recognize.

Eventually, she recognized the secretarial looking girl from the elevator, who was quickly walking over to her. "How are you? She asked. "I'm glad you made it."

"Thanks, it was nice of you to invite me. It looks like you have a nice turn out tonight."

"Yes, it appears that the word got out. With this group all you have to say is free drinks and free food, and you're an immediate hit."

A young man in his early thirties, who obviously wanted to be introduced to her, walked over to them as they talked. This girl turned to him to introduce Amy. "This is Andy. You'll have to be careful with this guy, and never trust him for a minute." Amy felt shocked and puzzled by the comment made so openly in front of Andy.

He tightened his jaw, as he rolled his eyes. "Thanks, and I love you too."

Amy returned his smile. It had to be an inside joke. "I'm glad to meet you Andy . . . I think."

Andy laughed. "Don't listen to my sister. I promise I don't bite." He stared at his sister and cast an evil eye, but then added a playful grin.

"Remember, I warned you." She walked off, leaving them alone.

As Amy talked to him, she noticed his constant stare at her breasts. Obviously, he only had one thing on his mind. Perhaps his sister knew him well after all. When a new group of girls walked in, Andy quickly went after new prey, but promised to return soon.

Amy quickly surveyed the room to make sure Edward hadn't joined them. She saw no sign of him, but she did double-check several guys. With the hate; no, the detestation she felt for him, she knew she wouldn't be capable of holding it all together if she confronted him now. Amy noticed a table off to the side that was full of food—all kinds of foods. Wow! Now, this is what she had been looking for as she started walking toward the buffet where she casually picked up a plate and started adding things to it. She felt hungry.

As she watched two heavy set women worked their way around the table, Amy felt better, since she wasn't the only one hungry tonight. One of them glanced her way. "This food's looks yummy, doesn't it?"

"Yes, it looks fantastic."

Suddenly, the other woman stared at her before she asked, "Did you hear the news today?"

"What news?" Amy replied.

"About the agent who was murdered earlier. They say his face was cut so badly that it was impossible to immediately identify him. Did you hear about it?"

"I was at the bar earlier where I met a writer, Beth Sherman, who he represented. She was badly shaken by it, but I didn't receive many details. What else have you heard?" Amy asked.

"They've almost nothing to go on. Someone must've hated him, and I mean really had it in for him. Nothing was stolen, but his computer was smashed to pieces. I'm sure we'll see a major investigation into it. Apparently he really pissed someone off."

Thinking about Edward, she could partially understand how it could happen, but murder is one thing she doubted she could ever do. "Do they have any suspects?"

"Not that I know of, but I'm sure we'll hear more about it tomorrow at the meetings."

"I'm sorry to hear something so gruesome happening to anyone. It sounded like Beth Sherman was fond of him."

"I'm sure she was. The relationship between writer and agent can be very intense, and I'm curious as to how it will affect her writing in the future."

"Are you one of the book critics here?" Amy asked.

"Yes, that's why I get invited to these damn things. No one wants to piss me off."

"I see . . . so how do you like these conferences?"

Filling her plate, the lady raised an eyebrow and instead of answering, asked, "Who are you with?"

"I'm with a bookstore. They thought it would be good for me to attend."

"I agree. I wish we attracted more people like you here. In the final say, it's the people in the store who help push or kill a book. You're the one the reader can look straight in the eye and ask for an opinion. If they like your recommendations, they keep buying books. If they don't, you'll never see them again. Also, the placement of books is determined by you. The public thinks you'll place the best books on the front racks with easy access."

"At our store we receive directions from the corporate office as to where to place the books."

"Yeah, it always has been about the money. The publishers have extra money to pay for special placement. However, in the end, the bookstores are in the business of making money. They want to sell as many books as possible. They don't care if it's a good or a bad book, as long as they sell it."

"I hear what you're saying, and we do have many people in the store buying books based on recommendations by book critics. I see it all the time."

"I'm glad to hear it. I think good writers should be

rewarded, and those who have no clue what they're doing should learn to do something else."

"Is it hard to be a book critic?"

"I guess that depends on who you're asking. After all, everyone has an opinion, but some experts you can rely on more than others. To build a loyal base of readers, you need to build trust. It's hard to win and easy to lose."

"You sound like someone very wise. Have you been doing reviews for long?"

The lady suddenly grunted, as if being annoyed. "Only about thirty years."

Amy quickly understood that she must be talking to one of the masters in this field and had never realized it until now. Feeling too embarrassed to ask her name, she decided to wait and find out later. She should have done more research before she came.

Andy eventually returned and walked over to Amy to hand her a glass of wine. "Here, I think you'll like this."

That was Amy's third glass of wine, and the last thing she remembered.

CHAPTER 9

Amy's dream, or perhaps nightmare, of Edward vanished as her phone rang. Startled by the sound, she twisted in the bed and reached for it. "Hello?"

"Hello, girl," Lenny spoke in a solemn voice, unusual for him. "Are you up yet?"

"Man, I'm so out of it. What time is it?"

"It's eight thirty. Listen, I do know how you can over-sleep, so I knew to give you a call." Lenny waited on a response.

"Thanks, I guess I need to get out of bed and start getting ready."

"I saw on the news this morning that a literary agent was murdered. It's on all the channels. This isn't your agent, is it?"

"No, it's someone else. I heard about it here also, but I know very little about this agent. I met a girl who used him as her agent last night, and who apparently liked him very much."

"I was just checking. Don't do anything I wouldn't do. See you later, girl."

"Okay, and thanks again for calling me."

Amy lay still for a second, but with so much to see and hear today she knew she needed to hurry. Her dream from the night before haunted her. She couldn't remember it well, but she could see the beady eyes of Edward staring at her inches away. Goose bumps covered her arms. She felt sure they shared some laughs the night they met, but she had no clue as to exactly what went on. She hated it when she went blanked out like that. The same thing had happened last night.

She climbed out of bed and looked for her clothes. They were neatly hanging on a hanger. She couldn't remember hanging them up, and she usually just laid them out until the next morning. After rushing to get ready, she barely made it in time for the grand meeting kicking off the two day conference. Luckily she located some coffee and pastries when she arrived. As she studied the room full of people chatting in small groups, she hoped the free food would keep coming.

While she hoped to find someone familiar as she looked around, they all, however, looked new. Finally, on the far side of the room, she recognized some of the people from the reception. She couldn't remember their names, but it was at least a small way of easing into a conversation. "Hello," she ventured as she approached them.

They looked her over and posted quirky little smiles. "How are you this morning?" A short woman with an almost masculine appearance asked.

"I'm fine, except for a slight headache."

"I can understand that. You had quite a time at the reception . . . and at the bar later last night."

"Okay, I like having a good time." Damn, she didn't remember going to the bar last night after the reception. "How are you feeling this morning?"

"I feel fine, but of course I didn't have the fun you were having. Perhaps tonight I can get lucky. By the way, I'm Lucy."

"I'm Amy. I hope I didn't make too much of a fool out of myself."

Another girl flashed a smile. "I think this should be one of those things that goes on at a convention, and should stay at the convention." She added a wink. "My lips are sealed."

Oh shit. Since she had no idea of what she did last night, Amy decided to move on to the next person in the room to chat with.

Eventually she noticed Beth, who looked better than she had the night before, but only slightly. "Hello," Amy said, as she approached her. "I met you at the bar last night. How are you feeling today?"

Beth paused to study her before answering. "I'm better, but I think it will take a long time before I get over this. We were very close."

"I can only imagine. How long have you been working together?"

"For almost ten years. He was my first and only agent. I know his wife is hysterical right now and she needs all the support we can give her. As soon as I finish this panel discussion I'll be heading for the airport. It's a long flight, and I need to make it today if I can."

"Do they have any more information on who did it?"

"They have no leads at all. They suspect it must've been someone who knew him, but who obviously didn't like him. They reported nothing stolen at all."

"I'm sorry." Not knowing what else to say, Amy turned and walked away. Amy tried to mix in as often and as much as she could with other groups. The mixture of people amazed her. Amy saw book critics, of course, but many publishers, authors, agents, newspaper and magazine editors, and a few bookstore owners and employees like her.

Everyone appeared to have a place in this crazy publishing business. While she studied the delicate signs of trust and distrust scattered around the room hidden, or displayed as the case may be in the many smiles and hugs given and received, she also overheard the backstabbing.

The lights blinked several times, giving everyone notice that the meeting would soon be starting. This main introduction session would be followed by many small meetings throughout the day, and some on Sunday.

During the opening presentation, one of the ladies that she had talked to at the reception stood and spoke on something that shocked Amy. She pointed to a paper she held in her other hand. "It's easy to see how everyone likes a good review . . . except when it's concerning a competitor."

She paused and looked around the room. "And thank God all of us book reviewers are not of the same opinion. I wrote an article about one book and gave it thumbs up, but I recently read another article, and the critic shredded it to pieces. After reading her article, I admired her courage to take such a stand on a very popular author. Bestselling authors should have more scrutiny, and I think the reviewer was right on the money. In fact, this reviewer has actually changed my mind on this novel. But then again, when I looked at who the reviewer was, I was a little bit taken back. It appears he or she prefers to hide their true identity and write under the name of *The Literary Hawk*."

Looking around to assess the room, she continued, "But . . . after thinking about it, I think he or she might have a point. No one can approach him or her to corrupt their point of view, and they could probably move through crowds like this and be totally undetected. For all I know, he or she may be here today."

Since Amy sold her reviews to only about a dozen papers, she wondered how the speaker found one of them. She felt like the frozen deer suddenly caught in a car's headlights. One thing was for sure now; she would never be able to reveal her true identity as a book reviewer. However, she loved having this kind of publicity. The more newspapers she wrote for, the more money she would make. And, of course, the more newspapers that purchased her articles, the more of an impact she would have on ruining Edward. She had a hard time believing a noted reviewer would say she had changed her mind after reading another review. Amy considered the compliment as a sign she must be better at reviewing than she even admitted to herself.

When the speaker asked all of the book reviewers in attendance to stand, Amy, of course, decided to remain seated. The reviewers comprised about a fifth of the attendees. The others came to the convention to meet them, and hopefully influence their opinion. It's no wonder the comments by the moderator rang so true on the use of a pseudo name.

The meeting progressed normally, with many questions being asked from the audience on how they went about reviewing a book. Near the end, one woman stood and asked the man at the end of the row on the panel a question. "This question is for the syndication representative." This panel member who worked for a national syndication had been relatively quiet for most of the meeting. Everyone knew what it meant to have him pick you as a client and syndicate your articles. As he stood to answer a question on syndication, the room became quiet and respectful. "What is the best way to have your company pick up a new reviewer for syndication?"

He raised a microphone to answer. "I know how much everyone here has to work on reading a book and writing an article to make the few dollars paid by a newspaper, that is, unless you work for one of the large national papers. I can promise you that quality work doesn't go unnoticed, much as we heard at the first of the meeting. If you think your work is outstanding then contact me, and I'll evaluate it. However, I'll tell you that many of our greatest reviewers come from our own research into what is being published. We read a lot of papers every day looking for new talent. If you're good, we'll probably find you before you find us."

The meeting soon ended as Amy thought about Edward and wondered if he had walked into the room. She didn't see him earlier, but she still knew that he might be around. She became especially curious if he was there, since it was his client's novel that the other book reviewer reversed her mind on. The thought of such a small victory felt exhilarating.

After the meeting ended, Amy decided to walk outside to relax for a minute. She stopped along the way to talk to two of the reviewers she had met earlier. With a big smile, the middle age woman asked her, "What do you think?"

"I think it was very educational. I had no idea book reviewing was so important to everyone."

"It does have its perks at times, but you have to remain independent and objective. The large publishers would love to have you under their thumb."

"What do you think of the national syndication route to selling your work?"

"It has a place, but it has pitfalls as well. For one thing, they take most of your money. Then, they also put their rules on you, which is like having a boss again. Being independent is something most book reviewers take pride in more than anything."

"How many newspapers do you write for?"

"We work together and have maybe 100 papers, more or less."

"Wow, that's a large number of newspapers."

"Not really, considering the tens of thousands of papers worldwide."

"I guess I never considered it as such, but a hundred papers is a large number to keep up with." Amy could only imagine such numbers.

"Today, all the real work is done on the computer. It sends the articles and tracks the payments. It does the whole nine yards."

"That must be one nice program to have." With a little work Amy felt sure she could find such.

"They have them available all over the net. It's not hard, even for an old hag like me to use."

Amy enjoyed the way the ladies like to kid each other. She had much to learn, and it would be fun to get involved with a group like this. While she felt bad not being able to tell them she also reviewed books, she was now more determined than ever to learn this trade.

JOHNNY RAY

CHAPTER 10

"Girl, you look terrible," Lenny said as Amy walked into the bookstore. "What time did you go to bed?"

"I'm not sure I ever went to bed last night. I had one more book I wanted to finish before I went to sleep. Perhaps I should've called in sick today."

"Ever since you returned from the convention, you've been working like a crazy person. I really don't understand why you're trying to kill yourself."

"I think I've discovered something I'm good at, and for once I have a goal I really want to achieve. I've been such a fuck up all of my life. I need to prove something to myself, my parents, and others that I'm not so bad." She tried to suppress a yawn but failed.

"You need to worry about your health also. Night after night with little or no sleep is not good. What does Dr. Lankford think about you working like this?"

"The same thing you're saying. It's all about my crazy bipolar condition. As you know . . . sometimes I'm super active like this, but it generally doesn't last very long. I'm watching my medication and seeing Dr. Lankford, since this is a tricky time for me. Too much or too little medication can cause me to swing wildly in the other direction."

Lenny glanced around before he continued. "Personally, I think you need to just get laid and chill out for a while."

Amy rolled her eyes. "I think *kinky sex* is all you ever think about. You're the one I should be worried about."

Letting the comment roll off his ego, Lenny continued to speak. "It just appears that you're pushing too much on this revenge thing. Since the papers will only use one article a week, why are you writing so many?"

"I'm adding a few new newspapers to my mailing list every day. It's a lot of work trying to decide who to send it to at the paper. You can find their web sites easy enough, but trying to find the person you need to send it to isn't easy at all."

Lenny poured a large latte and pushed it over to Amy. "Compliments of management," he whispered. "I thought you already made a list of newspapers to send the articles to."

"I work with some of them and I have luckily added many to it thanks to the free publicity I received at the convention. The attendees representing the newspapers at the convention were eager to hear from me."

"How many newspapers do you have publishing your articles now?"

"I think about twenty-five or so. I'm not sure, it varies each week."

"Wow, you must be making as much or more than you make here now."

"I'm growing fast, but it's because I've worked so hard at it. Very soon it will be time to put my real plan into effect. It has taken some time, but I'll soon have all in place to pay Edward back for the letter he sent me."

"I think you're so obsessed with paying back this guy you don't realize that he's still destroying you much more than you are him."

"He'll soon feel the wrath of my articles being released on him. I've learned a lot about him, and perhaps know more about him than he does himself. I know who all of his authors are, which editors he uses, the name of all the people in his firm, where he went to school and his old friends. He's a workaholic and has little time for friends now. His whole life is consumed by working as an agent. When I take that away from him, he'll have nothing, like I did when he let me down."

"I hope I never get you mad at me. You even scare me sometimes."

"Thanks for the coffee. I need to check on his blog and find out what he's up to." She laughed. "It's easy to track someone who posts what he's doing everyday for the world to see."

Amy went to the computer and clicked on Edward's site. He had posted about his day and how he was working with some new clients now. "Can you believe this jerk! He said I needed to get help with my writing and that he didn't represent my kind of work. However, it's exactly what he sells, and now he's bragging about getting new clients."

Lenny looked over her shoulder and whispered, "You have to remember getting clients is what he's supposed to do."

"Yes, but his letter stated that he had no room for any more clients. I wonder who these new authors are." Amy clicked away at the computer and searched for the new names she didn't recognize. Then she recognized one of them. It was the girl at the convention whose agent had been murdered. "You scum bag!"

"What is it?"

"The writer I met at the convention who was crying so mournfully about her agent's death has signed with a new agent. It's that bastard Edward."

"I can understand she would need another agent that—"

"I can't believe this. I should've told her about him. Maybe it's not too late. I think I have her card somewhere. If not, I'm sure I can find her on the internet." Amy clicked on the search engine and started looking. She found it and clicked on the contact information to only receive an e-mail prompt. She then clicked on her calendar and studied the various book tours she was making. None of them were close to her. She eventually saw a convention she was going to attend in a few weeks. It wasn't close, but drivable. She clicked on favorites and would think about going to it.

After finishing with a customer, Lenny moved over and

patted her on the shoulder. "You are definitely a woman on a mission."

"I found another convention in a few weeks. I think I might need to go to it."

"What kind of convention is it?"

"It's a small writer's convention hosted by the English department of a small university."

"Let me know. I can cover for you again, but the way it looks you won't need this job much longer." He presented her with a sad puppy dog look.

"Don't worry. We'll always be friends. You've been fantastic to work with."

"Well, this has not been much of a job, and I am thinking of doing something else. There's this guy I know, who's willing to help me with my interior decorating career. He's making . . . just bundles of money showcasing houses for realtors."

"That sounds like something you would be good at."

"I think you're right, and the guys coming in here are just not paying me any attention anymore."

CHAPTER 11

The alarm clock blasted away as Amy tried to decide what to do. She had just fallen asleep after another night of reading page after page. This morning, however, she needed to see Dr. Lankford and attend the group session. She had promised her mother to make it and to be on time.

The book from the night before still circulated in her head. The words were well written, but the plot was hard to follow and tricky. She was like most readers; she loved to read for entertainment, and not to be confused by an author who didn't know what he was doing or where he was going. She saw plenty to criticize in this book and pumped her fist with joy, since it was one of Edwards' new authors.

With her room in disarray and the plate of snacks beside her bed still containing traces of donuts and chips, she glanced at her robe covering the floor next to her clothes from the day before. It had turned hot the night before and she had removed her nightshirt to sleep naked.

She hit the snooze button and turned over for an extra five minutes. It felt so good to lie still as she drifted off to sleep and started dreaming of dancing on a large floor. It felt so good to have someone hold her close and gentle while the music played slow and romantic under dim lights. The fairytale setting appeared familiar and felt so natural and cozy. Her slim partner stood taller than her, but he wasn't very muscular.

She pulled from him slightly to study his face, but then only focused on his eyes. They looked small, beady and intense. Her dream shifted from euphoria to nightmare in less than a second. She was dancing with Edward. He held her and stopped her from escaping. She breathed in deep and started to yell as the beeping of the alarm clock woke her.

She stretched and shut off the clock. The sweat beaded

on her body as she breathed fast and furious. Even in her dreams she must be going crazy.

As she got out of the bed and stumbled to the bathroom to wash her face, the idea of spending sexy romantic moments with Edwards in her dreams felt repulsive to her. She felt like throwing up, and maybe even like putting a gun to her head to put an end to all of this growing torment. *What am I thinking*? Amy needed to get a grip on things now, since she was smart enough to know that many bipolar people commit suicide, and it was something she had attempted once. That couldn't happen to her again. She had been doing very well lately. It was all Edwards' fault. He had to be taught a lesson. No one else could do what had to be done, and there was no way of knowing how many others he had screwed over like her.

The cold water on her face made her feel better. Without makeup, she looked plain and simple, but she didn't have much time for a long shower and serious work on her face because she didn't want to be late. She would do the best she could.

Moving as fast as she could on her three inch high hills, Amy rushed to the door and pushed it open. She had actually arrived early and saw some members of the group still standing in the front office, waiting for the meeting to start.

She saw most of the group: Stephen, Judith, Nancy, Wendell and Ernest smiling at her, but she didn't see Estella. Perhaps she was running late, as usual. The group meeting was supposed to bring members closer, but it hadn't been too successful yet.

Dr. Lankford opened the door to her office and waved gracefully at the quiet group waiting to come in. "It's good to see everyone this morning, and I hope everyone likes the new meeting time."

Like silent soldiers, they all entered the room which had been rearranged to accommodate the small group. Out of habit, each person went to the same seat they occupied at each previous meeting. The only seat left open was the one for Estella. Dr. Lankford noticed the empty chair and glanced at her watch. "I hope she's all right, but everyone knows it's like her to be late."

They all looked around and waited as Dr. Lankford made the rounds of shaking everyone's hand and saying hello. She reflected her usual confident self and full of concern for each person in the room.

Amy shifted in her seat as Estella finally walked into the room. She appeared accustomed to making grand entrances, and so this was nothing new for her. She looked like she had just stepped off a runway in a major fashion show. Her long blonde hair looked perfectly styled, and without one hair out of place. If she did her own makeup, she was a master at it. It looked flawless.

"I'm sorry I'm late. Something came up this morning I wasn't expecting." She walked across the room and found her place. Everyone either stared at her, or studied the grace in her walk. The outfit she wore looked beautiful and appeared to be tailored specifically for her. In all probability, it was custom made. The pink skirt with matching blouse contained eloquent designs of contrasting colors. Above the blouse she wore what looked to be a cashmere sweater. The coordinated four inch leather heels made her slim legs sexy.

As she moved into her seat, the dress resting slightly above her knees inched up and revealed more of her legs. Obviously, the guys in the room enjoyed the show. Estella acted, of course, like she didn't notice them.

Dr. Lankford waited and welcomed her as she did the rest

of her patients. "How is everyone's week so far?"

As if on cue, the room started to relate the current status of their moods. Amy heard little changes from the previous weeks, until she finally had to reveal her week.

"I'm working a lot this week, and it's hard for me to sleep, since I've so many new books I need to read. When I contacted several of the publishers and told them I was reviewing books and would like to be put on their advance read copy list, the books came flooding in."

Shifting in her seat for a second, she continued, "I still have nightmares about an agent I told everyone about earlier. I know we're not supposed to get mad and seek revenge, but every time I turn around I see or hear about him and it makes me boiling mad inside. Until he gets what's coming to him, I'll never rest. I'm sure he's not the only jerk in the literary business, but I'll never forget the rejection letter he sent me, or how he led me on."

Amy studied the small group listening to her talk. She felt like they knew what it was like to be looked down on or misunderstood, and how they had their own stories of being mistreated. For the first time, Amy felt like the group thing might not be so bad.

Even Estella looked like she was a little starry eyed, with a deep look of concern on her face. Amy had a hard time telling how old she was. The perfect slim body and heavy makeup made estimating difficult. From a distance she could easily be considered to be in her late twenties. Up close, she looked much older—almost forty. Never having children helped her keep an attractive girlish figure.

Amy looked over the room and continued. "I'm going to another convention in a few weeks. Since it's good to make friends and contacts, I hope I can keep this good mood for a few more weeks."

"I think you'll do fine. This is especially true if you properly take your medication to control your current mood," Dr. Lankford added.

"I wish you a good trip, Amy." Estella also added with a deep compassion in her voice. "It sounds like you're working hard."

"Yes, perhaps too hard, but in a way it's good therapy for me. I finally have a constructive way to get back at the bastards in this industry. I'm still writing under a different name. Some of the arrogant agents coming to this conference will never know one reviewer is attacking them. Keeping my identity in the dark is the part that's kind of nice."

Estella looked up and glanced around the room. "I think I know how you feel. It's a terrible thing to not know how to fight back. While my family provides me with all I could want, they also treat me like a slave or a puppet. My mood swings are under control, but at the cost of everything else in my life. In fact, I feel like I have no life and no purpose most of the time. To me, this meeting is the closest I come to the real world."

"Do you think you're taking too much medication?" Dr. Lankford asked.

"It's either too much medication or too much to drink. Being lonely all the time can be very depressing. Sometimes I'm able to travel—I love it." A smile crossed her face as she obviously loved that one thing. "I especially love to discover new places on my own."

"Then, I think you should do more of it. What does your husband think about it?"

"He's scared for me to be on my own. It's like he does not fully trust me. I'll admit I've had times when I drank too much. I know it can be embarrassing for him, but I'm not sure why, since he works out of town all the time, and I don't see him too often anymore."

Stephen sat directly across from Estella with his eyes glued on Estella's legs that were pointed directly at him, which offered him a bird's eye view up her dress. Lost in his apparent imagination, he almost didn't hear Dr. Lankford calling his name as she walked over to him. A small laugh could be heard around the room as everyone knew what was on his mind.

He straightened his back and glanced around as he finally answered Dr. Lankford. "I'm doing fine, but it's hard to concentrate at work for long periods of time. Sometimes it takes longer to get a job done. The boss has a hard time understanding me. I think, like Amy, some people need to be dealt with personally, but if that's not possible, you have to do it anyway you can."

Estella suddenly spoke again. "I've never had children. Perhaps if I did I'd feel differently about many things. I hate to see anyone taking advantage of others. It's wrong when one person needs the help of another person, only to have that person take advantage of them."

Amy raised her hand before speaking. "That's exactly what I'm talking about."

Stephen also nodded with a big smile, as the rest of the room joined in. Dr. Lankford acted fast to get a handle on the situation. "I think constructive ways of resolving situations are always best, but there's a point where you can let your emotions get too carried away. That can be a dangerous situation for many people, especially for us who know we have violent swings in emotions."

Estella again added her opinion, which appeared strange for her. She usually acted like the quiet reserved one in the group. "I've often heard it said if friends don't help friends, then who can you depend on? I feel so helpless most of the time, and I would love to have a knight in shining armor rescue me and take me away to let me be me for a while. If I could help others, it would, at least, make me feel worth something for a while."

"Perhaps you could find some work you could volunteer

for."

"I've done the charity league thing before, but it's too bogus, even for me to enjoy for long." Almost like turning off a wind-up doll, Estella suddenly became quiet. Perhaps her morning medication had kicked in.

As the meeting soon ended, Dr. Lankford acknowledged each person in the group when they left. She had carefully watched each person's response. Sometimes letting someone talk freely offered her valuable insight into what was going on with that person. She appeared to have many unanswered questions on her mind.

CHAPTER 12

James Aaron's literary agency office, Washington DC, late night

James poured another cup of coffee as he wished he had more time to prepare for his presentation next week. Taking part in various workshops cost him so much time, but he knew it was necessary to maintain his image in the publishing world. He also promised himself he would work through his mounting e-mails of query letters, but he knew most of them would be ridiculous and be a total waste his few remaining minutes.

He hated the way some writers persisted and presented the same damn work to him over and over. A no meant no. Somehow this one writer had found a way around his spam filter. He added the e-mail address again to the spam registry, as he continued down the list, automatically sending one form rejection letter after another.

The last query sounded good, but not something he really wanted to pursue. He needed to concentrate on his own clients. When the coffee rush he had hoped for disappointed him, he decided to go home and catch some sleep.

He turned off and packed his laptop and one manuscript he wanted to look at first thing in the morning. That is, if he woke early enough. He envied the others working in his office. They always managed to leave early. Why couldn't he be more efficient and leave on time? Oh yes, he knew, because he owned the agency and had to pay the bills at the end of each month.

He walked around his office to turn out the lights and rearrange a few chairs pulled out of place during the day. The quietness of the office felt nothing new. He assumed he was the only guy left in the entire office building, which housed about ten other companies as well. However, this was Washington DC, and his office was not in the best of locations. The walk out to his car always made him feel a bit uneasy, and it was perhaps why most of his staff and the other agents left early.

After stepping outside, he locked his door as he heard the solid click. With a cold wind blasting his back, he pulled his overcoat tighter around his neck. He walked to the stairs and made the first flight. On the second flight, he heard a shuffle behind him. He didn't have to turn around, someone had rushed toward him. He thought about running—should he?

A voice confirmed his fears. "Stop where you are!" He complied, but forced his mind to forge a plan for survival. He attempted to face the voice. "Don't turn around."

He decided to lift his hands to indicate he wasn't going to fight back. Visions of being shot in the back of the head sent hairs on his neck standing. "What do you want?"

"We're going to take this slow. I want you to return back to your office. I have a gun aimed directly at your back. Do you understand?"

He nodded his head. "You can have my money if that is what you want."

"Shut up and move."

He felt an object poke his back. "Okay, just don't shoot me."

"Move." He climbed the stairs with his mind in overload. What could he do? As he reached his door, he felt the gun in his back again. "For your sake, I hope you remember to turn off your security system."

After unlocking the door, he stepped inside and turned to input the numbers in the alarm. The urge to glance at his abductor became almost too much to resist. He squinted as he finished entering the code. Tightening every muscle in his body, he prepared to make his move. He hesitated too long—a pain shot through the back of his head. His vision blurred for a second, and then all went dark.

Much later, James struggled with a dizzy, floating sensation to gain consciousness. While suffering the excruciating pain in his head, he groaned and tried to move. A new pain registered in his hands, which were tied by a thin wire that cut into his wrist. A lighter pain radiated from his ankles that had also tied together.

James forced his vision to clear as he attempted to survey the reception area. Was he alone? He saw papers and files scattered around him on the floor. He blinked his eyes again. Robbery, is that what this was all about? He had nothing worth losing his life over.

An image of someone moving about in his office materialized. He blinked again, hoping to see who it was. The person moved out of sight. He heard the eerie sounds of his office being trashed. His attacker soon walked out of his office and toward him. He saw someone much different than he expected. Why was this happening to him?

"I see you're coming to. Good. You don't have a clue why I'm here, do you?"

"No. If its money you want—"

He jerked backwards attempting to avoid a metal bat swung in his direction, barely missing his head. Again he managed to dodge a blow, which whistled inches above his head. He knew the miss was on purpose, but he trembled at thoughts of being hit. What could he do—nothing? He felt more files and papers thrown at him as the bat tapped the tiled floor with a creepy sound of a constant rhythm. "What do you want from me?"

His attacker leaned forward. "Nothing . . . but then again—everything. You're going to be an example of what happens to agents who think they can act as fucking jerks and get away with it."

"What did I do to you?"

The metal bat, which continued to tap on the floor,

slowly retreated only to return and smash into his face. The pain exploded throughout his head as several teeth broke inside his mouth. He yelled hoping for help from anyone. Of course, he knew no one would hear. "Please, oh God, please don't kill me!"

"What's the matter? You don't have someone bowing down to you and kissing your ass right now. Perhaps you want me to suck your dick to get you to simply look at my work. Is that it?"

His jaw hurt. Did the bat break it also? He felt a hand on his pants which quickly unzipped his pants. Now what? A vise like grip on his penis and his balls sent new waves of terror through his traumatized body. He forced a kick with both legs at his assailant, but he missed. The bat smashed his nose in response. The next blast shattered his last thoughts. However, he knew his torture had only begun.

CHAPTER 13

With her mood in a well-balanced mode, Amy cranked the motor to her car and headed south, knowing it was a long drive to the convention. She carried her road music with her, and she looked forward to the time of relaxing as she drove. She loved just getting her head out of the books for a while.

A few hours later she decided to stop at a fast food restaurant to rest and eat a quick burger. It wasn't too crowded, and it was near the interstate. She hoped to avoid eating too much as she looked at her stomach, but decided it was a lost cause, since she had no time to properly exercise.

Amy ordered a hamburger with fries and a coke before finding a seat in the front of the restaurant. After noticing a newspaper that a previous customer had left behind, she started eating the hamburger and looking through the paper. Since it was out of order, it was a few minutes before she read the front page.

When she noticed the headline, she dropped her burger. "Oh, my God!" She yelled loud enough to get the attention of others around her. Another literary agent, James Aaron, had been found brutally murdered. She had heard of him before, but didn't know too much about him.

He was found murdered in his office. While he had no close family, he did have an ex-wife, but she was not considered a suspect and she was cooperating with the authorities. The paper described the murder as brutal. He had been beaten and stabbed to death, making identification hard at first. The police had no suspects or motives. His work had been scattered and his office totally destroyed, but nothing was stolen that they could ascertain.

Amy knew she needed to search on her computer to find out more, since this sounded almost exactly like the first murder of an agent a few months ago. They even mentioned the possibility in the article of a serial killer targeting agents.

Amy lost her appetite; apparently someone hated agents more than she did, but Amy didn't hate all agents—just one. She felt sure the industry had some good agents.

At the convention she knew she would learn more about this murder, since it would definitely be the main subject of discussion. After quickly folding the newspaper, she walked out to her car with it. She didn't want her mood to swing too much, and this was the sort of event that could easily do it. As she entered her car, she turned her music louder before she continued on her way.

CHAPTER 14

Amy soon saw the hotel ahead on the right, and felt happy about the excellent time she had made. Eager to find out more about the latest murdered agent, she knew someone at the convention would have more information.

The hotel looked large, but not nearly as nice as the one at the last convention. This convention was tailored to new authors who wanted to become published authors, or those getting started in some fashion or other. Several agents and publishers offered pitch sessions to these want-to-be authors. Amy studied the information on the various meetings designed to help guide them along the way.

Amy hurried to the front desk to check in. After she handed the clerk her confirmation he looked at it, pulled out a file, and handed her a paper to sign. "Your room's all ready. You'll be in room 207 down the hall."

"Thank you." This was one of the fastest check-ins she had remembered in a long time.

The room looked nice and comfortable. While it would be nice to take a quick nap, she knew she needed some answers to the agent's death to be able to rest. She checked herself in the mirror, walked out the door, and headed to the meeting rooms.

At the entrance to the meeting rooms, Amy noticed several tables arranged to allow attendees to sign in. Some people were walking around and in no hurry, while others stayed seated at various chairs scattered around reading over material they had been given. Amy stopped at the counter and waited until a little lady who must have been in her seventies walked over to her. "Can I help you?"

"Yes, my name's Amy Jenkins and I need to register for the convention."

"Do you have your confirmation?"

"Yes, I think so. Give me a minute."

"Take your time, and I'll be getting your package together. Is this the first time you attended this convention?"

"Yes it is. Here's my confirmation, and where I prepaid the meeting fee when I signed up."

After searching the list of attendees, the lady located Amy's name and where she had in fact paid. "It looks like you're set to go. We're hosting a reception in the book signing room in about an hour. I think you might like to meet some of the attendees here. Also, look around at the books. The authors are here and they will be glad to sign them for you."

"Thanks. I do have a little time."

Amy walked over to an unoccupied chair and opened her package, which provided her with a list of attendees and speakers. While most of the attendees she didn't know, the main speaker was an agent who worked out of New York City and London, England. In his agency were several other agents who represented many of the top authors in the world. It was a huge honor for the convention to have landed such a high profile agent. Amy decided to give him the benefit of a doubt for the moment, but she wouldn't be surprised if he turned out to be just like Edward.

As the crowd started to move past her, she located the name she had been looking for—Beth Sherman, the main reason she had made the trip. How did she manage to get connected with such a jerk like Edward?

Amy placed the information back in her package and walked to the book signing room, which was busy with people of all ages standing and talking. Some were engaged in deep conversation with what would appear to be old friends, and some were standing around not sure as to what to be doing.

Amy walked over to the portable bar and noticed the drink prices. She stopped and considered it for a minute.

With money still not plentiful, she knew she needed to watch her spending. After a guy hurried to the bar and stopped in front of her, she watched him study her face for a minute before he grinned. "I think I know you."

Amy felt flattered, but confused. "This is the first time I've been to this convention."

"No, it was at a different convention. My name's Michael Hadcock. I was at a bar with my agent, Edward Lawson, when we met."

His face became clearer to her immediately. "Oh yes, I do remember you." Her stomach quivered as she quickly felt lightheaded. The notion of anything or anyone connected to Edward sent waves of anger through her.

"The last time I saw you and Edward, you two were dancing. You guys were hitting it off so well my buddy and I decided to leave both of you alone and try our luck somewhere else."

Amy was about to tell him what she thought of Edward, but decided to count to ten slowly. That was a mistake, since another guy interrupted Michael from behind before she could say anything. This man acted highly emotional and talked fast, but softly to Michael, as to not be overheard. Michael looked disturbed by the interruption, as he whispered to Amy, "This is someone I need to talk to for a minute. However, we do need to talk later so you can fill me in on you and Edward." He rushed off with the other guy as they started yelling at each other.

Amy felt the pressure mounting in her head, but this wasn't the place, or time. Oh yes, she would fill him in later, and it would be much more than he had counted on.

A shy looking girl in her early thirties slowly walked over to talk to her. "How are you?"

"I'm not sure. It seems like some people are always playing havoc with my life."

The girl didn't appear to know exactly how to take the

comment. Amy realized she had totally confused her. "I'm sorry. My name's Amy."

"My name's Rebecca. I noticed you talking to Michael Hadcock. Is he a friend of yours?"

"We met once and talked for a few minutes. Why? Do you know him?"

"No, but I'd love to meet him. You know he's one of the keynote speakers here. His books are doing extremely well."

Amy felt embarrassed. She hadn't done her homework well, and she hadn't recognized his name on the list of speakers. "I only made plans to come here at the last minute, and I didn't study the names of the presenters."

Amy had written a book review on one of his books and had criticized it savagely. It was really not too bad, but anything connected to Edward was a justified target in her mind. It was too bad if others had to get hurt in the process.

"Are you a writer?" She leaned toward Amy in an attempt to keep the conversation going.

"I've written one novel, but haven't had anyone seriously look at it. How about you?"

"I've written two. The first one is on the sales desk if you're interested." Rebecca's eyes sparkled as she pointed to the books being sold by authors in attendance.

Amy flashed a big smile. "So this is your first book!"

"Yes. I had to self-publish it, but I think it will help push me to the next level."

"Good for you! If you'll sign it, I'd love to read it."

"I'd love to." As Rebecca signed the book, Amy had a second to think of the quick conversation with Michael. She wondered what he meant when he said he left Edward and her alone on the dance floor when they started hitting it off together. Damn! She wished she could remember that one night better.

Amy eventually walked around the room and outside to the hallway. Michael had disappeared. Yes, she needed a good drink as she headed for the bar.

"What would you like to have?" The bartender asked at the small portable bar, as he waited on her to decide.

"Right now, scotch would be in order and on the rocks, even better."

Within minutes, the drink produced its expected result. She went to the sales counters and started talking to some of the other authors who brought their books with them to sell. "Hello, how are you?" Another girl moved closer and extended her hand toward Amy.

"I'm doing fine." And so it went for the next hour as Amy went from author to author while she waited for Michael to return, but he never did.

Later, another author walked over to her. "Several of us are going to a bar about a block away. Many of the attendees are going. It has been kind of a watering hole for the convention for years. You're welcome to walk over with us if you want to."

That was the best offer she could count on at this time, and perhaps she might catch Michael coming in later. She also needed to find Beth Sherman at the convention somehow. Amy knew she was there somewhere, and she needed to talk to her. She wanted to know how Beth had tied in with the likes of Edward. "Yes, I'd love to go, since I know almost no one here. Thank you for inviting me."

After two more girls joined them, they headed out of the room and down the hallway. While all three appeared to be in their late twenties or early thirties, none of them approached beauty queen status, but they didn't look too bad either. Making new friends would be fun.

At the end of the block, Amy studied the flashing neon lights that illuminated most of the surroundings, with colors rotating from pink to green. One guy stood by the door and talked on a cell phone as a tall blonde haired girl dressed in a black party dress patiently waiting on him. She smoked a cigarette and displayed an attitude in her mannerism which told everyone to stay away. No one said anything to her as they quickly entered the front doors.

The inside of the place looked crowded and sounded loud, with a band playing on the far left side of the bar in front of a dance floor. On the right side, she noticed a game room with about ten or twelve pool tables. She followed the other girls moving to the left side of the joint. Walking toward the band, the bar on the right of them had perhaps three or four bartenders working hard to fill their patron's orders. Being crowded, they had to weave between many people standing in the way chatting with others. Many of those were also waiting for either a chair at the bar to open, or a table on the left side to clear.

The crowd made their way impassable as they stood and waited for a path to open. It was kind of a local's bar where everyone knew each other. As Amy looked around, she noticed both young people and old people. The front girl in her group suddenly turned and yelled at her entourage, "Stay close and we'll make it to the dance area soon."

Amy considered leaving, since it was too crowded and had some weird guys looking at her, which gave her the creeps. However, she did notice some good looking guys occasionally. Being in this far, she decided to stay for a few more minutes.

When the crowd dispersed slightly, the lead girl forced her way through, but on the other side they found much of the same. At the end of the bar, the space opened onto a dance floor with many tables scattered around it. The lead girl continued to push her way onward until she located some open ground. "It's really crowded tonight," she yelled at those behind her.

After one of the other girls pointed to a table in the process of clearing, they all made a dash to it to make sure they arrived before others set up ownership. The band was playing a vibrant dance song, with a tremendous beat, which was driving the crowd wild as they packed the dance floor. Amy and the three other girls shared a big smile as they felt lucky to find a table close to the band so fast.

After settling in her chair, Amy started to look around to assess her surroundings, while trying to recognize anyone. With the dim lighting and the intense crowds, it would be useless to try to make any contacts in here.

A waitress walked over to the table and finished clearing the glasses before retrieving her tip. Amy assumed she was in her early twenties, perhaps an energetic college student needing to make some extra money. She wore her long black hair in a pony tail pulled through the opening in the back of a baseball cap. "What can I get you?"

Amy and the rest of the girls placed an order for beer, which appeared to be the popular drink in the place. Knowing it would be hard to tell if any of the people from the conference were mixed in this crowd, Amy leaned over to the girl on her right. "Do you think we'll find anyone else from the conference here?"

"I'm not sure, but I think some of them might be in here. I know some of the regular attendees who like to come to this bar. We should see them in a little while."

Amy again surveyed the bar, which contained the usual people you would expect in a bar, including the bleached out blondes looking for any guy including the pot belly guys hoping to get lucky. She also noticed, however, some unexpected, but very classy people scattered around who dressed nice and looked physically attractive.

At the end of the song, the dance floor cleared with many of the dancers heading for their table to finish drinks or order new ones. The staggering movements of the guys following the girls back to their tables indicated that they had already been drinking for a while. Some guys were attached to their dance partner, while others quickly left them and started looking for fresh territory. In minutes, the table with Amy and the three other girls became an object of interest as several guys rushed over to their table.

One guy who rushed to arrive at their table first quickly pushed some chairs out of his way before grinning like an actor auditioning for a part. Because of the loud noise, she had a hard time hearing him the first time. He leaned forward to talk above the crowd. "Hi, would you like to dance?" He pointed to the floor and motioned for her to join him.

She felt glad to be asked, but stopped and shook her head. "Not now, maybe later." She hadn't had time to catch her breath, and wanted to check out the place first. "We've just arrived, and I haven't had anything to drink yet."

He turned to the girl on Amy's left and extended his hand. She reached for it without hesitation. "Why not, I'm not too good, so bear with me." He reached for her hand to help her from her seat. He wasn't that bad looking, perhaps in his late thirties and in good physical shape. His hair was a little long and needed cutting, but he dressed well with a dark blue dress shirt that was clean and neat.

"I'll be back in a minute when the drinks arrive." She followed him to the dance floor, which was filling up fast.

As soon as they ordered drinks, the other two girls accepted chances to get on the dance floor as well. This left Amy in charge of guarding the table. Amy looked at the walls and all the banners signs advertising various brands of beer. They must really believe in nothing but beer here, she thought, as she saw no other drinks being advertised. The stories that could be told here were probably incredible.

Another guy who dressed in a light colored polo and dark grey dress pants walked over to her table. With his well cut, dark hair combed to one side, he looked like a professional. His voice definitely sounded smooth and masculine. "Would you care to dance?" he asked, as he extended his hand toward her.

Since all the girls at her table were now dancing on the floor, and she didn't want to be the only one sitting at the table, she decided to give it a try. "Sure, but just one, I'm waiting on my friends to return to the table soon."

His eyes sparkled as he moved behind her to help out of her chair. He acted like a perfect gentleman in a rowdy bar, which was a pleasant surprise for her. She felt his hand on her back as he helped guide her to the floor that was overcrowded with many dancers. The pounding music sounded even louder on the floor.

As he started gyrating in a free style move which had no particular name to it, the movements accented his well-toned body. His dark-brown hair reflected the circulating lights above the dance floor. While hard to make out too many details in the low light, his face appeared to be well shaved, making him look not too bad at all. She joined in and started swaying to the music. She recognized no patterns to the dances around her as the crowds bumped into her from all sides. This guy directed his attention at her, and while it made her feel good, it made her feel a little bit intimidated at the same time.

When the music came to a stop, Amy backed away from him. "Thank you." She said as she turned and headed for her table. It was obvious he wanted to dance more, but he politely thanked her and followed her to the table.

As she returned to her seat, he turned and surveyed the table. "Perhaps we can dance some more in a minute. Thank you again." He offered her a nice smile as he turned and walked away.

The waitress soon hurried over with the beers. "Here you go. Do you want to pay me now, or run you a tab?"

"I think it will be good to run a tab." The waitress made a note on her pad and turned and left. She appeared flirty in her outfit, but extremely busy running beer also.

The girls returned at the end of the next song, bringing the guys with them. It was easy to see that they wanted to pull up a chair and stay, but they knew it was still early. As the guys retreated, the girls started talking to each other.

The girl to her right spoke first. "That was not fun. You have to watch some of the guys in here."

"Why?" The girl across from Amy asked.

"Someone fondled my rear on the way back from the dance floor. Apparently some guys here think they can put their hands on your ass with no questions asked." Everyone turned, trying to decide which guy it was she was talking about, but he had disappeared into the crowd on the jam-packed floor. It was the center of attention, and space was a premium.

Amy lifted her glass, as the other girls followed. Since the loud bar noise made talking next to impossible, she offered no spoken toast, but everyone exchanged big smiles when the glasses touched in the center.

The girl to her right stopped drinking and pointed to one of the dancers on the floor. "That's one girl who is here every year. She's wild and going to get herself in deep trouble one day. She's playing with dynamite, and I'm not sure if she knows it or not."

This dancer looked tall, and slim, but with large breasts that she candidly displayed with a blouse opened enough to reveal her cleavage. The bra she wore highly accentuated their shape, and had thus captured everyone's attention.

"Do you know what her name is?" Amy asked.

"She's a writer who writes very sexy and erotic novels. Her name's Angelina Martin."

"I can see that she lives what she writes."

"Yes, she's a wild woman. You'll see as the night goes on, and at the convention too." An almost self-righteous look crossed her face, but Amy also acknowledged a little envy as well.

106

Amy watched Angelina dance on the floor, as she teased all the men around her. She had flirting down to a science with her white, skin-tight pants she wore radiating brightly on the dance floor. With her ass twitching with each beat of the band, her dance partner appeared to be having the time of his life, and ignored the constant flirting of Angelina with the other guys on the floor. After all, he was still the one with the honor of dancing with her for now.

The first beer didn't last long. The next one also quickly disappeared as the girls stayed busy critiquing the dancers on the floor. While they considered all the girls on the dance floor to be sluts or bar prostitutes, it didn't stop them from joining in when other guys asked them to dance. They all came to have fun.

Another guy came soon to ask Amy out on the floor. He looked short and chubby, but had a pleasant smile on his face. The engrossing beat of a popular song convinced Amy that it was time to get back on the floor. "Sure, it would be good to dance."

He turned and walked to the floor, but he was not nearly as charming as the previous guy she had danced with. On the floor, he moved to the center and waited for her to join him.

Amy started free style dancing in front of him, until he looked around and started dancing on his own. Amy quickly stopped as she watched him come alive. His dancing was terrible as he went through some ridiculous movements, trying to act like he was a kid who was only sixteen. It felt embarrassing, as he tried hard to become the center of attention. He had no idea people were continuously laughed at him behind his back. *Oh, my Gosh. How much longer is this song going to last?*

Luckily, the song quickly ended, but as Amy prepared to walk back to her seat, he grabbed her hand. "We just stepped on the floor. Please, let's dance at least one more," he pleaded.

While Amy could hear the girls at the table talking about her, it was such a short dance, and she felt obligated to stay for at least one full song. She didn't know the next song would be a slow dance song.

In a way it was a relief, but then it made her feel a little bit apprehensive in dancing slow with someone she didn't know. As he raised his arms and moved in close to her, she accepted his frame. He appeared to be intent on proving his dancing skills, not only to her, but she was sure for all around him.

On the first turn, Amy noticed Angelina dancing with a tall guy who had dark, black hair combed straight back—perhaps he was Italian. He demonstrated fantastic skills as a good dancer as he directed Angelina gracefully around the floor

As Amy's partner looked over his shoulder to see what she was looking at, he yelled over the loud music, "They're good dancers. It's always fun to watch them."

"Yes, it is. Do you know them?"

"Oh yes, I know her. We published some of her books when she first started writing."

"You're a publisher?"

"Yes. I work in my family's business. We're a small press and specialize in helping beginning writers self-publish their books."

"That's good to know. So, you're here for the convention?"

"Yes, but since you know about it, then I assume you're here for the same."

"Yes I am. I'm one of those want-to-be authors."

"That is good to know. I hope to talk to you at the convention. We have a booth you need to visit, and I think you'll like what we have to offer."

"Okay, I'll stop by and see."

He looked over his shoulder at Angelina again. "She has certainly done well after her books started selling." He moved in closer to Amy and tried to lead her through some turns of his own. With his unclear signals and awkward movements, Amy did the best she could to follow him. He pulled her closer as he whispered. "You're a good dancer."

What a line. Amy knew he only said that to try to *butter her up*. She watched the others on the floor turning cozier while the smooth romantic music swayed them softly to the beat. He tried to get intimate also as his hand slipped lower on her back, sliding a little at a time, but so obvious. Amy kept waiting for the song to end—the sooner the better.

When his hand reached the top of her butt, she pulled away and lifted his arm while giving him a defiant stare. He grinned and acted like it wasn't a big deal. Again, he moved in close to dance with her some more, but inched his hand lower again.

Suddenly, she saw the first guy she had danced with walking in her direction. She quickly moved toward him. "There you are," she shouted over the music.

He looked at her and opened his arms. "I see you're having a good time."

"I'm trying to." The song ended as all three stood looking at each other.

He looked over at the publisher. "Do you mind if I have one dance with her? She promised to dance with me earlier."

Since the publisher didn't know how to answer, he offered a goofy smile. "Sure, we're just finishing." He turned and went after new prey as Amy flashed a big sigh of relief.

Unfortunately, the band leader looked at the group and raised his hands. "We're going to take a five minute break. It's a good time to order some more beer, and if you have a special request, just write it on a twenty dollar bill and give it to us," he said in a joking fashion. "Really, we have a pen and paper in the basket here. Tell us what you want to hear. And, oh yes, we do like tips, or free beer." When he followed with a big laugh, Amy could tell many people liked the guys in the band.

"By the way, I'm Ike," the guy who rescued her said as the noise in the room became bearable with the band taking a break. His white teeth looked perfect and made his smile fantastic.

"Hi, my name's Amy, and thanks for the rescue."

"No problem, I could see that you might need some help. By the way, what's your favorite song?"

"I have many. It all depends on my mood."

"In such a case, I think I'll select one for us. I hope you'll like it." He turned to go to the bandstand as Amy waited for him. He showed impeccable manners and was turning more intriguing by the minute. "I've some other friends here, but I'll come find you when the song starts."

"I'm looking forward to it. You know where our table is."

When Amy returned to her table another beer was waiting for her. The girls continued to chat as Amy slipped into her seat. Two new guys had pulled up seats to join the girls. Since Amy was tired from the dancing, she finished the new beer quickly as the conversation at the table quickly centered on the agent who was recently murdered. She had not thought too much about it for the last few hours.

No one knew him well, but all the girls at the table and the two new guys, also aspiring writers, had sent him query letters. He appeared to be well known by all in the group. The details of the brutality from the beating made her sick.

Eventually, the band members soon started tuning their instruments on the stage. They had five members in the band, four of which played a guitar and sang as back up. The leader of the band, however, played a keyboard while singing the lead. He sported a short beard and long, dark, wavy hair. When he glanced in the basket and retrieved a twenty dollar bill, he quickly announced to the crowd, "Will miracles never end? Believe it or not we have a twenty with a note."

The guy with the bass on the far right spoke in a deep voice. "I knew you should've asked for a fifty."

The leader looked at him. "I think we can play this one. This song . . . is for Ike and Amy."

Amy felt shocked. She didn't know he planned to give her name for all to hear. The girls looked over at her with questioning looks on their face. Then the girl to her right shouted, "You go, girl!"

When Ike walked to the center of the floor and waited for her, she rushed to him as the band huddled to discuss the song. He reached out and softly squeezed her hand as the band started playing *Unforgettable* by Nat King Cole.

While he slowly and gracefully started to dance with Amy, the floor eventually became crowded with many others wanting to dance to such an incredible song. She felt his arms around her waist giving her support and security, allowing her mind to relax and drift into a small daydream.

As she closed her eyes for a few seconds and made some small turns, it felt almost like being in a trance. When she opened them, she saw Michael Hadcock standing at the edge of the dance floor intensely watching her. His quirky smile brought back a flood of memories. She backed away from Ike to study his face as she became suddenly scared that she might be dancing with Edward. He looked confused, as she must have turned white with shock written all over her face. She quivered in his arms as he directed her into one last measured circle.

"I'm sorry. I had a sudden flashback I couldn't control. It would be too hard for me to explain. You appear to be a nice guy." She moved closer to him to complete the dance without saying another word.

As she finished the dance, she noticed Michael still watching her, but talking to some other guys. It was obvious they were talking about her. The words he had spoken to her earlier now echoed in her head. *Did I dance like this with Edward earlier? Why can't I remember what all happened that night?*

After the dance, Ike returned her to the table and the other girls, who were busy talking to other guys who had followed them to their table. "I think I need to call it a night. Tomorrow's going to be here before I know it, and I need some sleep. Thank you again for the dance, Amy." He then turned and disappeared in the crowd.

Since the girls were concentrating on the guys talking to them, and the night was fading, Amy found her waitress and paid her bill.

CHAPTER 15

The wakeup call the next morning came as expected, and Amy had slept well during the night and felt rested. It was the first time in a long time she had slept all the way through the night. The over-sized bed felt comfortable with the large soft-white comforter keeping her so warm and cozy. This was one of those mornings she wished she could stay in bed all morning and simply enjoy it. However, she knew she was going to be busy and had so much to learn and accomplish. While her mood felt good, she had no idea how long it would remain so even-keeled.

After making it to the conference rooms, she could smell two things. She loved cinnamon and she loved coffee, both of which filtered through the halls where many people scampered around. Although she didn't recognize anyone, she decided to help herself to the freebies.

Since the conference had many rooms arranged for individual meetings on various subjects, she checked her list and made mental notes of the starting times. It was about fifteen minutes before the first one started. After passing one room, she noticed several computers available for the attendees to use. This was thoughtful. She decided to check her e-mail and find out what was new in the world of publishing.

She had received many e-mails concerning her latest articles being purchased by several more newspapers, which made her proud as she realized the articles now made enough money for her to squeeze by on. Then she clicked on Edward's site and subsequently on to his blog, as she started to read. He was relaying his day and how proud he was of one of his new authors. He had completed a book deal for her in a large auction, which was one of the largest he had seen for a new author.

Amy's blood started to boil. Her critiques of his work hadn't fazed him at all. In fact, he was doing better than ever, and to top it off this author wrote a paranormal romance, something he told her in his letter that he didn't handle. This book deal could've been her book deal.

It was time to take off the gloves and turn up the heat. With her mood dissipating, she turned off the computer and headed for the first meeting. Since this panel discussion included Beth Sherman, Amy wanted to hear what she had to say.

The subject of this meeting was how to get an agent. Being the main reason many of the attendees came to this writer's convention, she knew she would find a lot of want-to-be writers optimistically attending, and hoping to find a way to make it to the world of being a published author.

When it became time for Beth to speak, the room became quiet and attentive. Apparently many knew she had lost her previous agent to a brutal murder.

"Hello, my name's Beth Sherman, and I'm a writer. I can relate to so many of you here today who are hoping to find an agent to represent you. I went a long time looking for an agent and received tons of rejection letters. It can be extremely frustrating. So, how did I find an agent?" She paused for several seconds as she glanced around. "I'd have to call it dumb luck, in a way." Amy watched her take a small sip of water, as she was obviously searching for the exact words. "I had saved up my bonus miles for a long time, and I finally decided to take a dream trip to one of the Caribbean islands. It was so fantastic to run away from work for a while. Since I knew it was a long flight, I had hauled my computer and notes on another novel I was attempting to write with me."

The suspense built around the room, but then again, it appeared some of the attendees already knew the story. "I noticed the guy next to me was watching me write and

114

checking my notes. He soon started asking me questions about what I was writing. Like most writers, I was glad to tell him. After all, that is what writers like to do . . . you know, tell a story. He was interested in me, and it made me feel good to have someone show attention. After receiving one rejection letter after another, I was willing to tell my story to anyone who would listen. Yes, even this perfect stranger who I had all to myself."

Beth had apparently told this story many times before and knew how to space it out to build momentum. "He was a sincere listener, and he asked questions which made me do some serious thinking. I was so deep into my story that I never asked him any questions. He was friendly, kind, understanding . . ." She raised her hand to her throat as she leaned over. " . . . and he later became one of the best friends I could've ever imagined."

She started to weep as her body trembled. "I had no idea I was sitting next to one of the most sought after literary agents in the world. I know I wasn't the best writer around. In fact, thinking back on it, I'm sure I was terrible in the way I presented my book idea to him. But . . . what I had that he liked was a passion for telling a story."

It took several minutes for her to recompose her emotions. "I accepted his advice and worked on the book, and rewrote it hundreds of times. I knew I had one shot. That book had to be perfect before I sent it to him. I had taped his card to the front of my computer to give me inspiration as I worked on it over and over again."

She started smiling as she was reaching the height of her story. "He told me he would love to see the manuscript when I finished it. I wasn't sure he was simply being polite or not, but I accepted him at his word and mailed him the entire manuscript three months later."

"A month went by and no response. I assumed he wasn't interested, and I was naturally concerned because I knew my career would never have a better chance than this one. Then I received a call from him. He loved the book! He did say that if he represented me, I'd have to agree to some serious rewriting. I sure wasn't going to tell him I had rewritten it a few hundred times already. That book sold, and led to several more book sales. To me, he'll always be the greatest agent who had ever lived."

The group stayed quiet, but tense. Some knew the story, but others acted puzzled by the comment. "That agent was Mitchell Lloyd, and as some of you probably know, he was recently brutally and senselessly murdered."

A low mummer passed through the room. They all knew how hard it must be for her to tell this story. She had to be an incredible person to live through this and tell about it. Amy felt sorry for her, but she still had the burning question of learning how she managed to connect with Edward.

As she waited patiently to see if Beth would continue with her story, an inpatient hand went up from the crowd. Beth decided to ignore it and cleared her throat as she looked around the room. "This has been an extremely trying time. I had several new projects in the works, and since he was the emotional inspiration for me, I knew I would have trouble finishing my commitments."

The hand in the crowd didn't retreat and remained firmly visible, as one attendee waited on an answer. Being annoyed by the hand, Beth finally decided to point to it. A girl in the middle of the crowd stood. "Wasn't there someone else in the agency who was able to help you?"

The moderator moved to her microphone. "I know many of you have questions, but in the interest of keeping this meeting on track, please wait until the end of the panel discussion to ask them. However, it's a good point, and I think she'll address that soon."

Beth continued after giving an appreciative smile to the moderator. "Since my agent was active with a large number of authors, it would be a challenge for all of them to be properly represented by others in the agency. In my case, I'm fortunate to have another miracle in my life."

Amy watched as many of the attendees leaned forward with anticipation to hear the rest of the story. "I was at a convention that I had already made plans to attend before he was murdered when I met a friend of my agent. He was also an agent with a different company. He had heard of the murder and offered his support to me in my time of need."

Amy's heart beat fast as she listened to the story. "He had given me his card and told me to call him if I needed anyone to talk to. His attitude was fantastic. I didn't know much about him, but did my research later and discovered he was also considered a top agent."

While still wiping her eyes with a small napkin, she continued. "I was extremely apprehensive when I called him. I know some agents don't like to be called on the phone, but he was friendly and supportive. When I told him I needed help with the current commitments, he agreed to represent me. I was happy to receive his help. He also knew how much I missed Mitchell. I still have some details needing to be worked out and so on, but it looks like I have a new agent to take care of me. I guess this is the first announcement of the change, and I'm happy to share it with you here."

Amy breathed harder. She knew it was Edward. He had already made the announcement on his blog. Maybe he jumped the gun. That would be an interesting development if she could persuade Beth to change her mind. Damn, she would love to have him embarrassed.

Beth beamed as she finished the story, but she then turned somber as she continued. "I'm not sure how many of you have heard, but another literary agent, James Aaron, was found a few days ago beaten to death as well."

The shock of the second death rumbled around the room.

Amy could hear various comments from those near her. Some had heard, while others asked people close to them for more details. "I think it would be appropriate for us to bow our head in a quiet prayer for his family and for the family of Mitchell Lloyd as well. The authorities are now thinking that a serial killer is involved who is targeting agents. " She lowered her head as the room became deathly quiet.

While the rest of the meeting focused on those wanting an agent, Amy concentrated on how to implement her plan. She needed to work on Beth.

CHAPTER 16

Nearing the end of the day, Amy finally received a chance to talk to Beth. She appeared charming and all smiles as one person after another walked in front of her booth to buy an autographed copy of her latest book. Every want-to-be author wanted that one piece of advice that could propel their career.

Amy slowly walked in front of her. "Hello, I'm not sure if you remember me or not, but we met recently at the book reviewer convention in Orlando a few months ago."

Beth put on a smile indicating that she did, but Amy knew she probably didn't. "How have you been doing?"

"I've been staying busy. I work for a large bookstore where they love for me to attend conventions. I guess I'm lucky in that."

"Then I'm sure you receive all the books you want to read at fantastic prices."

"Yes. I receive some benefits in working for a bookstore. When I met you at the convention, you had just received news of your agent's death. Charles was ordering you drinks."

"Yes, I remember that. I had too much to drink, and heavy drinking is something I usually never do."

"It's perfectly understandable. It sounds like you had a fantastic relationship with your agent."

"We became closer than best friends. He worked as a perfectionist, and demanded the best. Knowing he always had my best interest at heart, I always tried to give it to him."

Amy gathered her courage to talk about Edward. "How well do you know your new agent, Edward?"

Beth appeared to be a little bit shocked. "How did you know I was going to be using Edward?"

"I read his website this morning, and I saw where he had announced that he was your new agent."

Beth groaned low, but intense. She leaned forward to whisper, "We've been talking, but I still have to work out a deal with the agency where Mitchell worked before I tell everyone his name. I assumed Edward knew it would take some time. He's excited about me working with him, but he should've waited."

"Have you heard anything about him being investigated for unethical behavior before?"

"No, what have you heard?"

"Nothing really, but you know how rumors can start. I was just asking a question."

"Thank you for your concerns, and perhaps I need to think about making such a quick move since I'm still not fully back to being myself yet."

"I'm sure things will work out for you. Since Mitchell had one of the best agencies around, perhaps they can still find a way to make you happy."

"You may be right. I guess I need to talk to them some more."

Amy picked up a copy of the book and handed it to Beth. "I'd love for you to sign this for me. My name's Amy, by the way."

Beth signed the book. "I'm going to a bar around the corner later tonight. If you're interested, feel free to join me."

"I'd love to very much."

###

Amy hurried to the bar after showering and resting for a while. She knew the night might be long, and a quick nap would tremendously help her later. She felt happy, knowing she had picked the right words to make Beth have second thoughts about using Edward. Now, she needed to move in for the kill.

Amy rushed along the dark but thankfully very short street until she reached the bar without any problems. She hoped she could find some of the people from the convention to connect with, and return with later to the hotel. A doorman checking for underage party goers at the door nodded at Amy and waived her on through. The inside looked exactly as she remembered from the night before, with the exception of the pool room which was now crowded with what looked to be a tournament.

She walked to the left and into the maze of crowded regulars. The small walkway between the stools placed at the counter on the right and the tables on the left provided a narrow path with various people trying to go in both directions at once.

An older guy of around fifty looked her over as she passed by him. "How are you?"

"I'm fine," she ventured with a small smile as she pushed past him. A girl on her right with very long black hair glanced at her, trying to size her up. She appeared to be someone she didn't want to mess with. Amy had a funny feeling in the pit of her stomach as she made her way toward the back.

Several guys pushed by her, heading in the other direction. She felt sure they used the full advantage of the tight quarters to feel of her breasts, but all she could do was bare it and hopefully make it through soon.

Suddenly, she felt a hand from out of nowhere reach over and pinch her ass. She swirled around, and she was ready to fight, but with the fast moving crowd, she had no way of knowing for sure who pinched her. She quickly turned and pushed harder through the crowd.

Once she made it to the dance area, and the crowds thinned, she breathed deeply. While she saw many on the floor, she recognized no one. She walked over closer to get a better view and hoped for the best.

Across the floor she saw several people from the convention. She wasn't sure of all the names, but they looked like they were having a good time. She walked around the edge of the floor and made her way to them. Several of them recognized her as she reached the table, and yelled out loud, "Hey, come on and join us." They looked drunk, but enjoying the night.

"Thanks. I hoped to find some people here I knew."

One lady in her forties walked over and pulled a chair up to the table. "We always have room for one more writer."

"Well, hopefully one day I'll be a published writer, but for now I'm just trying to get started."

"It took me a long time, and I'm still learning the ropes, so join the club." She acted feisty, young at heart, and the kind of person you could really count on if you needed to.

"It sounds like you've been published before."

"I've self-published several books, but that's it. I'm still looking for an agent to take me on, just like many people I know."

"I know exactly what you're talking about."

"Now Judy has several books published." She pointed across the table.

"Okay, I see her. What does she write?"

"She writes mainly comedy and some light, funny, young adult. She uses her years of teaching as a source of inspiration."

"She used to be a teacher?"

"Yes. She went through a divorce and relocated close to here, and has never gone back into teaching, except for the occasional work as an assistant when her money runs low."

"Does she have an agent?"

"Yes, but I'm not sure she's happy with her right now. She would love to find a different one. That's why she came to this convention, but like all of us she hasn't had much luck. The number of agents attending is very disappointing."

"I wish they had more here also. I work for a bookstore, and it's good for me to meet writers, publishers and agents."

"Then you must be the one we need to talk to about doing book signings."

"I'm sorry, but I'm not the one who lines that up."

"Then, you must be the one who orders books?"

"Unfortunately, I'm neither. While I work in the bookstore day after day, it's getting a little old and I'm thinking about leaving soon."

"It might not be much, but I would bet it's more than most of the people at this table make," she cackled as the alcohol added to her laughter.

Amy stopped talking and watched Angelina Martin, the girl from the night before who wrote sexy erotic novels, walk onto the dance floor. Amy had forgotten about doing research on her, but made herself a new mental note to do so. At the book signing, she had never visited her table. Perhaps tonight would be a good time to talk to her. After pointing to Angelina, Amy asked her new friend, "Do you know her?"

"Angelina? I think everyone knows who she is. She's always on the dance floor flirting with several men at a time. She can really dance when she wants to, and she has one long reputation, but to tell the truth I'm not sure it's all true."

"Do you know who her agent is?"

"I'm not sure, but if she ever gets off of the dance floor, I'm sure she'll tell you. She can be friendly when she wants to be."

Amy watched her dance. She looked tall and lean, and perhaps she had danced some professionally earlier. One thing was for sure, she knew how to play the guys along. She was large breasted like Amy, but instead of being self conscious about it, she left them partially exposed to draw attention.

Amy searched around the floor and hoped to spot Beth. She also hoped to run into Michael tonight, since she had questions for him as well. The night was early, and perhaps they would come in later. After all, Beth is the one she agreed to meet in the bar.

When a large pitcher arrived at the table, compliments of one of the guys, he looked across the table and told the waitress they needed more glasses. She left and returned minutes later to place one of the glasses in front of Amy. The pitcher vanished in seconds, and the guy motioned to the waitress they would need another one. When all their glasses had been filled again, he raised his and shouted, "To top-selling authors and the rest of us—the undiscovered talent."

Everyone laughed and raised their glass. It was a fun group and everyone seemed to be fun-loving. As Amy suddenly recognized the guy with the small self-publishing company from the night before, she ducked lower and hoped he hadn't spotted her yet.

"What's wrong?" the woman next to her asked.

"I danced with him last night, and I would prefer not to do that again."

The lady laughed. "He's harmless. Sometimes he thinks he's a big shot and holds the keys to fame and fortune, but most of the girls here are on to him. I don't know if there's a difference between a vanity press and a bad agent sometimes, since both can be bad for you."

Most of the group at the table, who were listening to her talk, nodded their heads in approval. Amy couldn't allow this opportunity pass. "What do you know about bad agents?"

"I know of many web sites with a full list of them," one girl added. "One thing's for sure, never let someone talk you into paying a fee of any kind up front, and always check around, since word has a way of spreading among writers, especially with the internet these days."

Amy forced her voice to project. "I agree. In fact, I was talking to Beth Sherman today, and she was about to change agents before she discovered things about her new agent that she didn't know. She's now rethinking about using him."

Everyone leaned forward and concentrated on her words, since many of them had heard her speak that morning. "Do you know who she's changing to?" the woman next to her asked.

"The agent she was talking to was Edward Lawson. Have you heard of him?" A mixed review circulated at the table. "It appears he made an announcement before she cleared all the channels with the agency she was with. The agent she had used, of course, had been murdered, but other people in the agency are, I'm sure, willing to help her. It sounds like Edward may have been trying to pull a fast one." Amy felt amazed she had pulled this off so easily. This small group presented her with the perfect opportunity to perfect her skills in going after Edward.

The attention quickly shifted to the dance floor where Angelina started having problems with one guy on the dance floor that had too much to drink. He was insisting on dancing with her, but he could hardly stand. The crowd around them thought it was funny and encouraged the old man to keep after Angelina.

Trying to keep the party girl image, and keep control of situations like this required a real juggling act. Being on her own this time, she looked like a cornered chicken in a hen house with a fox after her. He came after her again with the intent on hugging her in a slow dance. She tried to push away, but he was larger and bigger.

As he reached for her again, a lone guy made it to the floor and stepped between them. The drunk looked at the younger guy at first, and then yelled at him to get out of the way. He didn't move. The drunk threw a punch that the younger guy easily avoided. The old man was so drunk that he fell to the ground after he missed landing the blow. Before he could get to his feet, the security detail at the bar made it to him. He appeared to be well known, as they helped him stand and then told him to go home for the night. At first he resisted, but he slowly appeared to recognize that he was outnumbered.

As the guy turned around, Amy recognized him as the gentleman she had met the night before—Ike. "I wish we had more men like that in here."

The woman next to her agreed. "Don't we all."

Ike escorted Angelina off the floor as he recognized the people at the table. He continued to help Angelina over to the table, where they said hello to everyone.

"Come on and join us," Amy said, as she moved over and made room for some chairs to be added from a table behind them. As Angelina accepted the seat, she continued, "We really have enjoyed watching you dance. You're really good at it."

Ike interrupted briefly as he waved at the group. "Please excuse me and I'll be back in a minute."

Angelina leaned back in her chair. "I'm not nearly as good as I used to be, and not as young either." She looked around the table and recognized some of the regulars. "How is it going tonight?"

The woman next to Amy spoke first, "We're discussing agents and how some are bad and some are good, and also how hard it is to find an agent in general."

"That's a subject I can write a book on. I've had my share of bad ones and good ones."

The girl across from Amy spoke next. "We're talking about an agent you might know. His name's Edward Lawson. Do you know anything about him?"

"I've heard his name. Why, what have you heard?"

"I've heard he's someone to avoid." Amy couldn't

believe it.

The rumor mill had already started as Ike soon returned. Amy looked over at Ike and glanced at the dance floor, where he recognized his cue. "Would you like to dance?"

"I'd love to."

As they made it to the floor, Amy noticed a couple dancing on the far side—Michael and Beth. She didn't know they knew each other. Both looked up as Amy and Ike made it to the floor. They stopped dancing long enough to say hello.

Beth spoke first to Amy. "I'm glad you made it here tonight. It would've been good to have time to talk to you, but Michael has asked me to go out to eat, and I'm hungry. Perhaps we can talk later."

"I hope so also. You two enjoy yourself tonight."

Michael glanced at Amy, but she knew what attracted his interest. "It's nice to see you again."

When Michael persisted with his frozen smile, she felt compelled to introduce her dance partner. "This is Ike, by the way. Ike this is Michael."

After the two men shook hands, Michael turned his attention back to Beth and walked with her toward the entrance. Amy knew she might not ever know what they said to each other about Edward.

CHAPTER 17

As Amy struggled with her large bag of books, she assured herself she had only selected the books she wanted to read today. There were just so many of them. She managed to get on the mailing list for many publishers that added her to those receiving advance reader copies.

The front door of the bookstore had been left wide open to present a feeling of openness they always wanted to display. They wanted customers to know they had opened and were ready to do business. The front entrance was lined with some of the newest best sellers, while posters on the wall advertised special discounts for members.

At ten in the morning the store wasn't too busy, which was perfect for Amy. She didn't work at the bookstore anymore, but she enjoyed the atmosphere and the access to many magazines and other publications she liked to browse through when she forced herself to take a small break.

This was one of those mornings she wanted to leave her apartment for a while, and a change of location would help her. The smell of coffee drifting through the store reminded her of what she needed. She headed straight for the small coffee counter to order her favorite—an extra large white chocolate mocha.

Amy saw her friend Lenny cleaning the counters and checking on supplies as she walked closer. His eyes twinkled when he recognized her. "Hello, girl, I didn't expect to find you here this early in the morning."

"I didn't expect to be up and moving about so early. It was another long night of reading. The books keep coming and new ones show up daily. I've no way to ever catch up."

"Hey, you need to talk to your boss about your hours."

"Which boss?"

"That's exactly what I'm telling you, girl. You need to

not work so hard, and just live a little. Go out and have some fun."

"I know you're right, but it's just that I enjoy reading, and some of these books can be intoxicating. However, others can put you to sleep. It's funny how such crap gets published. I feel sorry for the person who pays good money and is then disappointed. I'm sure they never buy another book for a long time."

"How many newspapers do you have carrying your articles now?"

"It varies, but I think somewhere around fifty or sixty. I send it out to four or five hundred, but many of them don't use it every week. I'm adding new newspapers to the mailing list all the time. It's a slow process, and it's getting more and more time consuming keeping up with the business side of accounting for the sales."

"I think what you're doing is incredible."

"I've started blogging more and more also. The amount of hits I'm receiving is outrageous. I'll show you in a minute on the laptop I have with me."

"I'll look in a minute. This place was a total wreck when I got here this morning. We're just going to have to talk to the night crew. They're terrible. I don't know how they stand to work in the condition they leave . . . things."

"Some things never change, do they? I wanted to drink some coffee before I started reading."

"If you don't mind come on back and make it yourself. You know how to do it better than I do."

Amy rolled her eyes, slipped under the counter and started making her favorite. "So, how's your life been going?"

"Oh . . . it's been going like fantastic, but don't tell anyone, since this has not been finalized yet. I've this friend who is thinking about setting me up in a small business soon, and it's something I always wanted to do. He's in the real estate business, and he's always complains about his clients never making his job easy. They don't properly decorate or what he calls showcase their property. He thinks I've a real knack for doing that." Lenny looked around to make sure he wasn't overheard. "He'll set up the clients for me to talk to. For a small fee, I'll help make their place sparkle. We'll see how it goes."

"I think you'll be good at it."

"He calls it staging a house."

"I've heard of this before and wish you a lot of luck in it. Perhaps you could start with my place." She knew that would definitely be a challenge for Lenny.

"Something tells me your place will be a major project."

Amy laughed. "You've no idea, since I've made several walls into project sites covering Edwards's life. It has taken some time, but I'm having an effect on him. He has no idea that I'm slowing destroying him. He lost another author last week." She felt a rush of pride.

"I would think you would be over this guy by now."

"I'll not quit until I put him totally out of business." She nodded her head several times. "I know he'll really love my latest article on his prized author."

"You are really one bad and evil girl."

"No, I'm simply one girl who's going to get even." After Amy finished making her coffee, she headed for her favorite place by the window where she plugged in her computer and placed it in front of her to check her e-mail. With her fan base expanding rapidly, she needed to send out replies to inquiries. Also, she had received several messages from newspapers that she needed to respond to.

Amy received the same trash spam everyone receives, and like every victim, she went through it deleting all the ads for Viagra, and free money she supposedly won. Then she saw an e-mail from World Media Publishing Company. She read the note with interest. "I've been following your book reviews closely. Your style is much different than anyone else I read. The name you write under is also intriguing, and I'll have to ask you to tell me about how you decided on that name later. Obviously, it's very important to us to have our books portrayed in the best possible light. After all, we are in the business of making money and selling books."

Before continuing, Amy scanned to the end of the article to see who it was from. It was signed by a Leland Grantland, someone she had never heard of before. She quickly returned back to the top to continue reading. "Sometimes I agree with you, and sometimes I don't. However, you have one thing most reviewers don't have. It's a passion for books. In some form or another, a book has to be entertaining and fill a need in the readers mind. I think you made a good point several times lately when you state either this is the kind of book which will bring readers back to buy new books over and over, or that this is a book which will end a readers desire to ever buy another one."

Amy blinked her eyes. That was exactly why she wrote her articles. "This is the kind of crystal ball we wish we owned at the company, since I'm the one who has the final say so on if a book is published or not. You may not be interested in what I'm proposing, but I feel like I have to give it a shot. Would you be interested in coming to our corporate office to talk to me and letting me show you around. I'll give you the full details of what I'm proposing when I see you. Please think about it, and let me know."

Amy sat in front of the computer for a long time trying to determine exactly why the editor wanted to contact her. If she went to visit him, it meant she would disclose her hidden identity. However, being offered a chance to meet one on one with a major editor was something hard to decline.

Amy eventually admitted that making a contact like this

was important, so she clicked on the reply button and started to type. "Thank you for your letter. I do enjoy what I'm doing, and since reading books has always been a passion of mine, writing book reviews only comes naturally to me. It would be good to meet with you to receive some insights of the publishing industry from an editor's point of view. However, I've one reservation. I've hidden my identity since I first started writing reviews. If I come, you'll have to assure me that it will remain private. I go to many conventions, etc. and wander around talking to authors, agents and editors. They will not be so open and candid if they know who I am. I also assume you plan on paying my expenses for the trip. I look forward to hearing from you, The Literary Hawk."

Amy finished her coffee, she walked over to Lenny. "I think I'll need more this morning."

He looked at her with a raised eyebrow. "What is it with you this morning?"

"I just received an e-mail from an executive editor with a major publisher who wants me to come see him."

"Wow, you may have really stepped on someone's toes."

She realized that he might be right. "I'm not sure. I think there's more to it than that."

"Are you going?"

"It's a long trip and a big city. I sent an e-mail stating they would have to pay my expenses. We'll see." It would be interesting to visit New York City.

"I've friends, as you know, everywhere. If I can help you at all, please let me know."

"Thanks. You've always been a good friend. I think I'll talk this over with Dr. Lankford tomorrow as well. This trip could be very emotional, and I don't want to flip out on something this important. We're having another one of those groups meeting tomorrow, but perhaps I could schedule some private time before we all meet. My mood has been steady for a while now, but I know it doesn't last forever, and the least little thing can set it off again."

Amy went back to her small table and reached into her bag to retrieve a half finished book. It felt like a good time to drift off into another world by reading one of her favorite authors.

CHAPTER 18

Amy walked into Dr. Lankford's office with a big smile, since she had good news to tell her. Even the receptionist greeted her with a smile and remarked on how cheerful she looked today.

Amy returned the smile to the receptionist. "I've several things that have me in a good mood. However, I've some things coming up which are going to put a lot of pressure on me. That's why I wanted to see Dr. Lankford in private before we meet as a group."

"She's in her office waiting on you. I'll let her know you're here."

"Thank you. I know she doesn't have a lot of time before she has the group meeting, but I can help her rearrange the furniture later, if she wants me to."

"Thanks, but I think she has already moved most of it."

Amy went over to her office and knocked on the door. She heard Dr. Lankford yell back, "Amy, come on in."

Amy peeked around the door as Dr Lankford shoved one of the last chairs into place. "You look nice today. You must be feeling good."

"Yes, and I need your advice. You know I've been writing my book review articles, and they've been doing well."

"Yes, it appears to be a stabilizing force in your life right now. It looks like life is turning around for you."

"I was contacted by one of the editors at a major publishing house yesterday who wants to see me."

"Why does he want to see you?"

"I'm not sure, but he made it sound important. He was very complimentary of my articles, and this is strange since most of the articles are critical."

"I've read several of your articles, and yes they're very

brutal, but I think honest. Some of the readers must be thinking you're right on, or you wouldn't be selling so many of them. You do have a special form of wit you use, which is very entertaining."

"My mood is stable right now, and I don't want to screw up."

"Yes, it's good to see you doing so well right now, and I hope you're still taking the medication as you're supposed to be?"

"Yes. I really don't think I need it, but yes I'm following your advice."

"Tell me about the trip. Why are you so anxious about it?"

"I think it's the unknown?"

"Do you think it will be better if you don't go?"

"Maybe, but I also know this could be a big opportunity to make an important contact. I still want to be a published author one day."

"When will you have to decide?"

"I'm sure I'll have an e-mail waiting on me in my computer. He's probably waiting on me to respond now."

Dr. Lankford became quiet for a moment as she appeared to be deep in thought. "This is one of those decisions about life events you'll have to deal with. If you decide to go, please let me know how it's going and check in with me frequently. I'd really like to see you reach your dreams."

"It would be fantastic. I hope they don't have some hidden agenda in luring me to New York."

"The group meeting will start soon. Will you share the good news with the group?"

"I think I might say a few things, but not too much. I'm sure they all know how much I want to be a writer, and how much I hate one agent."

"That's one thing you need to work on."

Amy bit her lip. She hadn't told Dr. Lankford recently

about all the pent up hatred she still had for Edward. It felt like a cancer growing inside of her. She hadn't totally accomplished her goal of destroying him. Yes, she still pulled the rejection letter out almost every day and read it. She was also still having the dreams about him that were both sweet and full of horror at the same time. The night they met was still blurry for her, even though she had tried over and over to remember what happened that night.

"Shall I stay, or do you want me to wait outside with the others?"

"Don't be crazy, stay in here. They'll be coming in any second."

Dr. Lankford assumed correct. When the door opened, they saw several of the members of the group waiting outside. "Come on in," she invited the group through the opened door.

In a few minutes everyone claimed the same seats as the week before. By knowing some of the problems each shared, they had slowly formed a familiarity and mutual acceptance of each other.

With Stephen not in his super drive mood, Amy assumed the medication he had changed to was helping him stay under control. However, it also made him look more like Wendell, who still looked like a drunk because of his deep sunken eyes. However, after looking closer at Wendell, Amy noticed a little twinkle in his eyes today, as he sat straighter than normal. She felt happy for him.

Estella walked in last, reflecting her normal polished perfect self. Her face reflected the usual plastic tone as she waited patiently for the meeting to start. As always, she became bored fast. She never mentioned her husband much in the meetings. Amy thought that what she needed was a time to be a woman, and have some fun on her own. But, then again, she wasn't the psychiatrist here.

Dr. Lankford started the meeting off in her usual way of

saying hello to the group one member at a time. They all respected Dr. Lankford, and she had mastered a means of bringing out people who usually didn't want to talk in front of others. The only one she had problems with was Estella, who had a hard time opening up, and didn't always smile at Dr. Lankford as the others did.

During one of the meetings, Amy remembered how Estella had told about her life and how her husband only loved her for her looks and body. She had told how she felt like she was nothing more than a sex toy for him, and that the medication provided him with a way to keep her under his control. That is when she saw him. She had reiterated how he stayed gone most of the time. A good writer could've made a whole novel off of that exchange. It must've embarrassed her, because it was the last time she had opened up to the group. Dr. Lankford had given her an evil eye the entire time she had talked.

After making the rounds, she looked at Amy. "Do you want to share your news with the group?"

As the group focused on Amy, she would have preferred to listen to others than to have to tell what was going on with her life. "As everybody knows I really want to be a novelist, and I've a chance to go meet with a senior editor at a major publisher. It's a long trip, and I'm not sure exactly how the meeting will go. I've had many times in my past when major events have triggered bad swings in my bipolar condition. Because of this I'm apprehensive in going, but after talking to Dr. Lankford, I think I'll make the trip. It'll be nice to know that my friends here are supporting me as well."

A small round of applause echoed around the room, since everyone was glad to have good news happening to someone in the group. Several members asked additional questions about the trip, and acted interested in her plans.

Estella face even became cheerful as if she grasped the

conversation. "Trips can be a lot of fun. You'll enjoy yourself. How long will you be gone?"

"It'll be a short trip; perhaps only a day or two."

"Nonsense, if you are making a long trip you need to take time to see the sights. I definitely would."

Of course she would. She appeared to have all the money she could ever spend. "I'll have to think about it."

"Have you ever found an agent to represent you?"

"Not yet, but after the last problem I had I'm a little bit apprehensive."

"I remember when you shared with us how much he hurt you. It sounds like most literary agents are the same. Are you still obsessed with seeking revenge?"

"Yes, I'm still having problems accepting what he did to me, but I think what goes around comes around, and it's only a matter of time before he receives his reward."

"I think you're right. Sometimes life can make you feel so helpless, and perhaps I understand that more than anyone."

Estella's smile suddenly faded as she looked off into space again. Amy had a hard time understanding her. Perhaps her medication made her unable to concentrate for long periods of time.

As the group congratulated Amy for attempting to face the challenges ahead of her, she knew it meant accepting a big risk, but she knew it was the right thing to do now.

CHAPTER 19

After a long plane trip, Amy's nerves tightened as she worried about just what the editor wanted to talk to her about. Amy had learned everything she could about the publishing house that had many separate subsidiary companies scattered all over the world. She had located some information on the editor as well. He appeared to be well respected, and had been with World Media for about ten years.

The ride in the taxi from the airport to her hotel provided her some time to see part of the city. She wished she had more time, but she knew she needed to hurry, since the editor wanted to meet her for dinner that night. He said it would be best to meet before she came to the office in order to help keep her true identity a secret. They had agreed to meet in the lobby of the hotel at seven, and eat at a restaurant nearby. He had said he knew she would be tired, and would let her turn in early.

She soon arrived at the lobby and walked around, enjoying the elegant decorations and paintings on the walls. The ceiling stretched several floors high, and offered an appearance of grandeur she didn't expect.

As she finished studying one massive painting for a while, she turned around and came face to face with someone she recognized instantly. After a long pause they both smiled, as Amy realized she had stopped breathing.

"Hello . . . Amy. Wow! I can't believe . . . you're the Literary Hawk, but perhaps I should've known it would be someone like you, someone who attended conferences and stayed slightly out of the spotlight."

"I didn't know you worked as an editor, either. You never told me at the convention."

"I don't think you ever asked." Ike reached out his hand

and accepted her hand in a soft but firm grasp. "I'm so glad you accepted my offer to come."

"You're welcome, but I'm still not sure exactly why I'm here."

"I do have a special reason I wanted to talk to you tonight before you came to the office. As you can imagine, my job depends on selecting the best books and selling them."

"I can understand. If I offend anyone with my articles, all I can say is—I'm sorry."

"You don't have to apologize for anything at all. You're honest and critical, like you should be. It would be great if some of the ass kissers at World Media would learn that."

Amy felt confused. "I thought you might not be happy with my articles."

"Let me tell you why I contacted you and asked you to meet me here tonight. I have many people who work for me. Most of them are very good, but some of them tell me what I want to hear rather than being honest. In this business, personnel continuously move from one firm to another, with everyone always watching their back. It's all about survival."

"I can understand, but what does all of this have to do with me?"

"As you can imagine, we receive a tremendous amount of book proposals coming in that we have to analyze. Some are good and we do our best to sell as many as we can. Others aren't so good and we learn to live with the losses. The secret is picking the right projects to run with."

"I know that a publisher has many people involved with making a project work, but to be honest I've never been inside a publishing house."

"It can be intimidating, which you'll find out tomorrow."

"I'm looking forward to seeing around the company. It'll be exciting."

Looking across at her, he glanced at his watch. "We need

to get to the restaurant. I know you're tired and want a good night sleep tonight."

Amy remembered how considerate he acted at the convention. He appeared to care about people around him, which was something she didn't expect from a busy editor.

He reached over and offered her his arm as they walked toward the restaurant. The front door opened and she saw a man dressed formally in a suit attending the door. "May I help you?"

"Yes, I've a reservation for two under the name of Leland Grantland."

He looked at his list and smile. "Right this way, Mr. Grantland, your table's ready."

Amy reflected on the name he used when they met. It would be nice to learn how he came up with the name of Ike. They followed the greeter to a table at the rear of the restaurant. The large table covered with a white table cloth could normally accommodate four people. The heavy oak chairs had the seats covered in a padded leather finish. Amy knew it was expensive to eat here even before she saw a menu.

Ike pulled Amy's chair out for her, and waited for her to sit. He then moved around to take his seat across from her. The waiter laid a napkin in both laps as he turned to Ike to ask about drinks.

Ike glanced at Amy. "What kind of wine do you like?"

"I like red wines the most, but I think you know wines well, and it will be fascinating to see what you select."

He looked pleased with her answer, as he called the waiter over to order an Italian Chianti using an impressive Italian accent.

When the waiter left, Amy turned toward Ike and offered a serious, questioning look on her face. He looked like he knew what she had on her mind. "I do have one question for you. How did you come up with the name Ike?"

Ike laughed as if he had been asked this question many times before. "If your father named you something like Leland Ikedo Grantland, because he considered himself to be a poet who always rhymed words, but also wanted to honor an old Japanese friend, which name would you use?" Thinking about it, she also had to laugh with him. "You now understand what I'm talking about." He laughed with Amy enjoying the attention. "Now tell me how you decided on the name of the Literary Hawk."

Amy felt prepared for this, thinking he might ask her. "I'm a want-to-be-author." She held up a hand with two fingers crossed. "It seemed like a good idea to not use my real name—just in case I did get published later. Payback can be hell."

"I can imagine you might be right. Do you think you'll pursue writing or keep doing reviews?"

"I'm not sure, and I'll take it one day at a time."

"Let me get back to why I wanted to talk to you. I think you have a keen eye in reviewing books. It's a rare trait. In my case, it's something I highly prize. Have you ever considered working in a publishing house?"

This conversation caught Amy off guard. "Are you offering me a job?"

"We'll do a lot of talking tomorrow and discuss some possibilities. Perhaps now you understand why I wanted you to come here, and why I wanted us to meet before you come to the office tomorrow."

"What exactly will I be doing?"

"I'll go over a long list of duties you'll be involved in, but I think the main job you'll have is reading—lots of reading."

"So . . . you want to pay me to read?"

"I want you to read in order to do what you are good at— giving me an honest critique of the book."

"That doesn't sound like too bad of a job."

"Trust me, it can be demanding. A lot of money is riding on all decisions of which books to publish. We receive a large number of submissions every day. While we have a policy to not look at anything that is not submitted by an agent, it's well known that many times the best ones are hidden in various stacks. We find out about them after another publisher prints them."

"Would I have to move here?"

"Unfortunately, yes. When you see the operation tomorrow, you'll understand how large it is. The beast is complex and furious. The pace is relentless, and where nerves can be stressed to the limit. It's a world which many can't handle for long, but some thrive on."

"I'm sure glad you told me this today so I can do some thinking on it tonight. I'm at a loss right now, and I don't know what to think."

"That's definitely understandable. While I have many assistants doing various functions for me, I'm considering creating a special position for you. It'll take care of an area where I have a major need."

Amy sat back in her chair and laughed. "And I assumed you asked me to come here so you could criticize me for being too critical in my reviews."

The wine arrived and the waiter presented it to Ike. He glanced at the bottle and signaled his okay as the waiter uncorked the bottle and poured a small amount in Ike's glass. Ike studied it for a minute before tasting. "That's perfect. Just like I hope the rest of the evening will be." He looked over to Amy for her approval.

After the waiter poured her a glass of the Chianti, she raised her glass and waited for him. He grinned, highlighting his bright white perfect teeth as he made a toast. "To a world of possibilities."

She touched her glass to his and added, "Ha ha, and to think I was so scared of this moment."

CHAPTER 21

Downtown bar, Chicago, two days later

Blake Ashman used his ipod to hunt for the e-mail he received earlier and considered the words carefully. A juicy celebrity memoir dropped in his lap could not have come at a better time. It would have to be ghost written, but hell, he had many writers who would give a right nut to get an opportunity like this. During his entire career, he had never met someone outside his office. However, he had dropped by this bar often, and a good drink sounded exactly like what he needed after another stressful day at his literary agency.

Two hours later, he realized he had been stood up. Frustrated, he paid his bill and walked out of the bar and along a back street where he left his car. He could hear his wife asking him where he had been. Damn, what a waste of time. He quickened his pace, almost to a jog as he pulled his overcoat closer to shelter out the on-setting cold winds Chicago was known for.

Approaching his car, a new BWM costing much more than he wanted to think about, he forced his head to clear from the drinks. The intense buzz made him wonder just how many doubles he had ordered. When the lock clicked and he pulled the door open, he felt the presence of someone behind him and attempted to jerk around to see who.

"Don't move. I have a gun pointed at your back." A hard object punched his back.

Blake raised his hands as he contemplated his next move. "Don't shoot me!"

"Don't do anything stupid. I want you to unlock the back door and take your seat. Be sure to keep your hand where I can see them on top of the steering wheel." As he started to comply, he felt the gun tap the back of his head. "Remember move slow, and don't be stupid."

He reached the control button to unlock all doors. The sound of the click was pronounced and clear. He shifted his weight to his left foot and prepared to slide into the driver seat. He breathed in courage and prepared to slam the door, hopefully allowing him to enter the safety of the car.

The gun moved to the side of his head, slightly above eye level. The opening of the barrel slightly out of focus due to the proximity to his head confirmed his worst fear. It wasn't a bluff. He hesitated for the longest second in his life. Finally, he made the controlled descent to the seat.

"Now, put your hands on top of the steering wheel. Do it now." The gun struck his head hard enough to draw a reaction. He forced himself to avoid making a mistake. Any second his life could end.

In seconds, he felt the assailant behind him in the rear seat with the door slamming shut. "Okay, be careful and close your door."

He closed the door. "Now what?" The gun smacked him in the back of the head again. "Stop that. You don't have to beat me. Is it money you want, is that it?"

"Crank the car and drive, I'll give you very clear instructions."

A half hour later, he pulled into an abandoned parking lot. Was he going to be killed? He reached for his back pocket to find his wallet. The back of his head exploded with pain as he felt a smashing blow. He tried to focus as another blow ended his efforts.

Later, he twisted in his seat fighting the pounding trauma to the back of his head. His back rested against the driver side door and his feet pointed toward the passenger side. When he realized that something was stuffed in his mouth, gagging him, he struggled to spit it out, but soon realized it had been tied in place. A fine wire tying his hands and his feet together was cutting into his skin with an unbelievable irritating sting.

After a vague image moved next to him he tried to yell, but only managed low muffled groans. He watched as a small metal bat tap on the dashboard. Is that what hit him? He quit groaning.

Suddenly his attacker spoke. "You don't have a fucking clue why you're here, do you jerk?"

He shook his head no, as he felt letter sized papers thrown in his face. He twisted in the seat, attempting to avoid the sudden shock of a new attack. The papers didn't hurt him, but made him worry about what was behind them.

"These are copies of your rejection letters you idiot. You have no clue how much you have hurt people with them. Yes, tonight is payback!"

He leaned forward to fight back as the bat smashed into his side, possibly breaking several ribs. He tried to strike out with his hands as the bat struck his face, breaking his nose. He tried to yell again.

"I know you want to live. I'll give you one chance." What now, he thought as he tried to endure the pain. "Show me how much of a big guy you are now. You get it up for me and I'll let you live. What's the matter? You never had trouble screwing authors before." He felt his pants being unzipped. He knew he was in the hands of a maniac as he struggled to speak, but only managed to groan.

At first, he felt a hot wet grasp around his penis, but the next second, he screamed as he felt the pain of someone chewing into his dick, and severing it in minutes from his body. The ensuing screams drowned out his remaining minutes as the blood spurted, leaving him no will to fight on.

CHAPTER 22

Amy folded more towels and placed them in yet another one of the boxes scattered all over her apartment. Deciding what to leave in and what to throw out was hard. She had never made a move like this before. Knowing the weather in New York City would be cold, and that she would have limited space in the small apartment she planned to move into, she needed to plan wisely.

She still didn't regret the decision to move, even if it totally disrupted her life. Well, what life she had. Reading books all the time didn't leave any time for much else. Of course, that is the life she planned to move to. However, she was going to be paid for reading at work. Now, how could she top that?

Lenny repacked her dishes after laughing at the way she had packed them. He had insisted on using much more wrapping to finish the task. "That should do it. You don't need to go to New York and have all broken dishes and glasses. It would cost you way too much to replace them."

"Thanks. I really appreciate you helping me today."

"Not a problem. I know you're looking forward to this job, but if it doesn't work out just remember I can help you pack to come home just as easy."

"Thanks. I think life for me in the city might help me rediscover myself, and I'll have a lot of room for advancement in this company. Listen, I know the competition is terrible, but the opportunities are endless."

"What are you going to do with this—Edward's wall?" Lenny pointed to the collage of photos and articles Amy had collected on him.

"I think I'll box it and take it with me, since he's still running his agency as usual. I had hoped my attacks on his authors would've hurt him by now, but it's hard to say if it did much at all. I know it's not over yet, and that I'll find a way to nail him one day."

"So you're still not going to forget what he did to you."

"I still have nightmares about him, and even with Dr. Lankford working with me on this many times, she doesn't know why I'm so determined to ruin him. However, every time I bring the letter back out, I can almost see him in front of me talking. He played me for a fool and led me on. I know I blacked out the night we met, but I remember him saying he wanted to look at my work."

"Maybe he says that to all writers wanting to send him material."

"I don't know, but if he does this to everyone, then I'm justified in letting it be known. He destroyed me with his comments about my needing to learn how to write. How dare him. I know how to write!"

"Calm down, girl. I know your English skills are second to none. I've seen your reviews."

"It's because of his letter that I haven't started on a new novel. Becoming a writer was my dream, and he took it all away from me."

Lenny reached over and gave her a rare hug. He had always acted as a good friend, and had never showed any interest in her other than as a very close buddy. Amy always considered it strange how good looking guys sometimes prefer other guys. It was such a waste, but she knew it was something she would never ridicule Lenny about.

"Amy, if you ask me, I think he has problems we don't know about and may never know. Time is what you need. You'll write again, and I know it."

Amy walked over to her computer and clicked on the file holding all the information on Edward. She had accumulated tons of facts about him. He had become successful, but he worked all the time. While she wasn't sure if any of her hard work produced any effect on him or not, she knew she wouldn't quit until she had completed what she started.

Lenny looked over her shoulder. "I think you need to just call the guy and tell him what a jerk he is, and then just get on with your life."

"I don't think I could do that. It would be too easy for me to flip out and appear to be nothing but an idiot. I think it's best if I keep working on it. I know that eventually it'll have the desired effect on him. At the new job, I'll be going to many conventions to meet authors. It'll give me the perfect way to completely destroy him."

Lenny looked at Amy with a desperate but compliant smile. "I guess you'll have it your way, but I can hope this move might help you get over this."

Amy glanced at Edward's blog. He had posted a new entry. She gasped out loud as she read.

"What is it?" Lenny asked.

"Take a look at this."

Edward wrote, "I have bad news to share today. A friend of mine, Blake Ashman, who is also a literary agent, was discovered murdered last night. There appears to be a serial killer after agents. He is the third known agent who has been viciously murdered in the last few months. I'm sure it will be all over the news today. I'll leave in a few hours to be with his family. Everyone will have to understand if I'm slow in responding on any material I've requested."

The entry appeared short for him, as he appeared to be in a hurry to leave. Someone must be much more pissed off than she was. While she wanted to ruin one particular agent's career, becoming a murderer was something she would never knowingly convert to.

Amy's concentration shattered when she suddenly heard a knock on her door. She rushed over and opened the door to see her parents standing outside with large smiles.

"Hello, do you need some help?" Her dad asked.

"Yes, where have you been?" She hugged both as they entered the room. "I have Lenny helping me, but I'm hopeless."

"I'm not sure how good we are, but tell us what we can do." Her dad looked around, but waited for instructions.

"My clothes are what I'm worried about. I hate to have to send everything to the cleaners to be pressed after I get there. I also don't know which items to take and which ones I need to throw away."

Her dad threw up his hands. "I think this is one call you'll need your mother's help on more than mine." They all laughed until her dad continued. "We're going to miss you. Are you sure this is what you want to do? You'll be a long way away if you need us."

"Thanks for your concerns, but I'll be fine. Dr. Lankford has asked me the same thing, but she has finally agreed that the change might do me some good."

"We want you to call us if anything at all comes up and affects your mood swings. I still hate it that you will be so far away from Dr. Lankford. She has done so much for you."

"Dr. Lankford has already made arrangements for me to see one of her friends who is practicing in New York if I need help. However, I really think I'll be fine. My mood is stable right now."

"We understand," her mother added. "However we know how it can change so fast."

CHAPTER 23

Amy rushed along the sidewalk toward the mammoth building housing World Media. It stretched into the heavens, intimidating her. She knew by looking straight up, she signaled to all around her she was a visitor, but she didn't care today. After all, it was her first day to go to work in the city.

The inside lobby looked as impressive as she remembered. Amy went straight in, and walked to the desk where the guard, a slim elderly black man with a strong sturdy posture studied her. "May I help you?"

"Yes, I'm starting to work here today and I'm supposed to see Mr. Grantland this morning."

He handed her a sign in pad and a badge as a visitor. "They'll give you a permanent badge today, so please be sure to bring this one back to me later."

"I will. Thank you," Amy said as she accepted the badge.

She hurried to Ike's office and located his secretary, Ginger Swendel, sitting at her desk in front of his office. "I'm glad you made it. Did you have any problems?"

"Since I just arrived yesterday, I still haven't unpacked much. It'll take a while for me to settle in, I'm sure."

Ginger looked toward Ike's office. "He's in an emergency meeting this morning, and I'm not sure how long it will last."

"It sounds like the pace is fast and furious here."

"You'll get used to it, and I think you'll like it."

"I'm looking forward to it." Amy waited for instructions on what to do while Ike was busy.

"Let me show you around where you'll be working, and most importantly . . . the snack room and restroom."

"Thanks, that would be a great start."

After studying her office around the corner from Ike, Amy wondered if anyone called him by that name. He never did say how to address him in the office. She assumed it may be best to stay formal until she heard how others addressed him. "How long have you worked for him?"

"About five years. He's a great boss, but can be demanding at times. He can be under a lot of pressure from many sources at one time." Ginger walked into the cubical where Amy would be working. "I know it doesn't look like much, but you're welcome to decorate it basically like you want, within reason."

Amy glanced at the computer and telephone resting on a plain metal desk with a side credenza. "I think I can make it look a little better in time."

Ginger laughed and then waved at the girl across from her in an adjacent cube. One piece of paper stapled over the previous one covered the walls of her cubical, while a large stack of files completely hid her desk. Other projects, she appeared to be working on, also covered her floor.

The small girl with sassy, dark-brown hair and black glasses, which were much too large for her small head, had earplugs in both ears and appeared to be rocking out with some funky music. She pointed to her chest and mouthed the words, "me?"

Ginger nodded her head up and down.

She switched off her ipod and pulled the plugs from her ears. Her perky smile looked friendly enough. "Do you need me?"

"Yes, I want you to meet your new neighbor. This is Amy Jenkins. She's starting today as an assistant."

"I think I remember you telling me about a new girl who was starting soon."

"Yes, it's an idea of Mr. Grantland to hire someone to look at all the book proposals in a more critical light." She offered a curious snicker of a grin. "By the way, this is

Renee Sanderson. She's a fact checker, and perhaps one of the smartest girls here."

"Thanks, does that mean I get a raise in pay?"

"I wish. Then you would have enough money to buy us all drinks when we go out."

Renee looked at the stack on her desk. "Sorry, I need to get back to this. They want me to be ready by lunch and I'm way behind."

"Okay. It was nice to meet you."

"And you too." Renee replaced her earplugs and went back to work on her computer.

"I need to walk you over to see the office manager. I'm sure she'll have many papers for you to fill out as well." Ginger said as she escorted Amy thru the maze of offices.

In the office manger's area, Amy watched many secretaries at work. An attractive young girl wearing a professional looking suit hurried over to them. She had her hair pulled back in a small twirl in the back of her head. Her high cheeks and perfect posture resembled that of a high fashion model. The high heels she wore only increased her elegant look. "There you are. I see Ginger's showing you around."

"Yes, Mr. Grantland told me to help her until he returned from a meeting," Ginger replied.

The woman held out her hand to Amy. "I'm Gloria Carroll, the office manager for this area. We have many items to take care of so you can start working here. Mr. Grantland will be in the meeting for most of the morning. I don't know if you've heard or not, but several literary agents have recently been murdered and the FBI is investigating heavily."

"Yes, I've been reading the news. It's horrible. Do they have any leads on the killer?"

"None that I know of. . . . We've a lot to cover, so I guess we better get started."

"I'll see you later." Ginger said as she turned and walked off.

After signing numerous papers and answering countless questions, Amy received her own badge as well as a large stack of reading material. "Mr. Grantland, I'm sure, will go over the job description with you in much more detail later. This is a new position we created at his request. As you can imagine, you'll be doing a lot of reading. We receive hundreds, if not thousands, of unsolicited manuscripts each week. Most aren't suitable for one reason or another for publishing. We also receive many from literary agents who hope to sell their clients work. Also many, if not most of the projects you'll work on are works in progress. Obviously, we want to publish the best and the ones which will make money for us."

"Yes, I can understand."

"Mr. Grantland wants to use you as a crystal ball to lend a fresh eye in critiquing the projects. You'll be looking at final projects and through the slush piles. You'll be basically an extra pair of eyes for Mr. Grantland. It'll be your job to tell him why a project will not work. He'll then decide how to fix it or turn it down."

"He told me a little about what he wanted, and I'll do my best. It may take a little time to discover exactly what he's looking for, but I'm thankful he considered me for this job."

"Don't worry, he's an intelligent man and he makes good decisions on picking the right people for his team."

Amy knew she needed to prove herself, and all she had to really worry about was keeping her mood in check.

CHAPTER 24

The last few weeks streaked by like a blur to Amy. She woke and went to work until she could read no more then went home. She had a nap and then read some more. The stack of manuscripts waiting on her exceeded her wildest dreams. However, she remembered how she didn't like receiving form rejection letters. She sent quick notes on all of them, and even those she could only partially glance at that needed much work and were, in fact, very bad.

Amy felt amazed how cheerful Renee managed to always stay. It must be something with the headphone set. Perhaps it drowned out all the sounds and worries around the office, and she managed to worry only about her job at hand. Renee's job required her to be an expert in everything or know someone who was.

While at her desk and reading one query and the first chapter of a submission, she began to love the plot and the writing, but it still needed some help. Amy found it appealing enough to hold her attention as she read further. She soon decided to ask for Mr. Grantland's opinion.

Ginger stopped typing as Amy walked nearer. "Is he in?"

"Yes, he's talking to one of our new authors. He's excited about his first novel, and will be sending in his revision later today for us."

"Sounds good to me. I'm looking forward to reading something different for a change. I've been wandering through the slush pile the last few days."

"Now you know why he needed some help in that area. Most of the time, it's looked at so little and with not much real interest."

"That's too bad, because sometimes it contains some good stories in it, you know, like the one I discovered here." Amy waved the pages she had been reading.

Ike came to the door and glanced at Amy. "Hi, I was going to call you. Come on in for a minute."

Amy followed him as he closed the door. "Ginger told me that you have a new author you're working with."

"Yes, I just finished talking to him. He's sending us a final revision, I hope, on a novel that looks promising. I really want your opinion on this one."

"I'll read it as soon as you give it to me."

"I know you've been working hard, and I appreciate it. You'll soon learn how to pace yourself. Rejection letters are hard to write, but they become much easier over time."

"I guess you're right, but let me ask you about this one. It has an interesting plot, and the writing isn't too bad. With some work it could be a decent book."

"Which agent sent it to us?"

"He doesn't have one." She yawned slightly. "It was in the slush pile."

"That's too bad. He'll have a hard time getting his project through all the reviews and into print."

"Perhaps we could recommend him to an agent and he could receive the help he needs."

"If you think he has promise and you want to follow it, feel free to give him a name of a few agents. It'll still be a long shot."

"Which names do you think I should give him?" This was an interesting question that she hadn't planned on asking earlier.

"Check with Ginger, she has a list of those we use often. However, if this maniac on the loose keeps killing them, he'll have less to select from."

Thoughts of the murders sent her mood lower. "Do they have any clues on who it is yet?"

"Nothing. It's obviously someone with a large beef with literary agents."

"It'll be nice to see what they discover. I hear the FBI is

investigating a lot of people."

"Yes, it will be. Some of the agents murdered represented authors of books we publish here." He paused to walk toward his desk. "Also, it's simply a matter of time until various agents will start to find out you're working here, Amy. They make every attempt to find an inroad into this publishing house. It would be good for you to meet some of them, and it's why I wanted to talk to you. I've a convention I had planned to make this weekend, but I'm not able to now. If you're interested, I think you should go and see if you can find any talent there."

"Wow, I love to go to conventions, and it would be nice to escape for a while."

Ike smiled. "Good, then it's settled. Ask Ginger to make arrangements for you to go in my place. I appreciate it."

Amy turned and grinned. She really did like going to conventions, but she needed to remember to not drink too much this time. That is when she tended to have her worst experiences.

Ginger was talking on the phone at her desk when Amy walked out of his inner office. "Guess what?"

"What?"

"Mr. Grantland wants me to go in his place this week to the convention. I love them. It's a good way to meet people."

Ginger looked at her in disbelief. "I think this will change fast. The first few may be okay, but they soon become old. You'll find out very fast."

"I know you might be right, but I also need a list of agents we work with. Mr. Grantland wants me to see if someone wants to help this guy get started. I think he has promise if he's giving an opportunity."

"You've a good heart. We'll see how long that last. This business can bury you before you know it." She handed Amy a list. "Here, take a look and pick a good agent."

Amy looked over the long list. She recognized many of the names, but some appeared brand new to her. When she saw the name of Edward Lawson, she immediately marked it off.

"Why did you do that?"

"It's a long story, but he's one agent I don't want to work with."

"Why? I've met him here before, and he appears to be a good guy and a hard worker."

"I guess I've a different opinion of him. I think he's a jerk."

Ginger looked totally confused, but decided not to push it. "Whatever. We've many of them on the list, and I think all of them will be happy getting a referral."

"Thank you for making the reservations for me. I need to get away for a day or two."

"Okay, but I promise you, it will not be a vacation."

CHAPTER 25

Amy enjoyed the smooth flight to Denver. While she still had the usual butterflies in her stomach in anticipation of the convention, she now attended in an entirely different role this time. She had seen the hungry look of want-to-be authors frantically making their pitch for their book before; in fact, she was one of them a few months ago.

The hotel was busy with guests checking in and organizers of the convention making final preparations. This was a large convention, with many guests making their journey from all across the country. An older lady wearing a pastel suit she must've owned for some time smiled at her as she approached. Her glasses held by a golden chain made her look like a college professor. "May I help you?" Her voice was formal, but pleasant.

"Yes, I need to register. My Name is Amy Jenkins. My boss, Mr. Grantland, sent me to cover for him."

"Yes, I remember talking to him. We hoped to have him here, and many people are asking about him. However, we're glad to have someone from World Media Publishing here."

"I hope to meet many people. He mentioned I'll have several events I'll need to attend, but unfortunately he didn't have much time to explain to me exactly what you needed me to do."

"I know it was a last minute change, but he was going to participate on a panel discussion on selecting an agent. It would be nice if you could fill in on that and answer questions the group asks."

"I'll be more than glad to. Anything I can do, I'll be more than willing."

She peeked over the top of her glasses trying to analyze Amy. "I know one thing most publishers hate to do, but the writers here love. Would you be willing to listen to pitches on books by new authors?"

Amy contemplated it for a minute. "I think I can work that out. I know how important it is to find someone to listen to your story."

The lady looked pleased. "I'll post a signup sheet at the desk here, and announce it tomorrow morning. You'll be busy."

Amy retrieved her material for the convention. "I'm looking forward to this convention."

The lady pointed down the hall. "Some of the attendees are meeting at the lounge. You might find some of the other speakers having a drink."

"A drink before finding something to eat is exactly what I need."

At the end of the hall she saw an open air type sports bar, with the usual extra large screens in front of loud customers. She saw tables spread all around the central bar area, with stools crammed side by side. A larger group of men on one side screamed at a TV as their team apparently scored.

She saw a lot more guys than girls, and in a way that could be a good thing. However, tonight she had more interest in a quiet table and a nice glass of wine. Perhaps she could ask someone where she could go.

As a chair became vacant in front of her at the bar she glanced around and decided to rest on it for a minute. The room generated a high amount of traffic which constantly flowing around her. When the guy next to her looked over at her for a minute she only returned a partial smile, as she wasn't ready to make friends in a new bar, especially if she planned to look for a different place.

The bartender finally walked over to her when he saw her by herself. "What can I get for you?"

"I'm not sure I'm going to stay or not, since I'd love to have a drink somewhere where it's not so loud?"

He grinned at her. "There's a lounge around the corner, but not many in it. Trust me you'll have much more fun here."

"You may be right. This place is apparently very popular."

"Yeah, it's the greatest and it's early. We have a full band starting around eight. They'll be just on the other side of those tables. The chairs will be cleared out to make room for a dance floor."

"It sounds like I'll be back later then, but I have some material I need to review for tomorrow."

"You must be with the convention starting tomorrow."

"Yes, I am."

"I thought so. I hoped to have some time off tomorrow and make some of the meetings. I've been working on a book for years, and I would love to talk to someone about it."

"When I come back perhaps you can tell me about it."

"I'd love to." He offered a million dollar smile. "Look me up, and your drinks are on me tonight."

"I can't ask you to do that. It'd get you in trouble."

"Not really. I'm also the owner." He winked and lifted a finger to his lips. "Our secret—okay, don't tell everyone here."

"I'll keep it a secret," She whispered back to him as she stood and walked out of the bar. She soon found a small door to a lounge that looked much different. With the music playing soft and the lights turned low, this was a perfect place to rest for a minute.

A gentleman in a suit stepped forward. "May I help you?"

"I would love it if you can find me a quiet place to enjoy a glass of wine." She motioned toward the sports bar. "I came from the bar."

"I see." A smile edged out of the corner of his mouth.

"Please follow me."

She followed him to a small table by a window which presented a panoramic view of some of the buildings in Denver. "Would this be better?"

"Oh yes, this is perfect."

A waiter hustled over to her as she slid into the seat. "What can I get for you today?"

"I'd like a good glass of red wine, perhaps a cabernet."

"Very good, or if you would like . . . we have a Pinot Noir from France, which is very good. Would you like to try a glass?"

"Yes, I would. Also, let me ask you something. I'm here with the writer's convention tomorrow. Do you know of any others attending it?"

"I'm sure many are here. Perhaps you'll find someone you know soon."

After two glasses of wine, she had relaxed and finished reading all the material giving to her about the convention. She expected to be busy, especially after having agreed to the panel discussion and the pitch sessions. She wondered about the panel discussion, as she could imagine the kind of questions she would be asked about finding a literary agent. She knew one she wouldn't recommend, since it would be much easier to tell everyone what not to look for in an agent.

Amy paid her bill and walked to the registration desk to see if anything exciting was happening there. While still busy with late arrivals and organizers scampering around her, the lady at the registration table that Amy met earlier waved at her as she walked over. "Hello, I'm glad to find you. It looks like your pitch sessions are very much in demand, and as I predicted . . . it's completely full."

"Wow! That's amazing."

"I can't say I blame them, since this is why many of them come. They all hope to be discovered and get published. I hope you can find something of interest to you."

"I hope so also, because it is why I also came." Visions of finding a great writer entered her mind, but she knew the odds.

"We'll have some breakfast for the speakers early tomorrow morning in the speakers lounge. I hope to see you then."

"I'll be there."

Amy left and turned toward the sports bar. It would not be too long until the band would start playing. After all, someone had promised her some free drinks, so why not. She soon walked in and saw a much more crowded bar than before, and with many girls present now who looked dressed to kill. Perhaps she needed to go back to her room and change. She knew she would dress better the next night.

With all the chairs full, Amy selected a small place she could stand and have access to the bar top, but soon decided to move over and out of the busy traffic around the central bar area. A bartender eventually shuffled over to her. "What will you have?"

"I talked to the owner earlier, is he here?"

"Do you mean Luke?"

"He never told me his name. He wanted me to come back and let him buy me a drink."

With a big smile he raised his head and glanced around. "That sounds like Luke. What would you like?"

"A glass of Pinot Noir if possible."

"You've got it. He'll be back soon. He left to take care of something."

"Thanks. I appreciate it."

The band started setting up as a work crew pushed the tables off to the side to be stacked. The dance floor looked much larger than she originally imagined. The lights were strategically placed to highlight two places, the band and the bar. Both were intended to be places that would be easily noticed. After all, that's what brought in the business and the money. As Amy examined the incredible design work, she knew that if this Luke had a hand in it, then he was a very smart business man.

When Luke reappeared, the bartenders flashed him a thumbs up, as to indicate everything was under control. They all appeared to be good buddies of his as well. This had to be an interesting place to work. The bartender who poured her the wine soon tapped Luke on the shoulder and pointed at her.

When Amy winked at Luke and raised her glass to him, he saluted her and winked back. She knew he was busy. He appeared to be a nice guy and in his late thirties. When he wasn't working, Amy assumed, he must be spending most of his time in the gym, since his muscular body busted at the seams in his pullover shirt. He possessed the jaw of a tough commando from a movie. She would love to hear his story.

The band eventually started playing a combination of many short tunes all tied together to kick off the night. With such a fantastic introduction, the patrons readily turned to watch them play. Only a few of the die-hard sports bar fans stayed glued to the large TV's.

Amy felt good and now looked forward to hearing the band. She turned around to see Luke in front of her holding the bottle of pinot noir and taking her glass to pour it full again. "I'm glad you made it back again . . . I knew you would."

"Thanks for the wine. However, I think this is all I need, and in fact, this is probably too much for me already." She knew she had surpassed her normal limit of two glasses and she would not be able to function well if she had more. This would be her fourth glass and she would soon not be able to maintain control. However, she knew it would be rude to say no to him, and she hoped to be able to just hold the glass and enjoy the music for a while.

"I'm sorry. I had to leave for a minute. One of my friends

told me someone from a publishing house has agreed to hear pitches tomorrow, and I had hoped to add my name to the list. I was too late."

A big smile crossed Amy's face as she reached over and extended her hand to him. "By the way, I'm Amy Jenkins," she whispered behind her hand, "I think I can add your name." It was a comeback to the secret he passed to her earlier.

His face failed to hide the expression of shock. "You're Amy Jenkins?"

"I'll add your name to the end of the list, and I look forward to hearing what you've written."

He looked flattered. Amy raised the glass and toasted him as she watched him pump his fist in victory before he turned back to his mob of customers. She heard his name often over the sound of the band and the chatting of the patrons. He appeared popular and known by almost everyone.

The guy she sat next to earlier walked over to her. "Would you like to dance? The band is really good tonight."

She started to decline, but he had such a sweet pleasing smile she decided to give him one dance. "Okay, but only one, and I'll warn you I'm not too good."

They headed for the floor and weaved through the heavy traffic that was constantly moving about as other guys went on the hunt for dance partners. Most of the available women had already walked onto the dance floor. With the effect of the wine swirling in her head, she planned to enjoy the night, but hoped she didn't embarrass herself like she had so many times before.

That dance was the last thing she remembered.

CHAPTER 26

Wow, what a night! Her body, especially her feet, still ached from the dancing, and her head was pounding with an aching pain. Like usual, she didn't remember much about the night before. *When am I ever going to learn*? But for now, she needed to hurry and make the breakfast and the panel discussion.

She quickly dressed in a professional suit she had purchased for this occasion. She now had the reputation of the publisher she had to consider, and she was still new at the job. She wondered why Ike sent her into the field so early.

The registration area was busy with volunteers signing in attendees as she entered the main meeting area. She recognized some of the people from the night before walking around, as she retrieved her name tag and placed it on her lapel. "Hello, can you tell me where the speaker's lounge is?"

The girl studied her name and pointed straight ahead. "It's on the left, half of the way down."

While Amy felt a little hungry, she wanted coffee more than anything. With the door open she went inside, where saw about twenty people inside walking around with small plates in their hands. The person closest to the door moved over to her first. "How are you?" He quickly recognized her name badge and her agency's name. "I don't think we've met before. I'm Jason Blair with the Blair agency. How long have you been with World Media Publications?"

"I've been with them for only a few months now. I'm an assistant to Mr. Grantland."

"Yes, I know him. It looks like he's already throwing you to the wolves, but we're glad to have you here."

Amy still wondered why everyone thought they were so

bad. "I actually like going to conventions."

He smiled. "I used to like them, and I guess to some extent I still do. It's however . . . a large drain on my time. I hope you can still say you like them a year from now."

"I do also. I tried hard to find an agent before, so I know what everyone is going through. Also, I'm reading tons of manuscripts from hopeful authors, and it's hard to be so cold and informal. I've promised myself to not be like some jerks I've met in the past, and especially one particular guy."

He laughed. "I can understand, and I hope it wasn't me." He raised his hands as if to say, "I surrender."

"No, it wasn't you. If it was, you would be scrapping your eyeballs off the floor."

"Wow! It sounds like you really have it in for one guy."

Amy picked out one of her cards and handed it to him. "If you have a good novel you think we should look at, please let me know. It's my job to do preliminary screenings. If I like it, I'm sure Mr. Grantland will want to read it."

"Thanks, I'll remember your name. Also, you're not the maniac knocking off literary agents, are you?"

Amy turned and sent him a cold stare before answering. "That wasn't very nice."

She recognized he meant it to be a joke, but it didn't come out the way he had planned for it to sound. "I'm sorry, and I know it's very serious. I was trying to make light of your dislike for this one agent. I hope you'll forgive me. By the way, I knew two of the agents who were murdered."

"I'm sorry. It's just that it's hard for me to understand how someone can murder someone so viciously."

"I agree. In fact, I was having second thoughts about coming."

"I think the reason I'm here is because of the murders. I think Mr. Grantland has to work hard to control situations caused by these agents' deaths. We have many authors who were represented by these agents, and it's taking much of his time right now."

"If there's anything I can do to help, I'm sure he knows he can count on us."

"I'll be sure to tell him, and I'm sure he already knows. It's fantastic how this industry is pulling together to help each other."

Another woman joined in by asking if Amy had gotten anything to eat yet.

"I haven't yet. It looks good, but what I want is a good cup of coffee." Another young woman overheard her and then rushed off to get her one. The others in the group moved over to her as they recognized who she represented.

The conversation quickly centered in on the murders of the agents and how the police still had no suspect. Several in the group mentioned they had been contacted by law officials in some form or fashion. With the FBI in the hot seat looking for answers, the news coverage had intensified. Someone passed around a newspaper with the latest information, which made some of the members act tense and apprehensive in discussing it.

The older lady she had met yesterday walked in. "I hope you're all ready. We've some energetic writers wanting to ask questions. I'll do my best to maintain control and keep this orderly. Try to keep your answers as brief as possible, and I'll try to keep you from being tied up for any extended period of time. If you need help, try to grab my attention." She came across with a lot of authority, and the wisdom of someone doing this before.

They all lined up behind her and headed out of the room. The large meeting room held about three or four hundred people. While the attendees contained a mixture of ages, sex, and nationalities, they all had one purpose for coming to this meeting. They all wanted to know how to go about finding a good agent to represent them, or a publisher to buy their work.

The meeting progressed without incident until the time came for an open-mic session where the attendees could ask questions. A super slim man in his late forties moved toward the microphone. His voice, however, sounded deep and smooth. "Is it possible to have a publisher look at your book proposal without an agent?"

Most of the members of the panel glanced over in Amy's direction, as the pressure of the moment sent butterflies fluttering in her stomach. She wanted to speak clearly and concisely in front of a large group. "Yes, it's possible; everything's possible. However, the probability isn't very good."

The poor man remained still, listening, waiting for a small crumb of hope. What he obviously wanted was a secret way of getting in to see a publisher. He must have been turned down many times from agents, but like all want-to-be authors, he wanted to have his work looked at and published. He raised his hand again as if he a small boy at school. "I've spent five years writing this book and all I want is someone to actually take a look at it. What do you suggest?"

Amy concentrated to assure she spoke clearly. "It sounds like you've received your share of rejection letters. I know it can be hard, but my best advice is to keep trying and keep learning. At the same time, you have to be honest. I'm not saying this about your novel, but in general, sometimes editors are not as interested in a subject as you are. Sometimes other writers know how to write much better than you. You have to remember you're in a competition with everyone else not only in this room here, but from all around the world."

The man still persistently stood in front of her waiting for more. "I've come to many conventions in the past and met many agents who promised to read at least part of it. To date, I've not had anyone say anything bad about my work. They seem to just disappear or forget who I am. If I wasn't so encouraged earlier I wouldn't be so determined to have it published now."

Amy looked at him intensely with a long pause. "Are you sure you can truly stand a critical review of your work? Don't ask for something you really can't handle. You have to remember my job at World Media is to be extremely critical of some of the best writers in the world."

The man stayed unyielding. "That's all I've ever wanted."

"I like the way you stay focused on what you want. You have my e-mail on the program. Send me a query letter and the first chapter. If it's good I'll ask for more. If I don't like it I'll be brutally honest. Is that fair?"

"Yes. That's all I want."

Amy looked around the room and watched many heads moving up and down in agreement with her decision to look at his work. She wondered how many other attendees she would have to agree to do the same thing for. Amy soon agreed to accept over one dozen more works. Glad to be saved by the bell, she tried her best to keep her company in a good light. She knew she needed to learn the ropes quickly in her new role.

As she made it out the door, one of the authors on the panel walked over to her. "I'll have to admit you did well today. I know how much time it takes to go through all the email you receive. Are you hungry?"

"Yes, I think I can relax some now. That was my first panel discussion. It feels so different to be on this side of the table, but I remember being in their place asking for help before."

###

Amy glanced at her desk in a small room they had procured for her to accept pitches, and at a stack of her cards placed in the center. Each person was given ten minutes to make a case for their book project. It wasn't much, but it was hopefully enough to give her a feel of the book and the author. After the first hour, she realized this was going to be wasted time.

Everyone appeared excited about their book, but they had no clue how to pitch it. She could understand why they couldn't find an agent or publisher. While she had hoped for a miracle, and she felt sorry for everyone, she remembered her life earlier and tried to impart some encouragement.

She eventually glanced at her watch and felt happy to see her duty time almost over. The last one contained a decent plot, but after talking with her, Amy knew it needed a lot of work before being ready to submit. She breathed deeply as the last one left and reached to place her cards back in her purse. Finally, she had time for a good glass of red wine.

As she made it around her desk, the door opened again and Luke stepped inside. She had forgotten all about him, and he apparently sensed that she had. "We can do this some other time, if you want. I know you must be tired."

"No, I promised you I would talk to you. You run a very busy bar, and I think I must've must have had a great time there last night."

"Yes, I can also remember you having the time of you life."

"Oh, my god! I didn't do anything stupid, did I?"

"Not too bad, but you can be a good dancer. I'll have to remember not to serve you so much wine tonight."

"I fully agree. However, one glass would be perfect right now."

"That's not a problem." He opened his cell and quickly dialed. "This is Luke. I need a glass of pinot noir delivered to room 207B. Thanks."

Amy leaned back in her seat. "That was easy enough. Didn't you want one for yourself?"

His face turned somber. "I don't drink. Sounds funny, I know, but I guess down deep I'm too much of a health nut. I spend almost as much time in the gym as I do in the bar."

"I can tell you stay in good shape." She surveyed his body, but lingered perhaps too long as he waited on her to finish. A small smile of embarrassment swept across her face, as she pushed herself to regain control. "Tell me about your book."

He reached in his folder and handed her a brief query letter he had prepared. It looked professional and short to the point. "I've written a mystery based on body builders that are being murdered. The authorities are working hard to determine who is killing them, while the investigations are discovering many secrets that are ripping the local government apart. The mayor's daughter has been having an affair with all the known deceased. The captain of the police is well known for his body building routine as well. Is he the next target, or part of the cover up? The mayor must make some major decisions that affect the lives of his daughter, the captain and city, and it all must be done quietly and in an unorthodox method."

Amy listened to him with interest. It reflected a short, sweet plot which was well presented. "That's the best presentation I've heard all day."

"I appreciate it. It has been a story that I've wanted to tell for a while."

"I know you're a body builder, which would help in knowing the territory. What kind of writing experience do you have?"

"This is my first novel. I have some articles I've written for some health magazines, but that's about it."

"You may have something I can work with. I can't make any promises. Have you tried to find an agent?"

"I've sent out a few of these query letters, but all I have received is the normal form letter of, 'thanks, but no thanks'."

"I can understand. I met an agent here I think you should meet. He's looking to build his clientele."

"Thanks. I've been frustrated in hunting for an agent. Is he still here?"

"He's probably over at the speakers lounge right now. We're all supposed to meet for a small reception at the end of the day."

"I'm sorry. I think I must be making you late for it."

"Not a problem. I enjoyed hearing your proposal, and I hope to receive it soon. It sounds promising."

"Will you come back to the sports bar tonight? I'd love for you to bring the entire group. I'll buy them the first round if you can talk them into coming."

"I'll see what I can do."

CHAPTER 27

Amy looked around her office, which was stacked high in every direction with files, manuscripts, papers and advance reader copies of books, which needed to be sent to reviewers. With her computer under it somewhere, she knew her phone rested next to it, that is if she could get to it.

Renee's head bobbed up and down in her own cube, as she appeared to be rocking out to one of the latest tunes. Amy wondered how she managed to concentrate on fact checking and the music at the same time. Perhaps, somehow it helped keep her from going insane. Renee suddenly pulled off her headset and yelled over at Amy, "Are we still going out tonight?"

"I'm not sure I can. They brought me another large stack of material."

"Hey, it's Friday night. A lot of hunks will be out tonight. We owe it to ourselves. I know Ginger has already bought a new dress and she looks so hot in it."

"Well, I'm glad she does. I think I still keep gaining weight."

Renee looked so tiny. She probably never knew what it meant to be on a diet. She stared at Amy. "I know one thing for sure. I don't receive the looks you do when we walk into a room. You're the one that has what the guys are interested in."

Amy rolled her eyes. "It is also the thing that attracts the wrong guys all the time. It would be nice to have someone look at me in my eyes first and not at my tits."

Renee shifted forward for a minute. "It would be fantastic . . . for guys to even notice that I had some. Listen, you work all the time. We need some time off."

Amy rubbed her eyes. "I want to find something good in all of this pile. I've always wanted to respond to a writer as

174

soon as possible, but it's getting impossible. It's so tempting to use the form letters I said I'd never use."

"Don't worry about it. Remember it doesn't have your name on it. It looks like it came from Mr. Grantland. That's why he hired you. There's no way he can read through all of these. Yes, you'll find a few good ones, but we both know not many will make it from the slush pile."

"I know it. Maybe, we can go out tonight for a little while, but when I get home tonight I need to read the ones close to being published. I need to concentrate on the ones important to him. He wants me to be the first book critic to ever read the material so errors can be corrected before it goes out to the general public."

"Good, then it's settled. I'll stop by your place at seven."

Amy studied the envelope on the top of the stack from the agent she had met at the convention. At the bottom of the envelope, she read a note that it included the completed manuscript from Luke, the guy who owned the bar. She felt glad to finally see it. "I think I need to take this one with me."

"What is it?"

"It's from a guy I met at a convention a few months ago. He had an intriguing plot, but he had no agent. I introduced him to one, and they have been working on this for the last few months. This is the final manuscript, and I hope it holds up to expectations."

"Tell me about this guy. Is he hot?"

"Very hot, if you're into body builders. He's also a nice guy to talk to and owns a sports bar. That's about the end of the story."

"No way! That's not even a good opening chapter. I think you can do better than that. After we pour some wine in you, I'll ask you again." She winked.

"Not fair. You know I talk too much when I have a few glasses."

Ike appeared quietly, as he came around a corner, but he had a serious look on his face. "What's up?" Amy asked.

"The agents being murdered are causing problems for everyone. It's slowing down production and causing many authors and agents to have anxiety attacks, which are further causing missed deadlines. The FBI was here again today. They're looking at all angles, and they still have not discovered anything in common between the agents other than they worked as literary agents."

"I know it's causing problems. You can feel it all over the building."

"How are you doing on the last revisions? This is the last chance before we go to press on them."

"I think they're good. Not perfect, but they'll pass most critics with good grades."

"That's good to hear. When will you have the reports ready?"

"I'm hoping on Monday, since I plan on working on them all weekend."

"Except for tonight!" Renee broke in on the conversation. Ike stopped and turned around. "Why is that?"

"She needs a break and we're going out tonight. I'm going to do my best to get her laid tonight."

Ike rubbed his chin. He would naturally assume Renee was a fun loving girl, but one who would make sure Amy would stay out of trouble. "Well, you two keep notes, I'm sure it'll make a bestselling novel one day."

"I guess we could, since Ginger is going with us tonight."

He raised his hands. "I can see right now the guys don't have a chance. Perhaps I should call ahead and warn them."

"Not on your life. Tonight is girl's night out, and we intend to enjoy it."

Amy looked over at Ike. "Don't worry, I'll have it all completed by Monday morning." She reached over to the new manuscript that came in and added, "I might have a pleasant surprise for you."

"Why, what is that?"

"I hope it's good. It's from a guy I met at the convention you sent me to."

"Let me know, but right now I need to concentrate on the ones in the house needing to make it to the book shelves." As he left he looked around the office. Most of the personnel had already left for the day. It was Friday, and the end of a long week for most.

"How much do you know about Mr. Grantland?" Amy asked.

"I know about as much as anyone here. He works all the time. I'm not sure he has much of a personal life or not. He never says anything about it. I've heard once he was married, but then from time to time I've heard talk about a girlfriend. I think he gets one and loses her when they don't receive much attention from him. So is the life in the publishing world. Other than that, I think he's a nice guy outside of work."

"He has been a nice guy since I first met him. It's funny how I work for him now and don't have much time to ever talk about anything but work. Perhaps one day things will slow down and we'll have a chance to talk. I think he might have some exciting stories to tell."

"Good luck. In this business it never slows down. If it did, you'll witness mass panic. Trust me on that one."

"I think I'll go home, take a shower, and relax for a minute before we go out." Amy lifted the carrying bag holding her reading material and headed for the door.

"You can't wait to read the one from the body builder, can you?"

Amy hesitated as she turned around. "It has been on my mind some."

"What about your slush stack? They're gathering dust."

"I read some of them. I don't know if I'll have time to

give a personal response or not, since Ike's pushing me hard to finish the reports."

"So, the dreaded form letter rejections are going out again. And who's Ike?"

Amy had to laugh. "When I met Mr. Grantland, he told me his name was Ike. That's the name he uses when he's not Mr. Grantland. I shouldn't have told you—you'll promise me not to say anything, I hope?"

"I promise. You'll have to tell me the story when we go out later."

Amy looked at the stack of query letters and partials. "I guess you're right, I'm turning into one of those cold and heartless agents or editors I hated before. I don't have enough time to respond to all the mail coming in."

CHAPTER 28

Amy felt tired. The night was too short and the work was too long. She loved to read. It used to be fun before the tight deadlines and the never ending stack of reading material. It caused more stress than even her medication could cover. Last night she had a long conversation with Dr. Lankford. Something had to be done.

With no personal letters coming out of the slush pile and only a slight review of some of them, she decided to concentrate on the current stack of final submissions and revisions. She needed some time off. Her boss knew it. Aware of the long hours and how it affected those under him, he had called her to his office for a meeting. She knew he planned to give her an employee review which was required after six months on the job.

Ginger twisted in her seat as Amy walked over to his office. She wondered how Ginger maintained control day after day. She did have one advantage. At five every day, she went home. Ike agreed to this when she came to work, and he had never asked her to do otherwise. The rest of the staff worked long hard hours. Not so much because he required it, but because they wanted to advance.

Amy opened the door and walked in. "Hello." She watched him leaning over some papers on his desk.

His eyes darted toward her for a second, but soon returned to what he had in front of him. "Come on in. I was looking over some numbers, and I also received a letter I want you to read. It's from one of the agents I think you'll recognize."

Amy opened the letter and started to read. "We are so glad to be working with such a professional publishing house. The support we receive from you is incredible. You have a way of hiring all the best people to work with you.

When we received the critique from your office, it was detailed and right on. It was performed by Amy Jenkins in your office. She has one of the best eyes in reviewing plots I've ever seen. The insight she provided has helped to make this book much better than we had ever hoped. It's because of people like her that I know my author will never look for another publishing house. Keep up the good work."

"Wow! That can really make you feel good. Thanks for allowing me to read it."

"You're building a name for yourself, and I think everyone knows how hard you work. We're going to have an opening soon for a junior editor position where you'll be able to work your own clients. Of course, it will still be under my guidance and approval, but it will give you much more experience. There're still some things you need to do to prove you're ready for this kind of position."

"I know that I haven't been working here very long. Except for the hours being so long, it's a nice place to work."

"You'll soon be able to breathe a little easier, since I think that you're learning how we have to spend time on projects that matter. It's too bad we have to be so cold, but it's the way it is."

"I think I finally understand it, and it would be so good to have a good night's sleep."

Ike nodded at her. "With a lot of turmoil in the industry now the personnel is rapidly turning over. We're losing some authors and trying hard to gain others. The scandal of the murdered literary agents has sent chaos all across the publishing houses." He paused. "The one skill you need to develop is attracting new authors, and it's by all means one of the most critical."

"I fully understand. I came to this job without the normal background most have here."

"Yes, you took a different route."

"I've attracted one writer, and he has done a good job on the revisions I sent him."

"Yes, it appears he might become a good author for us, but for now he hasn't proved himself. I hope he does."

"I'm sure he will, I can feel it."

He pursed his lips as he pointed to a book on the end of his table. It was written by Larry Waterman. "I've heard a rumor that he's not happy with his publisher. The house that lands him will be more than happy."

Amy recognized the name instantly. "I've met him before. He's a nice blond headed guy with a fantastic grin."

Ike's eyes blinked in astonishment. "You never said anything about this before."

"It's not like we're major buddies here. I met him and his agent at a bar when I went to a convention a while back." Amy sweated, hoping she could hold it together. She didn't need to go off the deep end and talk about Edward.

"It's not much, but it's all we have right now. If you can think of a way to get to this guy, I think your chances of receiving the promotion are a done deal."

"But . . . like I said, we only met once and had one drink together. I know nothing much else about him."

"What about the agent. How well do you know him?"

Damn, Amy hoped this would never come up. "Not well. I was hoping to have him represent me, but it didn't work out." That sounded short and sweet. How could she tell her boss she hated one particular agent with all of her heart and soul? And, not to mention, an agent she spent a long time trying to destroy.

"Do some research and let me know if you can find an angle." The next hour they went over her performance to date. He had all good things to say about her, but she wasn't listening, since she was concentrating on how she could work herself out of this jam she found herself in.

CHAPTER 29

Amy planned to sleep late until the phone rang. After all, Ike had insisted she take a day off. He knew she looked tired and ordered her to do nothing but rest. "Hello."

"Hi, this is Dr. Lankford, how are you?"

"I'm fine, my boss gave me a day off and I was sleeping late."

"I'm sorry. I tried to reach you at the office and they told me you went home, so I wanted to check on you."

"Don't worry. I needed to get out of bed."

"How is your mood right now?"

"It's not bad. The work load has been hard, but I do it to myself. It's a little bit depressing lately, but I think I'm going to be fine."

"I'm not so sure. I think you really need to see my friend in New York."

"I don't have any extra time. I'm close to receiving a major promotion. It's unreal. When I do, things will be much better."

"If you go into a manic mode, you'll not have a job, you know how it goes."

"I know what to watch for. I do think I need to adjust my medication slightly to compensate for the depression. Is that okay?"

"I think you're right. When will you be coming home? I would like to talk with you for a while. This has been a long time for you to stay in the normal zone."

"I'm not sure, perhaps in a month for a short vacation. I'd love to see my parents."

"I'm sure you would. Try to make it happen as soon as possible. It's important you let me know if you start losing control. Don't wait until the last minute. The group has been asking about you and how you've been doing."

"Really, I assumed they would have forgotten who I am by now."

"The group is coming along well. They're getting good at monitoring each other's moods. Their input is a big help to me."

"Tell them that I'm doing fine, and I hope to receive a promotion soon. I only have one problem in nailing it, and it's a big one. Do you remember the agent I can't stand? The jerk has found a new way to ruin my life."

"What?"

"My boss wants me to try to persuade an author who's looking to change publishers to try us. I met him before. The problem is he uses Edward as his agent. Can you believe the dumb luck I have?"

"Wow! What are you planning on doing?"

"I don't know right now. First off, I have to find out if Edward is aware I tried to ruin him. The bastard hurt me so bad the first time that it's crazy to think I have to deal with him again."

"You need to get over this obsession you have. It will only hurt you more and more."

"I know what you're saying, but it's not going to be easy. Tell the group to pray for me, and I'll see if I can make a meeting when I come home."

"I will. Please go and see my friend. He'll help you to regulate your medication."

"I'll see, goodbye for now."

Amy knew she was right. She felt like a ticking time bomb, and especially in a crisis setting like she was in. She fell back in the bed. It felt so good to lay still and not have to read for a while. She soon fell asleep again and started dreaming, where she soon found herself dancing again. With such a romantic moment it felt so good to be held close. The music flowed and the dim lights added to the sensation. She could imagine it being someone she met out dancing. Not anyone special, simply a guy at a dance hall. One day she hoped that she would meet that special person, but when was anyone's guess.

Then she turned and pulled away to glance at her partner. Her heart almost stopped, and she had trouble breathing. She could see those beady eyes of Edward again, but this time he was laughing. She pulled away from him, feeling dizzy. She could feel herself falling with a crowd of people watching her. The music stopped. She felt paralyzed and scared until Edward lifted her as she crumbled in his arms. Where was he taking her? She screamed as she woke.

For the next hour, she trembled as she stared into empty space. She later walked over to the cabinet and opened her medication box. With this being such a dangerous time for her, she needed to calm down fast. She called Dr. Lankford's friend and made an appointment.

The pill soon inflicted its intended effect and she went to sleep again. She experienced no dream this time and woke late in the afternoon, where she felt much better and ordered some pizza before she jumped into the shower.

Soon after, she wrapped in her bath towel and sat at the small kitchen table until the pizza arrived. She walked to the door with money in her hand. The door opened and a young guy, around eighteen, stood with the pizza in front of him. He grinned and pushed the pizza in her direction. She accepted the pizza and handed him the money as her robe opened in front of him exposing her breasts. He flashed all smiles as she tried to cover herself and lost control of the pizza. Without the quick reflexes of the young man, it would have spilled all over the floor. "Oh, my Gosh," she yelled.

"I got it." They kneeled face to face with each other.

She felt embarrassed, but what could she say. It wasn't his fault she had flashed him. As she stood, she realized she hadn't put on any panties either and had now exposed her whole front side. She wrapped herself tighter and whispered in a shy weak voice, "Thank you. I hope you'll not tell anyone about this."

He lifted a hand. "Not a word."

She knew he lied, but shook her head and headed back inside. "I can't believe I'm so stupid."

She walked over to the table and the computer she used so often. With it already on and connected to the internet, she needed to do catch up work on her Edward research. She had stayed so busy in working at the publishing house, she had started to forget the pain he had caused her. In a way, she could now understand why agents used form letters now.

His blog was the first place to start, since he posted regularly and openly, giving advice to new writers. She read the indication of sincerity in his post, which made him look like a trusted friend. Boy, if people knew the truth about him.

She pulled a pillow off the bed. It would take some time to read his blogs all the way back until the time they met. Then she needed to check the web for notes about him. She felt sure she would find some of the critiques she wrote under the name of "The Literary Hawk".

He never acknowledged the assault she had launched against him. Either she had almost no effect on him, or he played it so cool. In any case, she assumed she was safe so far.

Next, she clicked on his calendar out of curiosity. He stayed busy with lectures and conventions. She hit the print button and printed out the list of dates.

She then started looking for a list of all of his clients, but couldn't find exactly what she wanted. That made sense, since other agents might target your whole list, or someone like Amy could destroy all of your work. However, she did remember finding it before. She located a link to Larry Waterman's site and clicked on it. It contained a large impressive photo of him on the right side. He looked like she remembered. A list of his books displayed on the far left. He worked as a prolific writer. He also posted a calendar of tours and events which she immediately clicked on.

Again she printed the page and added it to Edward's file. She located one common appearance—a convention in Hawaii. Now this is living the life, so to speak.

The phone rang. "Hello, girl. This is Lenny. How are you?"

"Hi! I'm so glad you called. I'm in a jam and trying to work my way out of it. You're not going to believe what has happened."

"What?"

"I have a chance to land a large promotion."

"Do tell. That just sounds like fantastic news."

In a pouting voice she continued, "I only have to land one account the house is after. Take a guess which agent this author uses?"

"You have got to be kidding. Is it really Edward, the jerk?"

"The one and only. I've been thinking about it, and I'm working on a plan. My boss has received word that this author, Larry Waterman, is unhappy with his publisher and is thinking of changing. It's the agent who usually handles this for an author. I'm wondering how close the connection between the two now is. If I could persuade the author to change to a different agent and bring both into the house, I'll be a hero and accomplish my goals as well."

"You are one wicked lady. I love it!"

"I'm not wicked. I want satisfaction, there's a difference."

"I'm sorry. I was only playing with you. What can I do to help?"

"I can think of nothing . . . that is, unless you own a place

186

in Hawaii."

"Dream on, girl. My new company's doing fabulous, but I'm not that famous yet."

"How is your company doing . . . really?"

"It's doing fantastic. I really can't believe it sometimes."

"I was checking on the places both Edward and Larry would be appearing in the next few weeks, and I noticed that both of them are going to a convention in Hawaii in two weeks."

"Now I see why you want to go to Hawaii. I have never been there, but I'd love to go sometime."

"Well, if you can figure out a way, let me know. It has to be expensive."

"I'll do some asking around. You never know what I can come up with, girl. I'll call you back in a minute."

"Thanks. I need to do some more research while I have the time."

For the next ten hours, Amy became obsessed with knowing everything about Larry. She read excerpts of several of his latest novels, and studied several book reviews on them. He was definitely a gifted writer.

The phone rang again—Lenny. "Hello, girl. I have some news, you might be interested in. I was talking to one of my clients who knew someone who owned a place in Maui. They called me and said if I did some work for them I could use their place for free. I played not interested at first . . . but let them talk me into it."

"You've got to be kidding me! That will help tremendously. Now all we have to do is come up with the airfare. Are you planning on going to Hawaii also?"

"It's the only way I can find you a free place to stay. Don't worry. It's a large house with several bedrooms."

"I can't believe you worked it out. I really owe you one for this. How long will we have use of it?"

"We have a whole week."

"Wow, now all I have to do is get permission to take off for a week. I'll call Ike at home. I know he'll want to hear what I'm proposing. I'll call you back in a minute."

Amy went and washed her face, she must be dreaming. She might be going to Hawaii!

She called Ike, who answered in a happy sounding tone. "Hello."

"This is Amy, how are you?"

"I'm doing fine and finishing the manuscript you handed me. He's good and a rare find. He should do well."

"I'm so glad you like his work and I agree. I also have been doing some research—."

"You're supposed to be taking a break and getting some rest."

"I know I was, but you know how it is. There's a writer's convention in two weeks in Hawaii."

"Yes, it's a large one they have every year. I know it well. However, it's not on our budget this year to attend."

"Larry Waterman is speaking at the convention and his agent, Edward Lawson will be with him, also participating in a panel discussion. A friend of mine has already located us a place to stay at no cost."

"It sounds tempting, and this is something I really should attend, but I don't have the time right now or the money budgeted for it."

"You know my doctor has been asking me to take some time off. If I could take a week of vacation, I can make the trip myself. If the company could pay the cost of the convention and airfare, I'll find some way to cover everything else."

Amy waited for a long pause.

"I think I can work something out, that is, if you're willing to try to get him as one of our authors. I wish I could cover more of the cost, but if you're successful I might be able to find you a bonus."

"I appreciate it very much. Somehow, I'll get the rest of the cost covered."

"Okay then. We'll work it out on Monday when you come back to work."

As she disconnected the phone call, she let out a yell, "I'm going to Hawaii!"

CHAPTER 30

Amy glanced out the window of the plane. Hawaii—wow, nothing better than a dream trip to lift her out of a depressed mood. Amy felt sure her medication helped, but she also knew to watch for a mood swing in the other direction. For right now, she felt happy and excited about the trip.

Lenny had fallen asleep next to her. He had pulled off one miracle after another in making this trip possible. The convention on Saturday, the day after they arrived, would last until Tuesday morning. The rest of the week, they could have a relaxing vacation and enjoy the islands.

A stewardess stopped by and asked, "What can I bring you to drink?"

"I would love some red wine."

"And for him?"

"I think he'll want the same."

She glanced at both of them, went to the cart and returned with the two small bottles of red wine, a cabernet, which sounded fine with Amy.

Amy opened the file she had built on her targets. She needed to know everything she could about them. Nothing could be left to chance. While both were single, she still discovered nothing written about either one of them having a girlfriend or a family life. In fact, she couldn't find any hobbies or distractions for either.

She remembered they both liked drinking beer, or at least they did the night they met at the bar. While Edward appeared to enjoy dancing, details of the night were still hazy.

Larry loved to write mysteries, and most of them were written with an international setting. He had been raised in Europe and Asia but had received his education at Yale, where he received his Master's degree in English. It appeared he started writing as soon as he graduated and never worked at a salaried job. It was like he knew what he wanted to do and never ventured from it. He had his first novel published at twenty three and followed it with over thirty since then.

When the plane landed in Honolulu, Lenny appeared rested and ready to go. "This is going to be so much fun."

"I agree. You slept the entire trip. You're amazing."

"I plan on having fun here, so while you're out stalking the guys, I plan on taking in my own sights."

She held up her hand. "I don't even want to know."

He laughed. "We're not there yet, we still have to make the trip over to Maui. It won't take long. And . . . one last thing, you know the old saying, "What happens in Hawaii stays in Hawaii."

"I agree with you, for sure."

###

After landing in Maui, the taxi driver drove them straight to the house they would be staying, which looked huge and impressive. This, she could get use to. "Lenny you hit pay dirt on this one. I'm not sure how you managed to arrange this, but . . . WOW!"

"I'm not surprised. They're a very wealthy family. They also wanted my opinion on updating it for them. I'm looking forward to going to work on making some recommendations for them."

"We have so many things we can do here. I would love to go whale-watching, learn how to skin-dive, or maybe go snorkeling. I know they have schools here to teach you how to surf. This week is going to go by so quick, it was a shame we didn't have more time to get ready for it."

"I know what you mean. I'm as white as a ghost.

However, I have no intentions of turning into a red lobster while I'm here."

"The convention doesn't start until tomorrow, but it would be good to locate the hotel and see if anyone arrived early like us. Do you want to go with me?"

"I want to head over to Lahaina, since it's supposed to be the party place on the island and check it out. You can call me later, and we can get back together."

Amy didn't want to separate so early, but agreed to it because she wanted to be able to find out if Edward and Larry had arrived already. She needed all the time she could have to make contact with them. "I'll call you as soon as I see what's going on."

She called for a taxi and hurried to her room to unpack and retouch her makeup. She wanted to make a good impression if she ran into them tonight.

"Wait for a minute and I'll ride with you. It'll keep me from calling a taxi."

"I've already called one. You better hurry."

It felt amazing that he would probably take much longer than her in getting ready. He was particular in his looks and worked hard at it. "Oh, my gosh," he yelled as he hurried to his room.

The taxi arrived about an hour later. Cab drivers never hurried on the island, which was much different than the city she came from. The weather looked perfect, with deep blue skies. As they walked out to the taxi, a small lizard scurried off and startled Amy. The driver laughed. "You must be here for the first time. You'll get use to them, they're harmless."

"Yes, it's the first time here, and I can already tell it will not be the last. It's so beautiful here."

The trip to the hotel was short—too short, considering how much Amy loved the scenery. "We're going to have to do a guided tour. I'm sure we're passing many places and missing any background story."

"That's a very good idea. We'll arrange it as soon as the convention is over. I know you'll be busy until then." Lenny darted his eyes around trying to act mysterious as his voice descended into a deep harsh baritone. "By the way, if you need me to go under cover for you in following these guys, you let me know."

Amy raised her hand to cover her open mouth. "I didn't know your voice could go so low."

"I'm full of surprises when I need to be."

As the taxi pulled in front of the hotel, Amy laughed and held her hand next to her ear indicating she would call him soon. "Take care."

Amy walked through the lobby and into the grand station, which was full of flowers everywhere and had some small waterfalls on the far side. She saw many people with different nationalities walking around and talking in foreign languages she couldn't understand. Hell, she didn't even know exactly which country they were from. She knew this convention attracted attendees from all over the world.

She felt little prepared for the meeting tomorrow, so she decided to find the local watering hole. After locating it directly across from the waterfalls, she studied the crowded entrance and the smell of food. With a line forming to enter, she edged over and waited.

For some reason, Amy turned and looked over her shoulder, where she noticed two guys hurrying toward the front of the hotel. While not absolutely sure, she had a shocking sensation it might be Edward and Larry.

She hurried, trying to reach the exit. After forcing the heavy door open, she rushed outside to watch a taxi pulling from the curb. She searched for the next cab and saw one about a block away. Her prey would be gone before it arrived. She turned to the doorman. "Do you know where the men were going who got in the cab that just left?

They're friends of mine."

He shouted and pointed toward the cab. "Do you mean that one?"

"Yes, I saw them leaving and I wasn't able to catch up with them."

"I heard them tell the driver to head toward Lahaina. They didn't say where in Lahaina. I assume they're going out to some of the clubs. That's the best I can do."

"Mahalo (Thanks)." She handed him a five. "I need to catch them if I can."

He whistled and waved for a taxi to come forward. She jumped in the back seat as the taxi driver listened to the bellhop speaking in Hawaiian before springing into action. He turned and yelled over his shoulder in poor English. "I try and catch you friends."

Although the driver made a valiant effort for a few blocks, she surveyed the streets covered in cabs and knew that it would be impossible to know which one they were riding in. She reached in her pocket, pulled out her phone, and called Lenny.

He answered after a long series of rings. "Hello."

"Lenny, this is Amy. I'm heading your way. Edward and Larry jumped in a cab heading for Lahaina while I was at the hotel. Only . . . I don't know where they'll go when they get there. I need you to look out for them and call me if you see them."

"With all the photos you posted on your hate wall, I think I can remember what Edward looks like, but I don't have a clue what Larry looks like."

"He has long, well about shoulder length, straight blond hair with a Swedish young boy look. He's slim and in good physical condition. I don't know how else to describe him."

"I'll do my best. I've discovered many places I want to visit tonight, maybe he'll show. Call me back again later, girl, and I'll let you know where I am."

"I will and thanks."

Amy went from club to club but never located Edward or Larry. While the clubs looked fascinating and would be nice to visit later, at one in the morning, she finally searched all she could. Tomorrow would be a new day and another chance. She needed some sleep.

She hailed another taxi and called Lenny. "I'm heading in. Do you want to ride with me?"

"Not now. I just made some friends, and we're going to eat some breakfast in a little while. I'll be home after that."

"That was fast."

"I guess I'm the lucky one tonight. We'll see you soon, girl."

The ride was short and sweet, and she felt sorry she hadn't moved fast enough earlier to catch Edward and Larry. As the taxi pulled into the long driveway, she studied a car waiting at the front entrance and leaned forward. "I don't know who that is. Can you wait on me for a minute?"

"Sure, I'll be glad to." The driver opened his door and moved around to open her door. As he escorted her to the front steps, the doors to the mysterious car opened and two men stepped out.

CHAPTER 31

Amy arrived early at the convention the next morning and wandered around the organizers setting up last minute tables and posting directional arrows. Luckily, she hadn't been asked to take part in any panel discussions or hear pitches. Her last minute entry helped her keep a low profile.

She was still shaking slightly from the visit by the two FBI agents last night. They had watched her following Edward and hunting for him. They had alerted Edward and Larry and had them ushered back to the hotel. With all the investigations into the murders of the previous agents, she realized she had come under their watchful eye. Only a quick call to her boss in the middle of the night saved her from spending the night answering questions at their headquarters.

Amy didn't know what they told Edward and Larry, but it sure wasn't going to make her job any easier for sure. Lenny made it back to their place just as she planned to leave. He considered it very funny, but he had been too tired to hear all the details.

Amy first planned to attend a general assembly meeting to discuss the state of the art of writing, so to speak. This is the meeting Edward had agreed to participate in as one of the panel members. With her nerves stressed, she wondered if he would remember her or not. And if he did what did he think of her? Also, did he know the pseudonym she wrote critics under?

She walked into the large meeting room and studied a few people scampering around. After continuing to the front, she laid her light sweater across a chair. She wanted to be up front so she would to be able to make eye contact with him.

Next, she went to the room Larry would speak in at

eleven. She slipped some papers on a seat to mark it for her later. She had her plan perfected and only needed a little luck.

The smell of fresh coffee greeted her as she walked into the hall. An attractive Hawaiian girl walked in front of the cart and handed her flowers to put around her neck. "Aloha, it's good to have you here."

"Aloha. It's good to be here." Amy reached over, accepted the flowers, and placed them around her neck. "Mahalo. It's beautiful." The coffee smelled better up close, as Amy motioned to it. The girl poured her a cup. "Mahalo. It smells so good."

"You're welcome. Have a beautiful day."

Amy spent the next hour pacing the floor and chatting with other attendees. Most became very interested in talking to her when they discovered she worked for a publishing house. Perhaps she should've waited until the last minute to come in. She didn't need to get tied up with other people, since she did have a mission to complete.

She walked back into the grand meeting room, which was coming alive with attendees clustering in small groups. She passed a man in his late forties wearing a professional business suit, who glanced at her name tag and the name of her company. He tilted his head to one side. "I didn't know anyone from your company was attending."

"It was kind of a last minute decision for me to come. My name's Amy Jenkins." She reached out her hand to shake his as she read his name tag—Brent Awkward, attorney-at-law.

"I represent many people in the publishing world. World Media has a good reputation."

"Thank you. That's very good to know. I've been with them for a short period of time."

"I generally represent celebrities who want an attorney to negotiate their contracts for them. Most of their books are one time deals and are usually ghost written. Tell me, what do you do for World Media?"

"I work for the executive editor, Mr. Grantland, as a book reviewer. I have the terrifying job of tearing books apart."

"That's definitely a job that brings you a lot of friends."

"Yes . . . but it's necessary. I'm still learning how important it is. The competition is fierce, and only the best will make it."

"Anyway . . . have you been able to find any new talent at conventions like this?"

Amy nodded as she glanced around, hoping to avoid talking to him. "I'm still looking, but I did find one not too long ago."

"Here's my card. Perhaps I can lead someone to you later."

"I'll be glad to take a look at anything you think is good." She pocketed the card and headed to her seat.

Some of the panel members soon moved into their seats as she glanced over her shoulder to study the room filling fast. A man in the corner caught her attention—one of the FBI agents she had talked to the night before. He looked like a statue who was coldly observing the room. She couldn't tell if he was specifically focusing on her, or if he was studying the room in general. Her stomach hurt. She obviously hadn't told him everything, and she hoped they wouldn't find out about her real stalking behavior of Edward.

As she turned around, she caught the first glimpse of Edward moving into the room. He looked tall and lanky, just as she remembered. While big enough to be an athletic type, he looked more like a gentle giant in appearance. His dark brown hair showed signs of balding, which appeared to be something premature for a man of around thirty. He appeared to be a quiet reserved man who would rather be reading a book somewhere than receiving all the attention he received as he made his way forward to the table in front of the room.

He dressed comfortably in dress slacks and a pull over t-shirt. A light beige sports jacket made him appear almost like a college professor. With his posture slightly bent, it looked as if he had trouble adjusting to his height. He also had the small beady eyes that she remembered well. While he was not an attractive guy by many standards, he did offer some interesting and unique qualities.

Amy concentrated on him as he made it to his seat, where she examined one detail after another. Either he recognized her, and he didn't want to acknowledge her, or he stayed deep in thought preparing for the meeting. Since she was directly positioned in front of him, sooner or later he would have to recognize her.

The president of the association facilitating the convention eventually called the meeting to order, and welcomed everybody before going over the agenda. She appeared especially proud and excited about the gala dance scheduled for Sunday night.

Amy started concentrating when they introduced Edward. This is what she had come. She wanted to find out more about him. He raised his hands and started to speak. "I'm so glad to be here today, and it's nice to see several of my authors and friends here. It's hard to believe I've been a literary agent for seven years now. This is the one thing I know, and I'm so thankful I get paid for doing what I love to do."

He paused for a few seconds as he paced himself. "I think it's important to remember several agents who are not with us this year. There's a serial killer determined to target agents out there, and who is still at large. The FBI is doing all they can to track down this murderer, but isn't having much luck. If anyone has any information regarding these killings, please don't hesitate to contact them. One of the agents from the FBI has agreed to address this convention in a few minutes to ask for help. I know this isn't on the schedule, but I feel like it's important to everyone here." Edward waved at the FBI agent in the corner to come forward. The agent walked over as requested.

When on the stage beside Edward, the agent reached out to shake his hand as Edward turned to the crowd. "This is Agent Jackson. Please listen to what he has to say."

"I hate to put a damper on the festivities here, but we've been receiving a lot of pressure to find out who's behind a string of murders. The common denominator on all of these murders is that they're all agents. And all of them had been brutality beaten to death by what appears to be a baseball bat, and all had their faces slashed repeatedly. Nothing was stolen, but all were covered with form rejection letters taped to their bodies. The person we're looking for is thought to be a writer who has been rejected and now has it in for agents. That isn't a lot to go on, but it's all we have at this time. That is why we're here asking for help. If you know of anything that might be useful, please let us know. We'll be here all day today, and we will be easy to find."

He offered a small question and answer session, but soon held up his hands and said he needed to thank Edward for the few minutes he was allowed before turning the meeting back over to him. Everyone applauded as he left the stage. They wanted to thank the FBI for doing what they could.

When Edward regained control of the meeting, he continued, "Now, for the part of the meeting I'm sure you're all interested in—the State of the Art in Writing—I think that is what we're calling it. To start with, anything I say today will be outdated within a few weeks. Computers are taking over the world. Now, that sounds like nothing new, but I've been doing some thinking about it. Our whole life is consumed with electronic gadgets from the time the electronic alarm goes off in the morning until the late night show ends at bed time. During the entire day, we interact with machines, not humans. We, those in the business of writing, I mean the author, agent, publisher and bookseller, are working harder than ever to keep up. I think I might be one of the worst at it, and I'll admit that I also need to get out and enjoy life more often."

He appeared to be looking around to see if he was getting across his message to the audience when she felt he noticed her for the first time. At first he looked stunned, and then the expression on his face changed, as he apparently remembered their meeting and the query letter she had sent him. He paused for a moment to gather his thoughts.

"It's becoming harder and harder to break into writing, and much easier at the same time. I know what it takes in the commitment of time and effort to write a book. The number of large publishing houses is shrinking every day. They're flooded with writers wanting to become published. On the other hand, I see so many alternate forms of publication available today. We'll continue to see electronic publications grow. E-books will outpace print books forever now."

"What I hate most about the way things are going is the loss of personal service we don't have any more. We would love to have the time to work with some of the bright new writers and develop them. And, it does happen from time to time. I think I have a good relationship with my clients and publishing firms, but it's something I have to work at. It's hard to believe sometimes when you receive the typical rejection letter from an agent, but remember that every time an agent or editor takes on a new author, he or she is taking time from a trusted friend they're working hard for also."

He glanced over at Amy and paused for a minute. It appeared he planned to say something, but changed his mind. "I could talk about this all day, but I think it's best if I open the floor, take questions, and try to answer them."

Amy listened while trying to memorize every word. At first, she didn't believe anything he said, but she knew she had to keep smiling for now. She needed him to be able to get to Larry. However, she heard a truth in his words she recently recognized in her own work. He spoke the truth about the limited amount of time and the pressures of responding to all the various query letters. There really wasn't enough time. At the same time, the publication houses had all the manuscripts they could publish.

As the hands went up across the room, Amy had one question she wanted to ask, but knew better. She wanted to know why agents encouraged writers to send query letters or partials to them, while they fully knew they have no time for them. Why couldn't they be honest, and save the heartache that followed?

One girl behind Amy came close to asking the question for her. "How would you go about finding an agent to do a full and honest critique of your work? I want to learn to be a better writer, and I'm willing to do the work and put in the time."

He grinned and looked around the room. "I know this is harsh, and I hope you understand. An agent isn't in the business of doing critiques and being a mentor, except to those he represents and feels like he can sell."

The room turned silent as if they were hearing the dreaded truth for the first time. "This is a business. It's one where an agent only gets paid when a book sales. It's my job to convince a publishing house that you're going to be successful, but how can I do that . . . if you can't convince me you can be? I'm just the middle man."

It made sense to Amy. However, she still fought with the one burning question of why lead someone on and encourage them to send in material? Perhaps one day she'll find her answer.

The meeting finished with a lot of unanswered questions.

Edward glanced in her direction several times. It was like he was waiting on a question from her. She wasn't sure if she missed an opportunity, or not. Only time would tell.

Amy prepared to leave by packing her papers in her bag when she noticed Edward moving off the stage. She moved over to the side of the tables so she would be directly in his path, just in case he had a second to chat.

He chucked as he approached her. "I think we've met before." He stopped to study her badge and wrinkled his face. "You . . . work for a publishing company? I thought you were a writer."

"I wanted to be a writer. It never happened, but I managed to find a job with World Media. I'm one of the assistants to Mr. Grantland."

"I know him . . . but not as good as I should, and we've worked a few deals together. Is he here with you?"

"No, I'm here on my own. Call it part work and part vacation."

"Are you still writing?"

"Not any more. After I received your rejection letter, I decided to try other things."

"That's too bad. I was hoping you could find a good agent. After the night at the convention, I was surprised you sent me a query letter. That's a night I think I'll never forget."

It was a night Amy wished she could remember. "I must have really made an impression on you that night."

"I think we all had too much to drink. I'm sorry if I got out of hand."

Amy decided to confess. "I'll be honest, I don't remember much. . . . Let me restate that, I don't remember anything after we met. I have this tendency to block things out of my mind when I drink too much."

Edward looked at her, trying to analyze her words. "Are you saying you don't remember what happened?"

Amy blushed. "That's exactly what I'm saying."

He whistled softly. "That . . . explains a lot to me. Perhaps we need to have another drink tonight to clear this up and to let me apologize to you. Perhaps I have a way to make it up to you. I'd like to talk to you about World Media. Larry isn't happy with his publisher right now. You have to keep it quiet, but I'd love to hear your opinion."

"You name the place, and I'll buy the first round." She wondered what he wanted to apologize for. She blinked her eyes and hoped she really didn't do what she dreaded with him—surely not.

"We went to a place last night and couldn't stay long. It would be good to go back. It's called "McCray's Bar"".

"I can be at McCray's around six, is that good?"

"Yes, six is doable. I'm looking forward to it, and Larry will be with me." As he turned and started talking to other attendees with questions, she knew he wouldn't have any more time right now to talk.

Amy felt the excitement in her swelling. This was much easier than she had hoped. As she walked out into the lobby, she flipped on her phone and called her office to tell Ike.

Ginger answered the phone, "Mr. Grantland's office. May I help you?"

"Hi, this is Amy. How are things? I wasn't expecting to catch you at the office on a Saturday."

"Hi, I agreed to come in for a little while to type some letters and have them ready to go out after the meeting he's in now. How's Hawaii?"

"Hawaii is a dream. I've some fantastic news to give Mr. Grantland. However, it sounds like he's unavailable now."

"Yes, he'll be in these meetings for a while, as usual. What's the news?"

"I'm having drinks tonight with Edward and possibly Larry tonight."

"Wow, it sounds like you're on the right track. I'll let

him know when he returns to his office. It sounds like you're having a blast in Hawaii."

"Yes, it's going to be a really good week I think. We're planning on seeing what we can after the convention. Tell him I'll call back tomorrow."

"I will, and enjoy yourself . . . I know I would!"

After she finished the call, she walked into the meeting room where Larry was scheduled to give his speech. The chair she had marked with papers was exactly as she had left it. A smile on her face glowed like the proverbial cat that ate the canary. She felt happy, as the goals of getting even with Edward slowly disappearing—well, sort of.

She reached in her bag to retrieve her writing pad to make notes when a large figure stopped in front of her. She glanced up to see Edward standing above her. "Is this chair taken?" He pointed to the chair next to her.

After flashing a quick smile his way, she answered, "Please help yourself, I'm by myself today."

"Thanks, it would be good to have a front row seat to hear one of my best authors."

"I've read some of his work. He's an extremely intelligent person with a real gift in writing. He's well known for developing unforgettable characters. To hear him discuss how he creates them would be fantastic." She knew this would be the time to butter him up. While trying hard not to overdo it, she thought she handled it well.

"I'm sure Larry would appreciate you saying this. He'll join us tonight, so you can tell him then. I'm sure he'll remember you."

"I was that unforgettable?"

"I think both of us were. Tonight, I promise not to drink too much again." He raised his hand giving his best boy scout sign.

"I hope to hear more about it tonight. I've no memory of what happened."

He lowered his voice, and leaned forward. "I need to tell you one thing about Larry, but you have to promise to keep this quiet."

She felt flattered to be gaining his confidence, which surprised her, but made her appreciative. "You have my word."

"I think Larry has homosexual tenancies. He doesn't openly display them, but I can see it in the way he looks at me. It makes me uncomfortable, but I've learned to live with it. I can't wait to see how he reacts when he finds out you're joining us tonight."

"That's unexpected. I had no idea. You have my promise on this."

Larry walked into the room as she heard his name whispered by the people behind them. They both turned to watch him making his way to the small table and chair on the platform. He looked as she remembered him, with his long blond hair reinforcing his strong Swedish look.

She couldn't forget what Edward told her about Larry possibly being gay. Much like her friend Lenny, she considered it such a waste to have such intelligent good looking men not interested in women, but perhaps that's why she hasn't ever been able to find anybody.

After being introduced, Larry started his speech. When he discovered Edward on the front row he waved him over toward him and told the crowd he owed much to the wisdom and direction of his agent. It was then that he noticed Amy. He paused for a minute before giving her a quick wink. She didn't know the exact meaning of the wink and it confused her. She hoped later she would have an answer.

CHAPTER 32

Lenny had already left by the time she had made it back to the house. He left a note asking her to call him later, as he had planned to meet the friends he had made the night before for cocktails.

She didn't know how long the meeting with Edward and Larry would last. It would be good to visit some of the bars tonight, but she didn't want to go solo either. All she could do was play it by ear.

###

The taxi driver soon dropped her off at the bar where she agreed to meet them. It looked normal for a Hawaiian bar, but had a young crowd coming and going. A Japanese man with a tall blonde walked in front of her. It was hard to know for sure, but the tall blonde offered the impression of being a call girl for a Japanese business man who was out on the town and wanting to have some fun. But, then again, she never knew.

The dim lights provided mainly by hundreds of candles placed around the bar highlighted the typical native flowers, and was much in contrast to the neon lights advertising name brand liquors. It impressed her as being a place to have some real fun.

She moved around the customers to check out the place. Running late, she assumed they would've already arrived. From across the bar she saw a large guy stand and wave at her, while Larry stayed in his seat. Amy saw where they had both purchased Hawaiian style shirts, and, of course, the drinks in front of them looked tropical, inviting while sporting little umbrellas in them. Edward pulled a chair out for her. "I'm glad you could make it."

"I'm glad to be here." She glanced over at Larry. "How are you?"

Larry raised his glass. "This is the life."

"I agree. It's the first time I've ever been here, and I'm looking forward to exploring it next week."

Larry spoke next. "How long are you going to be here?"

"We're going to be here for a week. I know that's not long, but we'll take in everything we can."

Larry picked up on the *we,* and asked, "Are you here with someone else?"

Amy felt her face blush with heat. "Yes, I am. A friend of mine arranged a place for us to stay. It's one place you'll have to see."

Edward looked surprised. "Where is your friend tonight?"

"His name's Lenny, and he left me a note saying he was meeting some friends he made last night for cocktails somewhere, and I was to call him later."

Amy noticed the quick glance between the guys. She tapped her fingers against her chin. "It's not what you think. He's an old friend, and we share nothing romantic. We worked together for a while at a bookstore. He has recently started his own interior decorating business."

They didn't appear to be convinced, but willing to play along for now.

A waitress walked over and asked Amy, "What can I get you?"

"I normally order red wine, but tonight I think I'll try something different. What do you recommend?"

Edward spoke first, "These are good, and I think you'll like one."

"I'm in."

The waitress nodded and turned to retrieve the drink.

"I hope this drink isn't too strong. I want to remember this night tomorrow."

Edward cleared his throat and looked over at Amy. "I want to apologize for the last time we had drinks. It's not like me to drink so much."

Larry laughed before leaning forward to take a sip of his drink.

Edward looked at Larry with a smirk of a grin edging out of the side of his mouth. "I think you're the only one sober enough to remember everything. I know you've teased me enough about it."

Larry looked at both trying to decide how to start the story. "I can't remember who had the most to drink the night we met. I think the other author, Michael Hadcock, was the only smart person when he talked us into turning in early. Michael and I had no luck in attracting any girls. You two were busy dancing on the floor, and you both must've been drunk, because you started slow dancing to some fast and funky music."

"You're kidding." Amy's voice carried an edgy embarrassment.

"I'm sorry to say it, but you were putting on quite a show for the crowd."

Amy covered her face. "I'm so embarrassed."

Edward tried to cover his laugh with his hand. "I guess I'm the one who should say I'm sorry."

"I think everything would've been fine, if it hadn't been for the young girl who walked over to you."

Edward let his head sink quickly as if he knew what was coming.

"She stopped you on the floor and told both of you loud enough for many people to hear that she thought you two should leave and get a room somewhere."

Amy looked at Edward for verification. He readjusted his posture, but didn't say a word. "Oh, my gosh, maybe that's why I couldn't remember anything."

"You came close to passing out, and I helped you back to

your room. I'm sorry, but I remember a few intimate moments, but I managed to stumble back to my room. I don't think I've ever been that drunk before. I'm sorry for anything inappropriate I may have done. Needless to say, I was surprised when I received your query letter a few weeks later. I honestly didn't know how to respond to it."

Amy used her hands to cover her face again. "I'm not like that. You must have terrible thoughts about me."

Edward raised his glass as Amy's drink arrived. "I think we should drink to a new beginning, if that's okay with everyone."

Amy scrambled to pick up her glass. "I'll definitely drink to a new beginning."

Amy's phone rang as she finished the toast—Lenny. "Where are you, girl?"

"I'm having drinks with Edward and Larry at McCray's Bar. Wow, do I have a story to tell you!"

"I would love to hear it. We're not far from you. How is it?"

"It's really nice. Come on over and I'll introduce you."

"I've several friends with me. Let me see if I can talk them into it."

"Okay, I'll see you soon."

She turned to the two guys. "That was Lenny. He'll come by here soon. It appears he already has a traveling group of friends with him. He's always like that, but I guess I need to warn you, Lenny's lifestyle is a . . . little different."

Larry's eyes lit up ever so slightly as he glanced over at Edward to see if he read things as he did. "Now, I think I see why you don't have any romantic interest in Lenny."

"Exactly, we're friends who respect each other."

Larry looked over at Edward as if asking for permission to talk. "I find your words comforting. Some people aren't so . . . opened minded; my current editor for one."

Edward looked at Larry. "I know you have some books

210

you want to write that are . . . different, but the image you've been groomed for is necessary to promote your books your publisher is selling now."

"Then perhaps I should write under a different name. It's not like it's the first time it has been done."

Amy spoke, as she studied Larry closer, "I think you might have a good point, and I can understand where you're coming from."

Larry had a big smile. "We need to talk more at a later time. Moving from one publisher to another can be tricky." He faked a jab at Edward. "But . . . that's why I need this guy."

Edward returned the smile. Amy knew Edward needed to keep Larry happy.

Lenny and six other guys soon walked into the bar. He had them all in tow, like little children on the way to a playground. Lenny waved when he saw her. After the three stood when they approached, it took several minutes to make all the introductions.

The conversation soon centered on other nightclubs in the area. It appeared Lenny and his group wanted to make all of them, if they could. Larry appeared to be all ears as it sounded like a lot of fun to him. He constantly studied the group and acted at ease with everyone.

Lenny turned to Amy. "What are your plans tonight?"

"I'm just going to go with the flow I guess." She looked over at Edward for some guidance. Edward, in turn, glanced at Larry.

Larry finally confronted the group. "If you don't mind, I think I'll just fall in with these guys. If you want to go somewhere with Amy, I'll understand."

Edward spoke. "I think that sounds good to me. We can all meet later if you want, but I do need to get some sleep tonight."

Edward looked over at Lenny. "I promise I'll take good

care of Amy tonight and keep her out of trouble."

Lenny looked over at him and whispered, "She's a two drink limit type girl. You'll learn that about her."

He grinned back at him. "I think I've already learned."

\###

After hailing a taxi, Edward and Amy had quickly asked the driver for advice on a quiet place they could hear some authentic Hawaiian music. He had quickly promised to take them to a small place where locals went to relax. When they arrived, it looked exactly like what they wanted—he hadn't disappointed them.

With the music of the slack key guitar playing, Edward continued to study her as he ordered her one more drink. "This is the third one, are you okay?"

Amy felt warm and relaxed, but she still like she could maintain control. "I'm fine."

A presumed local girl started dancing around the club in a grass skirt, she appeared to be not so much into putting on a performance for tourists, but simply enjoying the music and having a good time. In other words, she didn't appear to be part of a paid entertainment. Amy watched several local, cute, and friendly Hawaiian-looking guys flirting with her. This girl's movements became mesmerizing as she swished her hips so smoothly and in rhythm with the music. The graceful flow of her hands perfected the dance.

Amy could only imagine learning how to dance like this girl, as she turned to Edward. "I'd love to learn to Hawaiian dance."

"I've heard of many places here teaching Hawaiian dancing."

"It's going to be such a short week, but perhaps I can work it in. What is it you want to do here?"

He lowered his drink, tossed his head back, and closed

his eyes tight before opening them to refocus on her. "I'm not what you would call the athletic type, but I have a list of things I'd love to try."

"Such as . . ."

"Such as . . . hiking to one of the volcanoes early one morning, and maybe riding a bike back for starters. I've heard the best and easiest place to learn to surf is right here in Maui. What about you, what do you want to do here?"

"I'd like to go whale watching, and maybe go for a balloon ride with a nice bottle of champagne. If I had the money, it would be nice to take a helicopter ride." She remembered she had limited funds available.

Edward started watching the girl dance around the bar. "I can see why people come here and never go back."

Amy studied Edward again. While not a dreamboat, he radiated his own subtle charm. She would love to do some things with him, but she didn't know if it was idle talk tonight, or if he would invite her later.

Edward turned back around to look at Amy. "I think I need to go get some sleep. Tomorrow will be a long day, and we have the Gala tomorrow night."

"Yes, I almost forgot about it. It's supposed to be nice."

"Is Lenny taking you to it tomorrow night?"

"No. He loves getting all dressed up, but he thought he wouldn't know anyone. I think he really wanted to explore the places here, and it looks like he has already made friends."

"In such a case, perhaps I can talk you into going with me."

Amy reflected on the event. "I think going with you would be perfect."

He reached over and squeezed her hand. "I think we need to take you home soon."

She waited for him to lean over and kiss her. She knew he contemplated it, but he hesitated. Feelings of confusion built inside her as she tried to remember her mission. She hoped she could hold it together for the next few days.

CHAPTER 33

Mathew Kinley loved his job—who wouldn't. His life revolved around Hollywood where he made one party after another to keep his contacts in place. Attempting to clear the champagne from his head, he checked his ipod for the next event. He patted one shoulder after another on the way out of movie producer Gary Batonie's massive home, which was full of beautiful people who were all involved in his latest project. Yes, the movie was based on a book his agency handled. He knew he would sell many more to him, but Gary's funds were depleted on this one for now.

After staggering to the front door, he called his wife while he waited on his car to be brought around for him. He wanted to make sure his son completed his project that was due tomorrow at school. Mathew felt proud of the amount of creativity his son had spent on it. Damn, he almost forgot that he had promised his son he would bring home some photos he printed out at work that he needed for his poster. He checked his watch. If he hurried he would have some time.

The trip cost him much more time than he had anticipated. He half jogged to the front door, unlocked it and hurried in. It would only take a minute, so he left the door open. As he switched on the lights, the office came to life. He hurried through the reception area toward his inner office. Why did he forget to take them earlier? Mathew scattered papers around his desk, as the frustration in not locating them angered him. He tried to focus. They had to be here somewhere.

He heard the distinct clink of the lock to the front door. He held his breath and turned his best ear toward the door, but only heard a deathly quiet engulfing his office. He knew he was not alone, as he stepped toward his desk and tried his best to act normal while hoping his gun had not been moved. His shoe creaked on the chair guard protecting the carpet under his desk. He stopped and glanced toward the door.

At first, he breathed easier as a pleasant smile greeted him. Then, he saw the gun leveled at him. He raised his hand slightly to indicate he wasn't armed. "Who are you?"

"Shut up, and do as you're told."

"What do you want—money?"

"No. Just you."

A pair of handcuffs pulled out of a side pocket startled him. Frightening thoughts ran through his mind. Could he make it to his gun? Should he try? His eyes darted toward the drawer.

"I wouldn't try it, if I were you." He caught the handcuffs tossed in his direction. "Put them on, and I mean behind your back."

"I don't think so."

The pistol lowered to his knee. "I can start with one knee cap and then switch to the other. It's all up to you."

The concentration in the eyes gave him no doubt of the resolve to follow through with the threat. "I don't have much money on me, but you can have what is in my wallet."

He watched the intensified strain in the hand holding the gun. Damn, he had no choice. He lifted the cuffs to examine how they worked. He pulled them to his back, turned and snapped them in place as he heard steps approaching him from behind.

The pain of a smash to the back of his head shocked him at first as he stumbled. He attempted to turn and saw a bat swinging directly at his face. His attempt to dodge failed as his jaw popped sideways. He wanted to yell, but another blow silenced him. He staggered toward his desk. The bat hit his back, sending him to his knees.

"You have no clue why you are going to die, do you

jerk?"

He tried to talk, but his broken jaw wouldn't work. He groaned, begging for mercy.

"You're no better than most literary agents. Well, maybe even worse. Yes, everyone knows you're a married man, but in your case, you screw your clients royally as you managed to also get your dick taken care of often, don't you jerk?"

He fell to the floor with his back up against his desk. The words sounded confusing, crazy. "What did I do to you?" His voice mumbled amiss his groans

He watched as papers on his desk showered him. Then, one object after another from the top of his desk hit him in the face.

"You arrogant bastard! How does it feel to have your world torn apart?"

He watched the bat shatter the top of his desk directly above his head. Images of his head suffering such a blow registered.

"Funny, I wonder if I had given you a blow job if you would still reject me also. You jerks are all alike."

The bat continued to tap the top of his desk in an eerie rhythm. Should he pretend to pass out from the pain, to fake his death perhaps?

He started to close his eyes as he watched hands unzipping his pants. What the hell! This was so crazy. Then he felt the vise like grip around his balls and penis. He yelled out loud for the first time, managing to find his voice.

"Oh, I'm sorry. Did that hurt? Here let me make it feel better for you."

He felt a warm, wet sensation sliding over his penis. This is so insane. Then he felt the teeth chewing into him. His vision blurred with pain as the thought of losing his dick sunk in. He knew he was bleeding heavily. He screamed one last time.

CHAPTER 34

Amy watched Lenny become as frustrated as she felt. He obviously knew the importance of the Gala to her. However, he never called himself a hairdresser. Nevertheless, he had agreed to help her, but she knew he tried more or less for psychological support. When she had purchased the dress, she knew it fit perfect; now, she had all kind of reservations.

While her hair didn't look bad and the makeup looked as good as it could be, it was her large hips and breasts that caused the problems. She needed a dress not so revealing. Yes, she had a shawl that could hide much, but she knew she wouldn't have it on all night. This was especially so if they started dancing. The music could be lively and inviting her to dance.

Being a Sunday night, Lenny had planned to stay in and catch some sleep after returning home late from the night before. He looked tired. "Girl, that's about as good as it's going to get. You look . . . spectacular."

"Thanks. I don't know. He'll be here soon. You know it's kind of sad that I haven't dated much in my life. But now, with all the butterflies in my stomach, I can understand why I never tried too often."

The door bell rang. Edward had insisted on coming to pick her up. "He's here . . ."

"Don't worry. I'll answer the door for you and tell him you'll be ready in a moment." He walked off before she could object.

She went back to checking the details. She felt too old to act like this. It was just a stupid Gala she was going to. She eventually lifted her head and walked toward the living room, where she could hear their voices.

Edward was dressed in a dark suit, white shirt, and a bright red tie. His shoes looked highly polished. Wow, he

218

looked nice. However, it was his beaming bright smile which dominated her attention.

"You look fantastic, Amy!" His eyes sparkled as he walked over to her.

"Hey, you're not so bad yourself."

Lenny joined in, "I think you both look fabulous. Now, I wish I was going. You two are going to have a fantastic time. Give me a second, this looks like one of those Kodak moments." He hurried to find his camera.

Edward glanced around the house. "This is a fantastic place. It's huge!"

"Yes. We're lucky to have it."

"Lenny told me he's planning on recommending many changes. He seems so excited about it."

"Unfortunately, we haven't had much time to talk while we've been here."

"I meant to ask him how things went last night with Larry."

"He told me Larry didn't stay out all night with the rest of them, and he thinks Larry is more of a curious on-looker than gay."

"That's more like what I think also."

Lenny walked back into the room. "Give me a big smile, or you'll just hate yourself later." Lenny snapped their picture several times. "I know you're going to have the best time ever."

They soon stepped out of the front door and walked over to a taxi waiting on them. "I'm glad you decided to go with me. It's always a little awkward for me to go by myself."

"I'm sure you have many girls to choose from, and as far as I know . . . you have a girl in every port."

He smirked like a little boy. "I wish. My work doesn't allow for much of a social life. I meet and talk to a lot of people as you know, but when I have free time I prefer to be alone and regain my senses."

They slipped into the back seat of the taxi and drove off. Amy looked around the inside of the cab as she felt acutely aware of Edwards's presence next to her. He appeared gentle and kind and something she didn't expect—a little shy.

The taxi pulled in front of the hotel, where many people in formal attire walked toward the gala. Amy hoped this would be a night to remember.

Then, it happened. A man whose face was both serious and intent recognized Edward and rushed over to him. "Have you heard the news?"

"What news?" Edward responded.

The man looked over at Amy and then back to Edward. "Another agent has been found murdered in his house a short while ago."

Edward's face went stone cold. "Who was it?"

"His name was Mathew Kinley. Do you know him?

Edward glanced at Amy "I don't think I know him."

Amy made a frown. "Me either."

"He operated a small practice and represented celebrities on one time book deals. He lived and worked in L.A. where he also worked in brokering screenplays."

"Do they have any leads on who the killer is?"

"Nothing much. It's the same story as the others."

The man saw someone else and hurried off to tell them. Edward offered a reserved smile as he left. "At this rate, we won't have many agents left."

The news quickly put a damper on the festivities as she watched many people huddle in small groups talking about the recent murder. However, they soon entered a large ballroom decorated in Hawaiian style with native flowers everywhere and they could hear a slack key guitar tuning up. Edward reached over and held her hand as they walked around the tables looking for their name. "I called this morning and asked if we could be put together." He stopped when he discovered his name, and then her name resting next to his. He nodded his head in appreciation of the accommodations.

Amy started to remove her shawl, but she decided to wait for a little while. She placed her purse on the table and studied the room.

He glanced at the open bar. "Would you like some wine?"

"Yes, I think some wine would be good."

They walked over and greeted many attendees along the way. Many writers slipped them a card, or made sly pitches that they hoped would make an impression. Eventually, a bartender looked at them, waiting on their request.

"I think we'll order a red wine, if you have any," Edward said as he leaned forward.

"I have some Merlot and some Cabernet, which would you like?"

He glanced at Amy who shrugged her shoulders, indicating it didn't matter. "I think the Cabernet would be good."

An older woman in her fifties hurried over and stepped directly in front of them. "I think we've met before, my name's Catherine."

"Good to see you again." Edward appeared to be at a loss of words to say anything else.

"I'm so glad you made the dance tonight." She looked over at Amy. "I hope you don't mind me stealing at least one dance with him this evening."

Amy looked over at Edward. "I guess I can let you have one dance." She sneaked him a quick sideway wink.

The lady seemed pleased as she turned and left to chase after other targets. "Now, I think I remember why I don't like coming to these things," Edward whispered.

A couple bumped into them from behind as the busy location next to the bar grew. For the next twenty minutes they tried hard to make it back to their table, and felt lucky when the band started to play some music to allow some dancing before the awards presentation. They both enjoyed the escape opportunity to disappear from the constant parade of people.

The music played soft and measured—perfect for slow dancing. His suit made him look charming and pleasant, and it also had a tendency to make him stand straighter and not slump as he so often did. He raised his arms in a small frame, but his elbow was lower than it should have been. At least he made an attempt.

She stepped into his frame and noticed his eyes. They still looked beady, but not as haunting as before. It's strange how a person's appearance can change over time. He stood much taller than Amy, so she had to reach high to place her hand on his shoulder.

His large hand engulfed her much smaller right hand as he held her in position. He danced with a simple two step, as his eyes stayed focused on her face waiting on her to look up. She could feel his stare. "What?"

"I was thinking of the first night we danced."

She laughed. "From what I've heard, I think it's a good thing I can't remember it."

He returned the smile and continued to dance. "I guess I'll agree that perhaps it would be good for us to start over." The music soon ended, and the lights blinked, indicating it was time to eat and start the presentations.

At the end of the presentations, the speaker announced a winner in a raffle. "As you all know, this allows you to have your query letter, outline, and first fifty pages reviewed by no other than Edward Lawson. He's considered one of the top literary agents in the business, and I'm sure we would all agree this is an incredible honor." She motioned over to Edward for him to stand. As he stood and looked around he flashed a large smile, which made Amy proud to be sitting next to him.

With the presentations over, the band started to tune up again. The lady who asked for a dance earlier rushed to the table with large puppy eyes. Edward glanced over at Amy as if to say 'save me soon—please.' Amy started to laugh at the situation, but this laughter changed when several guys headed her way as she became a sitting duck.

And so that's the way it went, on and on, during the night. Several hours later, when they finally had a free minute together, they searched for an exit to escape.

They walked the hallway to the hotel lounge where Edward stopped to ask, "Do you want to have a drink here?"

"We could if you want."

"Or, we could go somewhere else if you want?"

She considered his question for a minute before answering. "You know I haven't been to the beach since I arrived, have you?"

A smile curled out of the side of his mouth. "I think a walk on the beach at night would be perfect." He looked at his suit. "Perhaps I should go change and then take you to your place. What do you think?"

"Sounds like a plan to me."

Amy felt glad they decided to change clothes before going to the beach as she quickly slipped into clothes much cooler and more fun. Edward looked pleased as he waited on her to join him in the grand ballroom of the large estate-sized house. "I think we both will be glad we changed later." They went out to the waiting taxi at Amy's place. A warm breeze blew which added a festive feeling to the air. Edward leaned forward to talk to the driver. "We don't know the area well yet, but would like to go to the beach somewhere to walk, what do you recommend?"

His wide smile looked genuine, and as if he had been

asked this question before. "We have two beaches close to here. The names of the beaches are Kapalua and Kaanapali."

"I don't know one from another. Which one do you think would be best? And by the way, I would love to stop and buy some champagne and glasses."

"Not a problem."

###

The taxi driver soon let them out right at the beach where the lights from the hotels and condos lit it up with a soft glow. Amy watched the waves pushing in toward the beach which offered everything she could ever dream of. Edward reached for and squeezed her hand as they walked. The water felt warm and pleasant as they ventured timidly into it. Neither said a word as they glanced around at the beautiful coastline. They continued for almost thirty minutes before either spoke. Edward carried the bottle of champagne, which was far from cold now, and the glasses as he nodded toward several chairs left close to the beach by someone. "What do you think? I don't think anyone will care if we borrow these."

"It looks good to me." They occupied the seats as he started working on the cork which soon exploded, throwing the cork into the surf. They laughed as he turned to pour the two glasses. "I think I had visions of doing this one day, but considered it all an impossible dream."

"This is a fantasy I'm sure many people have dreamed of," she said as she accepted the first glass.

After he poured his glass he raised it in a toast. "To Hawaii, friendship, love and . . . what else did I miss?"

"I think you have about covered it." They touched their glasses and sipped some of the champagne. It perfected a beautiful night, and helped them to both relax as the champagne soon disappeared.

224

After walking the beach, and having a little champagne, it felt incredible to her as to how she could tell someone her feelings and opinions. She slipped her arm around his waist, and he placed his arm over her shoulders to keep her close to him as the night turned cooler during their walk.

As they came to one point where the walk turned difficult they decided to turn back, but he hesitated in front of her for a minute. The focus of his eyes roamed around her face. Since she didn't run or move away from him, he perceived this as a sign of acceptance and moved in closer to her. Both hands moved to her waist and slid to her back as he pulled her closer to him. He leaned over to her and kissed the top of her forehead while she closed her eyes and breathed in the moment.

His hands grazed the side of her head as his fingers weaved through her thick blonde hair and offered her a gentle massage. "Your hair feels so soft and smooth."

"Thanks," she whispered. "Your hands feel good."

Apparently satisfied, he lowered his eyes to her lips and studied them as he adjusted his head to reach her height. He tilted his head to one side as he offered a soft contact with her lips. While not a firm kiss, and more of an exploratory first touch, he pressed so close she could feel him breathing. Her throat felt dry as she waited for him to return. She hoped he didn't notice her body tremble as she waited. While this felt new and thrilling to her, she didn't want him to know she was so . . . inexperienced.

His lips pressed hers the next time with more authority and warmth. She stopped breathing. The scenery around her vanished as he became the only item in her world. His hands pulled her head harder into him as he continued melting into her. The moisture of his lips felt intense as the kiss continued to drive her into a world of fantasy she wasn't prepared for.

When she felt him pull away from her lips, she could still

feel his presence so close to her. She opened her eyes to see him staring into her eyes as if to ask how she liked it.

Offering a small smile of pleasure she stared deep inside his eyes. "Wow!"

"Thanks. It was good for me also." They turned to walk along the beach. She snuggled as close to him as she could. He did the best he could to keep her warm. He whispered in a deep vibrating voice, "I never dreamed I would find a girlfriend at a convention like this."

Wow, he's already using the word "girlfriend" this soon. "It's funny how fast you can get to know someone when you let yourself be open and responsive."

"I agree."

She knew now might be as good a time to tell him something as ever. "I've never had a boyfriend before; at least not a real one, anyway."

He laughed. "My life hasn't allowed for a girlfriend before either. Keep this a secret, but all of this is new for me."

"You've never had a girlfriend before?"

"Never. I'm really surprised at myself tonight. This is totally out of character for me. It appears you have a way of bring me out of my shell when we meet."

She recognized the reference to the first meeting and laughed. "I've had guys interested in me before, but I'm sure for only one thing. Being full-size isn't always a blessing."

He laughed as he glanced in their direction. "I'd say that I haven't noticed them, but I'd be lying if I did. In fact, I've been trying hard not to notice them. I didn't want you to think I was a pervert or something."

"I guess I'm sensitive about them. One day I'll have to tell you some stories, but it will be much later."

"That will be fine. I'm sure you have much more experience than me."

She didn't know how to take the comment, and decided to stop for a minute. "There's one thing I think you should know and this is embarrassing as well."

"What?"

She paused and breathed in a large breath of air to be able to say, "I've never really had a boyfriend as such."

He intuitively paused for a minute before he turned to start walking again. He then stopped and whispered as he moved closer to her. "This is going to be fun, and I think our secrets are safe with each other."

"Yes, very safe."

###

They explored the island for most of the week on an almost nonstop sightseeing and exploration expedition. The hike up and back down the trail to Haleakala, which means "house of the sun", had exhausted them, but it was well worth the trip to see the volcano site. They had both returned covered in sweat from the trip.

After having decided to go to Edward's hotel first to let him shower before going to Amy's place, she fell on the bed exhausted as Edward headed for the shower. He glanced over at her and teased. "You could . . . join me if you want." His eye brows arched upward in his humor.

"In your dreams." She joked back.

He closed the door with a small laugh.

Amy knew the week would soon be over, and they did have a lot of fun. What would happen to them when they left the day after tomorrow was unclear, especially since they both worked all the time.

She had put him off several times when he made small advances. In reality, she wished he tried harder, and she had come close to giving in several times. Edward was, as he admitted, inexperienced in getting her excited enough to throw caution to the wind.

As she lay on the bed she became more and more aware of her inner desire, one which grew like a craving which wouldn't recede. It finally built to the point she knew she couldn't resist any longer. "It's now or never."

She stood and lifted the tank top over her head before reaching around to unfasten her bra. It dropped to the floor as she studied her breasts in the mirror. They looked too large, but they were still a little firm and upright. However, she knew that wouldn't last forever.

As she began to unzip her pants she started to reconsider, but when she heard the water starting to run, she lowered them to the floor. She looked at her image again in the mirror for a moment as she slipped out of her panties and her completely nude and vulnerable body reflected in the mirror.

Since he had left the door unlocked, she eased it open and watched the steam escaping from the shower. She shut the door and walked over to the curtain. "Do you have room for one more?"

He snatched the curtain to one side. With his hair dripping wet, water droplets falling off his eyebrows, and soap suds covering his slightly hairy chest, he pulled the curtain open wider to make room for her. "Absolutely."

She stepped into the shower and against his wet body, trying to huddle under the hot water with him. He pulled her close as he wrapped his arms around her. Her breasts pressed into his upper stomach and lower chest as the water and soap made her melt into him. Her curly hair went limp as the hot water bonded them together.

He grazed his fingers behind her back as he started massaging her with his hands, moving in larger and larger circles. She felt motionless as she rested beside him, and held onto him, as if she was in a dream that she never wanted to end.

When he reached up to her shoulders with his hands, he pushed her slightly away from him to look directly in her face. As her eye makeup ran around her eyes, he grinned and reached for a small wash cloth to wipe it. He soon dropped the cloth and leaned over to kiss her deeply.

She felt fully aware of all of his body. His hand worked its way lower to her breasts and he used his thumbs to make circles around her nipples that instantly made them hard and rigid. She tried not to moan, but lost the battle as he relentlessly made them harder and harder.

His penis pressed close to her and expanded moment after moment. She had tried hard to avoid looking at it when she entered, even though she wanted to know what he looked like. Now, she felt it pulsating faster every second.

She sucked in another breathe of air as he played with her nipples between his thumb and finger. He released one as he reached for her hand and enclosed it in a small squeeze. His mouth parted for a minute as she turned her head to one side offering her neck to him, which he kissed before he began sucking on it.

He squeezed her hand again as he guided it to his waiting penis. She tensed as she felt her hand touch it. Then she opened her hand and cupped her hand around it as it expanded more with a pulsating reaction to her touch.

He reached back around her and pulled her close to him again. His hardness thrashed at her in uncontrollable movements of his hips. He leaned over to be able to reach her butt. His large hands established a good enough hold to lift her off of the ground. *Oh my god, this is it! I'm actually going to make love to him, and in a shower no less.* She opened her legs to wrap around him as she let his penis slide along her stomach toward her.

"Are you nervous?" His voice barely in a whisper turned to a moan.

She felt her face blush as he held her closer to him. "You

know I've never done it like this before. I hope I don't disappoint you."

"I don't want to hurt you. Are you sure you're ready? Once I get started, I know it will be impossible for me to stop."

She moaned again as he caressed her rear he was holding. "Perhaps we should wait until we get to the bed for the first time."

CHAPTER 35

Amy felt like a fulfilled woman all day as she explored the island for one last time. She had never made it back to her place the night before. Edward had stayed constantly beside her, laughing and joking. Lenny had called to check on her and had wanted to meet with them for lunch. She knew that he enjoyed the week and had made many friends from all over the world, and he was now discussing the possibility of moving his interior decorating business to Hawaii permanently.

They planned to meet at a small café on the Kaanapali beach she heard offered some interesting Hawaiian food like a Kalua pig cooked in an imu. While they waited, they enjoyed some tantalizing java from the Kona Region they visited earlier.

Lenny spotted them instantly as he arrived. He walked in alone and wore a loose-fitting Hawaiian shirt that was unbuttoned in the front, and some new white shorts. His walked appeared to be stiff and awkward. As he came closer, Amy started to laugh. She knew she shouldn't, but she couldn't help herself. He looked red—very red.

"Don't say a word. This is just not the least bit funny." Lenny glanced at her from underneath a large hat he had purchased to provide better protection.

"What happened?"

"I meant to tell you on the phone last night when we talked, but I was too . . . well, embarrassed."

"I would have been glad to help you. It looks like it hurts."

"I'll be fine. I just can't believe it. I went to the beach for a quick look yesterday morning. I saw some, humm, these European guys walking on the beach." He raised his head upward as in praise. "I hope I can get the chance to thank the guy who designed swim suits for European men." Amy rolled her eyes as Edward sat and grinned. "I just didn't know they were planning on walking all the way around the island. I must have followed them like a little stray kitten."

Amy couldn't keep from laughing. "I'm sorry, I really am."

"Anyway, I've had a very memorable time here, and I'm so sorry it's almost over." Lenny examined his sunburned arms again. "We need to pack and clean the house tonight before we leave. It's the least we can do to show respect for them letting us, you know, use it for free."

"I agree." This would cost her some time, but she knew it was needed.

"I have some plans on decorating it. If they like what I propose, they may let me come again. We'll see." He turned to Edward and looked around for a minute to make sure he wouldn't be heard. "I'm not so sure if Larry had a good time or not."

"What makes you think such?" Edward asked.

"He's confused on who he is. I think he wanted to be with me and the friends I made, but when it comes time to party, he excuses himself. He's kind of shy, but intriguing none the less."

"He's a good writer and he's been looking forward to this trip. We're supposed to see him here soon also. I think he did have a good time, and I want to thank you for spending time with him for me."

"In that case, I think I'll leave before he sees me like this. Perhaps after a nap and a little attention to these burns, I'll look better. Tell him I'm sorry I missed him." He winked and headed for the door.

"I wonder why he left so fast." She watched him make a hasty retreat. "There appears to be more to the story than he told us. He'll talk to me more later on tonight."

Edward held Amy's hand as they drifted off into their

own world for a while. The golden moments of silence slowly itched into her mind as she wished this would last forever. However, she knew it would soon be over, and she would have to go back to the real world.

Larry soon walked in. He stood tall and his hair had lightened from the sun to a shiny yellow glow. He looked happy as he recognizing them. "Hello, you two. It's nice to see that you're still together."

"We're enjoying some great coffee. This . . . I'll definitely be taking back. It's exactly what I'll need, staying up late and catching up on all my back reading,"

"I'm so glad I made this trip. I had many questions I've been trying to answer and now I think I know." Larry continued to nod his head as he spoke.

"That's good to know," Amy said.

"And . . . I think seeing the two of you together has helped me to realize something." Amy and Edward turned to each other with a puzzled look on their faces. "I thought I'd never be able to find a perfect girl for me, and that maybe it was me, and I wasn't good-looking enough to attract one."

"Don't be silly. You're a nice looking guy," Amy replied.

He blushed slightly, as he continued. "I assumed maybe I was destined to be with guys like your friend Lenny. He's an interesting guy by the way. Maybe a little strange, but all of us are."

"Lenny's a great friend, but he's who he is, and nothing else."

"The two of you made me think maybe someone else is out there for me, and that it's simply a matter of time."

Amy reached over and wrapped her hand around Edward's arm. "I used to think the same. I can now tell you that you're absolutely right."

CHAPTER 36

Amy hurried along the sidewalk. With this being her first day back at work in the city, she wanted to find out how far behind she had fallen. The books she had dragged with her to Hawaii were still unread, but she felt glad for taking the time off. Now, however, she had to pay the price. At least she had some good news regarding Larry, who would probably be switching to World Media as soon as all the details could be worked out. Edward would be calling soon to talk to Ike.

Ginger sat at her desk when Amy walked in, but she didn't offer Amy her normal jolly smile. "Mr. Grantland has been waiting on you." She touched her intercom button. "She's here."

"What?"

"Go on in." Ginger then offered her a thumb up. "I think everything will work out fine."

Amy was confused. "What's up?"

Before Ginger could answer, the door opened and Ike walked out. "Hello. I know you had a busy trip, but we have a visitor this morning who wants to talk to you."

She walked in as he closed the door. A man in a dark suit setting at one of the chairs in front of his desk stood and faced her. She recognized him in an instant as the man from the FBI she had talked to in Hawaii.

"How are you? I heard you had a good time in Hawaii after I left."

"Yes . . . as a matter of fact it was the best time of my life."

He turned to Mr. Grantland. "It would be good if we could talk in private, if you don't mind."

"I agree. Let me move you to a private meeting room around the corner." Ike walked out to find a room.

"Thank you." The agent offered as Ike left.

Amy worried about what was going on. "Am I in trouble? Do I need a lawyer?"

"You're not a suspect in any crime. However, it's possible you're responsible. I'll explain everything in a minute."

After Ike returned, the three walked to a small meeting room. As they walked in, Ike asked, "Is there anything I can get for you?"

"I think we'll be fine, but I have a lot of questions for Amy, and this may take some time."

"I'm sure she'll help you in any way she can. We also want to do our part. Some of these guys were friends of ours here at World Media." Ike nodded at Amy as he turned and left.

"I know you're a little bit anxious in this meeting, but I assure you we've checked out your background intensely. If you were going to be arrested, we would have already charged you with a crime."

"I still don't understand." Her hands began to sweat. She would definitely need to increase her medication tonight.

"First let me say that you created a large panic in Hawaii. When you went after Edward, I thought you might be connected to the serial killer we've been searching for."

"I'm not a murderer!"

"I can believe you. Our investigation indicated you were never close to the murders."

"Then what do you want with me?"

"I decided to do some follow up investigations on you after I found you following Edward in Hawaii. I discovered you've been stalking him for a long time."

"Stalking?"

"Yes. I think stalking might be a good word. You've been doing everything possible to destroy his career, from writing bad book reviews on the books he's associated with, and bad mouthing him to others . . . shall I go on?"

Amy waited in quiet indifference as the expected panic smothered her. She had been caught. "However, legally you haven't broken any laws—at least not federal ones." He pulled out a seat next to her and looked her square in the eyes. "I need to ask you some questions." She sat quiet while he indicated he understood what he was up against, but continued to smile. "I'm going to ask you some questions, and I hope you can help me."

He placed a folder he was carrying on the table. "I need to know what you know about any of these people in these photos." He placed the first one in front of her. The man in the photo appeared to be in his late forties with dark hair and a genuine pleasant smile. "Do you recognize him?"

She glanced at the photo several times and shook her head. "I don't think so."

"His name was Mitchell Lloyd, the first literary agent to be murdered. He wasn't only beaten to death, but his face was sliced repeatedly with a knife, leaving him completely unrecognizable. His fingers were pounded until they left nothing but blood stains and shattered bones." He paused. "And . . . his sexual organs had been given the same treatment."

Amy raised her hand to her mouth in horror at the words she was told. "Why are you telling me all of this?"

"We know you weren't in the same cities when these murders occurred, but what we think now, is that someone has copied your extreme dislike of this one agent and amplified it. After the first murder, the killer has become addicted to it and is now our serial killer."

"That's terrible. I could never kill anyone!"

"Let me show you why we think this." He reached in his bag and retrieved copies of e-mails and her published articles. It felt like her heart rocketed through her throat. He did have lots of research on her. She looked at the e-mails and the articles he made copies of. "Now, I want to show you something which isn't general knowledge. I first need to warn you these photos are very graphic."

The muscles in her stomach tightened as she forced a smile at him, because she could only guess what he was going to show next. The agent reached into the file and retrieved another photo. It was a crime scene photo of a bloody corpse. The office around the victim looked totally destroyed and like a bomb had exploded. Then, she saw a paper size note on the front of his chest which read "REJECT THIS, JERK". His face had been so badly cut she had a hard time recognizing him as a human. She needed to turn away. She felt sick.

"I know this is hard on you, and I'm sorry for all this. What attracted our attention is the fact that the agent you didn't like, you used the word "JERK", just like this in the note.

She understood exactly what he was saying now as it became perfectly clear. "I didn't mean for anyone to die."

"We know that."

"I never knew this agent, so how can you say I'm connected to him?"

"We don't know the answer as of yet. That's the reason I'm talking to you now. I'm hoping you can fill in some holes in our theory." His attitude was forceful and unrelenting as he continued to push.

"I'm not sure what I can do." She started sobbing as the information sank in.

He paused for a minute before he continued asking questions. "The second agent was James Aaron. What can you tell me about him?"

"I know he's well known. I'm not positive, but I think I may have mailed my book query to him. That's about all I remember."

He pulled the next one out. "This is Blake Ashman. Can

you tell me anything about him?”

“I remember hearing he was murdered, but that’s all. And I also heard he had a family.”

“Yes, he had a wife, and two little boys that don’t have a father anymore.” He didn’t stop. It was as if he wanted the impact of the series of murders to sink in. He watched every little movement and sign she made, obviously looking for clues.

“Were all the guys killed in the same fashion?”

“All were murdered in a similar fashion. Its close enough we have little doubt that we’re dealing with a serial killer.”

“This is very scary. You’ve got to have some idea as to who this is.”

“We’ve received thousands of leads and tips, but nothing has proved credible. It appears the only connection we can make is with your articles.”

Amy lowered her head as she processed an overload of information and guilt. This wasn’t good. She would soon need major help if this continued. “I’m not sure you know, but I have a problem with a bipolar disorder.”

“I know. That’s in your file. We contacted your psychiatrist, but we didn’t get anywhere with patient-doctor restrictions. I think she knows we’re going to talk to you, and if I needed to I could call her at anytime to help you. How are you handling this so far?”

“Not very well.”

“I truly understand. This will not take much longer.”

He pulled out another photo. “This is Mathew Kinley. He was also a family man.” Amy looked but acted unresponsive as he pushed the photo closer. “Can you tell me anything about him?”

“I never heard of him until his death. When I heard that he was killed, I was with Edward. He didn’t know him either.”

A look of interest crossed his face when he heard Amy

mention Edward's name. "Let me ask you about Mr. Lawson."

She knew this was coming at some time. "What do you want to know?"

"I'm confused. It appears that this is the guy you really hated with a passion. Yet, at the convention in Hawaii, I saw you two acting like two love birds running around."

"A lot has happened since I first met him. This is a long story. Let me say things have a way of changing over time."

"It may be long, but I think it would be useful to hear it later. It's surprising this killer hasn't targeted him. For all we know she may have, and she hasn't been successful yet. This may be why the killer has hit on other agents."

She lifted her hands to her face again. "Oh, my God, so do you think I might've placed Edward in danger?"

"That's exactly what I'm thinking now."

"How much of this does Edward know?" She hoped nothing, but assumed otherwise.

"He knows to be safe and that a serial killer is still at large. He's lucky in the fact he leads a quiet life, and that he is in his office or his apartment most of the time, both of which are extremely well guarded."

"That's good."

"But . . . if we can't find out who is behind these murders, then it maybe only a matter of time before he's one of the next victims."

Amy shivered as she realized he might be right. She then wondered how Edward would take the news of her being responsible for trying to ruin his career, and also placing his life in danger. "Edward and I are becoming close, and we had a fantastic time in Hawaii. It was the best time of my life."

"I saw for myself. It would be nice to know how this happened."

"Are you going to tell him about all of this?"

"We have an obligation to let him know his life is in danger, but since this is still all a theory we can't tell things we're not able to fully support. Even the FBI doesn't like to spread rumors."

"Thank you so much for that." She breathed in deeply.

"It's up to you to warn him if you can. I know that's not an easy job. For now . . . I want to ask for your help."

"What else can I do?"

"We're still trying to piece together who our attacker is. We would like for you to work with one of our profilers."

"I think I have no choice in this, do I?"

"You always have a choice, but I hope you make the right one this time."

Amy lowered her head again as these events pounded on her. "Sure, let me know what I have to do."

"I'm going to have one of our profiler meet with you. She's out of town, but she'll be here in a few days. I'll contact you tomorrow with a time and place."

"Okay. Let me know."

He stood and handed her his card. "I'm sorry for having to meet you at your office, but it was very urgent that we talk to you as soon as possible. We have no idea when the killer will strike again."

As he left the room, Amy lowered her head to the table and started to cry. Her heart raced, and she tried to control her breathing. She needed to maintain a clear head since she had no doubt she was losing control. This was so dangerous.

Ike entered the room in seconds. "What happened?"

"They're investigating the serial killings of the literary agents, and they think my articles might somehow be tied to it."

Ike shifted his weight from one leg to another. "That sounds ridiculous. If that was the case, we would all be suspects."

"I think they're looking under every nook and cranny

they can."

"I'm sorry. Perhaps I should've stopped him earlier from harassing one of our employees."

"It's okay. He showed me photos of the murdered agents. They looked gruesome."

Ike bit his tongue. "I'm so sorry. This isn't a good day back at work for you. If you want to go home and recover, it will be fine."

"Please, give me a few minutes and I'll be okay."

"Take all the time you want. I'll send Ginger in here to be with you."

"Thanks, I'll be fine." But . . . she was wrong.

CHAPTER 37

It was almost nine that night when the phone rang. "Hello, this is Edward. How are you?"

Amy sat still as she responded, "I'm fine. How are you?"

"I'm swamped. You wouldn't believe the messages and e-mails I received while I was gone. I really have to pay for the time off dearly now."

"I'm sorry. It's my fault I pulled you away from your work at the convention."

"Don't say a word. I enjoyed it."

"I wish I could help you catch up."

"I'm sure you have your own stack to work on, but it's hard for me to get you off of my mind. You've been on it all day."

"Really!"

"Yes. Do you have time to talk?"

"Sure, I'm at home recovering from jet lag I think."

"I was talking to Larry today, and he's still interested in exploring a change in publishing companies. He's committed on the one he's currently writing, but will not sign any extensions with the current house. We'll hear some screaming, but it will work out."

"That's good news. I know you'll love working with Ike."

"Who's Ike?"

"I'm sorry; many people don't know him by his nickname. That is Mr. Grantland."

"It sounds like you know him well." His voice carried an exploratory tone.

"He introduced himself to me as Ike when we first met. It's a long story regarding how I came to work for him. I'll tell you one day."

"I think it would be an interesting story. I know we both

returned from a vacation of sorts, but I've something I hope I can talk you into soon."

"What's that?"

"I'm such a workaholic that I've devised a way to keep my sanity. Every other week or so, I go to a cabin I own in the Catskill Mountains. Almost nobody knows about it. I take a bag full of reading material, and simply chill out and read with no distractions."

"Sounds like heaven. I'd love to see you again."

"Me too. The cabin has worked out good for me for several years. I'd love to spend some time with you there."

"Give me a little notice and I'll try to work it out. I'm sure my boss will let me if he knows I'm reading material for him."

Amy slid lower and dug in deep under the covers. She knew that one day she would have to tell Edward the whole story. It wasn't going to be easy, but she would have to figure out how to do it.

The conversation lasted until late in the morning. She didn't realize how late it had become until she glanced at the clock. "I have to go."

"I'll call tomorrow if that's okay."

"Tomorrow will be good."

CHAPTER 38

Amy made it to the federal building with time to spare. She felt nervous and her stomach was all tied up in knots. She slept very little the last two days and she knew she showed signs of fatigue in her large drooping eyes. As she walked through the large front entrance as a security guard greeted her, "May I help you?"

"I'm here to see Agent Arrington." Amy tried to smile, knowing she failed miserably.

He walked over to a counter and retrieved a pad. "Please sign in." As she accepted the pad and started to fill out the information, he asked, "Do you have any weapons or knives with you?"

"No. I don't have any."

He pulled out a metal detector and scanner her anyway. "Go to the elevator and the seventh floor. Her office is straight ahead."

"Thanks." She didn't like this place. It looked too formal and intimidating. After she made it to the seventh floor, she walked toward a woman in front of her at a desk. "I'm here to see Agent Arrington. My name's Amy Jenkins."

"How are you?"

"I'm fine . . . I think."

"She's expecting you, so let me direct you to the meeting room you'll be using." She stood and walked along a hallway, leading the way to a small room with a conference table and a small TV on one side.

After the receptionist closed the door, the quietness of the room quickly overwhelmed her as she waited. She didn't know how much longer she could keep it together. Just as soon as this meeting ended, she had planned on visiting her psychiatrist's friend for advice on her condition.

A woman in her late thirties soon entered the room and

smiled. She didn't look like an FBI agent at all, as she reached out her hand and shook Amy's hand firmly. "I'm so glad to have you come in today."

"I still don't know exactly what I'm doing here."

"I know you're a little anxious, but I promise you've nothing to fear here. We need your help in solving several cases we're working on."

"How can I help?"

"It's my job to give the guys in the field guidance in describing a suspect in a murder as best I can. It's not always an easy job, but it's what I'm trained to do. The more information I have, the better I can predict."

"I've watched the FBI on the movies. That's about as close as I can guess what you do."

Agent Arrington laughed. "I promise you, it's not near as exciting as it's portrayed in the movies. It involves long hours of digging and digging. Then it all comes down to an educated guess."

Amy twisted in her seat. "I'm not trained in this."

"We know that, but what we do today is important. For one thing, I know you showed feelings of anger and hostility when you received the infamous rejection letters from literary agents."

"I think everyone feels the same way when they receive them—they hurt."

"Yes, I'm sure they do, and I'll be asking you many questions about them today."

"But why ask me, rather than someone else?"

She slowed for a minute and refocused a serious look on her face. "As I think you were told, the killer is probable someone who has read your articles or e-mails, or had some contacts with you, and then decided to do what you couldn't dream of doing."

"I find this hard to believe."

"I'm going to give you some police reports to read which

are confidential, but I think necessary for you to understand where I'm coming from." She handed a file to Amy. "I'm going to get some coffee, would you like some?"

"Yes, I think I might. I haven't slept much the last few days."

Amy started reading the files. In all cases, she noticed many similarities. The word "JERK" was written on a note or scratched into either the victim's body or furniture. The face, fingers and often groin area had been battered, cut or mutilated repeatedly to the extent of being totally obliterated. Whoever the killer was, acted viciously, and apparently insane in their killing methods.

Amy started noticing other details in the killings. It was always men in their early thirties, and while several of them had families only one had none. In each case, the rejection letters they sent out were poured out over them or distributed around them. Their files had been destroyed as well as, in most cases, their computers smashed.

Agent Arrington walked in with the coffee which smelled good. "I see you're studying the files. It's gruesome, I agree, but they tell a story that we need to be able to read."

"I'll have to agree it appears to be someone who has been rejected by an agent, but with the number of requests they receive it could be anyone."

"Our job is to lower the number as much as we can. While we've little to go on, we believe the killer is a female with long blonde hair."

"Why?"

She looked straight at her without emotion. "It appears several of the men were being treated to oral sex before they died, and we've recovered several long blonde hairs at the scene."

Amy didn't ask how they knew this, but knew they had some information she really didn't want to hear about. "I see."

246

"Why the face and fingers are mutilated after she kills them is still a mystery. Why the groin area is mutilated is obvious. It appears the killer has strong jaws."

"Perhaps the fingers are mutilated so they'll never be able to type again."

"Perhaps, but we think this is done after the victim's dead."

"It sounds like you have a wacko on your hands."

"That's an understatement. This'll be one for the records."

"Couldn't you do a check of all the rejection letters these agents sent out and find a common name?"

"I'll assure you that we're trying to do that, but it's not working so well."

"Why is that?"

"We may be hunting for someone who has never written anything and is using this serial thing as a cover, or may not like agents for some other unknown reason."

"I've seen sites all over the net of agents who are on black lists of some kind or other. Have you checked them?"

Agent Arrington paused for a second. "That's an idea I've considered. I'll put someone on it immediately. Excuse me for a minute."

Amy studied the photos and the police reports. This was the first time she had ever been involved in an investigation. She considered one thing which made sense—killing agents would never get a writer published.

Arrington returned in a few minutes. "It will not take long to research the internet sites."

"I was thinking of something you said about it might not be a writer. But, if not, who could it be?"

"That's what is so hard about this case."

"In my articles, I never mentioned specific agent's names. Yes, I had one agent I was unhappy with, and I tried to get even with by writing bad articles about the books he was involved with, but he's safe and doing fine. In fact, we've since reconciled and are close now."

"It could be that he's so well protected, she couldn't get to him."

"I hope he stays safe."

"Don't worry. He's under a careful eye right now."

Amy rubbed her eyes for a minute. "I also know of many blogs that agents, publishers and writers use. Maybe you can find a connection in them somewhere."

"Perhaps." The agent looked over at Amy again. "I want you to do something for me if you have some time."

"Sure, if it will help."

"We've accumulated as many of the rejection letters as we could from the computers and files of the deceased agents. Would you be willing to go through them and see if anything would trigger such a series of murders in your opinion?"

"Yes, but I'm not sure what I'll be looking for."

"Trust me. We've read these many times, but a fresh set of eyes might see something we haven't seen."

"I know you're constructing a profile on the murderer. Can I ask what you've come up with so far?"

The agent looked first like she was going to evade the request, but tapped her fingers on the table as she changed her mind. "I think maybe it would help if you know what I know, to some extent; however, I can't tell you everything as you would guess."

"I know that."

"I think we're looking for a young middle-aged blonde haired woman who is attractive and has the ability to travel at will. She probably has mental problems in the past, but still highly educated and well read. She's definitely right handed. How am I doing so far?"

"Good, but still a long way from narrowing the field."

"That's why we're hoping you can help."

"What have you told Edward?"

Her stare at Amy intensified. "He knows to be safe right now. He scared us when he went to Hawaii."

"I bet he did."

"It'll take a while to go through the rejection letters. Most of the time agents will make side notes on a standard rejection letter. I'm sure no records of these exist."

"Fortunately, many agents also make notes on their computers of writers they want to follow up with and sometimes they send rejections notices by e-mail. I know it's not a lot, but please look and see if you see anything we missed."

"I'll do my best."

"I'd like to get back with you in a few days after you have time to think about what we've discussed. I'll remind you to keep all of this confidential, as we're still investigating these cases as hard as we can."

"What am I suppose to tell the people at work?"

"Tell them we talked, but you're not at liberty to discuss it."

She knew that won't go over well at the office. "I'll do my best, but I'm sure my boss will ask me questions."

"He has been helpful and he is cooperating with us also. Some of the victims were agents he knew."

"I hope you catch this person soon. It worries me a lot to think Edward may be at risk, and it may be my fault."

"I'm sure we'll catch this person soon. Try to get some rest. You look tired."

That was an understatement. Amy hoped she had the strength to get home. She was losing control again, and she hoped she didn't go into one of her blackout periods.

CHAPTER 39

Amy never made it to the psychiatrist's office, and in fact, she couldn't remember how she managed to make it home. Being half dressed, she felt safe hiding under the covers on her bed. The phone rang and rang, but she didn't care. Let it ring. She didn't want to move.

She drifted off to sleep again. The dreams shifted wildly from moments of ecstasy with Edward to nightmares involved in watching him die. The visions tormented her all night, making her feel tired and depressed. She needed help and soon, but couldn't move or make a call—she would later.

Several loud knocks on the door startled her awake as it turned thunderous, unrelenting. She forced one more moan as she heard her name vibrating through the door. She groaned louder and heard the door being hit with such a force it made her rise on her elbows for a second. She watched a gray form moving through the door. She groaned again as she fell back into her bed one last time.

\#\#\#

Amy opened her eyes and looked around. Her head felt dizzy and uncomfortable. She didn't recognize her surroundings. Where was she? She moaned as she tried to clear her head. A cool cloth touched her forehead—it felt good. She opened her eyes to see Ike standing over her.

"How are you?" he asked.

"Not so good. Where am I? And what are you doing here?"

"I found you at home and brought you to the hospital. They've given you something to sleep. You'll feel much better tomorrow. I didn't know who to call to stay with you, so I've been here, and I'll stay until tomorrow."

"Thanks. What happened?"

"Don't worry about it. Get some sleep."

###

Later in the afternoon the next day, Amy woke again with a nurse hovered over her, taking her vital signs. "I see you're waking up. How are you?"

"I'm tired."

"I'll find the doctor for you. He wanted to know when you came to." Amy looked around trying to clear her head. While the small room looked clean and simple, she also studied a strap across her chest restraining her.

She almost fell back asleep as she watched a doctor walking in. "Hello, Amy."

"Hello," she vaguely responded.

"We're doing some tests on you now to see what's going on with you. Can you answer some questions for me?"

"Yes," she struggled to answer.

"Are you taking any medication we need to know about?" She nodded her head yes. "Can you tell me what it is?"

All she could mutter was, "bipolar."

"Okay, but who is your doctor?"

"It's on the medicine bottle."

The doctor turned to the nurse. "Did she bring in any medication with her?"

"I don't think so."

"Send someone to her place and find it. We need to know who to call as soon as possible."

###

The next time Amy woke, Dr. Lankford stood in front of

her. She felt much better and able to concentrate slightly.

"How are you?" Dr. Lankford asked.

"I've seen better days."

"You let your medication get out of whack again. I think you'll feel much better soon. Your parents insisted I come with them to see you. They're waiting outside."

"Thank you so much for coming. I know it was asking a lot of you."

"We were contacted by the FBI. They think they're responsible for pushing you and causing you to collapse. This is too much pressure for you to handle."

"I'm really trying hard to control this."

"I know you are. I'll send your parents in now. They're worried about you."

Amy hated having caused more trouble for her parents; they had been through so much with her. "Tell them that I'm fine."

"You can tell them yourself."

As she left, they appeared in front of her. "Hello, how are you?" her mother asked as she rushed over to the side of her bed, obviously worried about her daughter. "You scared us."

"I'm sorry. The last few days have been hard on me and I guess too much for me. I'll be back in control soon."

"Perhaps you need to come back home and live with us again so we can watch over you?"

"Mom, you know it'll never work. I need some rest and to make some adjustments to my medication."

Her mother started to argue with her, but looked at her husband for advice.

"It's not a good time to discuss it now. We will when you feel a little better," her father said, as he leaned over and kissed her on the cheek. "We met your boss in the lobby while we were waiting. He appears to be very nice."

"Yes, he has been looking out for me a lot lately."

"He said he went looking for you when you didn't show

up for work. Many bosses don't do that these days."

"I guess I owe him one."

After a stern look from a nurse entering the room, her mother added, "We'll let you rest now and talk some more later."

"Thanks for coming and checking on me. I hate you needed to make the trip."

"The FBI insisted on it and is paying for everything."

Those comments made Amy feel a little better. She knew what a drain she had been on her parents over the years. "I'm glad."

The nurse started checking her vital signs. "It's good to have parents who care. They seemed so concerned about you. Your boyfriend has also been here the whole time."

"My boyfriend?"

"He'll be in here in a second. He has been here ever since he brought you in."

Amy laughed slightly. "Ike's not my boyfriend. He's my boss."

The nurse never changed the tone in her voice. "You could've fooled me."

Amy shook her head at the confusion and then thought about Edward. She hadn't talked to him since the other night. She had lost time and wasn't sure how long she had been in the hospital. She needed to call him as soon as possible. He had to be worried about her since they were supposed to talk again the next night.

Ike suddenly appeared in the doorway. "It's good to see you awake. How are you feeling?"

"I'm much better thanks to you. I heard you came to my apartment and brought me here."

"Yes, I had a feeling you weren't well when you left for the interview with the FBI the other day."

"Thank you for being a good friend."

"It looks like you're doing much better. The office is

calling me constantly with questions. I think I can now leave you in good hands now. Take some time off and rest, and I'll check on you as soon they release you. Don't worry about anything at the office."

"Thanks."

CHAPTER 40

Several days later, Ike waited outside as the doctor made his last visit before they released her. Her medication had started to stabilize her enough to allow her to go home. However, it would be several more days before she would return to work.

"How did it go with the doctor?" Ike asked, as he entered the room behind the doctor who had left.

"All's fine. He asked me to stay stress free for a while."

"I agree with him. The stress of the FBI was enough to cause anyone to have a panic attack." He reached over and picked up Amy's bag and waited for the nurse as Amy stepped into a wheel chair.

"I really don't think I need this."

"I know, but its standard policy here. We'll have you to the car in a few minutes," the nurse added.

Ike acted attentive. She knew she had disrupted his work schedule which always stayed hectic. Even for a nice guy this was a lot to ask. "Thanks for being here, it means a lot to me."

"It's not a problem. I want to make sure you get home without any problems at all."

She felt good as he headed home with her. She enjoyed being with him and all the attention.

###

After Ike left Amy settled into her bed, she decided to check her messages on her answer machine, since it flashed an indication of being full. She heard calls at first coming from Ginger at the office, but then eventually she heard Ike's messages. She realized what they must have been thinking when she didn't show up for work or return their calls.

Then she heard the calls from Edward. They started off cute and jolly, but eventually turned to inquisitive. Finally, they turned to "I guess you don't want to talk to me." She didn't have his number with her at the hospital, and she was too dopey to talk intelligently.

She worried about this moment often the last two days. How was she going to tell him she was in a hospital? It would be hard to tell him she had a mental condition with the chemicals in her brain not functioning properly sometimes. She hated the bipolar problems she had more now than ever, but she knew she could do nothing else about it. However, she knew he sounded worried and she needed to call him. She practiced over and over what she planned to say as she retrieved the phone and dialed his office.

The secretary passed the call through to him. "This is Edward, can I help you?"

"Edward . . . this is Amy."

She heard no response

"I'm sorry I haven't returned your calls the last few days." Still, she heard no response on the other side. "I've been in the hospital."

"The hospital—what happened?" New life entered his voice.

"I had some kind of chemical imbalance in my brain. They sedated me and forced me to stay for a few days for observation. I just got home and discovered the messages you left me."

"I've been worried sick about you."

"I had no way of contacting you. I'm sorry."

"It's okay. I thought you were brushing me off."

"Not at all, I think you're very special."

"Are you going to be okay?"

"Yes, I'll be fine in a few days. Don't worry about me.

My boss has been extremely supportive."

"I'm glad to hear that."

"Some of the girls from work are planning on coming by to visit me after work today."

"If you need me to, I can make arrangements to come by as well. I was going to the mountains, but I can change my plans. To tell the truth, I was hoping you could go with me."

"I would love to go later, but I need to build my strength up first I think."

"Yes, you need to take care of yourself now. Thank you so much for calling me."

"You're welcome. I'm sorry I couldn't call earlier."

"I'll call you back later tonight after I get home and check on you."

"I look forward to it."

As Amy ended the phone call, she felt better. He hadn't asked too many questions about what happened to her, but she knew he would want more details later.

###

Around six, Amy heard a knock on her door. She strolled over to let in Ginger and Renee who carried several bags between them. "How are you?" they both asked at the same time, and in cheerful voices.

"I'm doing fine." She offered a smile. They were doing their best to cheer her up and she appreciated it. They were basically her only friends in the city, other than Ike.

"We didn't think you wanted to go out to eat, so we stopped and grabbed some Chinese food. We hope you like it."

"Chinese sounds good to me. Thank you for coming."

"We planned to come see you at the hospital, but we knew Mr. Grantland was with you. He has truly taken an interest in you. It's extremely rare for him to take off work like this." Ginger sneaked a sideway glance toward Renee.

Amy grinned as she nodded her head up and down. "It appears I'm the talk of the office."

"Trust me, there are many girls in the office who would love to attract his attention," Renee giggled as she darted over to the couch.

Amy started feeling better, but not up to full strength. The medication would work, but she knew from before it would still take several days. "I'm so sorry I didn't have time to talk to everyone when I returned from Hawaii."

"I've already heard you brought in a major account. That's certainly one way to get to Mr. Grantland. He has bragged about you several times for taking such initiative," Renee added.

"I got lucky on this one. The author was looking to make a change, and I had met him and his agent once before."

"It was still slick the way you flew all the way to Hawaii to hunt for him. You didn't sleep with him to get the account, did you?" Renee jokingly teased her.

The comment came as a surprise, but she knew Renee loved every minute of it. However, she couldn't resist. "Edward's different from what I thought. We instantly hit it off and we spent most of the week together—."

"You slept with him—I knew it!" Renee's sassy hair bounced around as she slapped her knee.

Amy laughed, but turned her eyes back on Renee. "It's not what you think. We're kind of serious about each other, and we enjoy each other's company."

"Sounds good to me. Does Mr. Grantland know about this?" Ginger asked.

"He knows we spent all week together, and that I went after the account. I doubt if he knows we're lovers." There, she said it. There should be no more teasing or speculation.

The two girls' eyes met each other and giggled. Amy knew they wanted much more details now. Amy held her hand up as she said, "We're still a new couple, give me a break."

"I don't think Mr. Grantland knows all of this. It's going to be fun to see how you're going to tell him." Ginger eyes glanced over to Renee for advice.

"I think Mr. Grantland's coming by here later tonight to check on you. Boy, I'd love to be a fly on the wall here tonight," Ginger teased.

"You two are nothing but perverts." Amy teased back, enjoying the moment. It felt good to laugh and have fun, but she knew she had many problems with situations she wasn't prepared to solve, especially right now in her condition.

The fun continued until she heard another knock on the door. Amy opened the door to see Ike standing outside. "Hello, how are you doing now? I wanted to stop by for a minute to check on you."

"Hi, come on in. Ginger and Renee are here also."

He looked around the door and saw them inside. "Hi," he said as he ventured in, realizing he had been caught coming back to check on Amy. He knew word of his extra trips to see Amy would make for fascinating water-cooler conversation for a while.

"We're leaving," Renee announced. "I think we've worn her out enough tonight."

"I'm not planning on staying long either."

The girls offered Amy a quick hug and headed for the door. "We'll see you later."

Amy looked over at Ike, and felt a little flattered he had come back to check on her. "Thanks for checking on me, you really didn't have to."

"I know, but I feel like it's partially my fault for letting the FBI question you so much."

"I don't think you had much choice in it."

"When you return to work, we still need to celebrate your victory in Hawaii. That was a terrific job you did. You'll have to tell me how you pulled it off later. I'm sure you could write a book on it."

Amy knew it was a lot more exciting than he would ever know. "Yes, I really enjoyed Hawaii."

Ike appeared to be waiting on a clue from Amy as to if she welcomed him closer. She felt him testing the waters and not sure of his status. Being her boss can cause intricate problems, to say the least, and she knew to be careful.

"It looks like you're doing fine, but please call me if you have any problems at all. I mean it."

"I will . . . and thank you for being here for me."

He patted her on the shoulder and headed out the door.

Amy's heart beat fast. *Who would've ever thought I'd have this kind of problem—two guys*. She knew she had no experience in this kind of triangle at all.

CHAPTER 41

With the help of the medicine, Amy slept well all night. She hadn't heard from Edward and decided to give him a call. His secretary passed her call directly into him. "Hello, this is Edward, can I help you?"

"Hi, this is Amy."

"How are you today?"

"I'm fine. You never called me last night."

"I know, but from what I heard, I assumed it was best if you had a good night's sleep."

While not sure he told the truth, she decided to give him the benefit of the doubt. "I did sleep well last night with the help of the medication they prescribed for me."

"Are you going to be okay now? What happened to you? I still don't understand."

"Don't worry. I'm going to be fine. It's some kind of chemical imbalance in my brain which makes me depressed, and it's supposed to be controlled by medication. For some reason, it wasn't working as it should."

"I hope you're right. I was worried about you."

"How about you? I know you must still be snowed under from the trip."

"I'm doing fine. The FBI came here again today. They came to warn me about this serial killer again, and to take extra precautions until they catch whoever it is. I think they must be telling all agents the same things right now. They suggested I hire a private body guard, but I'm not going to hire a personal body guard until they catch this killer."

Amy wondered what all the FBI told him. She hoped they didn't tell him about her past attempts to ruin his career. Since he hadn't said anything about it, she assumed they had not, but she still wanted to know what they did discuss. "What all did they tell you?"

"They think the killer may be a tall blonde haired woman and cautioned me about meeting strange woman right now, as if I would."

"I agree that you need to be safe right now. I don't want anything to happen to you."

"Don't worry. I'm sure they're telling all agents the same thing. I don't think I've pissed anyone off bad enough to want to kill me."

Amy knew it was going to be hard to tell him the truth later. "Did they tell you anything else?"

"That was about it. Have they been to your publishing house?"

"Yes, they were asking questions here when I returned. They're working hard on solving these cases."

"I need to finish some papers before I have a meeting. Let me call you tonight."

"Please call me, and don't worry about waking me. I'm starting to get cabin fever fast."

Amy ended the phone call and hoped for the best. The quicker the FBI captured the killer the better. She looked at the large files containing rejection letters they had given her. It was a long shot, but she opened it and started glancing at them. She wondered out of curiosity as to how agents tracked query letters, if they did at all.

She located a file for each agent with a list of standard rejection letters they used. The "Sorry, it doesn't fit our need list at the current time" to the "We feel we must pass at the current time, however it's a subjective decision and another agent may feel differently. We wish you the best."

After being at the publishing house, she now understood how some of the agents must feel with all the query letters they receive. With the competition enormous, they only had so much time available to represent the best.

Amy studied a transcript of the entries in James Aaron's file from the daily journal he maintained. The comments regarding his rejection letter process was the center of discussion. He made one note that caught Amy's attention. He wrote, "I know this is going to place me on some black list of agents, but . . ."

Amy knew of many lists of predatory and bad agents. If someone planned to kill agents she considered jerks, it would be a good place to start. Maybe Amy needed to think like a killer. How would you determine which agent needed to be killed? How would she determine her targets?

She walked over to her computer and started searching the net. It would take a month to go through all the agents on these lists. Again, Amy tried to think like the killer as she spoke out loud. "If I were mad at agents in general, I would start with either the easiest ones to kill or the ones needing it the most. If I was going to send a message to the community as a whole, I would kill the most prominent ones."

Amy suddenly considered the oral sex angle. Perhaps these agents were perverts and spent time in kinky sex sites. Another fact was haunting Amy, however. Agent Arrington's theory was that she may have triggered this predator. If so, she needed to go back and match the dates of her articles and books she had reviewed to see if they matched any of the dead agents. That kind of research would take some time.

Since she used the name of *The Literary Hawk* in her reviews, she had few readers of the articles who knew her real name. The newspapers knew because they had to mail her a check. Her friend Lenny, of course, knew, but not even her psychologist or the group she was in knew her assumed name, or did they? Amy dug deep into her memory. She wasn't sure if she mentioned her name in any of the meeting or not. They knew she acted mad at an agent when she started the campaign, but they were such a small group and were not supposed to share what went on in the meeting with anyone outside the group.

Only one other person knew who she wrote as, and had discovered it by accident—her boss. Ike told her he would keep her identity a secret, but she couldn't write any more book reviews. If Ike could track her down, perhaps someone else could have just as easily.

All the agents appeared to be prominent and well known except for the last one. While her articles had limited circulation, the murders were scattered over many cities. These murders had been committed in different towns than the ones in which the newspapers that carried her articles appeared.

This killer appeared to be smart and planned her moves carefully. She couldn't understand exactly what triggered her, but Amy was going to keep working on it. She needed to contact the FBI agent again, since she placed Edward in a dangerous situation and she couldn't properly warn him. He thought he wasn't even at risk. Since he was her first lover and she felt so bad about the whole situation, all she could do for the rest of the night was to worry and cry over and over.

CHAPTER 42

After a long and agonizing night, Amy laid in bed trying to decide what she needed to tell Arrington. Amy had questions and some insights she knew might help. It felt good that Agent Arrington could meet with her on such short notice.

After she cleared the guard station, she soon faced her and said her hello, with Arrington motioning for Amy to follow her back to the same meeting room. "I heard about your trip to the hospital. How are you now?"

"I'm better for now. They have my medication regulated to some extent. It's a delicate balancing trick."

"I'm a psychologist also, so I know what you're going through. It was my fault in not recognizing your conditions better when we talked the other day."

"Then you'll understand what I'm going to tell you. At times, I think I'm absolutely brilliant, and at other times I can't even tie my shoes."

"Yes, I know how it is."

"I'm not trained in the way of catching the bad guy, but I've been thinking about some things. Do you really think my actions created a person intent on killing literary agents?"

"I've no way of knowing for sure right now, and I sure don't want to put you on another guilt trip."

"I've been thinking, and something has been eating at me. Not many people know I wrote under the name of the *Literary Hawk*, or for my reason for writing the articles."

Arrington paused for a minute and opened a file. "I'm going to show you the section in your articles which makes us think there's a connection." She slid an article over to Amy.

Amy recognized it instantly. "In order to not be

considered concentrating on one particular literary agent, I also read and reviewed many author's work. This is one of them."

"Look at the bottom of the article where you talk about this author's agent."

Amy read it again, as if for the first time. She had written, "It's amazing he had this book published or acquired an agent to sell it. Considering the way some agents act like jerks when they receive quality work from good, hard-working authors, it's unbelievable something like this gets published. I'm sure many writers know exactly what I'm talking about."

Amy remembered writing it as she read. "It was one of my first articles I wrote when I was out of control. I'm surprised it was published at all. Only a few papers ran this article. Perhaps I piled it on a little thick."

"Perhaps . . . do you remember who that author used for an agent?"

"I'm not sure I ever looked it up, but I'm sure it wasn't Edward."

"It was James Aaron, the second agent to be killed. The murder occurred two weeks after the article was published."

"Oh, my gosh. I didn't know."

"The article appeared in a few papers, and none of them were too large."

"That had to shrink the list of suspects a pretty good bit, didn't it?" Amy hoped for the best.

"Well, we're still working on solving the killings."

Amy cleared her voice and focused on the agent. "I've an idea or a plan. I'm willing to do it if you think it'll work."

Arrington leaned forward. "What is it?"

"I'm thinking of a trap. If I write another article with your assistance, it might make the killer strike again."

"We've considered it, and it's tricky. Some of the killings are at random. We don't want to be responsible for someone else being a target.”

“It will have to be controlled, but I’m sure that’s what the FBI’s good at.”

“It’s something we’ve considered. All of your contacts will have to be duplicated and monitored. Are you sure you’re up to it?”

“I feel like I owe it to myself and to the agents who’ve been killed. Also, I may have placed one more agent in line to be murdered; someone I care a lot for now.”

“I hate to say it, but you may need to distance yourself from him for a while to not place him in more danger. I’ll have an answer for you by tomorrow on how to work this out. It’s important you don’t talk to anyone about this, is that perfectly clear?”

“Yes. Please tell me what I have to do, and I’ll help in any way I can.”

“Don’t worry about your work for a few days, and I’ll contact your boss and tell him we need your help. I’m sure he’ll understand. Since he’s one of the people who knew who you were, he’ll have to be in on this to a small degree, but we’ll have to control that situation as well.”

CHAPTER 43

After Amy had packed what she needed for the trip home, she rested for a moment. Agent Arrington had rehearsed every line with her. With the entire plan in place, Amy simply needed to execute her part, and hopefully the trap would be set. The FBI had told Ike to not say a word about her trip or call her while she left on a recovery trip for her nerves. It all had to look natural, and not send any warning signs. The killer still could be anyone.

Amy's phone rang. After seeing Edward's name on the caller ID, she wanted to talk to him so badly, but the FBI told her to not have any more contact with him than was necessary until they caught the killer. She understood, and she didn't want to place his life in any further danger. "Hello."

"Hi, this is Edward. How are you feeling this morning?"

"I'm fine and preparing for my trip home for a few days."

"I'm sure your mother and dad will be glad to see you. When you get back I want to see you."

She bit her lip. "I would like to see you also, but I know I'll be so snowed under when I actually return to work."

Her heart pounded during a long silence on the line. "I thought we really had something special in Hawaii."

"Hawaii was the best."

Edward allowed another long silence. "I'm sorry to bother you. Call me when you have a chance." The phone died.

She sobbed into the phone. Then she whispered, "I'll make this up to you one day, I promise I will." The depression would set in if she let it, but this time she would fight back. She picked the last of her luggage and headed for the door instead of the bed which pulled at her. She felt determined to make up for all the screw ups in her life this time.

She needed to retrace her tracks the days before she sent out the article which may have started all of this madness. She had already prepared another article to be sent out to the original newspapers, which have already agreed to run them with another literary agent selected to be the target. She portrayed him as moving into New York City where Mitchell Lloyd had worked. He also presented a perfect match for the other agents who had been killed. Only this agent was a trained FBI agent with an elaborately fabricated past.

She decided to call Lenny and let him know she was coming home. He answered his phone on the first ring. "Hello."

"Hi, Lenny, this is Amy. How are you?"

"Hello, girl. I was just thinking about you. Your mother told me yesterday you were planning to come home soon."

"Yes, as a matter of fact, I'm on the way home now."

"Fantastic! They sounded so glad you decided to come home for a while. How long will you be here?"

"I'm not sure. It depends on how long it takes for my head to clear. I hate these bipolar problems I have."

"You were doing so well in Hawaii. What happened?"

"Some things have come up I haven't had a chance to tell you about. We've a lot of catching up to do."

"Call me as soon as you get here."

"I will."

###

Amy's parents acted glad to see her and thought it was a good idea to escape from the hectic life she had moved to. "I hope to see you resting and not worrying about things at work," her mother said as she helped Amy unpack her suitcase.

Amy couldn't tell her mom about all the work she had to do while she was home. All the details had been scheduled ahead of time. "Do you mind taking me to the bookstore where I worked?"

Her mother looked puzzled at first, and then relented. "If you want to I'll be glad to take you."

"I have a book I want to read."

"You said you were coming home to rest. Going to the bookstore sounds like you want to work."

Amy forced her eyes to plead her case. "Don't worry. This book is just for me to read and relax. However, I may write a book review on it, simply to stay in practice. It will be nice to see if anyone remembers me as the "The Literary Hawk.""

Her mother flinched and stared at her with apprehension when she heard the assumed name again. "I know you enjoyed writing those articles because it always kept you busy."

"The money wasn't too bad either."

"But then you had to become famous and move off to New York City."

"I don't think I'm famous. You can drop me off and I'll call you in a little while. It would be good to drink some coffee and see if any of my old friends drop by."

"Sure, but call me when you're ready for me."

###

Amy quickly exited the car after it pulled in front of the store. "I'll call you, Mom."

The car pulled off, and Amy breathed a sigh of relief. This would be one step completed on her assignment. Her mother now knew she was writing an article for publication. She hoped the word would spread fast.

Amy's old boss greeted her as she made it through the door. "Amy, how are you?"

"I'm fine. I came home for a few days and thought I'd stop by for some good coffee and to check out a few books."

"Okay, let me know if I can help you."

Amy made it to the coffee bar and ordered a white chocolate mocha which was always her favorite. The new guy turned his head sideways to study her. "Didn't you used to work here?"

"Yes, it wasn't too long ago."

"Lenny got me this job when he quit. I remember you working with him earlier."

"Yes, Lenny's a good friend of mine. In fact, he'll be here in a little while I'm sure."

"I hope so."

Amy accepted her mocha and walked over to the rows of books and selected the book she looked for. She then located a table in the front of the café section close to the coffee bar. Anyone coming to the cashier would have to pass right in front of her. She laid the book in plain view so it could be seen.

After finishing her first cup of coffee, she retrieved her phone and called Lenny. He was finishing with a client, and he eagerly agreed to meet her at the coffee shop.

Several old customers greeted her as she drank her coffee and read the book. She had set up her computer and made notes as she read. It would be obvious to anyone passing by she was doing research.

Lenny soon walked in the front door. Amy had to laugh a little at him as he came nearer. He wore a bright yellow Hawaiian shirt and knee length pants.

He nodded his head. "Okay, so I'm hooked on the style. What do you think?"

"It's definitely you."

"I think I'll take that as a compliment." He lifted his chin slightly in the air in a show of arrogance, but teasing in the same moment.

"It does take a while to come back down to reality. Hawaii was the trip of a lifetime."

He sat next to her and looked her in the eyes, which froze her in place. "So, why are you having these wild mood swings? It looked like all was going great between you and lover boy." He batted his eyes as he teased Amy.

"Everything was fine until I returned to the FBI waiting for me in the office."

"The FBI. What did they want?"

"They're trying hard to hunt down the serial killer of the literary agents. They came to ask my help in profiling her."

"That sounds . . . exciting, but why did they ask you?"

"They think my book reviews may have something to do with triggering her rage, or whatever you want to call it."

"You've got to be kidding me. They must be really reaching for straws on this one."

"This is serious, they think if it's true that I may have placed Edward in danger and he could become the next target for this maniac killer."

Lenny's face turned serious. "This is not good, girl."

"Tell me about it."

"Have you told Edward?"

"NO! How can I tell him I may have set him up to be killed? I know in the future I need to tell him the whole story, but not now. Later, when we are more firmly established, I'll find a way."

"That is . . . if he's still around." He raised his eye brows to extract an agreement out of Amy.

"I know what you're saying. The FBI is calling the shots right now, and I have to do what they say. They're telling me to not have much contact with Edward right now and draw attention to him. He's lucky he lives such a very sheltered life. He's either at work or in his apartment, which

272

I heard has excellent security in New York City.”

“I hope you’re right. So, what are you telling him?”

“I told him I have a chemical imbalance and need some time to recover. I know he thinks I don’t want to see him, but he’s so wrong.”

“Well, if I can do anything to help, please let me know. I have to rush off right now. I have a client who would like for me to design a tiki room out of their pool house addition. This will be a fascinating project.”

“Thanks for coming by, and please keep this quiet. I needed someone to talk to.”

“Okay, I’ll see you in a little while.”

Lenny stood and left Amy to her work. While it was quiet, she decided to call Dr. Lankford to see if she could see her for a quick visit, and maybe she could visit the group she used to attend also. This was another of her assignments she had agreed to complete.

Dr. Lankford wasn’t in, but her secretary made her an appointment for the next morning. “I’m sure she’ll want to see you as soon as possible. The group meets at lunchtime tomorrow and it would be good to have you join them. I’ll set it up for you.”

“Thank you. I’ll see you then.” Good, she crossed another item off her list.

Amy next checked in with Ike to let him know she had made the trip safely. Ginger answered the phone, “Hello, Mr. Grantland’s office.”

“Hi, this is Amy. Is he in?”

“No. He’s in another meeting. It appears we’re signing many new authors because of the agent shake up. He told several people you’ll probably be promoted to junior editor when you return. He’s proud of your work, but he’s concerned about you also.”

“Thanks. Please tell him I called, and that he can reach me on my cell phone if he needs to ask me anything.”

"I will. Are you doing okay? We want to see you back at work as soon as you can. We miss you around here."

"I'll be back soon, I promise."

She started to call Edward next but changed her mind. The images of the murdered agents tormented her too much. She couldn't let that happen to Edward.

CHAPTER 44

Amy opened the door to Dr. Lankford's office and looked around. Everything looked as she remembered it, including the secretary. "How are you?"

"I'm much better, thank you. Is she in?"

"Yes, and she's expecting you. Please go on in."

Amy felt glad to visit her doctor again. She was someone who was always easy to talk to, and who always acted concerned about how she felt.

"Wow, I think you're looking much better than the last time I saw you. It's good to have you back home," Dr. Lankford said, as she walked over and hugged Amy.

"It's good to have some time off. At the publishing house, the work load can be so heavy."

"I was thinking it might be. Is that what caused you to relapse?"

"I don't think it was the fault of the house. It was much more than that. The trip to Hawaii put me on such a high that when I returned to the city, it was hard to come back down to earth."

"That can be understandable. Was there anything else?"

"Yes, I've been contacted by the FBI."

"I know. They came here also."

"Really? What was the FBI here asking about you?"

"Well, like I told them, I can't disclose anything we talk about. It's privileged information."

"That's good. They think I may be responsible for the deaths of several literary agents."

"From the questions they asked, I thought they were thinking the same. I guess it's their job to investigate, but this time I think they're way out in left field."

"I'm not so sure. Do you remember the articles I was writing? They think the reviews may be sparking the flame of the killer."

"I think it's their problem to work out. My concern is you. That's way too much guilt to place on you."

"It's a lot of pressure and more so than I think you could imagine. I went to Hawaii and met with the agent who sent me the rejection letter I hated so much."

She lifted her head with a sudden jerk. "How did that go?"

"Believe it or not, it went well. He's not the jerk I thought he was. It was just me and this crazy bipolar condition I live with."

"That's good news. When you manage to work something like this out, you become stronger and stronger, and it helps you to make it through episodes like this."

"I still have a problem. The FBI thinks I may have placed him in danger. He might be targeted by the killer."

"Is this what the FBI told you?"

"Yes."

"It sounds like they may be highly irresponsible."

"I think they're doing their job. If I can help, I want to."

"It sounds like you're thinking clearer now. I'm proud of the way you snapped back this time."

"Me too." Yes, she was proud of herself also. The conversation continued until her time ended. "I'd like to come back for the group meeting after lunch."

"I think that would be an excellent idea, since I'm sure they'll all be interested in seeing you."

Amy left to find some coffee at a coffee shop nearby. She was glad to be completing her part of the plan, but needed help when she could receive it. Dr. Lankford was a trusted friend and easy to confide in.

###

Several of the members of the group arrived before Amy

returned. She saw Judith and Stephen, who appeared to be in a good mood. They immediately walked over to her and offered her a hug. It felt good to see them.

Nancy stayed in her chair and waved at Amy. Her face reflected the unhappy feeling so common of someone in a manic depressed state. Amy felt sorry for her and walked over. "How are you?"

"Not so well. It's been hard lately." Her eyes regained a slight twinkle. "I've heard good things about you and New York. It sounds like you're doing well."

"I have my good days and bad days like most people."

Wendell and Ernest were also sitting in their same places, as always, but forced small smiles as she entered the room. It was just another day to them.

Dr. Lankford walked into the room as all the seats filled except for Estella's. She thanked those in the room for coming and pointed to the empty seat. "She called and said she might be a few minutes late. We'll not wait on her, but I think she'll be here soon."

They all stared at the doctor while waiting on repeating the standard routine of telling how they were doing. Amy noticed how nothing much had changed while she was gone, and she felt sorry for most of the group. She was not sure if these sessions had accomplished much good.

Dr. Lankford finally turned to Amy. "I think we should all be proud of Amy because she's doing well in her new job."

Amy heard a small applause as she blushed. "I've received word I'm receiving a promotion when I go back to New York City." Another round of congratulations reached a higher level of enthusiasm, as everyone appeared to enjoy having positive things happening to someone in the group. It did offer all of them some hope.

After about thirty minutes, Amy heard a small knock on the door and Estella walked in. She looked as beautiful and polished as ever and again looked like a giant Barbie doll. She also exhibited about as much life as a kid's doll. "I'm sorry that I'm late. Please, excuse me."

She floated across the floor to her seat and turned around before glancing at the room and taking her seat. As she recognized Amy, a small smile grew. "How are you?" she whispered to Amy while trying to be polite and courteous, but without disrupting the meeting.

"I'm fine, and my life is about the same."

"They told us about you having to go to the hospital."

"Yes, the pressure of working at that pace with authors and agents is very stressful."

"I remember you talking about agents before. You seemed so hurt then, and well . . . I'm surprised you're still in that field."

"I'm making headway, but it's definitely slow."

"I wish you well in your work." Her face suddenly lost the genuine smile, and she went back to the frozen fake smile she normally portrayed. It appeared she could focus for one minute before floating to the next. Amy wondered how much medication she was taking.

Amy was glad when the meeting ended, as it left her feeling somewhat sad. And this wasn't what she needed right now. She needed to focus on completing the plan the FBI had devised for her. Her mother would soon arrive to carry her back to the bookstore where Lenny promised to meet her and take her for a late lunch. She felt hungry and needed to talk to him.

\###

Lenny had arrived early at the bookstore and had ordered a coffee while sitting up straight to watch the guys coming and going. "Boy, I sometimes miss this place."

Amy rolled her eyes while thinking about how many

times before she had responded to Lenny acting like that. "You're one of a kind."

He arched an eyebrow. "Well, I certainly hope not."

Amy let it pass. "I need to start going to agents, authors, and editors' blogs and web sites to post information. That's something else I did before the first agent was killed."

"Are you sure you can remember all the places that you went?"

"I'm sure I can't remember all of them, but they wanted me to spend the day doing that. The article will hit the papers in a few days, and we can hope the killer takes the bait."

"How is Edward right now?"

"I'm trying hard to avoid telling him everything." She bit her lip slightly. "I need to find the right time."

"Girl, I hope you're not making a big mistake."

Amy pulled out her laptop and started connecting to the internet. "Wow, the coffee smells fantastic."

"I do take it that you would like a cup." Amy fluttered her eyes as Lenny rolled his before going to retrieve her some. She went to her favorites on the computer and ran down the list. It was going to be a long day and night to make all the rounds of blogs and chat rooms she used to go to.

CHAPTER 45

On all the sites Amy blasted agents, and in particular one new agent that she repeatedly called a jerk. She hoped she wasn't laying it on too thick, but making her point, hoping the killer would notice her articles or follow her post in one of the chat rooms.

She felt tired, and she had forgotten that she had promised her mother she would call her to come pick her up before dinner. The sites looked different, but in some respect the same after a while. She tried to keep Edward off of her mind, but she knew the more she posted the more of a chance she could also be setting him up as well.

Her phone rang—Edward. "Hello, how are you?"

"Amy, I'm fine and I was thinking of you."

"That's good to know."

"As I told you before, I own a place in the Catskills. It's a perfect place to escape from the city and not be bothered."

"I remember you telling me before, and it sounded absolutely fantastic."

"I was hoping to talk you into going with me to my cabin for a few days."

"I'd love to visit the cabin sometime soon."

"I can make arrangements for you to fly and pick you up at the airport tomorrow."

"Tomorrow—I can't do it that soon."

"Sure you can, I'll take care of all the details."

Amy's heart started to race. She hated to turn him down, but knew the FBI put a plan into place and needed her to follow it precisely. "I have some things here I need to attend to."

She waited for a long silence she often experienced when he was thinking, or hurt. "I see. Maybe it's me and memories of our time together in Hawaii. I thought we had something special."

"Hawaii was very special, and I think you know that I like you very much."

"I'm going to be there for several days. If you change your mind, let me know."

"What? You're leaving now for the mountains?"

"Yes, I've already packed."

"That will not be a good idea. You know a serial killer's targeting literary agents."

"With so many agents in the world, I don't think I'll be a target."

Amy drew in a large breath. She needed to tell him some time, and this may be the best time to get it out and into the open. "I have something I need to tell you, and I hope you don't hate me."

"What is it?"

"I may be responsible for the killer's action. At least the FBI thinks so."

"How can you be responsible?"

"I use to be a book reviewer, and I wrote some bad articles criticizing agents."

He went silent again.

"While I was intent on ruining career of agents I considered jerks, it appears that someone else has gone further by actually killing agents. The FBI thinks my articles and other activities may have been what triggered this person into action."

"That sounds like the FBI has a wild imagination."

"They have a lot of facts to back up their claim that I can't go into. This is something I was going to tell you when the time was right, but it appears I need to do it now to save your life."

"What do you mean . . . save my life?"

"After I received the rejection letter from you, I thought you were the biggest jerk in the business. I hated you, and did some things I'm ashamed of now."

"We talked about why I sent you the letter as I did."

"I know and after meeting you, I have a whole different opinion of you."

"I still don't think I'm a target. This is absurd."

"Edward . . . I'm The Literary Hawk."

He turned quiet again for a long time. "I always wondered who that was."

"I'm sorry to have to tell you like this."

"Then why did you come to Hawaii?"

"I went to Hawaii to try to get your business, and more directly . . . the business of Larry."

"I see. Well I'll have to say you're very good at your job. I hope it was worth it."

"Edward, I told you things changed after meeting you and getting to know you. I was wrong about you."

"It's hard to believe anything about you right now."

"I know you're upset, but listen to me. I was told that you're safe in the apartment complex where you live. The FBI has also assigned an agent to watch your back right now. This will all be over soon."

"I think this is already over." The phone line died.

She dialed him back, but he didn't answer, as his answering machine picked up. "This is Edward, please leave a message."

"Please pick up. We need to talk." She left messages until his message box stopped taking them. It was no use. He wasn't going to talk to her any time soon. She couldn't blame him. It wouldn't be long before he'd know all of her efforts in trying to destroy him. She also knew he might pull the deal with World Media, which would make her look like an idiot in front of her boss.

She considered calling Agent Arrington, since she should know what happened. The thought of being in trouble with the FBI made her even more depressed. She was losing control again, but she forced herself as hard as she could to remain focused.

Edward may not agree right now, but he needed her more than he could ever imagine. She wished she could've told him about the sting going down with the FBI, but wasn't able to. She felt scared he might do something stupid.

Amy's mother appeared outside and waved at her through the window. Her poor mother had no idea what she was involved with. Her parents treated her too special, as well, to be put in harm's way. If she started this nightmare, she needed to find a way out of it. But how? She wasn't a trained agent. This is what people like Agent Arrington were for.

She looked up the number for Agent Arrington and dialed. "Hello."

"This is Amy. I need to talk to you."

"Why, what's happening?"

"It's Edward. He called me."

"You know how important it is to avoid him for right now. We don't want to draw any more attention to him than is necessary."

"It may be too late. He got upset when we talked."

"What did he get upset about?"

"He wanted me to go with him on a trip to relax and recover from my hospital visit. I know he's concerned about me, but he took the rejection the wrong way. I'm sure I didn't handle it as I should."

"I know this is hard on you, but it'll be over soon. The articles hit the newspapers tomorrow and we're ready with all contingencies covered."

"What about Edward? I'm worried about him."

"We have a man covering him."

"I've a feeling he's going to his cabin without me."

"What? That would not be good right now. It will make him too open and exposed."

"Exactly, and that's why I'm concerned for him."

"Let me make a call and alert the agent in the field. I'll call you back in a minute."

Amy knew her mother still waited for her in the car as she picked up her bag and placed her computer in it. She wore a smile for her mother and tried to keep her from worrying about her.

###

Amy's mood stayed steady during dinner, even when she excused herself several times trying to contact Edward. He never answered his phone.

"Are you sure you're okay? You've not touched much of your food, and I know you've always liked my spaghetti before." Her mother hovered trying to decide what was wrong with Amy.

"I'm a little worried about a few things, but I'll be fine." This time she wasn't going to let her bipolar condition get the best of her. She was going to somehow correct the errors she had made in the past. Just the same, she knew it would be good to call Dr. Lankford to ask her a question about her medication. "Excuse me for a minute. I think I need to call Dr. Lankford to check on something." Her parents looked at each other with exchanged frowns. They apparently knew Amy was fighting her emotional swings hard.

Dr. Lankford answered her phone on the second ring. "Hello, can I help you?"

"Yes, this is Amy. I had a fight with Edward."

"I see, and how are you doing?"

"I'm fine for right now, but worried about later. Do I need to increase my medication?"

"Not tonight, but it would be good to have you come by the office on Monday. That's the day after tomorrow. Do you think you'll be okay until then?"

"I'm not sure. I don't need to lose control right now, since I'm involved with too much right now to lose it."

"Calm down. I know how you feel."

"I think if I can work past this, I'll be fine. I've screwed up to many times before. I don't want to do that right now."

"I hope so. I'll be here to talk to any time. If you feel like you need to, I can arrange for you to go to the hospital."

"I'm not that bad. However, for once in my life, I need to know I'll be okay for a few days."

"It's good for you to stay busy, and to keep your mind occupied. Call me if you need me at any time."

"I will."

CHAPTER 46

Amy had slept very little last night as she forced herself to avoid give in to the temptations of depression. She needed to focus now more than ever. Edward had never answered his phone.

With the papers now on the street, Amy went online to check for her article, which she saw in several of the newspapers. She studied the changes made by the FBI. While she wrote it, she knew the FBI had carefully edited and perfected it for their purpose.

The article contained a major headline, which left no doubt that it came from her. Sometimes they even added a teaser on the front page that alluded to the article by the "The Literary Hawk".

The name of the new literary agent was Joseph Muller. He had purchased the agency from the family of the first agent to be killed, Mitchell Lloyd. The book she reviewed was a paranormal romance and nothing more than a copy of a previous work by another author presented as the new author's debut book. She ripped it to shreds from the beginning, questioned why the agent looked at it, and how he managed to get it published. She wrote it was a total waste of money to buy something as pathetic as this. Of course, the book never existed. She even called the agent a jerk.

She wondered how long it would take Ike to hear about the article. She knew he would be curious about it, but he had to be left in the dark about much of the operation for now. She would explain to him eventually all that had taken place, but it would be after the killer had been apprehended.

Agent Arrington called as she was thinking through the various scenarios. "How are you today?"

"I'm reading the papers today. Wow, the papers have

been accommodating, and even giving blurbs on the front page. Where were you guys when I first started?"

Arrington laughed. "I'm glad you're in a better mood this morning."

"I'm trying to force myself to focus. It hasn't been easy."

"Have you heard from Edward?"

"No. I've tried all night. He hasn't been answering his phone."

"I hate to tell you this, but it appears he left his apartment last night. His car is gone."

Amy felt like her heart was going to explode. "Oh, my gosh!"

"Don't worry. We're trying to locate him now."

"If he's gone, then I think he might be going to his cabin, and I've no idea where it is in the Catskills."

"At this point we don't either, but we're working on that option also."

"There's no chance the killer's after him right now, is there?"

"I hope not, but he has certainly made our job much more difficult."

"Call me if you hear anything at all."

###

Amy went back online to do research. She needed to find the location of his cabin. No one at his agency answered the phone, and, of course, he still didn't answer his cell phone.

She tried to reach Larry, but all she reached was a voice mailbox. She left two messages and hoped he would call her. Perhaps he knew where Edward had the cabin.

Her phone rang again—Agent Arrington. "Hello."

"Hi, I wanted to let you know Edward was reportedly seen heading toward the mountains. Our man is heading there now. He was by himself, and we think he's fine. He's going on his normal trip to the Catskills that he apparently makes often."

"Yes, but he's still vulnerable."

"Don't worry. He'll be under our protection again soon. And, I've one more piece of information."

"What?"

"We may have a nibble from what may be the killer. Our agent received an e-mail already by a woman claiming to be a new writer. She would like to meet with him and discuss her book proposal."

"An agent never does that. They hate to receive requests from want-to-be authors wanting to meet them."

"So true, but this author also sent a photo of herself, and it's, shall I say, a very sexy photo."

"Do you think the photo is really her? If it is, you'll have a photo of the killer?"

"We're trying to determine who she is right now, but it'll take a little while."

"I hope this is the killer and you find her soon. This is so stressful for me."

"Just hold on, you're doing fine."

"Would it be possible for me to see the photo of the girl?"

"It might help, but I'll have to clear it with the field first. He's going to contact her thru the e-mail in a few minutes. I'll call you soon."

CHAPTER 47

The day dragged as Amy waited impatiently for a call back from Arrington. Edward appeared in her daydreams, but he was no longer haunting her as before. She needed to warn him, but how?

Arrington called late in the afternoon, and after saying hello and asking how Amy was, she continued, "The agent sent the want-to-be author an e-mail. He stated he appreciated the e-mail and wished her well and the usually bullshit of a rejection letter, but added a note that he loved her photo."

"Sounds like he's leaving the door open for her."

"We hoped it would work and it has."

"Really? Tell me what's going on."

"I can't tell you much more, but we're sending another agent over to your place to be safe. It's hard to know what's going on in this person's mind. And . . . we're still not sure this is the killer or not."

"Have you found Edward?"

"Not yet, we're still trying to find him, but it has been harder than we had anticipated. Did he say anything about where his cabin was located?"

"No, he said that he owned a peaceful and quiet cabin. It was like I was telling my psychiatrist . . . I wish I knew where it was so I could go to see him."

"Right now, it might be good to avoid discussing his disappearance with anyone."

"I know you're right, but it's so hard to do nothing at all."

###

Amy wandered through the various blogs she once

visited. Life in the publishing world was much the same day after day. She eventually went to Larry's site. She discovered he had not posted for a long time. With nothing else to do, she went backwards on his post page by page for hours. Then she noticed something she might be able to use.

Amy located a photo of Edward and Larry in a mountain setting. She leaned forward as she read the post. The two had spent the weekend at Edward's cabin and had spent some time fishing. Wow! That meant Larry would know the location of Edward's cabin.

She found her phone and called Arrington. "This is Amy. I think I found someone who knows where Edward's cabin is."

"That's good. Who is it?"

"It's one of his authors, Larry Waterman."

"I think we have his number, I'll have someone call him. It's good you called. It appears the woman has contacted our agent again. She's not wasting any time."

Amy slowly inhaled a full breath of air. "Do you know who she is yet?"

"Not yet. She has asked him if she can come by and see him at his home tomorrow night. You wouldn't believe the photos she sent to him. It's enough to drive most men crazy."

"So, she has been seducing the men before to gain access to them?"

"Perhaps, we'll have to dig deeper into the evidence on the previous murders."

"Is there anything else I can do to help?"

"No, not now, I think this will all be over soon."

"I hope so, I'm still worried about Edward and the fight we had."

"Soon you'll be able to tell him the truth on all of this, and I hope you'll have everything work out for you."

Amy tried to call Larry again. With no answer, she

decided to call Lenny. "Hello, girl."

"Lenny, I'm so glad to reach you on your cell. They still don't know how to find Edward. We know he has a cabin somewhere in the Catskill Mountains, but no one appears to know exactly where it is."

"I've spent some time in the Catskills, but it was a long time ago. It's not the busy season, so it shouldn't be too hard to find him if he ventures out. However, if he holds up, you'll never find him."

"I located a photo of Larry and Edward together in the mountains. Larry doesn't answer his phone, but I'm going to keep trying."

"I might have a way of contacting him. Let me check on my phone to see if he gave us another number. I'll call you back."

Shortly after the call, Arrington called back. "I heard from the agent sent to check on Edward. He located the cabin, but it appears Edward is having some renovations made to it and has many workers on site. They said he planned to rent something close by and not stay in the cabin until they finish."

"Since we have no way to find him, the agent is going to come back in. He's needed on this case right now to provide further cover on the meeting tomorrow night. Don't worry, he'll be fine."

"But . . . you know for sure he's safe somewhere?"

"Our man said he talked to some of the workers who saw him."

Amy felt a little better knowing he had left the city. She wished she could be with him, and hoped she received the chance later. However, she still had the compelling desire to warn him and tell him more about what was going on. "I'm worried about him and will be glad when you locate this killer."

"We both will. Try to get some sleep, and I'll let you

know what happens tomorrow night."

She soon called Lenny back on the phone. "Lenny, did you find Larry's number?"

"Hello, girl. Yes I did and left a message. I'm sure he'll call back soon."

"I don't know why I'm so scared, but I feel like I need to warn him. Something doesn't feel right. I want to try to go there and find him."

"From Atlanta to the Catskill Mountains in New York is a long way."

"I know, but if we leave now, we can be in the mountains by tomorrow morning."

Lenny whistled softly but long. "Girl, you're something else. Let me get some sleep first, and I'll take the first shift driving."

"Then you'll go with me?"

"I'm not sure how I let you talk me into things like this."

"Thanks, and one more thing. Come on over now and I'll let you sleep while I drive the first shift."

All she heard was another long whistle as he consented.

CHAPTER 48

Amy drove all night as Lenny slept. With the sun starting to light up the sky, Lenny stretched and opened his eyes. "Where are we?" He glanced around attempting to gather his bearings.

"We're almost in the mountains. It'll take a while to find his place. I just hope the guys working on his cabin can help us locate him."

"I'm like so hungry."

"I am too, and we also need to buy some gas." The country road heading into the Catskills approached a small town with a gas station on the right, and she saw a sign which advertised a small café. It looked like a perfect place to start. "How does that look?"

Lenny glanced at it. "Well normally I would never go to a place like this, but I'm starving."

Amy swerved off the road and cruised to the pumps. Lenny's little sports car got outstanding gas mileage, and she had to admit it was fun to drive. She knew he would want to drive after they ate. Such a shame because driving in the mountains would've been fun.

"I'll fill it up and let you go find us a seat inside." Lenny pulled out his wallet to find his credit card.

"Put your card away, I'll pay as I go in. This trip is on me."

After filling the tank, Amy walked in the rustic country store and presented her card to a girl to pay for the gas. "Hello," a small girl with a boyish haircut said as she inched forward.

"Hello, I need to pay for the gas, and we need to eat something."

"We don't have many people in here yet, so help yourself to any seat you want."

Amy moved into a chair at the first table she came to and reached in her purse to retrieve a photo of Edward she had brought with her. "Have you seen this guy in here?"

The waitress glanced at it for a minute. "I'm not sure. We have so many people coming in here on the way to the mountains. He's not a bad looking guy. Who is he?"

Amy started to say her boyfriend, but stopped herself. "He's a friend who has a cabin in the mountains somewhere near here."

"I'm sorry; I wish you luck in finding him."

Lenny joined Amy as soon as the girl went to retrieve some coffee for them. He looked rugged and totally out of his elements. "Girl, you're going to be the death of me yet."

"I have coffee coming, I think you'll survive."

The coffee smelled good as the waitress placed it in front of them. Lenny tasted it and looked over at Amy. She saw that look before. "It's that bad, hummm."

"It's worse. We're going to need lots of milk and sugar. Did you ask about Edward?"

"Yes, but nothing. We have a lot of stops to make today. This may take some time."

"I kind of assumed it would."

"Here's a photo of him for you to show, we'll be working all the stops around here. I think someone must've seen him in here before since he comes here often."

"Have you tried to call him again on his cell phone?"

"Yes, I've tried several times and I've never received an answer, and his message box is full. With his office closed today, I've no way of reaching anyone to help me."

She heard the same story all morning as they went from place to place. Shortly before lunch Amy's phone rang. "Hello, this is Larry. Have you been calling me?"

"Larry. It's so good to hear your voice. I need your help. Edward may be in danger and I can't find him."

"What danger? He's in the Catskills fishing. In fact, I'm on my way now to join him."

"Good, we're here also. He doesn't answer his cell phone."

"He never does when he's fishing. We're supposed to meet at a café we go to at around seven tonight. We know the owner and he's always willing to clean our fish and cook them for us. It's a real mom and pop type place."

"Do you know where his cabin is?"

"Yes, it's at the end of scenic drive off Hwy 22. His mail box looks like an old eighteen wheeler on a post, you can't miss it."

"Where are you meeting him for dinner?"

"It's called "Lucky Lucy" and it's also on Hwy 22."

"I'll meet you there if we don't see you before then. The killer's moving in on the next kill—I know it. I've been working with the FBI."

Larry remained quiet for several moments. "So, you're serious."

"Yes, very serious. I've a lot of confessing to do when I see you and Edward later."

"I'm sure we would love to hear about it. Edward told me he thought you were someone he knew but didn't. He sounded upset, and I had planned to talk to him about it when I saw him again."

"The truth is . . . I think I've turned full circle and have now fallen in love with him. I hope he gives me a chance to fully explain everything to him."

"If I hear from him, I'll call you."

"Thanks, I appreciate it."

###

When they found the cabin from the directions Larry provided they couldn't find Edward, but they did talk to some workers busy on the addition to the cabin. It appeared to be a massive library and office combination. "This is going to be beautiful when you finish it." Amy continued to examine their work.

"Edward has wanted to do this for a long time. He must have a lot of books to fill all of these book shelves." The worker forced a low whistle.

"I'm sure he does. If he comes back today, please let me know." She wrote her number on a piece of paper for them.

Agent Arrington's name appeared on Amy's phone as it started to ring. "Hello, how are you?"

"I'm fine and how are you?"

"I'm fine, what's going on?"

"The killer may've spotted us setting up, at least we think so now, and she disappeared before we could catch her. It looks like we blew it this time."

"Do what?"

"We didn't expect her to show up early today to check it out. The picture we have on one of our cameras is close to the one she sent the agent. We at least now have a good photo of her. It will only be a matter of time before we catch her now."

"I would really like to see the photo if I could. I go to a lot of conventions and may recognize her."

"I'm in route to your home now to talk to you."

Amy bit her lip. "I'm not at home."

"Where are you?"

"I panicked and decided to go to the mountains to find Edward."

"That's not smart and you should've called me first."

"I was going to call, but I never got around to it."

"Okay. Do you have your laptop with you?"

"Yes."

"I'm going to send you the photos in an e-mail. The sooner we identify this woman, the better our chances are of catching her."

"I'll get it out and connect to the internet now, but I'll lose my phone while I'm on line."

"Okay. You'll have it in less than one minute."

Amy reached to the back seat, pulled out her computer and quickly connected to the internet. She then clicked on her e-mail account. The e-mail from Arrington was at the top of the list as Amy clicked on it. The photo was in an attachment she opened as her nerves continued to unravel.

"Oh, my gosh!"

"What is it?" Lenny asked.

"I know who she is!"

CHAPTER 49

Amy disconnected her phone from the computer and called Agent Arrington. "I know who the killer is."

"Are you sure you recognize her?"

"Yes, I think so. I've seen her many times before."

"Who is it?"

"She's in the group therapy class I was in with Dr. Lankford. All I know her by is her first name, which is Estella."

"Thank you. That information is a big help. We'll talk some more in a minute. I need to send someone over to Dr. Lankford's place now. Please hang on."

Amy looked over at Lenny. "You're not going to believe this."

"How is someone in your group therapy involved with this?"

"I've no clue. While she's quiet and strange, I've no doubt it's her in the photo. Here, take a look."

Lenny moved over to study the screen. He studied the photos of her posing in the initial photo with an evening gown pushing her breasts up high and together, revealing an impressive cleavage. She provided the million dollar look and the jewelry to back it up. She also studied a photo of her in another dress, looking almost like someone painted it on her. Even at her age, she would turn the heads of the youngest of guys.

"Now, look at these photos of the woman caught on the security video." She clicked on the other photos to examine a woman wearing a hood over her hair, but without a doubt, it was the same woman.

Agent Arrington returned to the phone. "A field agent's on the way to Dr. Lankford's home now. Tell me what you know about this woman."

"I don't know a lot. She's very quiet. I think she was born into money and married well also. She has a problem with a bipolar condition like all in the group. The exact extent I don't know. You'll have to ask Dr. Lankford."

"Did she ever say anything, or indicate an interest in your problems with agents?"

"She showed some interest, but only slightly. Like I said, she wasn't as open as the rest of the group. She always dressed to kill, and wore a fake smile all the time."

"Did you ever have any contact with her outside the group?"

"Never! And in the group we were only allowed to use first names, so I don't know her last name."

"In the group meetings did she say anything about her problems or how she was doing? I guess I'm reaching for straws here."

"I don't know much, but she always complained about not having a life and nothing to do. She said her husband controlled her and never let her work. She did open up one day and mention something about feeling like a sex toy for her husband."

"I see."

"I think she has been on medication for a long time. She likes to travel, and she has mentioned some of the trips she has made. I assume she must have someone to travel with her, as I doubt she could handle things on her own. I don't think that she's brainless. I think she's highly educated in books, but not in the way of the world, if you know what I mean."

"Of course I do, Amy. Our agent will be arriving any minute to talk to the doctor. I hope she doesn't give us a hard time with patient privileges and stalls us. We need to find this woman fast."

"I hope you do. The more I think of her, the more anxious I'm becoming. She always appeared to be so cold."

"Did she ever mention who her husband was?"

"No, she only indicated several times he was rich and she didn't see him much."

"This all helps, but the main thing is to sit tight and this will be over soon."

Amy bit her lips as the pain registered. "I think I need to tell you something."

In a formal but alerted voice Arrington asked, "What is it?"

"I'm already in the mountains looking for Edward."

"How did you get there?"

"We drove all night. After I couldn't reach him and after all that's going on, I felt like I had to warn him."

"Have you talked to him yet?"

"Not yet, but I hope to soon. He's having dinner with Larry tonight. We've been to his cabin also and talked to his workers."

"I think you're all safe, but I wish you had told me first. Be sure to keep your phone with you, since I'm sure I'll need to ask you some more questions as soon we reach Dr. Lankford."

"I'll have it with me. Please call me with any news at all."

"Please be careful, this isn't over yet, and we still don't know for sure that she's the killer."

"I will." Amy allowed the connection to end before putting her phone in her pocket.

Amy looked over at Lenny. "I hope this is over soon. This is driving me crazy. How could Estella be involved in this?"

"We've no way of telling what she might've been through. I'm sure we'll know soon enough."

###

Three hours later Amy received the next call from Arrington. "How are you, Amy?"

"We're fine. I'm sitting at a café and waiting on Larry and Edward to arrive."

"We had a long conversation with Dr. Lankford. She, at first, wouldn't tell us anything, but when she realized she might be going to prison as an accomplice she finally started cooperating."

"What did she say?"

"It appears that Estella is her niece."

"Wow, I would never have guessed that one."

"Yes, Estella has been an embarrassment for the family for a long time. She drinks heavily and goes on wild binges often. She has to be constantly guarded, but manages to fool everyone into thinking she's all right for a while only to relapse."

"But . . . how is she connected to my problem and the killing of the agents?"

"Dr. Lankford admitted Estella has been obsessed with your problems and constantly asked questions about you when they had their private sessions."

"Wow. I would never have known. But . . . why?"

"She saw you as an underdog being manipulated like she was. While she couldn't do anything about her situation, she thought maybe she could get rid of your problems with the "jerks" you were dealing with."

"This is wild and kind of hard to believe that she would want to kill people."

"Who knows what's going on in her mind? She has some serious problems, and I'm sure we'll hear much more soon."

"So, what happens next?"

"We have to find her fast. Someone is on the way to her house now. We hope her husband will be honest and open with us. With a little luck, we can apprehend her as well."

"I'm so sorry for her, but I will be so glad when this is

over."

"I'll call you soon. I would stay somewhere safe until this is over."

"I've a friend, Lenny, with me here."

"That's good. Call me if you can think of anything else you think I need to know."

Lenny was all ears as she talked. "This is becoming more and more exciting, girl. You're going to definitely be the death of me yet. I think I need a drink."

"I'll agree. Beer is all they might have here."

Lenny groaned slightly. "Beer will have to do." He lifted his hand and waved at the waitress who walked over to them. "Is beer the only drink we can get here?"

The small smile on her face indicated that was about it. "I think we might have some small miniature bottles of wine."

Lenny laughed. "Whatever . . . bring us some of those."

Amy rolled her eyes at Lenny. "This isn't exactly Hawaii, is it?"

"Not at all, but it's remarkable in a way. I'm still thinking of moving to Hawaii. The guys I met in Hawaii will help me build an interior decorating company, and it would be a dream life living there. The owners of the house we stayed at are impressed with my recommendations and are telling their friends. It's a great way to get started."

"That's a long way to go. I might not ever see you again."

"Don't be ridiculous. You can come any time you want and have a place to stay."

"That would be good."

"And who knows, you might want to get married one day in Hawaii to you know who."

"I'm not sure, since right now he's not talking to me. He might not ever believe me at all." The thoughts of how true this was made her lip curl slightly as a small tear dotted her eye.

She watched the waitress bring the small wine miniatures to the table. She found a red and a blush. "I hope you see something you like."

"This'll be fine."

CHAPTER 50

Amy's phone rang with Arrington's name registering on the caller ID. "Where are you now?"

"We're still at the café waiting on Larry and Edward."

"We met with Estella's maid. It appears her husband has separated from her a long time ago. It'll take some time to find him. The maid doesn't know where Estella is and not very cooperative either. We brought her in for questioning as a person of interest. Of course, she's not saying a word until she talks to an attorney."

"That will have to take some time. Doesn't she know how important it is to find Estella?"

"We're working on it. We're also going to bring in Dr. Lankford."

"I hope they help you with more information."

"We found out a little more. I hate to tell you this, but Dr. Lankford had talked to Estella the other day and told her about Edward. She also told her you said he was going to his cabin."

Amy's heart almost stopped beating. "You don't think she's on the way here, do you?"

"We're not sure right now. We're having our field office send the agent back out to cover this angle, just in case."

Amy started to cry again. "This is all my fault."

"I agree you've made some mistakes, but you're not responsible for another person's actions. Are you going to be okay?"

"Yes, I think so. Do you think you can catch her soon?"

"Like I said . . . we thought we had her, but she escaped us again, and we're not still one hundred percent sure she's the killer. We won't know until we catch her and bring her in for question."

"When was the last time she was seen?"

"She hasn't been seen since we caught her on the security video, but we've reason to believe she was in the area a few hours after that. We've issued an all-points bulletin on her car, but we have received nothing so far."

"I see. It's the waiting which is killing me. I think I need to get some rest, since I never slept last night."

"Yes, please do so. You need to stay healthy. I'll let you know of any changes at all."

###

At almost six, Larry walked into the café and smiled at Amy, who was sleeping while leaning against a wall before he motioned over to Lenny. "It must've been a long day."

"Very long . . . she has refused to go to sleep until she was sure Edward was okay." Lenny extended his hand toward Larry.

"I've been trying to call him also, and he still doesn't have his phone with him. He'll be here soon, I'm sure."

"I think Amy loves this guy. It'll be good if she can convince him after all of this."

"Edward's a nice guy, but you can never tell about him."

Amy barely nodded her head as she blinked her eyes. "Ohhh, hi. What did you say, Larry?"

"Hi yourself, you look bad. I heard you had a long day."

"Yes, too long. What time is it?"

"About six I think."

Soon seven displayed on a wall clock, and still no Edward. Amy felt the nervous twitches expanding along her back. "I can't stand the waiting. Maybe we should go back to his cabin and see if he returned."

"Don't worry, he'll be here soon."

But, as time slipped away, he still didn't show up. "I think I'll drive by his cabin. If you see him, call me. I need to think about what I'm going to say to him also."

Lenny and Larry looked at each other as Larry reached for his keys. "You can take my car if you want. We'll call you, if he shows up here."

"Thanks, but I know Lenny's car better."

"Okay, but call us if you find out anything."

\#\#\#

Amy drove to the cabin, thinking of how she planned to explain things to Edward. This was going to be the hardest thing she ever had to do. She needed to stay focused.

She noticed a car passing her with a tall blonde haired woman in the driver seat that looked out of sorts for the mountains. The car looked like a large Mercedes. Her first thoughts were surely it wasn't Estella driving around—not here. Then, she hit the brakes. She had to check it out. She had to know.

She pulled off to the side and turned around before gunning the motor to make up the distance as fast as she could. She didn't know if she could overtake the car before she lost it or not, but she had to try.

Within a few minutes, she knew she had lost the car. She pulled out her phone and started to call when she realized she was in a dead spot. She would have to wait a few minutes until she could get a signal. When she pulled onto a side road, she saw a Mercedes parked on one side.

A trail extended to a small walking bridge before going up the mountain. Amy opened her door and headed for the car. She saw nothing to indicate who the owner was, but decided to write down the tag number in case she might need it later.

While Amy walked across the bridge to see if she could find the driver again, she definitely hoped she could spot the driver before she spotted her. Half of the way across the bridge her phone rang, startling her. She fished for it out of her pants pocket to keep it from ringing and giving her location away. She moved too fast, and awkwardly, as the phone fell from her hands while pulling it from her pocket. It hit the bridge once before she witnessed the unbelievable bounce of her phone off the bridge and down to the small stream below. "Oh, my Gosh . . . this can't be happening to me right now. Not now!" she gasped out loud.

She looked around to see if anyone saw her. The mountain stream continued to be the only sound she heard as she quivered. However, she needed to know. She walked across the bridge and a few hundred feet up the trail. She saw nothing. This was crazy. She needed Larry and Lenny.

She turned to go back to the car and almost made the bridge when she watched the Mercedes turn back around and pull out of the side road. She had missed her somehow. She had to hurry.

Amy ran to her car, jumped in and cranked the motor. She had to catch the Mercedes this time. It was heading in the direction of Edward's cabin. Why did she do something so stupid with her phone?

Within minutes she arrived at Edward's cabin, where she saw no signs of anyone, even the workers had left. Still, she searched for the Mercedes. Perhaps she had already checked it out and left. That is, if she had been by the cabin at all. Amy knew it wouldn't be good to be seen by either Estella or Edward. She needed to hide somewhere close by, and most importantly, she needed to find a phone.

Being too far to go to the café now, she pulled out of the driveway and headed toward town to see if she could find a pay phone anywhere. She saw nothing and knew she didn't want to get too far away. She needed to warn Edward. As she turned around and made her way back to the entrance of the cabin, all she could do now was sit and wait. Since it would be dark soon, she hoped he would show soon.

As darkness settled in, she watched a truck slowly turn

around in Edward's driveway. It was a sports vehicle of some kind which could've been one of the workers or someone lost, but for some reason Amy decided to follow it.

In less than a mile, the truck turned off of the main road and onto a dirt side road. Amy pulled closer but stopped at the entrance. Being a short driveway, it didn't provide her with much to hide behind. She started to pull past the road until the vehicle stopped in front of a small cabin.

Amy saw Edward jump out of the truck, walk to the cabin, and disappear inside. This must be the place he was staying while they worked on his cabin. She quickly pulled into a spot next to his.

He returned to the front door to see who it was as she turned off the engine and stepped out of her car. He stood still and patient as she approached him. "Amy? How are you and what are you doing here?"

"Edward, I've so much to say to you. It's good to see you're safe."

"Why shouldn't I be?"

"The FBI thinks they know who the killer is."

He raised one eyebrow in an inquisitive gesture. "That's good to know, it's about time."

"Edward, I'm so sorry for deceiving you. When I received your rejection letter after meeting you, I think I lost control, and I did some stupid things. I hope you can find a way in your heart to forgive me."

He focused the same hard glaze at her for a long time. "The first thing in any relationship is honesty. Without that, we can never have much to build on."

"I agree, and I'll tell you everything, but right now we need to find somewhere safe."

"Why do you keep saying that?"

"I think the killer is after you, and it's my fault. That's why I drove all night to be here. The FBI will be here soon."

"The FBI?"

"Yes, I've been working with them to find the killer. Someone has become a copycat of my actions, but is totally crazy and is determined to come after you now. They almost had her, but she escaped. We had no way of contacting you."

Edward apparently became astutely aware of the situation, as if for the first time. "Come on inside and tell me more."

They rushed inside. He closed the blinds on the front of the house. "Who is this killer?"

"Her name is Estella, and she's a woman in my group therapy class." She was going to tell him about her conditions first, but knew she may have already said too much. She didn't want to lose him now.

"I wish you told me about your bipolar condition earlier." Amy lowered her head as he apparently knew. "If you had, perhaps I could've helped you sooner."

Amy looked up with puppy dog eyes. "What do you mean when you said that you could've helped me earlier?"

"If we're going to have any kind of life together, I have to understand what you're going through. That's one of the reasons I came to the cabin. I wanted to do research on bipolar disorder. Like many people I've heard of it and know a little, but that's it." He pointed to a large stack of books on the kitchen table.

Amy covered her mouth with her hands, she couldn't believe it. "You did this for me?"

"Yes, I wanted to help. I talked to Grantland and he told me the situation. When you started acting like you didn't want to see me, I knew then that I needed to understand this or lose you forever."

Amy walked over to give him a large hug. "You're absolutely wonderful."

Lights appeared from a car flying down the driveway. They both moved to the front window and looked out. An outline of another car pulled behind Lenny's car. They had company.

"That may be her. I think I saw her a little while ago, but I'm not sure. She was driving a Mercedes."

Edward looked outside again. "I'm not sure, but it might be one."

"I lost my phone a few hours ago. We need to call the police."

"It'll take a while for the police to respond here, we're in the middle of nowhere."

"Do you have a gun here?"

"No, I don't own one. I never had a need for a gun before."

Edward walked over to the kitchen and started looking in the drawers for a knife to use as a weapon. He retrieved several he could possibly use, and handed one to Amy. "You might need this."

She hesitantly accepted the knife and wrapped her hands around the handle. Her heart beat fast. "What are we going to do?"

"I think we have no choice but to wait and see what happens. However, I'll make the call to the police and ask how long it'll take them to get here."

Before he could reach for his phone, the back door crashed open like a thunder clap as a large metal bat shattered the glass in it. With no effort, Estella swung open the door and walked in. She was dressed in an expensive dark blue pants suit with elaborate details embroidered into it. Her long blonde hair looked expertly cut and styled as if she walked out of a salon. And as usual, she was decorated with expensive jewelry, mostly diamonds, everywhere.

"Estella, what are you doing here?"

Estella nodded at Amy. "I see I arrived just in time."

"In time for what?"

"To rescue you from this jerk."

"I think you have it all wrong. This guy isn't a jerk, he's my boyfriend."

"I can tell he has already brainwashed your mind, much like my husband has mine."

Edward stepped forward and pointed the knife at Estella. "I think this is enough of this."

Estella laughed at the knife and removed a small pistol from her pocket and pointed it at Edward. "I don't think we're even getting started, lover boy." Edward looked determined to hold onto the knife until she cocked back the hammer. He dropped the knife. "Now, kick it over to me. I don't want you to get any ideas later."

He kicked it as he was ordered, but moved closer to Amy. "Estella, you have to listen to me. This is over!"

"It's not over yet. I'm just starting. The world's full of jerks, and if nothing else I can do my part to make things right. Once I was happy and with a life, but others wanted to control me and make me into their own private play toy. It didn't work!"

"Estella, we can get you help."

"I don't need help! From now on, I'll make my own way. As soon as I finish here, my loving husband will be the next jerk. All is in line for me to leave the country and never be seen again. I hate how it will end like this for both of you, but I've no choice now. It'll look like a lovers' quarrel where you both killed each other."

They all heard another car rushing down the driveway. Estella looked surprised. She drifted to one side of the door and motioned for them to sit on the floor. As they complied, the sounds of footsteps running to the door increased. Amy gently touched her pocket to confirm the knife inside.

She heard large knocks on the door. "Edward, are you in there?"

Estella stayed still, waiting, as she held the gun in one hand and a small metal bat in the other, preparing to do battle if she needed to.

Something large hit the door. It almost opened, but didn't. Estella moved closer to the door. The next large blast to the door made it explode open, with Larry and Lenny rushing in. Estella raised her gun with what looked to be full intention of firing.

Amy removed the knife from her pocket and slashed out at Estella, cutting her upper arm. Blood spluttered from Estella's open wound, but she managed to fire a shot and raise the bat at the same time, forcing Amy backwards. Estella pointed the pistol at the crowd in front of her again. She had the weapon, but they had the numbers as she backed away.

She then turned and ran out of the back of the house as she yelled, "This isn't over yet!"

Larry dropped to his knees as blood covered the wooden floor below him.

"Oh, my gosh! You've been shot," Amy yelled. The blood bleeding from his arm covered his clothes. Lenny helped him to rip off his shirt and hold the remnants against the bleeding to help stop the flow. "We need to rush him to a hospital."

"Yes, but what about Estella? She's still out there." As a shot ricocheted inside the cabin, they all hit the floor. "We're like sitting ducks in here," Edward shouted, as another shot shattered a light above them. She acted determined. Something had to be done, but what?

The next fifteen minutes passed with deathly silence. No one moved, but they placed another call to 911. They would arrive soon, but not fast enough it appeared as Estella stalked outside.

Eventually, two cars swirled into the driveway as flood lights came on. A large voice boomed over a loud speaker, "Drop your gun now; this is the FBI."

Estella appeared to have no intentions of complying as

several shots rang out. While turning quiet for a minute, everyone was too scared to look outside until they heard a loud voice. "Those in the house; please raise your hands and come out now." They all proceeded as directed. As they exited the house, a man ushered to them from one side. "Is there anyone else with a gun?"

Edward answered. "No! There's only the one killer here, but we do have one guy shot." He pointed to Larry.

After glancing at him, the officer called for an ambulance.

With Estella face down on the ground with two agents guarding her, she moaned and screamed chilling sounds of anguish. Another agent was busy on the phone talking to a rescue service. "Yes, we've two confirmed people who've been shot, but they're not life threatening."

Agent Arrington suddenly appeared and walked over to the group to hug Amy. "We've been trying to call you on your phone."

Amy looked embarrassed. "I accidentally dropped it in a stream a few hours ago."

"That wasn't smart."

"Tell me about it." Arrington looked around at the group attempting to identify everyone. Amy picked up on her glances. "This is Edward, Larry and Lenny." She motioned to each one as she said their name.

Arrington examined Larry's bleeding arm and asked him to sit. "We'll have someone here soon to take you to the hospital. Are you going to be okay?"

He cringed with a painful glaze radiating from his eyes. "I've never been shot before, it hurts like hell."

"Hang in there, it will not be long before the medics are here." Turning to Edward, she continued, "I feel like I know you somewhat now. It's bad to have to meet you like this."

"It's going to be good to get some answers on what's going on." Edward eyes stayed focused on her.

"I know you have questions, and rightly so. I'm sure you'll have all of them answered soon."

CHAPTER 51

On the long trip to the hospital, Edward had a hard time following the two ambulances. Lenny had decided to ride in the ambulance with Larry to keep him company. Amy felt glad since it offered her a chance to talk to Edward, although they spoke little on the way to the hospital.

They eventually arrived at a small hospital, where a crowd of attendants, nurses, and a doctor were on standby inside to start to work on the two patients. Estella was unconscious, and it wasn't clear if it was from the shooting or if she had been given something.

The staff pushed the stretcher carrying them to small rooms to begin assessing the damages. "You're going to be fine." Lenny reassured Larry as he was pushed away.

Edward held Amy's hand, as Lenny walked over to them. "I guess there's nothing else to do but wait."

Arrington walked in and surveyed the group. "I need to get some more statements from everyone. Perhaps we can find some coffee here."

"Sounds good, but I still haven't had any sleep from the night before." Amy blinked her eyes.

They walked down a hall and quickly located a small coffee shop open to the public. They all ordered coffee and found a seat.

"Amy has told me a little about what's going on, but I would like to know more." Edward started off by asking Agent Arrington questions.

"I know you have concerns. On the way in, Estella did some talking. We also have her aunt, the psychiatrist, confessing in a letter she wrote concerning information she should've shared earlier about Estella."

Agent Arrington lowered her head respectfully as she continued. "I've something else, something important, I need to tell you. The stress of this apparently was too much for Dr Lankford. We discovered her in her office a few hours ago . . . I hate to tell you, but she appears to have committed suicide."

"Oh, my gosh! Oh, my gosh!" Amy started to cry uncontrollably with Edward trying to comfort her as the words sunk in.

Arrington patiently waited for her to regain control. "Another problem we have now is Estella's husband."

"Why is her husband a problem?"

"Her husband left her a long time ago. He still provides for her, but couldn't tolerate the bipolar problems she had. He left treatment to the aunt, Dr. Lankford, to do as best she could."

"I didn't know." Amy felt sorry for Estella.

"It appears he'll do the most he can to hamper this investigation any way that he can. We haven't been able to find him."

"Does he know about his wife being shot?" Edward asked.

"I'm not sure if he does or not. However, we don't think he's an innocent bystander."

"Why is that?" both Amy and Edward asked at the same time.

"Estella's husband left her many years ago and he is your boss at World Media, Leland Grantland."

"Do what?" Amy felt like she was going to faint. Her world started spinning around. How could this be? "Does he know she's the killer?"

"We're not sure yet, but we highly suspect that he might be behind the killings and using Estella to do his dirty work."

Edward's face blushed with anger. "Some of these agents murdered were friends of mine."

"I'm sorry, and you have my condolences. We're still

piecing things together, but I need to ask Amy some more questions."

Amy looked up with her eyes full of tears. "What can I tell you?"

"Why do you think Mr. Grantland went looking for you and hired you?"

"We talked about this. He said he read my articles and thought I would make a great reviewer and assistant with the publishing house."

"Did he know anything else about you before then?"

"I don't think so. We meet at a convention earlier, but he didn't know much about me then."

"What are you leading to?" Edward wanted to know.

"The first murder was slightly different than the others on several accounts. It was the only one that didn't have sexual overtures. We've discovered some bad fights between Mr. Grantland and Mitchell Lloyd."

"Do you think Ike killed him?"

"We're not sure, but it was fortunate for him. It appears Mitchell was going to move all of his authors to other publishers as fast as he could. When he died, the authors found new agents but stayed with Mr. Grantland's company. While he is the executive editor there, very few also know that he owns a large part of the company."

"What about the other murders?"

"They may have been covers for the original killing. Since Estella wasn't killed in this latest set up, we hope to get some answers out of her; especially since she'll not be under the control of her aunt and the drugs she had been given."

"I don't understand. Were the murders performed by Ike or Estella?"

"That is the piece of information we don't know yet. It's going to take a lot more investigation into this to be able to solve it. We're hoping Estella can provide the missing data to us when she wakes."

"How bad is she hurt?"

"We're waiting on the doctors to tell us now. She's unconscious and has lost a lot of blood."

Amy forced herself to sit straight as the stress intensified. "I don't feel so well. A night of not sleeping and all of this is just too much."

"I'm so sorry. There's nothing else you can do now. You need some sleep."

Edward spoke fast. "She's welcome to go to my place to sleep. Not the one where the shooting happened, but my cabin. I'll call the workers in the morning and tell them not to do any work tomorrow so she can receive a good days rest."

Agent Arrington looked at Amy for approval.

Amy reached for Edward's hand. "I think that would be exactly what I need."

Edward looked over at Lenny. "You're welcome to come, also."

"I appreciate it, but I think I'll stick around for a while and keep Larry company."

"Someone staying with him might be a good idea. Let me know when you need me to pick you up and I'll come back to get you."

CHAPTER 52

Edward's rustic cabin looked exactly as she remembered it, but with a charm all of its own. The scattered material from the work on the addition was messy, but she knew it was only temporary.

He opened his door, and moved around the car to open her door for her. "I hope you like it. It's quiet here and peaceful."

"Anything with a bed right now sounds like heaven."

He held her hand as she walked the steps to the front door. He opened it and turned on the lights. She studied the rich wooden glow coming from inside. The highly polished floors looked much different than she had assumed it would be from the outside. She would have to call this a country elegant look. "Wow, this is much different than I thought."

He seemed pleased at her comment. "I'm sorry about all the construction, but I think you'll be happy with it later."

"I see you're adding on. What are you building exactly?'

He looked like an actor auditioning for a part. "I want to have a full library here so I can store many books. I think I can do most of my work from here."

"I've heard you say before you carry some of your work here."

"It's a place to hide and read and read. The office in the city will always be necessary, but with the proper staff, I think I can make it work."

"It'll be nice to see if you can."

He walked over to the door leading to the addition. "It's not much to look at right now, but I think it'll be fantastic later. It's something I've always dreamed of."

The room looked much larger than Amy had first imagined. The ceiling stretched almost twelve feet high.

"You'll be able to store many books on these walls."

"I had planned for a certain size, but I recently met with the builder and made it much larger."

"Why was that?"

She watched him blush. "When we met and I learned you were also in the book business, I thought if we were to get together, so to speak, we would need a larger space."

She felt a chill in her spine as she listened to his words sounding like magic to her ears. "You never told me anything about all of this."

"I wasn't going to until this all happened. It was supposed to be a surprise until I thought you lied to me and only used me."

"I'm so sorry. I promise not to lie to you again." She raised a hand to make a scouts honor pledge that ended in a large yawn.

"I think right now, you need some sleep. The bedroom's down the hall." He led her to a massive bedroom with decorations reflecting the feel of the mountains.

"Thank you."

"The bathroom's over there." He pointed to the back of the room. "I'm going to make some calls while you're preparing to sleep. Is there anything else I can do for you?"

"Do you mind going to get my clothes? They're in Lenny's car which isn't too far away."

"Sure, I'll be right back." He reached over and gave her a small hug and kissed the top of her forehead. "All will be fine now." He then walked over to the door, opened it, and left. She heard the car start, and him speeding away as he left.

She looked around the room for a minute at his photos which were mainly of the mountains, and then decided it was best to not get caught snooping. She had heard them referred to as the Blue Mountains before and the photos depicted such a color scheme. However, she would need something to wear when she got out of the shower. She walked over to his closet and opened it.

Of the few clothes in it, she did manage to find a long polo shirt. As tall as he was, it almost made a dress for her. She yawned and headed for the shower, where she pulled the curtain back and turned on the water. A good hot shower is just what she needed. On the holder was a large white towel she could use. She closed the door and started to undress.

She remembered the time she walked in the shower with Edward and how exciting it was. It would be good to do that again. She dropped her pants and turned to look at herself in the mirror. "Oh my gosh, I need to lose some weight."

After she removed her top and bra, she worried about her breasts starting to show signs of sagging, in spite of all the support she had tried to give them over the years. As she looked over her body, she noticed the window to the outside and a thin curtain, which didn't provide much security at all. "That's one thing we'll have to change soon."

She removed her panties, pulled the shower curtain to one side and stepped inside. The water felt hot and terrific, and standing under the flood of hot water helped to melt away some of her tension. The body wash she helped herself to felt silky and sexual as she washed her body. It would've been easy to spend the entire night in the shower, but when the water started to turn cold, she knew she needed to quit and dry off.

As she left the shower she yelled through the door, "Edward, are you back yet?" After she heard no answer, she stood on a small rug to dry and looked again over at the window making her feel uneasy again. She wrapped herself in the towel and opened the door to look out in the bedroom. Since all remained quiet, she stepped back into the bathroom and slipped on the polo shirt.

She managed to find a small comb for her hair, but since

Edward had short hair, he had no need for a hair dryer. As such, she retrieved the towel and started working on it as best she could.

After opening the door to the bedroom and going outside, the quiet cabin invoked a spooky feeling as she walked around. She felt sleepy as she walked over to the bed and fell into the middle of it. Within minutes she fell asleep.

###

She wasn't sure how long she had slept, but when she woke later, she lay on her side with someone snuggled up close to her. He felt so warm against her body she immediately went back to sleep.

###

The light filtering through the windows encouraged refreshed eyes to open. While the previous day was a nightmare, Amy's body felt rested to some extent now. The bed felt soft, comfortable and warm as she reached behind her to explore the other side of the bed. There was no one there. Where was Edward?

She sat up, trying to remember last night, but could only remember very little at all. A sound of voices talking in the yard abruptly brought her out of the deep concentration. As she walked over to the window and peeked out, she heard Edward arguing with a man in the yard. Edward soon waved at him and headed for the front door.

As the front door cracked open and she heard footsteps she jumped back in the bed, pretending to be asleep. The bedroom door creaked as he opened it. She moaned as she turned over to face him.

He smelled fantastic as he leaned over the bed. "I'm sorry I was gone so long to return with your stuff last night."

"I think I slept like a log."

"Yes, you were asleep when I returned."

"I think I heard voices outside a few minutes ago."

"The men want to start on the house, and they didn't like having to wait until tomorrow, but it'll be okay."

"You didn't have to do that for me."

"Well . . . to tell the truth, I think I wanted to be alone with you today and relax, and to get to know you better. We have many things to talk about."

He leaned over to the bed to give her a kiss on the cheek. "How are you feeling this morning?"

She received the kiss with a big smile, as she rose and placed her back against the headboard. The polo shirt she borrowed from Edward's closet was oversized in some respects, but fully filled in others. "I hope you don't mind me borrowing your shirt. I had nothing else to wear."

He looked at the shirt and grinned. "I think it looks much better on you than on me."

Amy pulled back the covers to make room for him to slide over next to her. He hesitated briefly and then kicked off his shoes before moving beside her. She watched him study her breasts only so slightly concealed beneath his thin polo shirt. Her nipples in particular became pronounced as they attempted to poke through the shirt. "Maybe the shirt wasn't such a good idea."

"No, I think it's perfect." He looked back up and focused on her eyes.

She didn't feel threatened at all, especially since she had been with him once before, and it had only been a few weeks ago. However, it seemed like they needed to be reacquainted with each other again. Amy considered the slow gradual ritual they were performing, which was probably not too much different than any man and woman falling in love.

While not for sure, it appeared he wanted to make love to her right then and there. While she felt nervous about actually doing it again, she felt calm in knowing he would be gentle like the first time. Her feelings grew deeper for him than she wanted to imagine, and she knew it wasn't simply a lust thing at all.

He reached over and ran a hand through her hair to the back of her head where he gently massaged her scalp. He waited and watched her reactions as if he appeared to be analyzing her every thought. "I've dreamed about you all the time since I returned from Hawaii."

His words sounded sweet, and tender, and exactly what she wanted to hear. "I've thought about you as well."

As he slid in closer to her she worked hard to control her breathing. Becoming more and more excited, she wanted him to know she welcomed his advances. The craving she had for him mounted as he continued to drive her crazy with his slow but meticulous method. She moaned again as she put a small amount of pressure on his hand to indicate it felt very good.

Amy reached over and placed her arm around his neck as he leaned over and kissed her neck. The warm moisture of his lips melted into her body, sending it further into convulsions of pleasure. She couldn't contain the low moans of pleasure any more.

He brushed his hands across her nipples as they hardened. This brought a quick smile to his face. He moved his hand toward her face to brush it as he lowered his head to kiss her on the lips. They barely made contact, but it was enough to send further sparks racing across her body. "Oh, my Gosh," she whispered as she was losing control in a soothing, yet positive way.

He lowered his hand to her breasts again and whispered, "Is this okay?"

She didn't answer, but nodded her head up and down several short times. He then started to feel of her nipples between his finger and thumb. Amy's breathing increased, becoming faster and faster.

Edward leaned in closer and this time kissed her with much more authority. It was as if he now had the green light to proceed. She opened her mouth and let him use his tongue to explore her mouth. Her whole body generated heat, as the craving for more and the yearning to move on intensified.

RINGGGGGGGGGGGG. Edward's phone sent her heart into panic mode. The high volume and this precise timing sent both of them scrambling.

"Damn!" Edward cursed as he tried to dig the phone out of his pocket. It rang again as he finally retrieved it. He quickly turned it off.

"Who is it?" Amy asked.

"I don't know." While he acted exasperated, and embarrassed he had left the phone on at all, he quickly recognized Agent Arrington's name on the caller ID. "Okay, this may be important."

"Yes, answer it."

"This is Edward."

"Hello. I hate to call you so early in the morning, but I need to see you and Amy this morning at the hospital. It looks like Estella may be able to talk soon, and if she comes around we might be able to finally get some answers."

"I hope so. We'll come as fast as we can."

"Thanks."

"That was Agent Arrington who I met last night. She said it was important we come to the hospital as soon as possible. I'm sorry."

As Amy fought to breathe normal she couldn't believe how much she wanted Edward. It felt like she had years and years of pent up desires in her body, and it was almost released, but again life had a way of putting obstacles in her way. "I can't believe this timing." She offered a pout.

"Don't worry. It will be much better tonight when we

have more time to relax."

"I hope I can wait until then."

He laughed. "Hey, keep that motor running." He slid his hand over her nipple one last time as she moaned again.

As she closed her eyes, she felt him remove his hand and get off the bed. "I guess I need to get ready, hummm."

"Yes. She made it sound urgent."

CHAPTER 53

Amy and Edward walked in the front door of the small hospital and hurried to the SIC waiting room, where Agent Arrington and several other agents waited for them. "I'm not sure we're going to get anything more out of Estella. She's on life support."

"How bad did she get shot?" Amy asked.

"The shot wasn't too bad. She said she wanted to die. The slash you made to her arm made her bleed, and she intentionally let it keep bleeding. She wasn't able to cut her wrist herself, but she welcomed the cut you made. The shots she fired at the house weren't intended to kill you, but to keep you from getting help for her."

"How do you know this?" Amy asked.

"She told us this last night on the way into the hospital before she blacked out."

"What else did you learn from her?"

"We learned her husband is much more involved than we assumed. He used her to do his work for him. He had almost committed the perfect crime and got away with it."

"I still have a hard time believing all of this."

"It will not be long until we have him in custody. As long as he thinks Estella's alive and talking, he knows he's vulnerable. We think he was hoping she would be killed in one of the assassinations herself."

"You're painting him as some kind of monster."

"It's much worse than you can imagine. Estella did some fast talking before she passed out. She was told to prostitute herself to get the agent's attention. If she didn't do exactly as ordered, she was told that she wouldn't receive any more drugs."

"So, he had her strung out on drugs then."

"Her own aunt was ordering them for her based on what

her husband was telling her. They wanted to keep Estella under control, and thus not embarrass the family any more. It was Estella's father, Dr. Lankford, who was very wealthy before he died. Mr. Grantland stands to receive a large inheritance from Estella when she died and is why he never divorced her. However, he couldn't live with her highly bipolar disorder and depressed outbreaks."

"This is terrible."

"It's going to take a while to build this case, and I'm sure we'll discover much more we don't know yet. Again, some of this is still speculation."

"I still can't believe I started all of this."

"It could be that you didn't start this. I think Grantland devised a way to cover his first murder with you, and handle the problem with his wife all at the same time. He may have been playing you for a fool the entire time."

The harsh reality of her comment stunned Amy. "That's so . . . cold."

Edward moved closer to Amy and put his arm around her. He listened but didn't say a word, as Amy looked over to him and smiled. "I'm so sorry for getting you involved in this."

"It'll be fine. We'll put this behind us soon."

###

They waited for Estella to wake for several hours as the time slipped away. Amy decided to go for a small walk as Edward made calls on his cell phone. The hallway leading to the wing where Estella was in had a man standing by the door, obviously an FBI agent of some kind. She glanced at him, but continued to walk.

Later she saw an orderly walking by with his head lowered as he pushed a cart along. Amy tried to move out of his way, but the cart hit her right hip. "Ouch!"

The orderly looked up quickly. "I'm sorry."

At first, his face didn't register, but then the deep-green eyes locked in on her. "Ike! What are you doing here?" Her voice quivered as she stepped backwards.

He glared at her as he pulled a gun from his pocket and pointed it at her while partially hiding it behind the lab coat. "Don't say a word. We're going to walk slowly to Estella's room, and I'm going to follow you."

"Why are you doing this?"

"I'm not here to answer your questions. Just do as you're told."

Amy could see the barrel of the gun fixed on her chest, and the look in his eyes—so cold, so penetrating. She already witnessed Larry getting shot, and the idea of being the next one made her knees tremble. She managed to focus slightly as she turned to walk along the hallway.

The few hundred feet to Estella's room seemed like several miles as all activities around her shifted into slow motion. What was she supposed to do, and how could she warn the others? She felt Ike's presence as he walked close behind her.

As she made one turn, she turned toward him. "What do you plan to accomplish? You know she's guarded by the FBI."

"I saw her room. They only have one agent on duty. He'll be taken care of. Keep walking." Amy obeyed, but tried to think of any way she could signal for help and not be detected. He stayed too close and they would be there soon.

As they made the last turn heading for Estella's room, Amy studied the entrance to her room with the one agent in front of the door simply standing and watching them as they walked.

"What do we do now?" Amy whispered over her back toward Ike.

"Keep moving forward and act normal."

As they moved in front of the agent, the agent held out his hand for them to stop. He never flinched when Ike moved from behind the cart and brandished the gun under the lab coat. "What's this?"

"It's a meeting to discuss things. Don't say a word and open the door."

"I don't think I can do that."

"Then you'll have a dead girl in front of you, and it will also be the last thing you will ever witness. Do as I say."

Slowly, the agent moved to the door to open it. Ike moved around Amy to follow him in. As he entered the room, Ike pulled Amy behind him. Estella slept on the bed in the next room.

Before the agent could turn around, Ike struck him with the heavy barrel sending him stumbling forward. The agent tried to regain his footing only to be struck again with much more force. This time he collapsed to the floor with a dull thud.

Amy started to scream, but caught herself as Ike pointed the gun at her, inches from her eyes. "What's wrong with you?"

"I'm in a situation giving me little options. It's too bad you got involved with this."

"I don't understand at all. You never told me Estella was your wife."

"Yes, but in name only. We've been separated for over ten years." He checked the door and looked over at Estella.

"The FBI knows you're behind the murders. You have no way of getting away with this."

"The only evidence they have on me is what they might be able to learn from Estella. Since she's still legally my wife, she can't testify against me. Anything she has told them will not be acceptable in court." He looked over at her with contempt.

"How could you do this to her?"

"She has been a weight around my neck for most of my life. There's so much about her you don't know. Only her father's money and her aunt's drugs have allowed her to stay out of prison. The money I'll have when she dies is more than you can imagine, but I think I've earned every penny of it for what I've been through."

"You can't mean what you're saying. You'll be caught and convicted."

"I don't think so. I'm in this too deeply now to turn back." He walked over to Estella and checked one of the lines going to her arm. "It's important for me to know what she has told the FBI and what you know."

Thinking fast Amy answered, "I know she told them everything, and they also have her aunt to back up her stories."

"I don't think Dr. Lankford will be a problem. I hated it for her, but she was also a problem I needed to eliminate."

Tears flooded Amy's eyes. "Then you know about her suicide then?"

An evil smile crossed Ike's face. "Any evidence she had on me is now destroyed. Her letter was designed to remove any evidence connecting me with Estella."

"Oh my Gosh! You murdered her too!"

"It was necessary. I can't leave any evidence of any connection with Estella."

"But . . . she's your wife, and the FBI knows this."

"Yes, but proving I had any other connections will be impossible."

Amy started shaking and the dizzy feelings increased as the stress overpowered her. "Are you planning on killing us also?"

"I've no other choice." He looked over at his wife again and studied her. The bandage around her face made identifying her difficult, but considering what she had been through, understandable.

"I still can't believe you used her to kill people for you. I always thought she was highly strung out on drugs. How do you live with yourself?"

"With this behind me, I'll live fine. The first agent to die, Mitchell Lloyd, was causing problems and intended to move his clients to another house. I went to see him and hope to persuade him to change his mind. We ended up in a fight. He gave me no option, so I repaid him for his actions. I wanted it to look like a maniac had killed him."

"I saw the photos. Only a psycho would do that to someone. You've lost it."

"Perhaps. But it was a conversation with Estella that provided the plan for the cover up. She felt sorry for you and understood your feelings of wanting revenge. I simply provided the means for her to act. This made it look like a serial killer had targeted all the agents."

"You used her."

"Yes, I did. However, she advanced to the point she started liking it, and acted on her own in killing the last agent, Mathew Kinley. I'm surprising she got as far as she did. I hoped for sure she would've been killed in attempting to murder one of the other agents."

Amy tried hard to focus. It wouldn't be long until she blacked out, and she knew it. "So, you wanted her to die. That would give you the inheritance you wanted and cover for the murders."

"Precisely . . . I started liking you, and hoped all of this would be over soon. It was when I received the call from her aunt I knew I had to do something fast. Estella had discovered who Edward was and was now after him. It was only a matter of time before her aunt would tell everything to the FBI."

Amy hoped that another agent or Arrington would soon check on Estella. Now, if she could only keep him talking. "Estella's not capable of lining this up on her own. You had

332

to help her."

"Yes, I did help her, but it was her fantastic body and dependency on drugs that did the trick."

"The FBI told me she said she was forced to prostitute herself to do your dirty work."

The comment caught Ike by surprise as he moved over closer to Amy. His dark-green eyes penetrated her as he wanted more answers. "I need to know exactly what the FBI told you."

With the point of the barrel pointed directly between her eyes, she started breathing fast and almost to a point of hyperventilating. "That's all I heard. She said you made her prostitute herself."

"The truth is—she loved to tease men and flirt. The number of affairs and sexual encounters she had were numerous. When she went off drinking and disappeared it would take weeks to find her. The main reason I left her was because of this. There's no telling what kind of sexual diseases she's contracted."

Amy could believe this about Estella, but couldn't understand why Ike couldn't have been more supportive. "Her aunt's a psychiatrist. It's hard to believe she couldn't have done more for her."

"I'm sure she tried, but it was impossible. It was best to try to keep it quiet."

Ike moved over to Estella again to analyze the wires and tubes going to her. He was obviously trying to decide what his next move would be. The agent still laid on the ground with his skull cracked open. Ike reached over to check if he had a pulse. Being satisfied, he removed the agent's pistol and pointed it at Amy. "I guess the authorities will have to guess why you came in here and killed Estella, and the agent before taking your own life."

Amy now understood the plan, as her head kept spinning wildly. "Please . . ."

"I'm sorry, but I—"

"FBI, drop the gun now!" A voice of authority ordered from Estella's bed. Ike turned, flashing a face full of shock as he glared at a pistol leveled at his head. He had been tricked; it wasn't Estella in the bed. "This is the FBI. I said . . . drop the gun now!"

The door crashed in as several other agents rushed into the room. Ike swung the gun around toward the bed preparing to fire. Two bullets hit him before he had the chance.

The surrounding blurred and voices faded as she felt herself falling.

###

Much later, Amy gained consciousness and saw Arrington in front of her, as her mind replayed the shooting. "Is he dead?"

"No, he'll recover, and we're looking forward to hearing what he has to say later."

Amy nodded toward Agent Arrington. "I don't understand. What happen to Estella? Someone else took her place. Is she going to be okay?"

"We thought he might try something, and she will recover, but it will take some time. We still don't know what all of her involvement was, or even if she's capable of logical thought or not. It'll take some time to determine the facts."

"I feel so sorry for her."

"We all do, and by the way Larry stopped by this morning. It appears he'll be released later today and he'll be fine."

"Good!"

"His friend Lenny has stayed with him all night."

"I'm sure he's tired. Where is he?" Amy asked as she

attempted to stand.

"Hold on, I'll help you. I think it will be good for you to walk around for a minute."

They walked to another waiting room, one where she saw Lenny curled up on a sofa sleeping. Amy leaned over and kissed him on the forehead as he looked up with a dazed look on his face. "How are you?"

"Girl, like I keep saying, you're going to be the death of me yet." He looked over at Edward waking also. "I don't know if this girl's crazy about you, or just plain crazy, but I've had all the excitement I think I can ever handle."

Edward looked over at Amy. "Well . . . I think I can handle it from here as long as you come to the wedding."

Lenny grinned. "Damn, I wouldn't miss it . . . ."

THE END

THE MALIVIZIATI

1375 COASTAL INLET NEAR FRANCE

"Stay alert, men." Giovanni walked to the front of his boat, scanning the strange rocky shore for a good place to anchor, or if possible, tie onto a dock somewhere in this small port city. "Since we'll need this boat to get home, three men will stay here to guard it until we return from Avignon."

One of his best men walked behind him. "Do you think three men will be enough?"

"I don't really expect problems, but I've learned to be safe."

"I agree, Giovanni. If Marco, the pope who resides in Avignon, isn't here to greet us, I'll venture into the city myself and find him for you."

"Relax, I'm sure someone has seen us already and he'll be alerted."

While Giovanni had accepted this trip to the north, he had had his doubts, taking with him some of his best fighters, enforcers who were extremely loyal to him. He knew that Queen Joanna I of Sicily, and the countess of Provence, had sold Avignon to Clement VI for 80,000 florins, making some enemies along the way. He had only been persuaded to make this trip, however, after he was further told that the future of not simply Sicily, his home country, but of the entire human race depended on him.

As he walked about the front of his ship, he knew he would be told more when he went ashore. Marco had made

336

him swear to tell no one what was going to happen until after they had talked. Still, he had no doubt a new alliance of some kind was about to be formed. Sicily had always lived with the fear of one invading ruler after another, keeping them in the dark for centuries.

While their way of life in Sicily had developed because of these abusive rulers, the Mafia had learned how to combat these iron-fisted invaders that were inconsistent with their values and belief in justice. It was always better to handle matters internationally and tell these cruel bastards nothing.

As they positioned his boat next to an unused part of one dock, Giovanni saw the guy who had invited him. With a cautious step upon the dock, Giovanni handed Marco a flask filled with wine. "Hello, my friend. I was hoping you would be here to meet us."

"You're late, but I knew you would come." Marco offered him a hug. "We have much to talk about before we make the journey overland to the Papacy. This division in the ranks of the Catholic Church will soon come to an end, and the Queen may have major challenges ahead of her. While many think it will be better for us to return to Rome, I . . . and many like me, have our doubts. This has been a schism in the Catholic Church for a long time. While the eastern banks of the Rhone have often marked the edge of the French kingdom, the French have often exerted control over the city, at their will."

"If you think me and my men are available to fight as mercenaries, you would be gravely mistaken. I'll assure you the only interest we have is protecting our own, and learning why the Queen of Sicily, who resides in France, wants to see us."

"Giovanni, I share your interest. The way you have gained respect from your countrymen speaks well of you. Unfortunately, there are those in a certain ruling class who want to control all nations, and which has been our central conflict since back in the time of Babylon."

He really didn't need a history lesson, or to bother himself with problems involving others. He had plenty of his own to worry about. "We do our best to protect our own."

"Agreed. As you probably know the Vatican hasn't been the habitual residence of many popes for a while. It has been more of a Lateran Palace, or maybe I should I say a Quirinal Palace." Marco lowered his voice. "This will all change soon."

While it was good to be in the know of such a revelation, Giovanni replied with caution. "Perhaps I should be asking what this has to do with me."

"This ruling class of "born to rule dictators", the ones that have made life miserable for you in Sicily, are the same ones who challenge the freedoms of many societies everywhere."

"This is something we have had to live with inside Sicily for centuries, and something that we all can assume will plague us forever. We are a small region compared to the mighty lands to the north."

"Giovanni, my friend, you'll soon see that you have perfected a method of surviving that will lead us into a new world. There is talk of a new secret society, one that will directly oppose these arrogant rulers who think they're born with special privileges and the right to rule over others."

"As you can imagine, I made this trip for several reasons. Turning down the request of the queen that rules over us might have created some serious problems for us. We have learned to live under dictators, but control our own destiny in a more private way."

"Exactly, my friend, and it's just such expertise that we're looking for." Marco broadly smiled for the first time. "In this new society you'll be a hero, just like in Sicily.

While you have perfected the ability to quietly do things, this new society we're forming will require you to be even more secretive."

"Marco, since you keep saying "we" . . . it would be good to know who else is invited to this group."

"I hope you trust me for now, but it's others with an interest much like your own."

That would require a lot of trust, since he knew spies could come from anywhere. "For now, and since we have known each other for a long time, I will. However, one thing has me curious. What does this have to do with you, the Catholic Church, and this assumed move back to Rome?"

"I know you would ask this question, and I'll partially answer it now. The rest you'll be told when we meet with the queen." Marco glanced over his shoulder to make sure they were still alone. "While I feel sure that many of the Popes will be convinced to return to Rome, some of them, including me, know that we're very vulnerable being so much in the open like we are. A secret location to operate out of may be the best way of surviving in the future."

"Where?"

"This location will only be given to a few people. There is already an effort being made to recruit the best warriors the world has ever seen."

"That would be very expensive to maintain without a steady source of funds."

"Membership in this society will include many very wealthy people, but don't worry, these are people who are also oppressed by the group with whom we'll always be mortal enemies. These leaders are much like you, since they only want the best for their people and not come under the rule of one group that controls all the worlds."

"My friend, you know I'll reserve what I can offer until I meet those that are invited to this group."

"Giovanni, I would expect nothing less." He pointed to

the sails as the men began to lower them. "The winds are going to be stronger tonight. This is a very treacherous time, and until we have everything in place, we do need to cover our back."

"Agreed, and you know I will. Does the group have a name?"

"Yes, and it is one that I think you'll appreciate very much. It will be called the Maliviziati, a malice against those born rich and arrogant enough to think they can rule the world."

"Good! And how will this society survive while you're recruiting your mercenaries?"

A commotion behind them halted their conversation. Men on horseback were heading toward them. Their aggressive march would have them upon them in minutes. "Marco, do you know who these men are?"

"I can guess. Tell your men to be prepared to do battle, but to wait for my signal. This may be tricky."

Giovanni motioned to his men. While he was temporarily cornered, he at least didn't have to worry about his back. All of his men knew how to kill.

As the two lead men on the horses got within shouting distance, they stopped and waited for the rest of their forces to join them. One man stepped from his horse before he yelled at Giovanni. "We were informed that a boat from Sicily was on the way here. You must be the captain."

Giovanni stepped forward with Marco beside him. While he prepared to answer, Marco did so for him. "This envoy has been summoned by the queen herself. As such, it would be good for you to step aside and not interfere."

He heard their leader laugh. "If you were important to the Queen she should have provided you with a protective escort, don't you think?" Since the words made sense, Giovanni studied his friend who looked calm–too calm.

Marco stepped forward, as if to accept the challenge.

340

"What makes you think that the Queen hasn't anticipated you interfering?"

The leader of the group glanced around. "I see no soldiers anywhere, and we have been in port for a while, waiting for this boat to arrive."

Another surprise waited for Giovanni as he listened to this posturing. Marco motioned to the hills around the outside of the port. "Perhaps you're looking in the wrong places." Marco raised his hands higher.

Within seconds, one man after another stepped out of the forest that surrounded the port. Giovanni knew they were planted there, as if Marco had anticipated this attack. The attackers gathered in a circle as they quickly realized they had been surrounded. Still, they vastly outnumbered the small group of men approaching them from the forest.

When the leader of this group saw the small number sent to oppose him, he laughed again. "Like I said, the Queen must have not thought highly of your visit."

Marco's voice boomed over the laughter. "To the contrary, these are the men that will make sure you have a quick journey into hell." Marco yelled as he raised his hand again into the air. The attack came immediately.

While Giovanni considered joining the fight, he waited to study the initial attack. These men from the forest aggressively attacked from all sides and within a few minutes it was over. Whoever they were, they were some of the most fearless warriors he had ever witnessed.

The last few minutes of the battle were even more brutal, as these mountain warriors made sure all of this group sent to attack them had been killed. They had no intentions of taking any survivors.

Finally, they turned their attention to Marco, and spoke in a strange language, but one which Marco appeared to understand. It was a strange combination, a man of the church, a pope no less, and vicious mercenaries of some kind acting like good friends. There had to be much more to who they were. For the moment, however, Giovanni felt glad they appeared to be on the same side.

After a quick hug offered to his comrade, Marco turned to one side to introduce the leader of these mountain men. "Giovanni, this is Johann. He and his men are very dedicated to the Catholic Church, having taken special oaths to always defend it and its popes. They will also be the defenders of the Maliviziati, and have already taken steps to establish a base of operation in their mountain domain in the Alps east of France."

Giovanni stepped closer to study the rugged character in front of him. "I don't understand his language."

Johann smiled, but spoke in Giovanni's native Sicilian language. "We pride ourselves in knowing many languages. You will be safe traveling with us, but I hope you understand that you won't be allowed to see or record the way we go. It will always be best this way."

"So, I assume we're not going to Avignon, are we?"

"We have been instructed to make sure you have a safe trip to Baltonia." Johann stopped to study him. "The Queen also won't be allowed to see the way in or out, but she'll be waiting for you there."

While Giovanni and his men were blindfolded, they were allowed to keep their weapons and had their hands untied. These special guards sent to escort them appeared to be totally fearless. Keeping the destination of their base a secret only heightened Giovanni's desire to know more.

Johann's voice eventually broke the long silence of a long third day of riding horseback. "You may remove your blindfolds." As he complied, all remained dark around him except for a single torch held by Johann. This torch soon ignited others as the walls inside of a large cave reflected the flickering flames. "Stretch your legs for a minute. We have a long walk ahead of us in the tunnel."

Giovanni felt the cold dampness inside the cave, with the flickering light reminding him of many dungeons he had seen earlier. Was this a trap? A quick glance confirmed that his men had the same concerns.

Johann stepped forward. "You have my word that you'll be safe. In fact, this is probably the safest place you'll ever know." He pointed ahead of him. "The Queen and many others are waiting for us ahead."

Many hours later they entered a large opening. This room was adorned like a magnificent inner chamber of a castle. With hundreds of men busy performing types various construction work of some kind, this still had to take lifetimes to build.

Johann pointed to the construction work. "This is but one room. There are many of them. We have created a network of tunnels and other facilities here. We also know that it might take another thousand years to complete what all has been envisioned."

Giovanni realized what this meant. Having several ways to come and go would make attacking it impossible–the perfect fortress. "This is very impressive."

Johann laughed. "We thought you would like it. Please have your men rest for a while. The others will be here soon."

Several hours later Giovanni was summoned to another meeting room. The walls reflected a golden light, as if they were covered in amber, while a large circular table made of a colorful substance he had never seen before demanded his attention. There was one place for a leader to sit above the others, but not so much as to be imposing.

Giovanni studied the others at the table. He knew none of them. Many of them looked strange. He cautiously walked to a spot away from the others and joined them, saying nothing. No one said a word.

Finally, the person he suspected was the Queen entered. As she rounded the table, he expected her to sit in the prestigious chair of honor, but she surprised him and walked on to another one.

When all of the chairs were occupied except the tallest one, he wondered who had been selected as the leader, and how he was selected. He had not been told and he had not given his consent to this.

Two of the guards walked in and stood on each side of the main chair, saying nothing, acknowledging no one. After several minutes, one of them spoke, first in one language then another, until he finally switched to Sicilian and glanced at Giovanni. "A leader hasn't been selected, as of yet. The reason for this meeting is to decide on one. Additionally, the power given to such has to be agreed to. We're only here to facilitate this meeting."

More guards soon entered, walking beside each invitee sitting at the table. The one beside Giovanni smiled. "I'll be your personal translator. My name is Igor."

Moments later, Marco entered the room. Since he spoke in Italian, Giovanni could understand him without Igor's help. "Thank you for coming. Today will be well remembered forever, but no one but those here in Baltonia will ever know that. I know you all want answers, and I hope to give them to you now."

Giovanni studied those around him. Would they be introduced?

Marco's voice boomed as he continued. "This group, which shall be known as the Maliviziati, shall serve everyone's interest in one major aspect. We all have our own secret societies from many corners of the world. Some of these are much more guarded than others. Our common interest, however, is maintaining it and not coming under a force that wants to control the world. I think we all know of which I speak. This evil society will stop at nothing to accomplish their goals."

Marco raised a wine goblet in front of him and suggested that all follow his lead. "In unity, we'll all maintain our freedom to do what we do best, and serve that which is good." Impressions of distrust soon vanished as smiles were exchanged between the various attendees.

After Marco finished his drink, he continued. "On a personal note, and as a leader in the catholic church, I know we can count on the guard to always defend us. Some of you know that the days of residing in Avignon will be over soon, and we will move back to Rome. There we'll face many attacks over the years, but by having a safe haven established here, we know that we can survive to serve into the future."

Marco stopped to study the others around him. "We also know that by gathering together, we can support each other in stopping the world dominance by our biggest foe." He paused. "You might not know the others at this table, but you'll become friends, comrades over time. At this time, I can only tell you that kings, queens, scholars, and some of the most influential people from many nations are among you."

Marco pointed to Giovanni. "I'm not a born leader, or one that can teach us how to maintain such a secret society, but you have become a master at it. The leader of this group isn't one of control, but one of teaching. I hope you will consider being the first leader."

Giovanni felt flattered to have been chosen, but he knew there must be more to the offer. He watched the stares coming from the others receiving the translated announcement. "And if I accept?"

"If you accept, you'll have a lot of work to do. You'll not be a ruler as such, but a servant to all. In this society, it's not about taking, but giving."

Interesting concept. "So, why would I agree to this?"

"Because you, like everyone here, has a love for others above yourself. If not, none of you would have been invited."

Giovanni had to think fast. "If this means building an army, I don't have any experience in doing such."

"There will be times when a physical intervention may be necessary. The royal guard here will take care of that. I think you saw them in action earlier. There are also many others here with knowledge of fighting discretely. This force, or special guards if you wish, will become the best in the world, but only a few will know of them."

Giovanni glanced around him. He had a lot of work to do. They all had a lot of work to do. He raised his cup again. "To the Maliviziati!"

In a show of solidarity, he watched all stand and salute him, including the Queen who had said nothing yet. To his surprise, she raised her drink and saluted him again. "To the Maliviziati!"